Darogah Haji Abbas Ali

An illustrated historical album of the Rajas and Taaluqdars of Oudh

Darogah Haji Abbas Ali

An illustrated historical album of the Rajas and Taaluqdars of Oudh

ISBN/EAN: 9783742840554

Manufactured in Europe, USA, Canada, Australia, Japa

Cover: Foto ©Andreas Hilbeck / pixelio.de

Manufactured and distributed by brebook publishing software
(www.brebook.com)

Darogah Haji Abbas Ali

An illustrated historical album of the Rajas and Taaluqdars of Oudh

AN

ILLUSTRATED HISTORICAL ALBUM

OF

THE RAJAS AND TAALUQDARS OF OUDH,

COMPILED AND ILLUSTRATED

BY

DAROGAH HAJI ABBAS ALI,

Government Pensioner,

Late Municipal Engineer, Lucknow.

ALLAHABAD:

NORTH-WESTERN PROVINCES AND OUDH GOVERNMENT PRESS.

1 8 8 0.

TO

THE HON'BLE SIR GEORGE EBENEZER WILSON COUPER, BART.,
K.C.S.I., C.B., C.I.E.,

LIEUTENANT-GOVERNOR, NORTH-WESTERN PROVINCES,

AND

CHIEF COMMISSIONER OF OUDH

Whose firm and consistent policy it has been

to strengthen and support

that loyal and enlightened aristocracy,

the Taaluqdars of Oudh,

these Memoirs are, by permission, respectfully dedicated

by

the Author,

ABBAS ALI.

CONTENTS.

PREFACE

INTRODUCTORY CHAPTER.

THE compiler of these Memoirs had a twofold object in his undertaking. First, it was his wish to collect all interesting details regarding the ancestral and present history of each individual taaluqdar in Oudh; and, secondly, to trace and chronicle the several circumstances of the past which have led to the existing prosperity of the province, and which have gradually secured for the taaluqdars themselves the high influential position which they now hold in the country. For this purpose he found it necessary to divide this work into two parts —the one, general, bearing on the history of Oudh, and the other, personal, on that of its baronial proprietors. It was not possible to gather anything like a continuous history of the province from the family records of individual taaluqdars. The circumstances attending the advancement of each to his present position vary in nearly every instance. A large number of them (or rather their ancestors) came from other parts of India, and many of them have acquired their possessions by purchase, or by adoption, or more recently as a reward for services rendered during the Mutiny. As a whole, the present aristocracy of Oudh cannot be said to have come in lineal descent from chiefs and nobles who held any prominent place in the early annals of the country. On this account it has been deemed advisable to keep the " Province" distinct from its " Land-owners," and to give a succinct account of both in separate parts of this volume.

It is as well, in passing, to say a few words regarding the photographic portraits attached to this work. A likeness of every taaluqdar in the province has been secured at a great expenditure of time, labour, and money, and photographs have been given in preference to any other kind of pictures as giving more correct portraitures. The compiler has introduced these additional attractions, first, because he thinks that the friends and relations of the subjects of the Memoirs will prize them; and, secondly, because it may be gratifying to posterity to have by them correct representations of the faces and forms of those to whom they are indebted for their wealth and position. There is no doubt, too, that portraits of this nature are not only gratifying, but also give those who come after very good ideas for forming an estimate of the character of those who have gone before. And here the compiler gratefully acknowledges the very great assistance given to him in this work by MAJOR DODD, B.S.C., who has very kindly revised the English version of the Memoirs.

With these prefatory remarks it is proposed to trace very briefly the earlier history of Oudh, and then to give a short account of the reigns of the several kings that ruled over the province from the earliest days to the annexation by the British Government, the annexation itself, the mutiny, and the subsequent circumstances which led to the present constitution of the country.

A

CHAPTER I.

EARLIER HISTORY OF OUDH.

OUDH, in old days, that is, upwards of 2,500 years ago, was called Koshalah, and its capital town was Ayodhya. There is, strange to say, great etymological similarity between this Koshalah and Kausham, the ancient name for the famous city of Kanauj. The rulers of Kanauj, no doubt, at one time held great power over the province of Oudh, but so little about them and other people connected with the early annals of the country has been translated into European languages, that our information on the subject is very limited.

As a matter of fact, Oudh has no early history as a distinct province. The city of Oudh, called Ayodhya, is a place of very great antiquity, and the legends of Rama give one some idea of the different races that held sway from time to time in that part of the country. The Aryan race were in possession apparently from a very distant period, and before them, the Bhars. Very little, however, is known of these Bhars, except that they appear to have been a civilized people, and to have been extirpated by the Muhammadan conquerors in the early part of the fourteenth century. Sultanpur was their capital, but it did not receive that name till it was taken by Allah-ud-din, Sultan of Delhi, or at least by one of his generals.

Another large tribe in those days were the Pasis, of whom almost numberless families still reside in Oudh. Their hereditary profession is robbery, and it is said that whenever disorder prevailed in the country they were quite ready to serve without any salaries, on the chance of making large profits by plunder. Many of these Pasis are known now as Rajputs, chiefly from acquiring great wealth, and so being in a position to give their daughters in marriage to influential members of the Rajput class. The pride of caste among these Rajputs was so great, that the difficulties in the way of approved marriages led to the terrible prevalence of infanticide, for which Oudh, till recently, has held an unenviable notoriety.

But till 1720 A. D., Saadat Ali Khan's time, we know little or nothing of the province of Oudh beyond the record of occasional conquests by invaders. Mahmud, the great Ghazni chieftain, took Kanauj in 1018. In 1195 the then Emperor of Delhi, Kutb-ud-din Aibak, through one of his generals, conquered nearly the whole of Oudh. In 1528 Babar led an army and drove all his opponents out of the province. The Afghan chieftain Baban, however, shortly afterwards succeeded in obtaining a footing in the country and captured Lucknow. When Babar died, Baban tried to raise an insurrection in Oudh, but Prince Humayun promptly quelled it. In 1559, taking possession of Jaunpur and the Doab, he also secured Oudh for himself.

From this time till Saadat Ali Khan took over the government of the province nothing of historical interest occurred.

CHAPTER II.

NAWAB SAADAT KHAN, BURHAN-UL-MULK, JANG BAHADUR, VAZIR-UL-MUMALIK.

THIS nobleman was the son of Mirza Nazir Sayyid Shams-ud-din, Neshapuri, Hussein, Musai, his father, being a descendant of Mirza Kazim. In 1118 Hijri his father went to Bengal and took with him his other son, Mir Muhammad Baqar. The two settled at Azimabad and were under the protection of the then Nazim of Bengal, Shuja-ud-daula. Shortly afterwards, in the year 1120 Hijri, Mir Muhammad Amin (the name by which Nawab Saadat Khan was called at his birth) also set out on a journey to Azimabad, in hopes of seeing his father, who, unfortunately, died before his arrival. After his father's death, accompanied by his elder brother, he went to Shahjahanabad, at which place his illustrious career first commenced. He is described as having been a brave, courageous man, a good scholar, and an able administrator (and, withal, an ambitious man also). Through the kindly assistance of Sayyid Abdulla Khan and Kutb-ul-Mulk, and as much also by his own zeal and ability, he rapidly rose from very minor appointments to that of Subadar of Hindon and Bagan in 1121, and subsequently received from Muhammad Shah the name and title at the head of this notice, i.e., Saadat Khan Burhan-ul-Mulk. He was at one time the leader of the Shia sect, but afterwards he joined the Sunnis and assisted in the massacre of his former co-religionists. In those times the Sayyids were great favorites with the emperors, and consequently were at enmity with the old noblemen of the country, chiefly the Nizam-ul-Mulk, Muhammad Amir Khan, and the Etmad-ul-Mulk. These noblemen naturally thought that if Sayyid Abdulla Khan and Sayyid Hussein Ali became masters of the position, there would be an end of the Iranis and Duranis. The latter nobleman therefore awaited his opportunity for finding Sayyid Hussein Ali off his guard and killing him. For the execution of this foul work, however, he could find no reliable friend. At last Saadat Khan and Mir Haidar Khan, Kashgari, agreed to cast lots with Etmad-ul-Mulk for the office of murderer. The lot fell to Mir Haidar Khan, and he killed the Sayyid.

On the 3rd November, 1720, corresponding with 1134 Hijri, Muhammad Shah's army defeated Abdulla Khan, and in the rejoicings over this victory the title of Bahadur Jang was added to the other titles enjoyed by Saadat Khan, and he was also appointed Subadar of Agra. The great friend of the Sayyids was Raja Ajit Singh, Governor of Guzerat and Ajmere, between whom and the reigning emperor a war shortly broke out. Saadat Khan, Burhan-ul-Mulk, Bahadur Jang, was called to the command of the troops, and every preparation for a severe contest was duly made, but owing to a conflict of opinion no further action was taken. Shortly afterwards, Saadat Khan, besides holding his Subadarship of Agra, obtained that of Oudh also, and he went to Oudh to take up the management of affairs. It was from the time of Saadat Khan's resumption of this new Subha that Oudh dates as a separate dynasty. At the time of this assumption an incident occurred which might have changed Saadat Khan's plans. On leaving Akbarabad (Agra) to take up his appointment as the Chief of the Government of Oudh, he nominated one Rai Nil Kant as his deputy in the former post. But Rai Nil Kant was shortly afterwards shot by a Jat while he was out riding. Saadat Khan was so wroth and grieved at this that he was anxious to return to Agra at once and avenge his assistant's death, but fortunately for Oudh, a substitute was forthcoming in the person of Raja Jey Singh Sawai, who was an old enemy of the Jats. He was appointed Rai Nil Kant's successor, with the twofold object of revenge and future good administration, and Saadat Khan was consequently enabled to remain at his post.

He, however, was not very long in his new charge before troubles began to threaten him. The Mahratta chief, Baji Rao, was at the time gradually extending his powers and possessions in the direction of Delhi. During these exploits, Mulhar Rao, in command of his army, advanced as far as, and commenced to plunder, the towns of Saadabad and Jalesar. Saadat Khan, who was then on a tour through that part of the world, accompanied by his army also, heard of this and resolved to withstand the aggressive prince. A severe battle ensued, the result of which was the defeat of the Mahratta horde and their dispersion from the country. The effect of this was so great and so widespread that all the Mahrattas were driven to a hurried flight to the Deccan. When Baji Rao heard of the discomfiture of his army, he organized preparations on a very extensive scale against the Emperor of Delhi. Saadat Khan received intelligence of the probable arrival of Baji Rao's army at Dholepore and repaired to the spot in hopes of an encounter, but on arrival he could find no trace of either Baji Rao or his forces. He then prepared to cross the Chambal in hopes of engaging the enemy in that part of the country, but while these preparations were going on he received a most urgent request from Khan Daura Khan to stay proceedings until he (Khan Daura Khan) could arrive with his army, and they could make a combined attack. Some delay, however, occurred first in Khan Daura Khan's arrival, and afterwards in feasting and entertaining, and in the meantime Baji Rao made forced marches, which brought him unopposed to Kalka, near Delhi. Saadat Khan reached Delhi shortly afterwards, and Baji Rao retired back to the Deccan. This was in 1737 A. D., corresponding with 1149 Hijri.

The next we hear of Saadat Khan was in connection with the battle-field of Panipat, where Nadir Shah was doing battle with Muhammad Shah. He arrived at the scene with a splendid force of artillery, which attracted a great deal of admiration and caused no little fear. But there was some jealousy among the troops. Nadir Shah's men did not wish to be allied with Saadat Khan's force, and as a result of this difference a fight ensued. Shortly afterwards Nadir Shah and Saadat Khan made them friends, and from that time forth till Saadat Khan's death Nadir Shah's admiration for him knew no bounds. Saadat Khan eventually, by paying two crores of rupees, obtained the appointment he had all along quietly coveted, viz., that of Amir-ul-issa, Vizier of Delhi. But the attainment of his ambition brought out his worst qualities, though fortunately for his former reputation and for those brought under his influence, his career of oppression and cruelty did not last long. His treasonable advice to Nadir Shah mainly led to Nadir's disgraceful work of spoliation at Delhi. All the treasure and jewels of the Imperial Court were taken, and every one who did not make a clean breast of his wealth was tortured most unmercifully. In this work of spoliation Saadat Khan took part, but his days were happily cut short, some say by a carbuncle or cancer which formed on his back, but more than probable by poison administered either by himself or by some one of the many thousands who groaned under his ruthless treatment.

Thus ended the life of the famous Saadat Khan, a man who had risen to his distinguished position as the first founder of the dynasty of Oudh solely by his own ability and great courage. This latter quality in his character is proverbial, his own personal bravery equalled his great military skill. Even his Hindu foes have recorded with awe "how he slew in single combat Bhagwant Singh Khichi, and how his troops, when almost beaten, rushed again to the combat when the long white beard of the old chief was seen in the thick of the battle."

Saadat Khan was succeeded in Oudh by Abul Mansur Khan, better known in history as Safdar Jang, whose memoir now follows.

CHAPTER III.

ABUL MANSUR KHAN, SAFDAR JANG.

SAFDAR JANG was both nephew and son-in-law of his predecessor, Saadat Khan. Not much, if anything, is known of his early days. The first event of note in his career was his joining Mirza Ahmad at the time when hostilities were going on between Shah Abdali and Muhammad Shah in Sirhind. It is said that it was chiefly owing to the very effective service of Safdar Jang's guns that Shah Abdali was defeated three times. On the way back from Sirhind Mirza Ahmad heard of the death of his father, Muhammad Shah, which led to his succession to the throne. He immediately appointed Safdar Jang his Vizier, and the appointment thereafter became hereditary in Safdar Jang's family. It was soon after his appointment as Vizier that he became involved, chiefly by his own doings, in one of those complications which were so frequent in those days. Safdar Jang always had an ill feeling against the Rohillas, principally on account of their somewhat dangerous proximity to his jurisdiction. In course of time Ali Muhammad Khan, the chief of the Rohillas, then styled Ruler in Rohilkhand, died, whereupon Safdar

Jang wrote to Qaim Khan, son of the ruler of Farukhabad, and instructed him at all risks and cost to prevent any of Ali Muhammad's sons coming into their father's possessions and government. In obedience to these instructions and also from personal avarice, Qaim Khan attacked Saad-ulla-Khan (Ali Muhammad's son) in the fort at Budaun. Saad-ulla Khan sued for peace, but none of his entreaties were regarded by the enemy. At last, in a fit of desperation, he made a sortie with the whole of his forces, and not only drove back the invaders, but also succeeded in killing Qaim Khan himself. Safdar Jang at once turned the tables, marched to Farukhabad and secured possession of all Qaim Khan's country, leaving only Farukhabad itself and a few villages for the support of the deceased's widow and mother. He then left as his Assistant in charge Newal Rao, an Oudh man, who came and settled there and made Kanauj his capital. Among the spectators of Safdar Jang's conduct was one Ahmad Khan, Qaim Khan's brother, a member of Safdar Jang's service. The treatment of his father and brother so exasperated Ahmad Khan that he deserted the Vizier and attacked, and eventually killed, the new Assistant, Newal Rai. This was in 1163 Hijri, corresponding with the Christian year A. D. 1750. This occurrence roused Safdar Jang into action against the Pathans, but he was defeated by them and also wounded. After this defeat he went to Delhi, but found his position there as Vizier in an exceedingly critical condition, and it was only by extensive bribery he was enabled to maintain his footing there at all. In the meantime Ahmad Khan had followed up his victories and had taken possession of Allahabad and of Oudh also. Safdar Jang, after re-establishing himself at Delhi, immediately set to work to wipe off the stain of the severe defeat he had met with at Ahmad Khan's hands. He procured the assistance of the Mahrattas, and with their help fought and gained the battle of Hussenpore in the year 1751. It is estimated that quite 10 or 12,000 Pathans lost their lives in this action ; anyhow the result was so decided that the Mahrattas, in consequence, became possessors of the country from Jalesar to the Himalaya. The behaviour of the Mahrattas and that of Safdar Jang became so oppressive that, in a state of despair, the Pathans made peace with them.

After this followed a period of favour and disfavour with the Emperor of Delhi. At first it was all favour, repeated interviews, and promises. Then came the interference of the favourite, Khwaja Serah (the eunuch), the friendly invitation to dinner, the cowardly assassination, and in consequence, the displeasure of the Emperor. Safdar Jang ultimately received the royal permission to go to Allahabad and Oudh, but when the time came to start, he hesitated, hovered about the city, and in the end, finding no hope of better things, but, on the contrary, a chance of meeting with violence and possibly death also, he decided on making a stand. He summoned whatever chiefs he could find, and the war, if it may be called a war, commenced. The old quarrel of Iran and Duran between the Shias and Sunnis was raked up, and Ghazi-ud-din

Khan, commanding the opposition forces, despatched a distinguished messenger to the camp of the Rohillas to persuade them to come over to the Emperor's side; indeed, the messenger had barely started when an appeal was made to the men of Safdar Jang's army on the subject of their regard for the Sunnis, which was responded to at once by the whole of the Pathans going over to the Emperor. In addition to this, Ghazi-ud-din Khan also sent to Holkar for assistance, but Holkar declined, first because he did not like to attack his co-religionists, the Jats, and also because he had some scruples about joining against his friend Safdar Jang. All these appeals and overtures caused delay, nearly six months being wasted with mere personal, or at most small encounters, and no decisive action being taken. At last peace was made. Safdar Jang submitted, and went, after all, apparently satisfied, to his Subadhari of Oudh and Allahabad.

A short time after in 1107 Hijri (A.D. 1754) Safdar Jang died and was succeeded by his son, Shuja-ud-daula. Safdar Jang had the reputation of being an able statesman.

CHAPTER IV.

NAWAB SHUJA-UD-DAULA.

SHUJA-UD-DAULA (or as he should be more properly called Tillah-ud-din Haidar) seems to have inherited much of the character of his father, and perhaps, in a more marked degree, that of his grandfather. He was a statesman of no mean ability, but he is chiefly remarkable for his manliness and great courage. His enemy even describes him as active, passionate, and ambitious, and as second to none of his predecessors in valour and strength. The first we read of him is in connection with the great conflict which was going on at the time between the Mahrattas and the Abdalis. Ahmad Shah sent Najib-ud-daula (the then Vizier of the King of Delhi) to summon Shuja-ud-daula to the scene of action. The summons was obeyed and Shuja-ud-daula started with 10,000 cavalry, but at the same time he did not discontinue his correspondence with the Mahrattas. In fact, all along he was a sort of link between the contending parties, the Mahrattas suing for peace through him, and the Abdalis making him the channel for communicating their intentions to fight to the bitter end. A decided victory for Ahmad Shah's army shortly followed, on which occasion Ali Gauhar (who, by the way, was not at Delhi at the time) was crowned Emperor of Hindustan and Shuja-ud-daula was made Vizier; this occurred at the beginning of 1761. Shuja-ud-daula then started to take charge of his possessions at Allahabad and in Oudh, reaching the former place in safety after defeating the garrison at Jhansi *en route*.

Two or three years after this came about the most remarkable event of Shuja-ud-daula's career. He found himself doing battle for

the first time in his life, in fact for the first time in the history of
Oudh, with British troops. This event came about as follows:—It
appears that about the middle of 1763, Mir Kasim, the Nawab of
Bengal, was forced into hostilities with the British Government by
certain actions which led to the seizure of Patna. Mir Kasim was
defeated and so utterly routed that he had to seek protection in
Oudh, at the hands of Shuja-ud-daula and the Emperor Shah Alam,
who happened at the time to be encamped at Allahabad. Shuja-ud-
daula espoused the Nawab's cause and at once made a demonstra-
tion with his army, with a view to recovering Patna, but in this
undertaking he was driven back with heavy loss. Then followed
some little cessation from hostilities, owing first to mutiny among
the British troops, and subsequently to the setting in of the mon-
soons. However, after a time, the English army under Major Munro
commenced an advance and shortly afterwards encountered the
Oudh army at Buxar, which it repulsed with serious sacrifices to
itself, but with still more extensive damage to the enemy. On this
defeat Shuja-ud-daula deemed it advisable to try and come to some
terms with his opponent, but as he wished for the separation of
Behar from the jurisdiction of Mir Jafar, which stipulation the
English declined to accept, and as his opponent demanded the surrender of Mir Kasim, Shamru and others, which he refused to effect,
negotiations came to nothing and the war was in consequence
renewed. But while Shuja-ud-daula was unable to come to terms,
his ally, the Emperor, conceded a great deal in order to secure
British favor and support. He gave up Gházipur, a portion of the
territory of the then Raja of Benares ; the English, on the other hand,
promising the Emperor to put him in possession of Shuja-ud-daula's
dominions. The British forces marched into Oudh, and Shuja-ud-
daula withdrew his family and his treasure to Bareilly. After this,
several attempts were made to secure peace, first through Major
Munro, and subsequently by the personal intervention of Captain
Staples, but so long as the condition was the surrender of Mir
Kasim, Shuja-ud-daula remained firm and declined to relent. But
the time occupied by him in attempting to make these negotiations
also gave him time to seek for aid elsewhere, in the event of their
failure. He tried many, the chief of whom were the Mahrattas and
the Afghans. The Afghans promised assistance, but gave none. The
Mahratta chieftain, Mulhar, accepted the invitation and sent a force
to his support. But Shuja-ud-daula's forces, combined with the
Mahrattas, could not withstand the British. On the 3rd of May,
1765, General Carnac routed them near Kora in Oudh, and subsequently near Allumpur. Shuja-ud-daula, after the second defeat,
sought refuge with Ahmad Khan Baksh in Farukhabad. By Ahmad
Khan Baksh's advice, he made overtures of peace, a few months afterwards, with General Carnac. Peace was eventually concluded in the
following terms:—(1) Shuja-ud-daula had all his territory restored to
him except Allahabad and Kora, which was given to the Emperor ;
(2) he had in return to contribute a good sum towards the expenses

of the war; (3) give up the fort of Chunar; (4) levy no duty on the East Indian Company's goods passing through his territory; (5) was not to receive Kasim Ali or any of his followers into his (Shuja-ud-daula's) service; and (6) he was in no way to interfere with the British ally, Balwant Singh.

Shuja-ud-daula's administrative ability, as displayed after the conclusion of this treaty, was such as to secure much admiration, so much so as to raise a feeling of jealousy in the British Government. He placed his finances on a sound footing; he paid off all the debts of his property; with European (generally supposed to be French) assistance he re-organized his army and made it thoroughly efficient, and so rapid and sound was his progress that the English Government were obliged by a fresh treaty to curtail the strength of his forces. This strength was fixed at some 35,000 men, and none of the force were to be equipped and drilled like English soldiers. At first Shuja-ud-daula was disgusted at this act of the British, but three or four years afterwards he had reason to be grateful for the help the English afforded him. In 1772 a powerful force of Mahrattas had overrun Rohilkhand and had seized nearly all the possessions belonging to his old friend, Ahmad Khan Baksh of Farukhabad. The Rohillas, in their despair, entreated Shuja-ud-daula to procure British aid and offered to pay a handsome sum for its support. The aid was procured, the Mahrattas had to retire, but the Rohillas were not faithful in the execution of their promises. Here Shuja-ud-daula threw them over, some assert unjustly, after all the assistance they had rendered him in his days of distress. For a comparatively insignificant sum these people were sold to him by the British, who also made over to him Allahabad and Kora, the property, as noted above, of the Emperor. Rohilkhand was not invaded by Shuja-ud-daula, but he dealt badly and cruelly with the Rohillas after the conquest. He appears, from Colonel Chapman's report, to have behaved badly throughout the action. However, he not only secured British support, but also that of the Emperor, Shah Alam. He did not long survive his ill-gotten gains, for an abscess that had formed on his thigh compelled him to retire to Fyzabad, where he died in 1775, at the comparatively early age of 46. He was succeeded by his son, Mirza Amani, who assumed the title of Nawab Asfadaula.

<hr>

CHAPTER V.

NAWAB ASFADAULA, *alias* MIRZA AMANI.

ASFADAULA's career differed greatly in almost every respect from those of his predecessors. His father and grandfather were both men of battle; they delighted in military exploits, were always ready for aggression, and never willing to surrender a concession without a struggle. Nawab Asfadaula, on the contrary, was a man fond of home and ease; he was indolent and sensual, and rather than risk the loss of the pleasures of his Court life, he was prepared to concede any point to his would-be aggressors (chiefly the English). Some maintain that no intelligence or money, not even such as his father and grandfather possessed, would have sufficed to thwart the ambitious designs of the British in those days, but still there is no doubt that Warren Hastings and others made the most of their opportunity and profited considerably from the extreme weakness of this chieftain.

He had hardly taken his seat on the throne before it was declared to him that all the engagements made with Shuja-ud-daula had become null and void by his death, and that if he intended to secure the services of the English Government, he must acquiesce in more stringent terms than those which had been accorded to his father. Barely six months after his father's death, Asfadaula attached his signature to a sanad, by which he ceded to the British Benares, Jaunpur, and Gházipur, as well as Raja Chait Singh's *ilaqa*, and he also consented to pay Rs. 2,60,000 monthly for the maintenance of a brigade of English troops. In return, the Kora and Allahabad property, which was sold to his father, was given to him. The Nawab, however, found that he was not equal to the payment of the Benares revenue, which he had guaranteed, and he had resort at last to oppression to act up to his promises. But this was not his sole financial difficulty, for the British Government, in their impecuniosity, drew enormous sums of money from Oudh, besides from time to time imposing on the unfortunate Nawab the expense of maintaining large numbers of additional troops. Affairs went on in this ruinous way for some little time, when at last Asfadaula grew desperate and appealed to the Governor-General for protection. On this appeal, Warren Hastings met the Nawab at Chunar, September, 1781, and by the treaty signed there he was relieved of nearly all the charges he had met hitherto, but on the condition, discreditable to both parties, that he plundered his grandmother, the Bahu Begam, and his mother, of all their money. It will be remembered that this condition made by Warren Hastings formed one of the most serious subjects in connection with the impeachment of that statesman by Mr. Burke.

Shortly after this a fresh difficulty besetted Asfadaula's path. Under the treaty of 1781 all the troops had to be withdrawn from Oudh, a movement which at once suggested disaster. It was highly probable that, seeing the country denuded of all military protection, the neighbouring enemies, especially the Mahrattas, always on the alert for an opportunity, would at once invade the province. In his embarrassment he had resort to Faizulla Khan, who, it may be remembered, was allowed by Shuja-ud-daula to hold Rohilkhand. Asfadaula applied to him for 5,000 cavalry to replace the British troops that had been withdrawn, and on his intimating his inability to comply with the requisition, Asfadaula took measures to despoil him.

Matters went on in the usual unsatisfactory way from this period to the close of the Nawab's career—exorbitant money demands from the British Government, then the expense of maintaining new cavalry regiments, all raised from loans which Asfadaula was quite unable to meet. All the time from the conclusion of the treaty of Chunar, 1781, to the day of his death in 1797, things went from bad to worse. Lord Cornwallis did something towards ameliorating his sad condition, but he was far from completely remedying the evil, while Sir John Shore's subsequent action led to oppression as widespread as it was before.

We have already recorded Asfadaula's character at the commencement of this Memoir. His love of home and ease had one good result: it led to the establishment of one of the most beautiful cities in India,—Lucknow. When Asfadaula first took up his residence there, Lucknow was merely a village. By the time he died, it possessed all those elegant buildings (palaces, mosques, bridges, *imambaras*) for which now it is so famous. He was very liberal with his money, so liberal that it used to be said in his praise—

" Jis ko na de Maula.
Usko de Asfadaula "
" To whom God does not give, Asfadaula will give."

But unfortunately for the people, his liberality was secured from others' money, and the province was ruined by these whims. His life on the whole must have been a miserable one. The only two bright points were his succession to the Viziership of Delhi and the satisfaction of being able to lavish money on undertakings, such as the buildings at Lucknow and his son's wedding, that pleased him.

CHAPTER VI.

NAWAB MIRZA ALI, *alias* WAZIR ALI KHAN.

THE reign of Mirza Ali was a short one, and by no means a bright or happy one. He was said to be the son of Asfadaula, and as such laid claim to succession to the throne. But there was a powerful faction against him. Saadat Ali Khan, as eldest surviving brother of the late Nawab, protested against Mirza Ali's succession, on the ground that Asfadaula really had no legitimate offspring, and the then Governor-General was called upon to decide on the claims of the disputants. Asfadaula's mother and widow were both desirous that Mirza Ali should obtain the place, and so also was the population generally. The result was that Sir John Shore gave the case in favour of Mirza Ali, and he was recognized accordingly as heir by Government.

But he had not many months of the sweets of Court life. Ihtias Ali Khan, a man of high standing in Oudh, and withal a cordial hater of the British Government, set to work to undermine Mirza Ali's position. While the Governor-General was in Lucknow, the young Nawab was laid up with an attack of measles, and the opportunity was taken to form conspiracies against him. Sir John Shore himself encountered great difficulties in connection with these intrigues. Strong evidence was adduced to show that Mirza Ali was not the son, not even the illegitimate son of Asfadaula; that his mother's husband was still alive; that the mother was a nurse in the late Nawab's household; and that when Mirza Ali was born, Asfadaula purchased him for Rs. 500. It was further shewn that it was not an unfrequent freak on the part of the late Nawab to bargain with pregnant women, and to bring up their children as his own. After a short time, Sir John Shore was convinced that these statements were substantiated by facts, and he made up his mind in consequence to depose him in favour of Saadat Ali Khan. Mirza Ali was sent to Benares, from whence Saadat Ali Khan had come, and a lakh and a half was granted to him as a pension. He subsequently killed the Resident, Mr. Cherry, and broke out into open rebellion, but he was eventually given up to the English, and was sent as a prisoner to Calcutta, where he died in 1817. Nothing much is known of young Mirza Ali's character, except that he was a man of impracticable temper.

CHAPTER VII.

NAWAB SAADAT ALI KHAN.

As had hitherto been the case with his predecessor, the accession of Saadat Ali Khan to the throne was the occasion for the signing of a fresh treaty, such treaties, oftener than not, involving increased payments to the English Government. In Saadat Ali Khan's case the payment was increased to 76 lakhs a year and the surrender of the Fort at Allahabad. He had further to maintain a British force of a minimum strength of 10,000 men; he had, too, to pay the pension allotted to his predecessor, Mirza Ali, and to see that his (Mirza Ali's) relatives were tolerably well provided for. In return, the British Government undertook to protect Saadat Ali Khan from all foreign aggression and to assist to keep his rebellious subjects in order. So great were the demands made upon him that Saadat Ali at one time seriously contemplated abdication. Lord Wellesley, who was then Governor-General, would gladly have acceded to his wish, had the abdication been in favour of the British Government, but Saadat Ali was not prepared for this, even in his greatest extremities, and so that question was not mooted further.

Shortly afterwards in 1801, the Governor-General wrote and warned Saadat Ali Khan that Jami Shah had crossed the Indus, and would in all probability invade Oudh; warning him at the same time that such an invasion would be an easy matter, as the Rohillas were against Saadat Ali Khan, and that, after all, the Nawab had only a rabble force wherewith to defend himself and his possessions. The Nawab admitted all this, and offered even to proceed at once on an indefinite pilgrimage, provided his rule met with no opposition. A lengthy correspondence followed, in which it is said Saadat Ali Khan considerably distinguished himself by his statesman-like proposals and arguments; but the whole ended only in a fresh treaty, according to which so much of the Doab yielding a revenue over Rs. 1,00,000 was made over to the British, the Nawab's force was reduced considerably, and free navigation of the Ganges and other rivers was to be permitted.

Nothing historical is recorded of Saadat Ali Khan from the time this treaty was signed, the 14th November, 1801, to the day of his death, 11th July, 1814. The opinions regarding Saadat Ali Khan's administration during this interval, and of his character generally, are varied. He is acknowledged by all to have been a parsimonious man, and a wise man in his generation; but while some native accounts comment severely on his tyrannical habits, his extortions and oppression, some European historians assert that these 13 years were marked by an administration characterized by prudence, self-denial, and conspicuous ability such as has not been equalled in the history of native government. In fact, it is said that it was by his judicious management and sound enterprise that Oudh obtained in his reign the title it has since ever held as the "Garden of India." Commencing his career in bankruptcy, it is believed that at his death his treasury contained no less than 14 million pounds sterling. He was succeeded by his eldest son, Nawab Ghazi-ud-din Haidar.

***

CHAPTER VIII.

NAWAB GHAZI-UD-DIN HAIDAR.

THIS Nawab's career was comparatively an uneventful one. It is chiefly distinguished on account of the amount of money the British Government was enabled to borrow from his treasuries, and the circumstance that during his reign Oudh was formed into a distinct territory and the title of King was conferred on Ghazi-ud-din Haidar and his successors.

On the Nawab's accession, a treaty was drawn up between him and the Governor-General, in which all the engagements made by Saadat Ali Khan were held to be binding on him and on the English Government. The first thing Ghazi-ud-din Haidar did was to carry out the promises of his predecessor to give Lord Wellesley a crore of rupees. Lord Wellesley demurred to taking the money as a gift, and so in lieu he accepted it as a loan at 6 per cent. In 1815 more money was required by Lord Moira towards meeting the expenses of the war with Nepal. This sum was duly paid, and in return the British Government made over to the Nawab the marshy forests of the Terai, which, far from being a profitable acquisition, was a source of annoyance and danger, from the fact that it soon became the refuge for all the rebels and dacoits of that part of the country.

Ultimately, in return for these money loans and many other substantial acts of pecuniary assistance, but really, it is believed, with a view to stir up a useful jealousy between the Courts of Delhi and Lucknow, the Nawab was permitted to assume the title of King. This was in 1818. In 1825 another loan (these, as a matter of fact, were perpetual loans) of a crore of rupees was borrowed from Ghazi-ud-din Haidar. The following year another loan of half a million was obtained, it was said at the time, for a period of two years only. Ghazi-ud-din Haidar died in October, 1827, having lent, or rather given, the British Government four out of the 14 millions he found in the treasuries on his accession to the throne. He is said to have been an enlightened and a popular man. His career would no doubt have been a more successful one had he not been surrounded by a body of fraudulent men, chief among whom was the unscrupulous Agha Mir, his minister.

CHAPTER IX.

NASIR-UD-DIN HAIDAR.

NASIR-UD-DIN HAIDAR, or as his real name was Sulaiman Jah, was the eldest son of Ghazi-ud-din Haidar. He came to the throne under very fair auspices. The treasuries were full, and the young Nawab seemed anxious to lay out his money to the best advantage. His first request was that the interest on the money lent by his father, and also on the further 12 lakhs then lent, should be settled on the ladies of his household and their followers, but the British Government would not accede to the proposal. He also tried to make Agha Mir refund the money he had misappropriated during his father's reign, but in this matter also the British Government thwarted the designs of the young King by covering the traitor's retreat to Cawnpore. After a ten-years' uneventful reign Nasir-ud-din Haidar died, some assert, by poison. His character, though at first it gave signs of being good, was evidently a weak one, for ill-advised, or not advised at all, by the British Resident, and surrounded by courtiers of the vilest description, he soon gave way to sensuality and commenced to neglect all the reforms which at one time seemed probable of accomplishment under his rule. He had the makings of a second Saadat Ali Khan, but he failed under the bad influences of those about him.

CHAPTER X.

MUHAMMAD ALI SHAH.

MUHAMMAD ALI SHAH's accession to the throne was not unattended with difficulties. He was the uncle of Nasir-ud-din and brother of Saadat Ali Khan, and according to the Muhammadan practice his title to the kingdom was indisputable. But there was opposition in the way in the person of Badshah Begam, the widow of the late Nawab. It appears that Nasir-ud-din had a son called Munna Jan by a lady named Afzal Mahal, but he had disowned him out of enmity to the Badshah Begam, whom he greatly disliked in the latter years of his life. On the occasion of the proclamation of Muhammad Ali Shah, the Begam went to the palace, at the same time, with an armed multitude of followers and had Munna Jan proclaimed instead. Colonel Low, then Resident, took timely action in the matter, and making some excuse for leaving the scene of these rival claims, he obtained a small armed force and arrested Munna Jan, who was pronounced illegitimate by the English Government and sent to Chunar. It is said that upwards of 100 persons were killed in this emeute.

There was nothing worthy of record in Muhammad Ali Shah's reign. He promised to adhere to the treaty with his predecessors, but he failed to fulfil his side of the agreement. The East India Company were obliged, under the circumstances, to conclude another less favourable treaty with him. He was no longer permitted to keep up an army of his own, but in lieu to maintain one, consisting of not less than two cavalry and five infantry regiments, to be officered by Europeans, and involving to him a regular annual payment of 16 lacs of rupees. This treaty he of course accepted with great reluctance. In May, 1842, he died. He had a character for prudence, but otherwise he was not remarkable for any particular qualities, either good or bad.

CHAPTER XI.

AMJAD ALI SHAH.

MUHAMMAD ALI SHAH was succeeded on the throne by his second son, Amjad Ali Shah. Nothing good, bad, or indifferent is recorded of this King. The government of the country during his reign, though perhaps not so bad as in the days of his successor, was about as bad as it well could be. There was little short of anarchy throughout the whole of Oudh. He was only five years on the throne, dying in February, 1847. He was succeeded by Wajid Ali Shah, the last King of the province.

CHAPTER XII.

WAJID ALI SHAH.

WAJID ALI SHAH's career will be chiefly remembered by the annexation of the province during his reign, and by his deeds of misrule which ultimately forced this action on the British Government. Wajid Ali Shah himself is described as a man of some literary attainments, but utterly devoid of all business habits and all governing powers. On his accession he found Oudh practically under the control of the barons of the country, and he had not sufficient authority to hold his own, not even in the matter of procuring a reasonable amount of revenue from them. In fact each baron or taaluqdar was really the king of his own particular ilaqa, plundered his people in order to erect fortresses for his own protection, and acted in any way he wished, independently of the laws of the land or of the edicts of the King. From all this arose the question of annexation, to the history of which the following chapter is devoted.

CHAPTER XIII.

THE HISTORY OF THE ANNEXATION.

THE beginning of the end of Oudh as a separate Native Government commenced with Lord Hardinge, who was Governor-General of India when Wajid Ali Shah came to the throne. Lord Hardinge did his best to secure some improvement. He took all the trouble of going to Lucknow on purpose to confer with the King on the subject. He then pointed out to him all the details of his maladministration, and the serious results to him personally if remedial measures were not immediately adopted, concluding with the grant of two years' grace to carry out the reforms that were necessary. By the close of these two years Lord Dalhousie had received charge of the Government of India. He called upon Sir William Sleeman to make a tour through the province, and afterwards to report fully on the condition of affairs, in the light of the instructions given to the King by Lord Hardinge. Sir W. Sleeman's report was about as unfavourable as it well could be. He described the King as a " crazy imbecile " completely in the hands of eunuchs, fiddlers, and utterly unscrupulous ministers; and added that " what the people of Oudh really want and most earnestly pray for " is that the Government should take upon itself the responsibility of " governing them well and permanently." But with all his pitiable description Colonel Sleeman did not express himself as an advocate for complete annexation, but only for the supersession of the corrupt native agency, by the exercise of a general control by European officials.

In 1854 Colonel Sleeman was compelled by ill-health to take leave, and his successor was nominated in the person of Colonel Outram. On assumption of office Colonel Outram found everything very much the same as his predecessor had reported. He, too, was called upon by the Governor-General to institute careful enquiries and report as fully and as quickly as possible his views on the condition of affairs. Four months after he furnished a most elaborate memorandum, dealing with every point that had come under his notice, or on which he had been able to procure information from the records left by those who had been deputed on a similar undertaking. The conclusion Colonel Outram arrived at was that affairs in Oudh were, if possible, worse than they were in Colonel Sleeman's time; that the King had made no attempt whatever to carry out the improvements peremptorily demanded by Lord Hardinge seven years ago; and that he felt compelled, much against the principles he always advocated with regard to our policy with Native States, to recommend recourse to extreme measures as the only means of securing to five millions of people such a system of government as would be "conducive to their prosperity and calculated to secure them their lives and property." Colonel Outram's Minute was supplemented by an equally strong one by Colonel Low, who was then Member of the Governor-General's Council, and whose experience of the state of Oudh was invaluable at that particular time in its history. He pointed out that Lord Hardinge had distinctly given the King only two years in which to carry out reforms; that seven had passed with results which showed that things were worse instead of better; and that now, in his opinion, to avoid resort to extremities was no longer incumbent on the Indian Government.

These powerful records against the effete and incapable dynasty of Oudh were laid before Lord Dalhousie, who, in "an able and elaborate State paper," submitted the whole subject for the consideration of the Court of Directors. Before the end of the same year (1855) the order had gone forth for the annexation of the province.

The execution of this difficult and delicate task was entrusted to Colonel Outram. Military preparations were at once made to carry out the plan, and on the 30th January, 1856, the Prime Minister was distinctly informed of the intention of the Government of India to take possession of the country. Three days' grace was allowed to the King to acquiesce in the proposals made by the Governor-General, which proposals, briefly stated, amounted to the transfer of the administration of the government of Oudh into the hands of the East India Company, the King's title, honours, rank and dignity being carefully preserved, and His Majesty's authority being absolute so far as his own palace and his own household were concerned. The three days passed and Wajid Ali Shah still expressed his unwillingness to attach his signature to the treaty, and so Colonel Outram had no alternative but at once to carry out his instructions. Accordingly, on the 7th February, 1856, he issued the Proclamation announcing that the British Government "had assumed to itself the exclusive and permanent administration of the territories of Oudh." No disturbance followed the execution of this difficult work. Civil officers were appointed to the charge of all the divisions and districts, and a thorough re-organization in every department of the public service was commenced. To all matters, even to those of the minutest detail, Colonel Outram gave his closest attention. The process of assumption under the circumstances could not fail to create a certain amount of dissatisfaction among those who had profited from the extravagance and imbecility of the King's rule; but, on the whole, whatever view may be held regarding the soundness of the policy which dictated the movement, it is readily allowed, by all acquainted with the delicate nature of the undertaking, that Colonel Outram carried out his part in the annexation with a firmness and care deserving of all praise.

CHAPTER XIV.

From the Annexation to the Mutiny.

The measures adopted for the general administration of the province of Oudh by the British Government were very much the same as those which had been carried out with such marked success in the Panjab. Judicial and Financial Commissioners were appointed, also Commissioners of the Revenue Divisions and Deputy, Assistant, and Extra Assistant Commissioners of districts; Colonel Outram's own title being changed from Resident to that of Chief Commissioner of Oudh and Agent to the Governor-General. All public buildings were taken possession of, police control was organized, jails and charitable dispensaries were started, a Public Works Department was formed, Civil and Criminal Courts were established. It was further determined that the settlement should, in the first instance, be made with persons actually in possession, village by village, but their proprietary right, either formal or indirect, was not recognized by the Government. This settlement was to last for three years certain. On one point the Government of India were very explicit. They declared it to be their intention to deal only and solely with the actual occupants of the soil—that is to say with village zemindars, and on no account to allow the interposition of middle men, such as taaluqdars, farmers of the revenue and such like. The claims of these latter class, if they had any, were to be investigated and settled individually by the Civil Courts.

As regards the King himself certain concessions were made which doubtless would have been even more favourable to him had he signed the treaty presented to him just immediately before the annexation took place. On account of his refusal to comply with the wishes of the Government of India in the matter, he placed himself in entire dependence on the future will and pleasure of the British Government. Lord Dalhousie, under the circumstances, was not prepared to give any guarantee or any promise of hereditary succession to the Royal title. Apart from this, however, the Government dealt liberally with Wajid Ali Shah. It allowed him a stipend of 12 lakhs a year, it arranged for the maintenance of the families of the former rulers of Oudh, and it directed that all deference and respect and every Royal honour should be paid to him during his lifetime.

But much as a vast number of the people welcomed the introduction of the reforms of the British Government, there is no doubt that by the changes many were thrown out of employment and were, in consequence, greatly discontented. Not calculating the thousands who earned a livelihood formerly by their evil deeds, there were others also, a large number of artists, workmen, soldiers, and even civil officials, whose occupation was now gone. The work, for instance, which formerly devolved on upwards of 300 administrators of high rank was now performed by 12 Deputy Commissioners. This, doubtless, produced ill-feeling among many men. Again, the taaluqdars were not likely to accept with cheerful submission their deprivation of influence and other means of amassing money. It was held by them, and, it may be added, by other unprejudiced persons also, that this wholesale degradation was a great mistake on the part of the then Government of India, which, however, it was soon to be one of the results of the mutiny to correct.

CHAPTER XV.

The Mutiny in Oudh.

So much has been written on the subject of the mutiny, and also particularly of the mutiny in the newly acquired province of Oudh, that it is proposed in the following record to give a mere cursory review of this the greatest event in the History of India.

Sir Henry Lawrence was appointed to the Chief Commissionership of Oudh in March, 1857. A month later, rumours began to prevail throughout the country regarding the composition of the cartridges issued to the Native Army. It was as well for the province that so able and so sympathetic a statesman as Sir Henry Lawrence was at the head of affairs during this critical period. He found himself surrounded by discontent, in many instances amounting to sedition. The taaluqdars, of course, were wroth, thousands of discharged sepoys crowded the city, and as many Court followers and unemployed professional men in all directions were harbouring enmity to the British rule. The province also was under the great disadvantage of containing, it is said, the families of upwards of 40 or 50,000 soldiers, while at Lucknow itself were located several disaffected regiments of infantry and cavalry. The 71st Native Infantry were the first to mutiny, and they invited the 7th Bengal Cavalry, 48th Native Infantry, and others to join them, till gradually all except those who remained faithful to the end joined in opposition to British authority. Sadder and sadder news in the meantime reached Sir Henry Lawrence from all sides, both in his own province and from all parts of India, and it became necessary to take immediate steps to take up some place of defence and to store ammunition and supplies against a protracted siege. At first it was hoped that both the Muchee Bhawan and the Residency could be held by the garrison, but ultimately the former was given up as untenable, its walls being unable to resist artillery, and the drains under it affording a too favourable means for mining. Then followed all the terrible events of those days—universal mutiny, massacre, flights and privations, the unfortunate reverse at Chinahat, the concentration of the remnant of the English people for the siege, the melancholy death of the good and great Sir Henry Lawrence, and further, all the anxiety and danger to which this brave little garrison was exposed, till relieved by the arrival of reinforcements under General Havelock and General Outram. The reinforced garrison had still to hold their own for two months more, within the defences of the Residency, till the final relief was effected by Sir Colin Campbell in November. The retreat which followed the relief is perhaps one of the most perfect military combinations on record, a model of discipline and exactness. So well arranged was the movement that the whole garrison, men, women, and children, was withdrawn from the heart of the city of Lucknow to its very outskirt, not only without molestation from the enemy, but even without the enemy, some 50,000 or so, being aware of its taking place.

After this retreat had been accomplished, it was held that, though the British force was not strong enough to hold Lucknow altogether, the total withdrawal of the English troops from Oudh would have an unfavourable effect at that time. So the Alam Bagh was occupied, and a small army left there under the command of Sir James Outram to keep the city in check, while Sir Colin Campbell and the main body of the army moved back to Cawnpore. This force was constantly harrassed by the enemy for upwards of three months, but was as constantly successful in repulsing all attacks that were made upon it. Eventually in March, 1858, Sir Colin Campbell, with a large body of troops and a heavy siege train, arrived from Cawnpore, to relieve the garrison at Alam Bagh and to capture the city of Lucknow. With comparatively trifling loss of life this purpose was completely effected before the close of the month. The great stronghold of that part of India being now in possession of the British Government, it was a mere matter of time, and numberless small engagements, to clear the whole province of rebels and to restore English rule and supremacy from one end of the country to the other. In less than two years, all the terrible storm of almost universal rebellion and disaster that had burst upon Oudh had completely cleared away, and peace and security reigned to a much greater extent than it ever did before in every village and every house in the province.

CHAPTER XVI.

FROM THE MUTINY TO THE AMALGAMATION.

(With special reference to the Taaluqdars).

ON the British occupation of Lucknow it became necessary for the English Government, through the Governor-General, Lord Canning, to make known the policy it proposed to adopt in regard to the future administration of the country. Lord Canning lost no time in enunciating his views, which were embodied in the celebrated Oudh Proclamation, and which probably aroused more interest and comment than any proceeding of the Government during the mutiny. The Proclamation in question involved nothing more or less than the confiscation of all land property in Oudh, with the exception of that in the possession of six of the chieftains named below :—

Raja Digbijai Singh of Balrampur.
Raja Kalwant Singh of Padwala.
Rao Hardeo Baksh, Taaluqdar of Kathari.
Rao Kashi Parshad, Thakur, Sakodi.
Zahar Singh, zemindar, Gopal Kheri.
Chandan Lal, zemindar, Morawa.

It was further added that such taaluqdars as would give up their arms to the Chief Commissioner and cease to be rebels would receive pardon on condition that they had not been parties to the murder of any Europeans. This Proclamation was received with great concern by many of the Oudh officials, but by none more so than by Sir James Outram, whose views and influence in the matter carried no little weight with the Home authorities. The end, however, was that the Proclamation, with certain modifications from the Board of Control at the time presided over by Lord Ellenborough, did come into force shortly after its issue by the Governor-General. Its issue at first created great consternation, but afterwards, on further reflection, men came to see that they had too hastily condemned it, and its results would not be so severe as at one time they had anticipated. In the meantime Sir James Outram had made over his office to Sir Robert Montgomery, and in June, 1858, the taaluqdars were summoned to Lucknow, and were told distinctly the conditions under which they would be allowed to retain possession of the land they held before the annexation. The result was that two-thirds of the taaluqdars made their submission to the British Government, and eventually through them all the revenue of the province was paid into the treasury. Sir Robert Montgomery was succeeded by Mr. Wingfield, who carried out the policy of Government with still greater earnestness. Under him the country gradually came under a thorough system of organization. The population was disarmed, the police had a certain military training, and Oudh gradually was converted from a warlike province into one of the most peaceable and contented countries in India. It is said that no less than 1,562 fortresses were destroyed, and that 720 pieces of cannon, 192,307 firearms, 579,554 swords, and 694,050 miscellaneous arms, or a total of 14,66,641 weapons of sorts, were destroyed.

From that time the position and dignity of the taaluqdar in Oudh have been steadily on the ascendant. He is no longer the worst enemy the people have, the bitter opponent of the Amils, always at feud with his neighbours and the Government, but he has become a link between the rulers and ruled, a loyal, peaceful, enterprising subject of the Throne. Such taaluqdars number some 3 or 400 men, and at Lord Canning's durbar in 1860 no less then 177 of them were present. Many of these have since become Honorary Magistrates and some Assistant Commissioners, thus taking an active part in the general administration of the country. Subsequently, in Lord Lawrence's time, some attempt was made to modify matters in favour of the tenantry; but, on the whole, the rights of the taaluqdars were maintained on much the same footing as that on which they were in the first instance placed by Lord Canning.

In Oudh, now, there are about 25,842 villages, each village being on an average one mile square. Out of these villages, 15,553 have 410 owners, and each of these owners pay a Government demand to the extent of Rs. 5,000 and upwards. The owners of the remaining 10,290 villages are 9,650 shareholders. The old taaluqdars were owners of three-fifths of the land.

In many respects Oudh has made great strides in the way of general improvements. The Civil and Judicial Courts have effected much good and other departments also have left their lasting mark. But with reference to no matter, perhaps, has such a change been effected as in education. There are now numberless schools scattered over the province, in which whoever cares can receive a sound education. The Canning College, too, has borne good fruit, while Munshi Nawal Kishore's Press has contributed much towards the diffusion of wholesome and useful knowledge among the people. Added to the above, the taaluqdars have formed themselves into an Association, where much advantage is gained by themselves and by the Government, by a periodical interchange of thoughts and sentiments among the aristocracy of the province.

CHAPTER XVII.

THE AMALGAMATION OF OUDH WITH THE NORTH-WESTERN PROVINCES.

For some time rumours had been circulated to the effect that the Government of India intended to amalgamate the province of Oudh with the North-West, and in January, 1877, the measure was really adopted

The occasion was an opportune one, for Sir George Couper, the Chief Commissioner of Oudh, had just been appointed to officiate as Lieutenant-Governor of the North-Western Provinces. The chief changes have been in departments only. The law of Oudh and the position and rights of the people have not been affected by the union. For many reasons Allahabad was preferred as the seat of Government, though the Lieutenant-Governor was invited to remain two or three months of the year at Lucknow.

Many thought at first that the amalgamation scheme would alter the position and injure the interests of the taaluqdars, but, happily, these anticipations were ill-founded. In March, 1877, Lord Lytton dispelled all these ideas in open durbar. He told the taaluqdars that they need harbour no feelings of uneasiness on the score of the amalgamation, that it would in no way change their rights and privileges, and that all the laws and rules that previously governed Oudh would remain exactly as they did before.

CHAPTER XVIII.

CONCLUSION.

WE cannot conclude this History of Oudh, so far back as its history is known up to the present day, without congratulating the province on the share of Government favour and Government attention it has invariably secured from the earliest period of its existence. In old times Government felt itself bound to interfere with the affairs of Oudh, but time and experience has shown that, almost in every case, the interference has been for the real good of the country. Before the influence of England ever found its way to this province, we well know how things and people fared ; no security from the invasion of an outside foe, no protection from the oppressive Chiefs, not even safety from the intrigues of one's household and immediate friends. Men went fully armed to till the ground, and they returned in fear and trembling to their homes, night after night, not daring to think what might have happened in their absence. Now all is different. The Government, by being kind and considerate towards the taaluqdars, have led them to be kind and considerate towards their tenants ; there is no oppression, no uncertainty of the present or the future, and every sense of injustice is appealed to the British authorities, through the medium of the Civil and Criminal Courts. Five and twenty years ago there was no province in India where there existed such malversation, misrule, insecurity of life and property, and such wretchedness, and now probably there is no province in the country so conscientiously governed, so prosperous, and so contented.

List of Taaluqdars of Oudh, arranged by districts.

Page of illustration.	Darbar number.	Name of taaluqdar.	Name of estate.
		Lucknow.	
75	232	Muhammad Husain	Ghazipur.
11	42	Raja Chandar Sikhar	Sisendi.
66	200	Qutub-un-Nisa	Gauriya kalan.
12	47	Rani Sitar-un-Nisa	Salempur.
6	23	Raja Jagmohan Singh	Raipur Yakdariya.
43	129	Babu Jadunath Singh	Mahganw.
60	143	Muhammad Ahmad Khan	Kasmandi khurd.
44	131	Muhammad Nasim Khan	Sohla Mau.
75	233	Mirza Jáfar Ali Khan	Bihta.
63	192	Saiyad Nazir Husain	Ahman Mau.
		Unao.	
36	107	Thakur Baldeo Bakhsh	Pursaini.
18	56	Makrind Singh	Rampur.
18	57	Kunwar Harnam Singh	Manager of Bauudi.
74	230	Saiyad Muhammad Ali Khan	Unchganw.
74	...	Saiyad Husain Ali Khan	Ditto.
58	174	Mahip Singh	Kantha.
14	52	Har Prashad	Maurawan.
14	52	Ram Charan, partners	Bihta.
14	52	Bisheshar Prashad	Thalendi.
15	52	Madho Prashad	Daretha.
15	52	Debi Dayal	Amawan.
15	52	Sheo Dayal	Deoni Kandawan.
15	52	Ram Narain	Lnasinghan Khera.
16	52	Balmakund	Atwat.
16	52	Kalka Prashad	bachhrawan.
16	52	Chandka Prashad	Ditto.
16	52	Mohan Lal, and 5 others	Asrenda.
17	52	Beni Prashad	Birwakalan Talenda.
50	61	Mahant Harcharan Das	Maswasi.
47	142	Fatch Singh *alias* Fatch Bahadur.	Sarausi.
28	84	Nau Nihal Singh	Muhammadabad.
47	140	Balbhaddar Singh	Gaura.
47	140	Darshan Singh	Husainabad.
76	235	Mahpal Singh	Malauna.
58	175	Sultan Singh	Galgalha.
61	183	Saiyad Ramzan Ali	Unao.
13	49	Raja Daya Shankar Dichhit	Parenda.
66	203	Daya Shankar Bajpai	Kardaha.
86	...	Beni Madho Bakhsh	Akbarpur.
64	195	Mahesh Bakhsh	Patenbihar.
64	195	Arjun Singh	Ditto.
14	59	Babu Ram Sahai	Maurawan, &c.
73	225	Shekh Wasi-uz-zaman	Miyanganj.
86	...	Mahpal Singh	Jaja Mau.
84	...	Raja Sheo Nath Singh	Bihtar.
83	251	Sheo Gobind Tiwari	Bihta Bhawani.

Page of illustration.	Darbar number.	Name of taaluqdar.	Name of estate.
		BARA BANKI.	
61	185	Girdhari Singh	Gokalpur aseni.
74	231	Shams-un-nisa	Jismara Malikpur, &c.
75	234	Shekh Talib Ali	Dinpanah.
...	...	„ Karim Bakhsh	Ditto.
62	186	„ Mansab Ali	Sidahar.
...	189	„ Muhammad Amir	Shahabpur.
63	...	„ Gulam Abbas	Ditto.
51	152	Sahib-un-nisa	Kharka.
5	16	Raja Farzand Ali Khan	Jahangirabad, &c.
40	123	Qazi Ikram Ahmad	Satrikh.
42	123	Hakim Karam Ali	Gotya.
59	177	Pande Sarabjit Singh	Asadanau.
51	153	Mir Bunyad Husain	Jhunnau.
51	153	„ Amjad Husain	Suhailpur.
50	151	Thakur Sheo Sahai	Samrawan.
36	108	Shekh Ahmad Husain	Gadya, &c.
..	...	„ Wajid Husain	Ditto.
76	236	Rukman Kunwar	Tirbediganj, &c.
59	178	Shekh Inayat-ul-lah	Saidanpur.
...	...	„ Ikram Ali	Ditto.
60	...	„ Inam-ul-lah	Ditto.
46	138	„ Nawab Ali Khan	Maila Raiganj
38	114	Kazim Husain Khan	Bhatwamau, &c.
11	43	Raja Sarabjit Singh	Ramnagar.
71	219	Dan Bahadur Singh	Muhammadpur.
...	2 7	Har Prashad	Lilauli.
76	237	Shekh Muhammad Nasir-ud-din	Mirpur.
65	199	„ Riyasat Ali	Shekhpur.
20	64	Chaudhri Murtaza Husain	Bhilwal, &c.
...	63	Ratewuz-zaman *kaimakam* Bech-un-nisa,	Sikandarpur.
17	64	Babu Mahpal Singh	Surajpur.
7	25	Raja Narindar Bahadur Singh,	Harha.
40	120	Rai Ibram Bali	Raupur.
43	139	Shekh Mahbub ur-rahman	Barai, &c.
...	...	„ Inayat-ur-rahman	Ditto.
...	...	„ Abd-ur-rahman	Ditto.
44	...	„ Fazal-ur-rahman	Ditto.
47	141	Saiyad Raza Husain	Narauli
62	188	„ Muhammad Abid	Parai.
63	1 1	Shekh Ihsan Rasul	Amirpur.
6	21	Raja Bhagwan Bakhsh	Pakhra Ansari.
76	238	Thakur Parthipal Singh	Ramnagar.
77	239	Babu Lal Bahadur	Akhyapur.
63	190	Gulam Qasim Khan	Usmanpur.
64	197	Bhaya Antar Singh	Rani Mau.
66	201	Muhammad Husain Khan, son of Nisar Ali Khan	Banaura.
77	240	Wazir Ali Khan	Barauli.
77	241	Babu Kishun Datt	Pali.
77	242	Diwan Kishun Kunwar	Yaqubganj.
		SITAPUR.	
62	187	Sita Ram Khattari	Bhagupur, &c.
34	117	Thakur Jawahir Singh	Basi Dih, &c.
39	119	Thakur Maharaj Singh	Kaoh Mau, &c.

Page of illustration.	Darbar number.	Name of taaluqdar.	Name of estate.
		SITAPUR—(concluded).	
40	121	Mirza Ahmad Ali Beg ...	Qutub Nagar, &c.
33	118	Thakur Durga Bakhsh ...	Nil Ganw, &c.
38	113	Mirza Muhammad Ali Beg ...	Urangabad.
45	136	Seth Raghbar Dayal ...	Muiz-od-dinpur, &c.
45	136	„ Sita Ram ...	Ditto.
27	68	Thakur Pratab Rudr Singh ...	Rampur, &c.
39	116	„ Fazal Ali Khan ...	Akbarpur.
83	Without number	Nawab Muhammad Baqar Ali Khan	Kunwaukhera.
12	44	Raja Shamshir Bahadur ...	Saadatnagar &c.
29	88	Thakur Sheo Bakhsh Singh ...	Katesar, &c.
48	143	„ Anand Singh ...	Rampur, &c.
44	...	„ Jagan Nath Singh ...	Ditto.
45	...	„ Hardeo Bakhsh ...	Ditto.
45	...	„ Ganga Bakhsh ...	Ditto.
38	113	„ Hari Har Bakhsh ...	Saraura.
3	10	Raja Muhammad Amir Hasan Khan.	Mahmudabad, &c.
6	20	Raja Muhammad Kazim Husain Khan.	Paltepur, &c.
64	207	Thakur Ganga Bakhsh ...	Ramkot and Hajipur.
68	209	„ Kalka Bakhsh ...	Ditto.
84	Without number.	Raja Jagar Nath Singh ...	Wazirnagar.
49	146	Chaudhri Ram Narain ...	Mubarakpur.
44	132	Mir Muhammad Hasan Khan,	Rajapara, &c.
57	171	Mirza Abbas Beg... ...	Baraganw.
78	243	Maulvi Mazhar Ali ...	Mahiwa.
78	244	Thakur Kalka Bakhsh ...	Saadatnagar.
78	245	„ Raghuraj Singh ...	Rajpur.
		HARDOI.	
2	6	Raja Tilak Singh... ...	Katyari, &c.
5	18	„ Randhir Singh ...	Bhatawan, &c.
29	86	Chaudhri Khaslat Husain ...	Kakrah, &c.
29	87	Thakur Bharat Singh ...	Atwa, &c.
37	111	Saiyad Wasi Haidar ...	Bhigetyapur.
37	112	Chaudhri Muhammad Ashraf,	Asatpur, &c.
37	112	Muhammad Zain-ul-ab-din ..	Bhagyari.
37	112	Muhammad Fazil ...	Durgaganj.
38	112	Saiyad Muhammad Abrar ...	Dhundhpur.
40	122	Maulvi Fazal Rasul ...	Jalalpur, &c.
35	105	Thakurain Dalil Kunwar ...	Lahrasatpur.
51	154	Deb Singh	Sujpur Sakrav.
36	110	Thakur Lalta Bakhsh ..	Khajrahra, &c.
10	39	Begam Amanat Fatima ...	Basti Nagar.
31	90	Wazir Chand	Sarawan Bara Ganw.
31	90	Durga Prashad	Ditto.
73	246	Thakur Sarabjit Singh ...	Pawayan, &c.
56	166	Imtiyaz Fatima	Gopa Mau.
56	Without number.	Bhag Bhari	Karam Bhola.
79	247	Safdar Husain Khan ...	Bhanapur.

Page of illustration.	Darbar number.	Name of taaluqdar.	Name of estate.
		KHERI LAKHIMPUR.	
8	31	Rani Sahib Jan, widow of Musharraf Ali Khan.	Bahadur Nagar, &c.
44	133	Saiyad Fida Husain Khan	Atwapiparya, &c.
72	222	Muhammad Sher Khan	Raipur, &c.
23	72	Raj Milap Singh	Shahpur Majhgain,
23	72	Gumau Singh	Ramnagar Daulatpur.
23	72	Gobhar Dhan Singh	Bichhwanighasan.
23	72	Dalip Singh	Bichauriya Jagdespur.
72	221	Fazal Husain, son of Chand Bibi,	Kutwara, &c.
83	262	Widow of Niamat-ul-lah Khan,	Mirzapur, &c.
7	24	Raja Krishen Datt, son of Raja Anrud Singh.	Oel, &c.
13	51	Thakur Balbhaddar Singh	Mahewa, &c.
10	38	Raja Narpat Singh	Khamra, &c.
17	55	Thakur Ranjit Singh	Isa Nagar, &c.
14	41	Raja Muneshar Bakhsh Singh,	Mallaupur, &c.
10	37	„ Indar Bikrama Sah	Khairigadh, &c.
54	160	Rai Ram Din Bahadur	Pela, &c.
85	Without number.	Alexander Douglas	Aira, &c.
85	...	Pauline Annie Orr	Nagra, &c.
85	...	Louisa Fanny Orr	Jirabojhi, &c.
84	...	L. D. Hearsey	Kiman Buzurg, &c.
		FYZABAD.	
1	3	Lal Pratab Narain Singh	Mihdanna, &c.
24	73	Babu Udres Singh	Maopur Lhirwa.
24	73	„ Chandres Singh	Ditto.
70	214	Gaya Din	Mudera.
70	214	Sabhjit Singh	Ditto.
24	75	Saiyad Gazaffar Husain	Pirpur.
25	75	„ Baqar Husain	Ditto.
72	224	Mir Ashraf Husain	Katariya.
25	76	Babu Ugardat Singh	Bihti, &c.
29	85	„ Mahindradat Singh	Khajrahta.
32	94	Thakur Bisheshar Ba'hsh Singh.	Sahipur.
31	91	Thakur Anand Bahadur Singh,	Khapradih.
49	145	Babu Azam Ali Khan	Deoganw, &c.
34	102	Lachmi Narain, son of Babu Kishan Parshad Singh.	Barhar Chandipur.
35	104	Shamshare Bahadur, son of Babu Sheo Pragash Singh.	Barhar Raj, Sultanpur.
34	105	Babu Hardat Singh	Barhar Chandipur Haswa.
35	106	Sheodist Narain Singh, son of Babu Mahape Narain Singh.	Barhar.
49	147	Babu Porthipal Singh	Tigra.
28	82	Malik Hidayat Husain	Samanpur.
79	248	Lala Auant Ram	Rasulpur.
		BAHRAICH.	
8	28	Raja Mahindar Bahadar Singh,	Payagpur.
5	17	„ Jang Bahadur Khan	Naupara.
7	27	„ Sitla Bakhsh Singh	Gangol.
6	19	Son of Raghu Nath Singh	Rihwa.

Page of illustration.	Darbar number.	Name of taaluqdar.	Name of estate.
		BAHRAICH—(*concluded*).	
33	97	Bhaya Udepratab Singh	Bhinga, &c.
67	205	Thakur Fateh Muhammad	Tiparha.
67	206	„ Nirman Singh	Ainehapur, &c.
49	144	Thakurain Jaipal Kunwar	Mustafabad, &c.
59	176	Shekh Niwazish Ali	Ambhapur, &c.
60	181	Mir Zafar Mahdi	Ali Nagar.
61	182	Saiyad Kazim Husain	Pera Qazi.
32	96	Niwazish Ali Khan	Nawabganj Aliyabad.
73	227	Sardar Hira Singh	Jamdan.
74	229	Saiyad Sardar Ali	Sisai Salon, &c.
73	228	Baghhale Singh	Bhanghia.
85	Without number.	„ Jazjot Singh	Charhari, &c.
86	Do.	Lachhman Kunwar	Ditto.
4	1	Raja Rajgau Jagat Jit Singh Bahadur, Maharaja Kapurthala.	Baundi, &c.
		GONDA.	
1	2	H. H. the H. Sir Drig Bijai Singh Bahadur, K.C.S.I	Balrampur and Tulsipur.
9	32	Shambudat Ram, *kaimmakam* of Raja Kishndat Ram.	Siugha Chanda.
9	34	Rani Saltanat Kunwar	Mankapur.
9	33	„ Janki Kunwar	Paraspur.
12	46	Raja Sher Bahadur Singh	Deoli, &c.
41	125	Thakur Mirtunja Bakhsh Singh,	Shahpur, &c.
41	124	„ Raghbir Singh	Dhannwan, &c.
45	135	Thakurain Iklas Kunwar	Paska, &c.
47	134	Babu Sukhraj Singh	Ata.
65	198	Bhaya Har Ratan Singh	Majhgawan, &c.
79	250	Pande Har Narain Ram	Akbarpur, &c.
57	169	Ude Narain Singh	Bhunni Pair.
12	45	Raja Mumtaz Ali Khan	Bilaspur, &c.
57	170	Lal Achal Ram, husband of Brij Raj Kunwar.	Birwa.
		RAE BARELI.	
1	4	Raja Sheopal Singh	Murar Mau, &c.
4	12	„ Surpal Singh	Tiloi, &c.
4	14	Rana Shankar Bakhsh Singh	Thalrai Khajurganw, &c.
32	93	Babu Bishan Nath Singh	Katgadh.
6	22	Rai Bisheshar Bakhsh, son of Raja Jagmohan Singh	Harsinghpur, &c.
7	26	Raja Rampal Singh	Kori Sudauli.
8	29	„ Jagmohan Singh	Atra Chandapur, &c.
21	64	Thakurain Sheopal Kunwar	Simri, &c.
21	65	„ Darya Kunwar	Simarpaha.
21	66	Thakur Chandarpal Singh	Koribarsitawan.
21	67	Thakurain Achal Kunwar	Gaura Kasithi.
27	81	Thakur Shankar Bakhsh	Pabu Gulariya.
33	99	„ Bishan Nath Bakhsh	Hasanpur, &c.
3	8	Raja Lal Madho Singh	Amethi.
33	100	Babu Sarabjit Singh	Takari, &c.
46	137	Musammat Daryao Kunwar, widow of Bishan Nath Singh.	Narindpur Charhar.

Page of illustration.	Darbar number.	Name of taaluqdar.	Name of estate.
		RAE BARELI—(*concluded*).	
46	137	Thakur Ajudhiya Bakhsh	Narindpur Charhar.
46	139	Thakurain Ude Nath Kunwar,	Hamir Mau Kola.
52	156	Muhammad Zaman Khan	Amawan.
52	156	,, Said Khan	Ditto.
52	156	,, Sultan Khan	Ditto.
53	157	Zulfiqar Khan	Pahra Mau.
53	157	Karam Ali Khan	Ditto.
53	157	Shahamat Khan	Ditto.
53	157	Asad Ali Khan	Ditto.
54	158	Thakur Bhagwan Bakhsh	Udrehra, &c.
54	159	Mithan Kunwar, widow of Balbhaddar Singh.	Bahrauli, &c.
60	179	Mir Fakhr-ul Husain	Banaubra.
69	210	Thakur Jagmohan Singh	Deogaua Girdharpur.
69	211	Jagraj Kunwar	Hardaspur.
80	251	Babwain Anand Kunwar	Ausa.
80	252	Maharaj Bakhsh	Palkha.
80	253	Sita Ram	Sihgaaw.
80	254	Balbhaddar Singh	Kahjuri.
81	255	Thakur Bakhsh	Kesarwa.
81	256	Babu Bakhtawar Singh	Dihli.
81	257	Ganga Bishun	Mainharkhera.
67	207	Fateh Bahadur Khan	Bahwa
13	50	Raja Sukh Mangal Singh	Shah Mau, &c.
71	208	Sheo Ratan Singh	Pinhauna.
65	196	Babu Madho Singh	Nur-ud-din-pur.
69	212	Mahpal Singh	Bara.
25	77	Rudr Pratab Singh	Seoni Siwan.
60	180	Subhan Ahmad	Azizabad.
84	Without number.	Shahzada Shahdeo Singh	Bhandri Ganesh.
18	58	Captain Gulab Singh	Bhira Gobindpur.
18	68	Sardar Atar Singh	Khoreti.
19	58	,, Narain Singh	Bela Bhela.
33	98	Babu Bihuaraujan Mukarji	Shankarpur.
68	174	Mir Ahmad Jan	Raghupur.
70	206	Saiyad Farzand Ali Khan	Kathwara.
83	Without number.	Major A. P. Orr	Lodhwari.
81	258	Saiyad Muhammad Muhsin	Alipur Chakai.
82	258	,, Muhammad Shafi	Ditto.
82	259	Beni Prashad	Mahgau, &c.
		SULTANPUR.	
52	155	Babu Ashraj Singh	Meopur Dihla.
79	249	Sheo Raj Kunwar	Sultanpur, &c.
3	9	Raja Muhammad Ali Khan	Hasanpur.
4	13	Rani Kishan Nath Kunwar, widow of Madho Pratab Singh.	Kurwar, &c.
54	161	Hafi Khasam	Maniyarpur.
55	163	Lachhman Prashad	Bahduiyan, &c.
65	163	Bishun Nath Singh	Ditto.
66	202	Thakurain Daryao Kunwar	Garabpur.
82	260	Sheo Shankar Singh	Pratabpur.
82	260	Arjan Singh	Ditto.

Page of illustration.	Darbar number.	Name of taaluqdar.	Name of estate.
		SOLTANPUR—(concluded).	
28	83	Anant Prashad	Rampur, &c.
28	83	Bikarmajit Singh	Ditto.
2	7	Raja Rudr Partab Singh	Dihra, &c.
172	55	Bijai Bahadur Singh	Shahgarh.
17	54	Iwaz Ali Khan	Mahona.
69	213	Dargahi Khan	Unchgaow.
8	20	Rani Har Nath Kunwar	Katari.
27	80	Ganesh Kunwar, widow of Jagarnath Bakhsh.	Jamau.
55	164	Sripal Singh	Barauliya.
67	204	Jagesar Bakhsh Singh	Baliwan Shahpur.
35	107	Ganesh Kunwar, widow of Arjun Singh.	Rehsi.
27	79	Jagannath Singh, *kaiwmakam* of Babu Hardat Singh.	Simratpur.
55	162	Jahangir Bakhsh	Gangeo, &c.
33	95	Babu Lalu Sha	Meopur Dihla, &c.
54	161	„ Sitla Bakhsh	Nana Mau, &c.
21	74	„ Amres Singh	Meopur Baraganw.
		PARTABGARH.	
2	5	Raja Hanwant Singh	Kalakankar.
2	5	Rampal Singh	Rampur Dharupur, &c.
3	11	Raja Bijai Bahadur Singh	Bihlolpur.
4	15	Rani Dharamraj Kunwar	Parhat, &c.
10	36	Raja Mahesh Bakhsh Singh	Khetauli.
18	48	„ Ajit Singh	Sarwal, &c.
19	59	Rai Jagmohan Singh	Raipur Bichaur.
19	59	Bisheshar Bakhsh	Ditto.
19	60	Rai Madho Prashad Singh	Adharganj.
20	62	Lal Sarabjit Singh	Bahdri, &c.
21	69	Diwan Ran Bijai Bahadur Singh,	Patti Saifabad.
22	70	Thakurain Ajit Kunwar	Ditto.
22	71	„ Janki Kunwar	Pawansi Dahgos.
25	78	Sitla Bakhsh	Madhpur.
25	78	Lal Bahadur Singh	Ditto.
26	78	Kalka Bakhsh Singh	Ditto.
26	78	Udat Narain Singh	Ditto.
26	78	Nageshar Bakhsh	Ditto.
27	78	Chauburja Bakhsh Singh	Ditto.
30	89	Thakurain Baijnath Kunwar	Kamlrajit.
30	89	Chhatarpal Singh	Ditto.
30	89	Surajpal Singh	Ditto.
30	89	Chandarpal Singh	Ditto.
31	92	Dan Bahadur Pal Singh	Dandikachha.
41	126	Har Mangal Singh	Utiya Dih.
41	127	Bhagwant Singh	Daryapur.
42	127	Jagmohan Singh	Ditto.
42	127	Bisheshar Bakhsh Singh	Ditto.
42	127	Arth Singh	Ditto.
50	149	Babu Mahesh Bakhsh Singh	Dhayanwan.
50	150	Sarabjit Singh	Shekhpur Chauras.
56	167	Babu Hanuman Bakhsh Singh,	Dumepur.
57	163	„ Hardat Singh	Pirthiganj.
16	184	„ Bajrang Bahadur Singh,	Baispur.

Page of illustration.	Darbar number.	Name of taaluqdar.	Name of estate.
		PARTABGARH—(concluded).	
64	193	Babu Balbhaddar Singh ...	Sujakhar.
64	194	Umed Singh	Asanpur.
68	208	Thakurain Sagu Nath Kunwar,	Dasrathpur.
68	208	„ Kharak Kunwar .	Ditto.
70	215	Babu Sarab Dan Singh ...	Utwamaupur.
71	220	Drig Bijai Singh	Athganwan.
72	223	Mahpal Singh	Amrar.
9	35	Raja Chhatpal Singh ...	Nurpur. &c.
34	101	Sitla Bakhsh Singh ...	Dahugadh, &c.
34	101	Shankar Singh	Ditto.
73	226	Sheo Ambar Singh ...	Rajpur.
11	40	Raja Jagat Bahadur ...	Amri.

SHORT MEMOIRS

OF

EVERY TAALUQDAR IN OUDH

WHOSE PORTRAITS ARE GIVEN IN THIS VOLUME

(Arranged in the same order as the photographs.)

No. 1.

RAJA RAJGAN SIR JAGET JIT SINGH, *of Kapurthala, of Sikh descent, Maharaja, Taaluqdar of Baundi, Parsauli, and Bhatauli.*

THIS Maharaja is the chief of Kapurthala territories situated in zila Jallandar, Panjab. The loyalty of His Highness's family to the throne of England has always been conspicuous. This loyalty was exhibited in a marked degree by the present Maharaja's grandfather, Randhir Singh Bahadur, G.C.S.I., during the mutiny in 1857. When the mutiny was at its height, he rendered to Colonel Abbott, Deputy Commissioner of Hoshiarpur, services of the most important nature, which had a very marked effect on that part of the country. His Highness afterwards promptly responded to a call made on him by Colonel Abbott and Mr. Robert Montgomery, Chief Commissioner of Oudh, and placed himself at the head of a large force organised and maintained entirely at his own expense. With this force he reached Lucknow *via* Dehli, and from thence took part in a series of operations which reflected the highest credit on his own personal valour as well as on the discipline of his troops. In return for these eminent services, and in recognition of his steady loyal adherence to British authority in those trying times, Maharaja Randhir Singh Bahadur received from the Viceroy a gift of the *taaluqs* of Baundi, Parsauli, and Bhatauli (situated in zilas Gonda, Bahraich, and Kheri), yielding an annual public revenue of Rs. 2,00,478-13-1. His Highness died at Aden on his way to England, and was succeeded by Maharaja Kharag Singh Bahadur. The present chief succeeded to the *guddi* of Kapurthala on Kharag Singh's death. The Kapurthala estates in Oudh are under the management of Kunwar Harnam Singh, uncle of the now ruling Maharaja.

No. 2.

MAHARAJA SIR DRIG BIJAI SINGH BAHADUR, K.C.S.I., *Janwar, Taaluqdar of Balrampur, Tulsipur, Chardah, and Barawan Kalan.*

THIS well-known Oudh taaluqdar is a descendant of Maharaja Nainsukh Deo of Japaner, in the province of Guzerat, whose sixth son,

Bariar Sahi, in the *sambat* year 1325, came to Delhi and entered the service of Emperor Tajudin Shah Ghori. Following his new master to parganah Ekonah, in zila Bahraich, on a combined visiting tour and shooting excursion, Bariar Sahi was entrusted with the duty of reducing that turbulent part of the country to order, a work which he is said to have carried out with much success. For the tact and ability displayed by him on the occasion he was rewarded by the Emperor with the gift of the parganah in question, where he took up his permanent residence. Raja Madho Singh, sixth in descent from Bariar Singh, went over to Ramgarh Gauri (in the same parganah) and established himself there, giving away Ekonah to his brother Ganesh Singh. Balram Sah, second son of Raja Madho Singh, had a somewhat distinguished career. It was in those days that the name Ramgarh Gauri was changed to Balrampur in his honour. The fifth descendant, Raja Newal Singh, on succeeding to the estate, fought and won twenty-two battles with the neighbouring rajas and taaluqdars. After his death the estate fell to Raja Arjun Singh, who in turn was succeeded by Raja Narain Singh. In succession to this last chieftain the present Maharaja came to the *guddi* in the *sambat* year 1893, commencing his career by successful actions against the Rajas of Atrauli, Bhinga, and Tulsipur. His Highness, under orders from the Emperor, and with the consent of the British Resident, subsequently marched at the head of his troops against the then Raja of Tulsipur, Drig Narain Singh (who had forcibly possessed himself of the estate from his own father). Surrounding the latter, he compelled him to fly, and placed Drigraj in charge of the *ilaqa*, reserving to himself a *chauth* or quarter share of its income. By this latter engagement the Maharaja established so great a reputation for himself that no taaluqdar ventured to oppose him ever afterwards, and since then His Highness's good name and good fortune has been steadily on the ascendant. Shortly after the English occupation of the Province of Oudh, Mr. (now Sir Charles) Wingfield, Commissioner of Fyzabad, made him a present of a gun in return for his good and loyal services. For ever afterwards great mutual friendship and cordiality continued between the Maharaja and the British Government.

As soon as the Maharaja heard of the mutiny of 1857 (1264 fasli), he at once, at the peril of his own life, marched with his troops to Sikrauri and safely conducted the chief local officers back to Balrampur, where he gave them shelter and amply provided for all their needs and comforts during their stay there, a few days afterwards arranging for their safe escort to Calcutta. About this time His Highness himself was besieged in the fort of Batohan, and although the mutineers made three daring attempts to take the place, the Maharaja eventually escaped and the enemy were dispersed. After the suppression of the mutiny, His Highness, in return for his good and faithful services, received from the English Government a reward of the proprietary right of *ilaqa* Tulsipur and others, of a *khilat* of great value and high rank, of a considerable sum in cash, of the powers of an Honorary Magistrate, and of the free gift of two additional guns. As a further recognition His Highness's name was ordered to be placed at the head of the five select taaluqdars of Oudh prominently mentioned in Government records for their valuable services and conspicuous loyalty.

At a durbar held in Agra in 1866 the title of K. C. S. I. was conferred on this illustrious chieftain, and, as a special favour, a reduction of 10 per cent. on the assessed revenue was allowed in his favour at the recent thirty years' settlement, with the additional concession of no enhancements in any future settlements. He is exempt from attendance in civil courts. His Highness's relatives, dependants, and servants were also freed from the operation of the Arms Act, and he himself was appointed a Member of the Viceregal Council. The well-known enactments, viz., Acts XVII., XVIII., XIX., and XXVI., applicable to the Province of Oudh, were passed at his instance and mainly through his intelligent exertions. At the Delhi Proclamation on 1st January, 1877, the Maharaja's tent was pitched in a conspicuous spot specially set apart for the purpose, and his reception was on a par with that of the highest independent chiefs present on the occasion. A salute of nine guns was fired in his honour, and the same honour has since been accorded to him for his lifetime. His Highness's acts of beneficence and public-spiritedness are numerous. Among these are several charity houses, where paupers are fed without charge, and many hospitals, where the suffering poor obtain medicines free. He is the owner of houses throughout the province, and in Lucknow itself has a large and splendid hospital, a ganj, a sarai, and buildings, such as the " Wingfield Manzil," and others, all which are well worthy of a visit. The " Moti Mahal" is especially entitled to notice. Here *raieses* arriving from other stations find a ready reception, as also every comfort in the way of food and lodging at the Maharaja's expense (each according to his own position and rank). Managements are under the superintendence of a manager assisted by a competent staff especially kept up for the purpose. The *Dasehra* festival is celebrated with unusual *eclat* at Balrampur, and on the occasion of it, thousands of *fakirs* annually arrive at the place from long distances, stay there for about four months, are fed at His Highness's expense, and on leaving for their homes receive substantial presents in cash. His Highness is a good rider and an enthusiastic sportsman, and, both by himself as well as in the company of English gentlemen, is constantly in *jungles* after tigers, elephants, or any other game that is to be found in his rich preserves. Several caged elephants are to be seen in the vicinity of his palace. Literary, scientific, and sporting men of every kind and class find a ready patron and supporter in the Maharaja. He has also established a museum in Balrampur which is of great interest to thousands of his subjects. The comfort and happiness of his people occupy the Maharaja's closest attention, and their health, needs, and condition generally are constantly under his consideration. That this attention and concern are really appreciated by the people may be judged by the fact that they have raised a large sum of money by voluntary subscription among themselves for a lasting memorial in honour of His Highness. To him is indebted the *Anjuman-i-Hind* for its very existence, and to him the taaluqdars of Oudh owe much of their prosperity and influence.

The Maharaja of Balrampur owns 812 villages and 3 *pattis* situated in zilas Gonda, Bahraich, and Lucknow. These yield to Government an annual revenue of Rs. 5,34,724-14-5. In this family the practice obtains of a single succession to the *gaddi* by right of heirship or appointment, the estate not being divisible collaterally.

No. 3.

LAL PRATAB NARAIN SINGH, *Brahmin, Taaluqdar of Mahdauna, Bahrauli, Ahiar, Ochera, Tulsipur, Bisambharpur, and Mahdauna.*

THIS taaluqdar is a Sangaldipi Brahmin, and his estate and position date from Raja Bakhtawar Singh, who received the title from Nawab Saadat Ali Khan of Oudh. His younger brother, Raja Darshan Singh, was in charge of the Nizamat during the Nawabi *régime.* For his good services the title of Raja Bahadur, and subsequently that of Saltanat Bahadur, was conferred on him. Latterly, Sir Maharaja Man Singh Kaim Jang, son of the said Raja Darshan Singh, rendered some valuable assistance to the English during the mutiny, and was also instrumental in saving the lives of some European gentlemen. Man Singh was rewarded for these services with the titles of Maharaja and K. C. S. I. and the gift of the taaluq of Bisambharpur. He was held in much esteem among the taaluqdars of Oudh. After his death, his widow, Maharani Sobha Kunwar, succeeded to the estate, and recognized the heirship of Lal Triloke Nath Singh, son of Raja Raghubar Dayal Singh, a brother of Man Singh. But this recognition was set aside by a decision of the Privy Council, resulting in the estate being assigned to Lal Pratab Singh, grandson (by his daughter) of the late Maharaja. The Kunwar has followed the footsteps of the Maharaja, and he is like him in many respects.

Estate, 669 villages and 124 *pattis* in zilas Fyzabad, Gonda, Nawabganj, Bara Banki, Lucknow, and Sultanpur. Government revenue, Rs. 4,79,348-7-10.

In this family the same practice obtains of succession to the *gaddi* as has already been mentioned in reference to the Balrampur estate.

No. 4.

RAJA SHEOPAL SINGH, *Bais, Taaluqdar of Morarmau, Alluvion land Sangrampur. Title of "Raja" hereditary.*

THE clan of *Bais* owes its origin to Raja Salbahan (*Chattri*), who about nineteen centuries ago defeated (Pauwar) Raja Vikramadyta and obtained his daughter in marriage. About this time dates the era known by his name and which he proclaimed in supersession of that hitherto called after the vanquished chief. The foundation of Sealkot and Mungi-pátan was also laid by him about this time. In his twentieth generation were born Raja Abhai Chand and Prithi Chand. These brothers on one occasion went with troops to Sheorajpur, in zila Fatehpur, to bathe in the Ganges, and there found the beautiful wife of Raja Argil of Fatehpur (who had also gone to Fatehpur for a similar purpose) a prisoner in the hands of the Subadar of Allahabad (Prag), acting under orders from the Emperor of Dehli. Receiving intimation of the fair captive's anxiety to be liberated from her captivity, they attacked the vile instrument of imperial lust and tyranny with their forces. Prithi Chand was killed in the battle that ensued, but the victory of the day was won by the surviving brother. Abhai Chand escorted the liberated *Rani* to her husband, and in reward for his act of gallantry was honoured with the hand of his daughter and large estates as a dowry. He then returned to Sheorajpur, and getting the better of the *Bhars* in battle possessed himself of their *ilaqas.* These acquisitions form the basis of the present taaluq which is called Baiswara (*i.e.,* *bis* or twenty), from the fact of its founder having been of the twentieth generation from the original ancestor, Raja Salbahan.

In the tenth generation from Abhai Chand came Raja Tilok Chand, who had two sons, Harhar Deo and Raja Prithi Chand. Tilok Chand was taken dangerously ill one day, and Harhar Deo being absent at Delhi at the time, the former declared Prithi Chand his heir to the raj. Harhar Deo, however, returned shortly after, and at a subsequent period went to reside in Sehbasi, which gives its name to his descendants comprising the following "Sehbasi" houses :— Nos. 14, 65, 67, 137, 210, and 255.

Harhar Deo, some time after his return from Delhi, was installed into his father's *raj*, as will appear on reference to No. 14.

One of these descendants, Karn Rai, leaving Sehbasi, went to reside in Nahatha, and hence the distinction of " Nahatha Bais," by which are known taaluqdars Nos. 26, 64, 99, 140, 158, 195, and 255.

Fifth in order of succession from Prithi Chand was Raja Narsingh Deo, who, reclaiming the site of Morarmau from *jungle*, built on it the village which gives its name to the present taaluq.

Twelfth in inheritance from Raja Narsingh Deo came Raja Drig Bijai Singh, who for loyal services rendered during the mutiny received, in addition to the permanent recognition of his title of " Raja," the distinction of C. S. I. and the gift of taaluq Narsinghpur. The present Raja succeeded him in the estate.

This estate is one of the five "loyal taaluqs" and enjoys the benefit of a permanent settlement. It comprises 114 villages (inclusive of the Government gift) situated in zilas Unao and Rae Bareli. Revenue payable to Government, Rs. 56,471. The custom of inheritance to the *guddi*, as in the case of Balrampur, &c., before alluded to, also obtains in this family.

No. 5.

Raja Hanwant Singh and Rampal Singh, Bisain, Taaluqdars of Rampur (Dharapur), (Kala Kanker), and Aunujebna. Title of " Raja" hereditary.

These taaluqdars claim descent from Rai Homepal of the Chattri caste (gót Bais), a younger brother of Raja Jay Chand of Kanauj.

About six hundred years ago, the said Rai, who was then residing at Majhauli, zila Gorakhpur, made a pilgrimage to the junction of the holy waters at Allahabad. From there he accompanied Raja Manik to the latter's own *ilaqa* at Manikpur, and shortly after, having married his daughter, obtained from him the present of certain zamindaris. The descendants of Homepal by this union are known as Bisain Thakurs. In course of time and by degrees the said zamindaris came to be divided among posterity, and these divisions were subsequently raised to the position of taaluqs, comprising Nos. 62, 71, 89, 101, 149, and 150. The taaluqdars above are also among the descendants referred to.

The faithful services of Raja Hanwant Singh rendered during the mutiny were rewarded with the gift of taaluqs; the sanad of which however, at his request, was made out in the name of his daughter's son, Rampal Singh. The Raja some time ago sold the Government gift of Bhagalpur in zila Bahraich.

Rampal Singh is an English scholar and has imbibed the manners and customs of the West by a long residence in England. He is in the prime of life and holds a distinguished place among the nobility of the province.

Estate, 198 villages in zila Partabgarh and Rae Bareli. Government revenue, Rs. 86,568-8-0. In this family also prevails the custom of inheritance as in Balrampur, &c.

No. 6.

Raja Tilak Singh, Katyar, Taaluqdar of Katiari, Daulatpur, Murwan, and Fatehpur.

This taaluq was formed, on the basis of zamindaris formerly owned by the Dhanuk and Manihar clans, by Deoramdat, who came with a large retinue from Tom'r Katar (in Gwalior) to Singhi Rampur (in zila Farukhabad) to bathe in the Ganges. Seizing the opportunity of the mutual dissensions and quarrels then prevailing between the said clans, he espoused the cause of the more powerful Manihars and rendered them material help in defeating the rival Dhanuks. He next turned his arms against the friendly Manihars, and in a short time so completely got the better of both the clans that hardly a member of either retained his former possessions. He then established his own authority over their ilaqa and laid the foundation of the taaluq which has since formed the inheritance of his descendants. Among these, in later generation came Hardeo Baksh, who, for signal services rendered to the British Government during the crisis of 1857, obtained the gift of Daulatpur, &c., and also the title of c. s. i. After death he was succeeded by the taaluqdar (his brother) who now represents the family. This nobleman is the recognized head of the Katiari house, so called after ('Tom'r Katar) the place from which the founder, Deoramdat, came.

This is among the five "loyal taaluqs" of the province and has the benefit of a permanent settlement.

Estate, 64½ villages, 4 *pattis*, in zila Hardoi. Government revenue, Rs. 59,974. *Gaddi* system prevails in this family.

No. 7.

Raja Rudr Partab Sah, *Rajkumar, Taaluqdar of Dehra Amahat, Bhavao, Dih, Madanpur, Puniar, Ramunagar, Kishupur, Kumai, and Purasi. Title of "Raja" hereditary.*

About five centuries ago Raja Bariar Singh came to the Province of Oudh from Sambhal (Moradabad), and defeating the Bhars, occupied their possessions at Bhadaiyan and other villages in zila Sultanpur. He had four sons—Rasal Singh, Khokhay Singh, Ghotam Deo, and Raj Bhabhut Singh.

Baryar Singh was a descendant of the Chauhan family who at one time reigned supreme on the throne of Delhi. Apprehending the consequences to them of Emperor Ala-ud-din Ghori's determination to exterminate their house, the said son of Baryar Singh, gave up the hereditary family title of Chauhan, and Khokhay Singh assumed that of "Rajwar," to which belong taaluqdars No. 260.

The three others became known as *Barhgotis*. To Raj Bhabhut Singh were born three sons—Raja Bhup Singh, Raja Chukr Singh, and Raja Ishri Singh. From the first two of these are descended taaluqdars Nos. 13, 40, 59, 60, 69, 70, 76, 78, 79, 83, 85, 126, 127, 194, 208, 215, and 220.

The descendants of Raja Ishri Singh are known by the name of "Rajkumars," and they comprise the house heading the present notice, and Nos. 73, 74, 95, 155, 161, 163, 202, 214, and 249.

The Raja who is the subject of this memoir comes lineally from Jadu Rai (descended from Raja Ishri Singh), who, leaving the original ancestral seat of Bhadaiyan, came to reside in Dehra, a village which he himself built on a site originally covered with jungle, and by subsequent acquisition of other estates laid the foundation of the present taaluq bearing that name.

In his latter days Raja Rustam Sahi rendered good service to the Government during the mutiny, and received a reward of 118 mauzas, inclusive of Amahat and others.

This estate (including Government gift) comprises 187 villages and 183 *pattis*, situated in zilas Sultanpur, Fyzabad, and Rae Bareli. Government revenue, Rs. 1,02,914-11-1. The *gaddi* system also prevails in their family.

No. 8.

RAJA MADHO SINGH, *Bandalgoti, Taaluqdar of Amethi. Title of " Raja" hereditary.*

IN A.D. 1326 (during the reign of the Emperor Jalal-ud-din Akbar Shah) the first ancestor of this taaluqdar came to the Province of Oudh for the purpose of chastising the turbulent Bhars, whom he reduced to order and several of whose villages (situated in zila Gonda) he occupied. The estate continued in the hands of descendants in successive generations for a period of about three hundred years, until Raja Madho Singh made it over to Babu Sarbjit Singh of Tikari, No. 100.

Taaluq No. 172 is a branch of this taaluq.

Estate, 318 villages and 3 *pattis* in zila Sultanpur. Government revenue, Rs. 1,91,217-11-0.

No. 9.

RAJA MUHAMMAD ALI KHAN, *Bachgoti, Khanzada, Taaluqdar of Hassanpur, Jaisinghpur, Mungra, and Hatgaon. Title of " Raja" hereditary.*

IN a later generation from Bariar Sah (*vide* No. 7) came Tiloke Chand, who, becoming a defaulter in the matter of Government revenue, embraced the Moslem faith in the reign of Emperor Babar Shah and assumed the name of Tatar Khan. He had two sons, Bazid Khan and Jalal Khan. Husen Khan, son of the former, received the title of " Raja" from the said Emperor, and also the privilege of conferring similar titular honour by affixing the *tika* on the recipients after obtaining presents from them. He also established and gave his own name to the *basta* (collection of villages) after which the taaluq Hassanpur is called. In his twelfth generation comes the present taaluqdar. Nos. 162 and 165 are branches of this taaluq.

Estate, 104 villages and 7 *pattis* in zilas Sultanpur and Fyzabad. Government revenue, Rs. 52,532-7-0. The *gaddi* custom is also observed in this family.

No. 10.

AMIR-UL-DAULA, SAIED-UL-MULK, RAJA MAHOMED AMIR HASAN KHAN, BAHADUR, MUMTAZ-JANG, *Honorary Assistant Commissioner of Mahmudabad, Taaluqdar of Mahmudabad in the Sitapur District, of Konwan Danda in the Bara Banki District, of Basha in Lucknow, and of Mitauli and Kusta-ub-gawan in the Kheri District.*

WAS born at Belhera on the 23rd of Rajab 1265 H. Succeeded his father while a minor on the 9th of Ramzan, 1274. Was educated at Sitapur School, at Queen's College, Benares, and Canning College, Lucknow. The taaluqa was under the Court of Wards up to the 6th of March, 1867, when, the Raja becoming of age, it was restored to him. At the early age of 16 he was nominated a member of the Executive Committee of the Provincial British Indian Association. In 1871 he was selected successor of the late Maharaja Sir Man Singh, Bahadur, K.C.S.I., to the vacant post of the Vice-Presidentship of the above Association, and thus it devolved on him to take an active and leading part in the discussions and deliberations of measures and matters of public good affecting the political and social welfare of Oudh. For services which the Raja thus rendered to the Crown and the public he was publicly thanked in the Administration Reports (Revenue Report, 1869, page 32, and Administration Report, 1869): and as a mark of especial recognition was presented with a sword—an addition to his dress of honour—by the late Lord Lawrence in His Excellency's durbar at Lucknow. Again, Sir Henry Davies in his official letter No. 546, dated the 2nd February, 1871, to the Government of India, while expressing his own approval of the Raja's services, recommended him for the form of honorary address of "Amir-ul-daula, Saied-ul-mulk, Mumtaz-jang," and the Government of India authorized the Chief Commissioner to address the Raja in the terms recommended by Sir Henry Davies.

Further, the Deputy Commissioner of Sitapur, while reporting the liberality and generosity of the Raja in respect to the sufferers from the famine of 1878, wrote as follows:—" Raja Amir Hasan Khan was extremely lavish in the gratuitous relief—a fact of which I have satisfied myself while in the camp." His Honor Sir G. Couper, &c., &c., &c., Lieutenant-Governor, North-Western Provinces, and Chief Commissioner of Oudh, appreciated the behaviour of the Raja, and presented the Raja with a dress of honour in a public durbar.

LINEAGE.

The Raja is a descendant of Aboubakar Siddicke, the first Khalifah of the Prophet of Islam : the family are "Sheikh Siddiekees." The ancestors of the Raja came to India from Bagdad while kings of the Ghorian dynasty were ruling and settled at Amroha, a town in the North-Western Provinces. For four generations they were Qazis of the said locality ; later on, in about 1226 A.D., Qazi Nasrut-ullah, *alias* Sheikh Nuthan, accompanied Prince Nasir-ul-din to Oudh in his famous invasion of this province, and overthrew the principalities of the Bhars and Bhats then ruling Oudh. The monarch of Delhi appreciated his services and granted him the villages now forming the major part of the taaluqas of Mahmudabad, Belhera, Paintipur, and Bhutwa Mow, the zamindaris of Bishanpur, Mahanandpur, Sirouli, Babupur and Kutri, Achaicha, Rai Bhari and Mitoura, Niamutpur, Bhiuri and Sudrawan, which are up to this date in the possession of his descendants. Sheikh Nasrut-ullah died at Belhera and was succeeded by his son Sheikh Nizam, who was after his death succeeded by Gholam Mustapha, his eldest son, who was

2

succeeded by his son Daood, who was also a General in the armies of the Mogul Emperor Akbar, and was raised to the honorary distinction of " Khan Bahadur." From this date the surname of the family was changed from Sheikhzadas to that of Khanzadas, *i. e.,* the descendants of the Khan. Daood Khan valiantly fell in the battle of Rintamhour, at the very gates of that impregnable fortress, while leading an assault. Mahmud Khan, his son, succeeded his gallant father to his property in Oudh and as well in the North-Western Provinces, also to the command of the brigade of the army. He founded Mahmudabad after his own name, and died at Jounpur while foujdar (governor) of Jounpur. He was succeeded by his son Bayazied Khan, who divided the ancestral property between his kinsmen, Pahar Khan and Saied Khan, giving Bhutwa Mow to the former and Paintipur to the latter, and holding himself the estates of Mahmudabad and Belehra. He entered the service of the Emperor Jahangir, was governor of Jounpur and of other divisions of the empire, was presented by the Emperor with a sword bearing the name of Emperor Jehangir, which is still in the possession of the Raja. He was also honoured with the titles of "Ghazzufur-ul-daula, Umdat-ul-Mawali, Bayazied Khan, Bahadur, Muzuffer-jang " He died at Belehra, and was succeeded by his three sons, who divided the property amongst themselves.

Enayet Khan got Belhera, Fathai Khan Sudrawan, Hidayet Khan got Mahmudabad, of whom presently ; he was the youngest son of Bayazied Khan, and fixing his residence at Mahmudabad, founded Khudaganj.

He was fond of sport and died by a fall from his horse, and was interred at Mahmudabad.

Khalel-ul-Rahman Khan, the only son of the former, succeeded him and was married to the daughter of Marhamat Khan, grandson of Enayet Khan of Belhera, and had only one son, Hidayet-ullah Khan, who succeeded him at his death.

Hidayet-ullah Khan was a kinsman of Nawab Moniz-ud-din Khan, Bahadur, of Lucknow, the historic defender of Oudh. Hidayet-ullah Khan co-operated with the abovenamed chief in the expulsion and overthrow of the Bangashes, and recovered Oudh from them for Nawab Safdar Jang, the Governor of Oudh and Vizier of the Mogul Emperor of Delhi (the Imad-us-Saadat and the Sair-ul-Muta Akhareen.) He also met the Raikwar Raja of Rammagur at the famous battle of Chenlaha ghat, and with the co-operation of the Sheikhzadas of Lucknow under the renowned Nawab Moniz-ud-din Khan, Bahadur, the taaluqdars of Belhera, Bhutwa Mow, and Jahangirabad, and other Mahomedan chiefs of renown and influence, defeated the opposite side with great slaughter—(*vide Oudh Gazette,* Vol. 1., pages 257, 258). Hidayet-ullah Khan was himself slightly wounded, but he never left his saddle, though strongly advised by his bosom friends and loving relatives.

Hidayet-ullah Khan died without any male issue, and was succeeded by his cousin and son-in-law, Mahomed Ikram Khan, a grandson of Marhamat Khan, and great-grandson of Enayet Khan, who was married to the youngest daughter of Hidayet-ullah Khan.

Mahomad Ikram Khan had two sons, Sarfraz Ali Khan and Musahib Ali Khan,

Sarfraz Ali Khan succeeded his father Ikram Khan. After the death of the latter, was Nazim of Sundilah and Bangur Mow, now the districts of Hardoi and Unao. He was afterwards deputed by Nawab Asfadaula in the capacity of Nazim of the trans-Gogra districts, and was made an honorary commander of artillery, a distinction which continued till the days of annexation. He distinguished himself in the Rohilla war. Sarfraz Ali Khan died a bachelor, and was succeeded by his only brother, Musahib Ali Khan, who, like his elder brother, succeeded in rendering valuable services to his ruler. Nawab Saadat Ali Khan, Vizier of Oudh, paid a visit to Mahmudabad and was a guest of Musahib Ali Khan. It is said that all the wells of Mahmudabad, owing to the extraordinary consumption of water by the hosts of Nawab Saadat Ali Khan, ran short in their supply of the liquid with the exception of only one well, which has since been named and which still bears of "Dul Thumban," i. e., "Lasting to supply an army of 10,000,000." The Nawab, as a memorial of his visit, bestowed a dress of honour and the estates now known as Feel Khana, formerly the elephant stables of the rulers of Oudh.

Musahib Ali Khan died without leaving any issue. He was much loved by his tenants, and his memory is much cherished. The ignorant Mahomedans and Hindus do him honour by adoring his tomb. Hindus call him a *daiata*, and the Mahomedans look upon him as a saint.

Musahib Ali Khan was succeeded by his widow, who adopted Nawab Ali Khan, son of Amir Ali Khan, grandson of Muzhur Ali Khan, great-grandson of Mahomed Imam Khan, and great-great-grandson of Marhamat Khan, who was heir-presumptive of Musahib Ali Khan, to succeed her.

Nawab Ali Khan when he succeeded to the *gaddi* was only 20 years of age. He was a scholar and a soldier, also a poet. His poetical works have been published. He took active part in the politics of the province. Was employed by the Nazims Raja Darshan Singh and Nawab Baha-ul-daula in the reduction and overthrow of a good many refractory chiefs, notably those of Naupara, Mitauli, Bhinga, Oel, Kataisur, Rampur-Muthra, Easa Nagur Saroura, Bohyeah, Jhalyapara, Kasimganj, and Behtai. The Court of Lucknow by letters patent ordered Nawab Ali Khan to join in the pursuit of the notorious highway robbers Fazl Ali and Ram Bux, and also in the overthrow of the fanatical leader Moulvi Amir Ali of Raudouli.

For his services the Court of Lucknow first honoured Nawab Ali Khan with the title of "Raja Nawab Ali Khan, Bahadur," and some time after with the title of "Mukim-ul-daula, Raja Nawab Ali Khan, Bahadur, Kiam-jang." The mother of Nawab Ali Khan was a niece of Nawab Mouiz-ud-din. Nawab Ali Khan was married to a grand-daughter of Nawab Mouiz-ud-din Khan, and was succeeded by his only son, the present Raja.

No. 11.

RAJA BIJAI BAHADUR SINGH, *Sombansi, Taaluqdar of Bahlolpur. Title of "Raja" hereditary.*

FEAR of Shaikh Taki and Roshan Kamil, two notorious enemies and oppressors, who resided at Jhusi, in the Allahabad district, and had troops at their command, compelled Raja Bir Sibti, forefather of this taaluqdar, to leave his home about six hundred years ago and to settle at Soral, now called Partabgarh. His son, Lakhan Sibti, at one time discovered a considerable amount of some hidden treasure, and was by this means able to entertain the services of a good number of retainers. With the help of these men he got the better of the Bhars and became possessed of an estate. The title of Sah was shortly after bestowed on him by the then Government of Oudh. In course of time the estate came under partition among his various heirs, each of whom represented a separate branch of the family. These branches comprise Nos. 85, 48, 92, 167, 168, 184, and 193. Raja Bijai Bahadur, on coming to his inheritance, sold a portion of his own share to Raja Ajit Singh (No. 48).

Estate, 81 villages in zila Partabgarh. Government revenue Rs. 29,231-2-8. The *gaddi* system also obtains in this house.

No. 12.

RAJA SURPAL SINGH (*Thakur*), *Kanpuria, Taaluqdar of Toloi, Bhoalpur, Kutarraa, Mustafabad, Sartagarh, Rustamau, Chatra Buzurg, and Pirhi. Title of "Raja" hereditary.*

ABOUT seven centuries ago, Raja Manik (of the Thakur *Guharwar* caste) made a gift of his whole estate to an only daughter on her marriage with a Brahmin. Of this union was born a son called Raja Kan, from whom is descended the clan of Thakurs called "Kanpurias."

Raja Kan had three sons—Rahas, Sohas, and Rodan.

From the first of these came Jugga Singh, Madan Singh, and Man Singh.

In the family of Jugga Singh was one Balbhaddar Sah and Mitrjit.

From the former of these (generations after) came four brothers—Pahara Mal, Salbuhan, Tribhuwan Sahi, and Raj Sah.

The descendants of the first of these is now represented by taaluqdar No. 30, of the second by No. 107, the third by No. 204, and the fourth by Nos. 80 and 164.

From Mitrjit the descent of the taaluqdar noticed in No. 100 can be traced.

Madan Singh (from Rahas) was the forefather of Nos. 29 and 77.

Man Singh (the third of the brothers coming from Rahas) was the forefather of the taaluqdar who forms the subject of No. 196.

Houses Nos. 36, 223, and 226 are derived from Sahas, the second son of Raja Kan ; Rodan, third son of the latter, had no descendants.

The subject of this and of notice No. 50 claim for their latest progenitor Balbhaddar Sah above referred to.

In later days Raja Mohan Singh, grandfather of the taaluqdar heading this memoir, made large and valuable accessions to the original taaluq of Oel by means and resources of his own, and after death was succeeded by his son, Raja Jagpal Singh, from whom came to the inheritance the present Raja.

Estate, 100 villages in zilas Sultanpur, Partabgarh, and Rae Bareli. Government revenue, Rs. 95,964-6-6. *Guddi* system prevails with regard to this estate.

No. 13.

RANI KISHAN NATH KUNWAR (*widow of the late Raja Madho Pratab Singh*), *Thakur, Bachgoti, Taaluqdar of Kurwar, Majais, Maighat Kora, and Hatgaon. Title hereditary.*

FULL family details of the origin and history of this family are recorded in No. 7. The deceased Raja was sixteenth in generation from Prithipal (a descendant of Chakr Singh), who laid the foundation of this taaluq, to the succession of which the present Rani came after the death of her husband, the said Raja. Taaluqs Nos. 76 and 85 are branches of this family.

Estate, 136 villages and 20 *pattis* in zilas Sultanpur and Fyzabad. Government revenue, Rs. 59,870-2-0. The custom of *guddi* obtains.

No. 14.

RANA SHANKAR BAKHSH SINGH (*Schbasi*), *Bais, Taaluqdar of Thalrai, Khajurganw, Ibrahimganj, and Kardahia. The title of " Rana" hereditary.*

HARHAR DEO, son of Tilok Chand (*vide* No. 4), some time after his return from Delhi, was installed into the Raj of his father, in supersession of his younger brother, Prithi Chand. He also received the title of " Rana," and in later days founded the village of Khajurganw (so called from the fact of abundance of *khajur* or date trees originally growing on the site), which gives its name to the present taaluq.

In the third generation came Rana Shankar Singh, who had three sons—Rana Daman Deo, Rudh Sah, and Alam Sah—who shared the family inheritance as follows : the first receiving Khajurganw under notice, the second Sunarpaha (No. 65), and the third Karihar Sataon (No. 66).

At a partition of the family inheritance between the eight sons of Rana Daman Deo, taaluq Khajurganw fell to the share of the eldest of them, Ajit, his brothers receiving only small estates for their maintenance. The subject of this memoir counts eleventh in descent from the said Ajit Mal. The other descendants of Daman Deo comprise houses Nos. 67, 81, 93, 252.

The taaluqdars descended from Rudh Sah are Nos. 139 and 254.

The present Rana is an Honorary Magistrate and Assistant Collector, and enjoys a marked reputation for the efficient management of his estate and for his love of justice. During the severe scarcity in the province (fasli year 1285) he spent large sums of money from his own pocket for the relief of the suffering people. He also gave material assistance to the deliberations which resulted in the legislative enactments lately passed in the interests of Oudh. He is one of the six taaluqdars who received medals of honour in the Imperial assemblage of Delhi in 1877. For the relief which he gave to the poor during the famine of 1878, he received a testimonial in the durbar held at Lucknow. He is the Vice-President of the Provincial British Indian Association.

Estate, 130 villages in zilas Lucknow, Kheri, and Rae Bareli. Government revenue, Rs. 1,14,169-8-7. The *gaddi* custom prevails in this family.

No. 15.

RANI DHARM RAJ KUNWAR (*widow of Raja Mahesh Narayan Singh, Drigbans, Taaluqdar of Parhat, Raipur, Bichuur Mangoli, and Tonk.*

ABOUT four centuries ago, one Drig Sahi, who on account of domestic quarrel left his native place, Kalangarh in Jaipur, came to Delhi, and under orders from the Emperor marched against the Bhars, whom he fought and defeated. He then established his own authority over their possessions and laid the foundation of this estate, receiving at the same time from the Court of Delhi the title of "Raja." His descendant, the husband of the Rani above alluded to, deserved well of the British Government for loyal services rendered during the mutiny of 1857, and was rewarded with the grant of taaluq Mangoli and the title of "Raja" as a personal distinction. After him comes the present owner of the estate.

Estate, 30 villages in zilas Sultanpur, Partabgarh, and Rae Bareli. Government revenue, Rs. 12,251-9-0. The *gaddi* custom prevails in this family.

No. 16.

RAJA FARZAND ALI KHAN, *Shaikh, Kidwai, Taaluqdar of Jahangirabad, Ahyaon, Ranni, and shares in villages. Title of "Raja" hereditary.*

SHAIKH RAZAQ BAKSH, whose ancestors orginally founded this estate in the name of Emperor Jahangir, having no heir of his own, made a gift of it (fasli 1258) to the present taaluqdar. The title of " Raja" was conferred on him by the late *Sultanat* of the province.

Subsequent to the late thirty years' settlement, he made considerable additions to the estate by acquiring the zamindaris of Osmanpur, Simrawan, and others, which are not included in the *sanad* granted to him by the Government.

Estate, 81 villages and 34 *pattis* in zila Bara Banki. Government revenue, Rs. 78,118-14-7. The custom of inheritance to the *guddi* is observed in this family.

No. 17.

RAJA JANG BAHADUR KHAN, *Pathan (Tarwi), Taaluqdar of Nanpara. Title of " Raja" hereditary.*

IN the *fasli* year 1193, Rasul Khan, ancestor of this Raja, came as a " kiladar" to Bahraich, in the reign of Emperor Shah Jahan, and for his services in effectually subduing the *Banjaras* was rewarded with the proprietary gift of a tenth share of pargana Salon. In a subsequent generation (*fasli* 1215) the grant of taaluq Garganj was made to Madar Baksh by Nawab Saadat Ali Khan. In later days (*fasli* 1260) Karam Khan built a *garhi* (fort) in Nanpara, where he came to reside, and about this time he received from the reigning Nawab, Shuja-nd-daula, the titular honour of " Raja" and the gift of a *jagir* consisting of taaluqs Sangha, Bahraich, and Kahuwapur, &c. Since then has been in existence the estate now held in inheritance by the subject of this memoir.

Estate, 525 villages and 1 *patti* in zila Bahraich. Government revenue, Rs. 1,66,994-1-6. The *guddi* custom prevails in this family.

No. 18.

RAJA RANDHIR SINGH, *Bais, Taaluqdar of Bharawan, Basantpur, and Markapur. Title of " Raja" hereditary.*

THIS nobleman is descended from one Ram Chandr, who came to reside in Bharawan after his marriage with a daughter of the family of *Gaurs* who formerly owned this estate. The *Gaurs*, however, subsequently put the said Ram Chandr to death on a suspicion of their probable supersession by him in their possessions. His three sons who survived were Athsukh, Ruttibhan, and Lakhan, the first and third of whom won golden opinions during their service under the Emperor of Delhi. In lieu of an offer of *jagir* and other distinctions made to them by the Emperor, they asked for the supply of an adequate force to avenge the murder of their deceased parent, and their request being complied with, they marched against the *Gaurs*, whom they defeated and compelled to yield possession. This was about six centuries ago. In later days Raja Murdan Singh succeeded to the inheritance by right of adoption, and for services rendered during the mutiny of 1857 obtained from Government the gift of taaluq Marhapur and a *sanad* of the estate. After him came to the inheritance the present owner.

Estate, 45 villages and 4 *pattis* in zilas Unao, Hardoi, and Lucknow. Annual Government revenue, Rs. 34,629. The custom of inheritance to the *gaddi* prevails in this family.

No. 19.

The unnamed son of RAGHU NATH SINGH, *Raikwar, Taaluqdar of Rahwa.*

SALEO and MALDEO, descendants from Partab Sah and Dhunda Sah (two Surjbansi Rajput natives of Raika, in Kashmir, who came to Oudh some centuries ago), laid the foundation of this estate by defeating and killing in battle the *Bhar* Raja Dip Chand and taking possession of village Bamhnoti in his *ilaqa*. In a subsequent generation, Gajpat Singh, about a century and half after, secured the title of " Raja." In later days came Raghu Nath Singh, whose death brought to the succession his surviving infant son yet unnamed. The taaluq owes its present name of Rahwa to the fact of the washerman's clay " rehu" being plentiful in its vicinity.

Taaluqdars Nos. 43 and 68 come from this stock.

Estate, 55 villages and 4 *pattis* in zila Bahraich. Government revenue, Rs. 34,835. The *gaddi* custom prevails in this family.

No. 20.

RAJA MUHAMMAD KAZIM HUSAIN KHAN, *Khanzada, Taaluqdar of Paintipar and Belhera. Title of " Raja" hereditary.*

THE BELHERA ESTATE IN THE BARA BANKI DISTRICT.

Vide No. 10. This house and property date from Enayet Khan, who was the eldest son of Bayazid Khan, and succeeded him to this estate. He had five sons, *i. e.*, Kaim Khan, Asalat Khan, Moazzam Khan, Ghazanfar Khan, and Aolya Khan. The present zemindars of Mahumadpur are the descendants of Aolya Khan. None of the descendants of Moazzam Khan and Asalat Khan are now living, while those of Ghazanfar Khan, though still living, possess no estates. Kaim Khan, who took possession of the Belhera estate, left one son, Marhamat Khan. He won a complete victory over Bakhtawar Singh, a Raikwar chieftain of renown.

Marhamat Khan had four sons, of whom the first was Bedar Bakht Khan, whose descendants are the present zemindars of Bishanpur. His second son, Ghulam Husain Khan, *alias* Meyan

Sahib, was the progenitor of the present zemindars of Mitoura and Kutri and Bhinri. From Walajah Khan now remain no male line in existence. His fourth son, Mahomed Imam Khan, on the partition of the hereditary estates, received the Belhera estate, and co-operated gallantly with Nawab Moniz-ud-din Khan against the Afghans of the Bangash, and lately against the combination of several Hindu chiefs under the Raja of Ramnagar. Mahomed Imam Khan had two sons, Mahmud Akram Khan and Mazhar Ali Khan. The former, on the death of his father-in-law, Hidayet-ullah Khan, obtained possession of the Mahmudabad estate, and the latter took possession of his paternal estate of Belhera. Mazhar Ali Khan was succeeded by his son Amir Ali Khan, who fought bravely under Nawab Asafadaula against the Rohillas. His eldest son, Raja Ibad Ali Khan, succeeded to the Belhera estate, and in 1269 H. received the title of " Raja Ibad Ali Khan Bahadur" and the robes of honour from the Court of Oudh. In addition to his hereditary estate of Belhera, he received the Paintipur estate as a gift from the daughter of Khadim Ali Khan, the chief of that estate. His younger brother, Raja Nawab Ali Khan, the father of the present Raja of Mahmudabad, succeeded Musahib Ali Khan in that estate. Raja Ibad Ali Khan Bahadur was succeeded in the Belhera estate by his son, Raja Kazim Husain Khan, who is both paternal and maternal cousin to the present Raja of Mahmudabad.

Estate, 83 villages and 10 *pattis* in zilas Sitapur and Bara Banki. Government revenue, Rs, 48,326. The *guddi* custom prevails in this family.

No. 21.

RAJA BHAGWAN BAKHSH, *infant son of Raja Umrao Singh, Amethia Taaluqdar of Pokhra Unsari. Title of " Raja" hereditary.*

ABOUT seven hundred years ago, Raja Prithi Chand, the original founder of this clan, came from Shinpur to Narkangri, and after a visit for bathing purposes to Ayodhya went to Amethi, where he established himself. His descendant Raja Dingur Sah, a General, marched against and defeated the Bhars, and taking possession of their *ilaqa* laid the foundation of this estate. Subsequently Pokhra Unsari (formerly called *Lohi*) became the property of the victorious General's brother, Ram Singh, with whom his third brother, Dipak Rai, went to live, Dingur Sah continuing to reside in Shinrajpur. Eleventh in succession from Ram Singh came Umrao Singh, whose son now occupies the *guddi*. In consequence of the under age of the present owner the management of his possessions is just now in the hands of the Court of Wards. This nobleman and taaluqdars Nos. 22, 238, and 239 are scions of the same house.

Estate, 23 villages and 4 *pattis* in zila Bara Banki. Government revenue, Rs. 25,280-11-9. The *guddi* custom prevails in this family

No. 22.

RAJA BISESHAR BAKHSH, *Amuthia, Taaluqdar of Narsingpur, Kumrawan, Sikandarpur, and shares in villages. Title of "Raja" hereditary.*

Vide No. 21. The ownership of this estate can be traced back to one Araru Singh, a descendant of Prithi Chand. In a later generation from the former came Raja Jagmohan Singh, predecessor of the nobleman above, and whose title received the recognition of *sanad* from the British Government. Taaluqdars Nos. 251 and 256 are from this stock.

Estate, 28 villages in zilas Lucknow, Bara Banki, and Rai Bareli. Government revenue, Rs. 22,159-8-2. The *gaddi* custom prevails in this family.

No. 23.

RAJA JAGMOHAN SINGH, *son of Ratan Singh, Panwar, Taaluqdar of Raipur, Yakdariya, and Ituunja. Title of "Raja" hereditary.*

NINETEEN generations back, one Deo Rudh Rai, a native of Dharanagar in Gwalior, came to Oudh in the service of the Emperor of Delhi. Taking advantage of his brother's employment under the Kurmi proprietor of Mahona, he, in concert with the former, expelled the latter out of his possessions. He had three sons, Dankar Deo, Bahlan Deo, and Karn Deo, among whom at a partition his acquisitions were divided.

From Dankar Deo comes the nobleman above, from Bahlan Deo taaluqdar No. 129, and from Karn Deo Nos. 115 and 118.

Estate, 51 villages and 1 *patti* in zila Lucknow. Government revenue, Rs. 33,194. The *gaddi* custom prevails in this family.

No. 24.

RAJA KRISHON DAT SINGH, *Janwar, Taaluqdar of Oel, Baragaon, Bijauli, Maileni, Rasulpanah, Bhanwanpur, Barausa, Gharthannia, and Harrya. Title of "Raja" hereditary.*

FOR the first possession of the above taaluq Oel this family is indebted to Raja Buniad Singh, who founded it about three hundred years ago. His descendant Mehma Sah, having no issue of his own, sent for his daughter's son, Udip Sah, from Jaipur and adopted him. About a hundred and fifty years ago, disputes arose between Raja Katesur and Udip Sah, and the latter fled to Muttra. The estate was thus lost to the family. Subsequently however, in 1175 *fasli,*

Pitam Singh, a descendant of Udip Sah, managed to recover possession of Oel, and his successors now form the two separate houses of Mahewa (No. 51) and Oel. The *sanad* of this taaluq was first granted by the English Government to Raja Anrud Singh, father of the subject of this notice.

Estate, 160 villages and 10 *pattis* in zilas Kheri and Sitapur. Government revenue, Rs. 1,06,656. The *gaddi* custom prevails in this family.

No. 25.

Raja Narindar Bahadur Singh, *Surajbans, Taaluqdar of Haraha. Title of "Raja" hereditary.*

In 783 fasli, one Bisram Singh first obtained possession of this estate in lieu of moneys advanced by him for payment of revenue due to the Government of Emperor Timur Shah, and for which payment he had stood security for their former owner. He gave to this acquisition the name of Dhurwah, which in course of time has been corrupted into Haraha. In his eighth generation came Lachhmi Narayan Singh, who, depriving his brother Gular Sah of his joint share in the estate, allotted to the latter a separate share of it, now represented by taaluqdar No. 197. Raja Narindar Bahadur Singh comes ninth in descent and in inheritance from the said Lachhmi Narayan.

Estate, 50 villages and 16 *pattis* in zila Bara Banki. Government revenue, Rs. 53,796. The *gaddi* custom prevails in this family.

No. 26.

Raja Rampal Singh (*Nabatha*), *Bais, Taaluqdar of Kori Sudauli. Title of "Raja" hereditary.*

Vide No. 4. Karn Rai had three sons—Harsingh Rai, Narsingh Rai, and Birbhan. The first continued to reside in Nahatta, the second went to Narsingpur, and the third settled in (Bihar *khas*) No. 195.

Fourth in descent from Harsingh Rai, Aubai Chand resided in the taaluq above, and Mansuk Rai removed to Simri, No. 64.

In the fourth generation from Abhai Chand came Sidaq Singh, who obtained the title of "Raja" from the Imperial Court of Delhi, and fifth in succession to him came the Raja now in possession. Taaluq No. 99 is a branch of this.

Estate, 22 villages in zila Rae Bareli. Government revenue, Rs. 29,983. The *gaddi* custom prevails in this family.

No. 27.

RAJA SITLA BAKHSH SINGH, *Thakur, Janwar, Taaluqdar of Gangol and Jairainjot. Title of "Raja" hereditary.*

ABOUT 1325 *sambat*, one Bariar Sah, with the help of some troops supplied under orders of Emperor Firok Shah, ousted the Bhars from their possession of *Raj* Ekonah, in the district of Bahraich, and himself became master of it. Having shortly after obtained the title of "Raja," he remained in undisturbed exercise of authority for a period of thirty-seven years.

Several generations after was born Bhaia Pratap Singh, to whom was allotted for his share of the ancestral estate taaluq Gangawal, without, however, the title of "Raja." Fourth in descent from Bhaia Pratap Singh was Ganesh Prasad Singh. This last, under circumstances not clearly known, acquired the title of "Raja," and from him in lineal descent comes the present representative of the house, whose right and status have the recognition of a *sanad* from the British Government.

Estate, 54 villages and 6 *pattis* in zilas Gonda and Bahraich. Government revenue, Rs. 35,336. The *gaddi* custom holds in this family.

No. 28.

RAJA MAHINDAR BAHADUR SINGH, *Thakur, Janwar, Taaluqdar of Payagpur. Title of "Raja" hereditary.*

THE original founder of this house, Chaudhri Shyam Singh, about four hundred years ago, came from Guzerat to Delhi, and having been appointed a Resaldar in the army, obtained proprietary gift of the village Balapur Patra in Oudh, the reigning Vizier of which was then Nawab Saadat Ali Khan. He was succeeded by Payag Singh, on whom was bestowed the zamindari of Payagpur by the Delhi Emperor. Fifth in descent from Payag Singh came Bakht Singh, who obtained the title of "Raja" from the *Saltanat* of Oudh, and from the said Bakht Singh comes the present owner of the property.

Estate, 150 villages and 4 *pattis* in zila Bahraich. Government revenue, Rs. 74,989-4-9. The *gaddi* custom holds in this family.

No. 29.

RAJA JAGMOHAN SINGH, *Kanpuria, Taaluqdar of Atra, Chandapur, and Behikhori. Title of "Raja" hereditary.*

THE origin of the house to which this nobleman belongs has been escribed under No. 12. In the reign of Emperor Alamgir, Raja

Madan Singh came to Simrota from Manikpur, zila Partabgarh, and, having defeated the Bhars, erected a "koti." He also cut down a dense forest and called the place Chandapur (after the moon), in commemoration of light having taken the place of darkness. To the west of Simrota is parganah Hardoi, which was formerly known as Byalis. In this parganah lived the Bhars. Raja Madan Singh further took from the Bhars parganah Hardoi, and here he erected a large building which is called Atra. Since then the ancestors of the present taaluqdars have been in possession and always rendered material assistance to Subahdars from Delhi when they came for political purposes. For this service 27 villages in parganah Simrota were given as reward in *muafi*. After some generations came Raja Jagraj Singh, who assisted the Subahdar of Oudh in defeating the Bhars and made such arrangements as prevented highway robbery, dacoity, &c. For this the Government of Delhi conferred a valuable *khilat* on him, and 148 villages in parganah Simrota were given in zamindari and 5 villages in parganah Hardoi in *muafi*. Subsequently, Zorawar Singh, a scion of the family, was allowed by the Government at Delhi a khilat, salute of guns, and the use of "*danka*." After him Raja Dig Bijai Singh established almshouses and gave pecuniary assistance to a number of poor people to enable them to get their daughters married. When Raja Sheo Darshan came in possession, he made his nephew, Raja Har Parshad, the father of the present taaluqdar, his heir. Raja Har Parshad, however, having died immediately afterwards, Raja Sheo Darshan Singh made the present taaluqdar his heir. Raja Jagmohan Singh is a loyal subject of the British Government, and in a durbar was presented with a valuable khilat and a sword. He is an Honorary Magistrate and has been invested with the powers of an Assistant Commissioner. He is one of the six select taaluqdars who were specially honoured at the Imperial assemblage of Delhi in 1877 and received medals. It was through his exertions along with that of others that Acts XVI., XVII., XIX., and XXVI. were enacted. For the relief which he granted to the famished people in 1877 he received a robe of honour in the durbar at Lucknow.

Estate, 30 villages in zila Rae Bareli. Government revenue, Rs. 31,656-6-10. The *gaddi* custom holds in this family.

No. 30.

RANI HAR NATH KUNWAR (*widow of Raja Sarnam Singh*), *Thakur, Kanpuria, Taaluqdar of Katari. Title of "Raja" hereditary.*

Vide No. 12. This branch house was founded by Paharamal at the time a partition of the ancestral estate was effected between him and his three brothers, sons of Balbhaddar Sah, a descendant of Raja Manik.

Estate, 13 villages in zila Sultanpur. Government revenue, Rs. 10,403-4-0. The *gaddi* custom holds in this family.

No. 31.

RANI SAHILJAN *(widow of Musharaf Ali Khan), Sayyid, Taaluqdar of Bahadurnagar, Narsinghpur, Ahmadnagar, Magdapur, Bankapwa and Mansurnagar. Title of "Raja" heredi-tary.*

THIS estate comprises a jagir bestowed in the year 1605 by Emperor Jahangir on Nawab Sadr Jahan, founder of the family. After his death, and during the reign of Emperor Aurangzeb, it passed for some time into the hands of the Ahbans. The property, however, subsequent to the fasli year 1252, reverted to the family in the person of Ashraf Ali Khan, father of Raja Musharaf Ali Khan, the deceased husband of the widow above.

Estate, 54½ villages in zilas Kheri and Hardoi. Government revenue, Rs. 24,497-9-6. The *gaddi* custom holds in this family.

No. 32.

RAJA KISHN DAT RAM PANDE, *Brahmin, Taaluqdar of Singha Chanda. Title of "Raja" personal.*

WHEN in the year 1738 A.D. Nadir Shah invaded Hindustan Newazi Ram (original founder of this family) advanced to Nawab Saadat Khan Burhan-ul-mulk, Subahdar of Oudh, a loan of several lakhs of rupees to meet the pressure of the invasion. Subsequently his son, Baldi Ram Pande (coming from Delhi), demanded repayment of this loan from Abul Mansur Khan, son-in-law of Saadat Khan, after the latter's death, and Abul Mansur made over to Baldi Ram the taaluq of Gonda, &c., in *jamogh.*[*] Some time after a grandson (by daughter) of Baldi Ram, at the request of Raja Sheo Prasad of Gonda, accommodated the latter with an advance of Rs. 3,00,000 to meet the provincial Nazim's demand of Government revenue, and the Raja's inability to clear this loan ultimately resulted in the cession of certain villages by him to the creditor, which villages formed the foundation of the present taaluq Singha Chanda. Considerable additions to this taaluq (both by purchase and *nankar*[†]) were made by Mardan Ram, a predecessor of the present owner.

Estate, 324 villages and 78 *pattis* in zila Gonda. Government revenue, Rs. 2,09,760-6-6. The *gaddi* custom holds in this family.

---

[*] A process sanctioned under native rule, by law or custom, by which the lessor of a village or estate, not having confidence in the lessee, might send his own servant to collect the rents, an account being kept of the same, the lessee being entitled to the profit or liable for the loss accordingly as the collections exceeded or fell short of the sum for which the village had been leased.

[†] An allowance or deduction from the rent of land made to the person who engaged for the revenue in the nawabi; it was at once an acknowledgment of his proprietary right and an allowance to him for managing the village.

No. 33.

RANI JANKI KUNWAR (*widow of Mahipal Singh*), *Kalhans, Taaluqdar of Paraspur. Title of "Raja" hereditary.*

IN 739 Hijri, or about five hundred years ago, Sahaj Sahai (a descendant of Raja Bharjeo of Baglana) left his own country, Ghamoj, and marching at the head of a large number of troops took possession of the parganah of Kuransa, now called Gonda. At this time the throne of Delhi was occupied by Emperor Nur-ud-din Jahangir. From Sahaj Singh descended one Nahal Singh, who had three sons—Dula Rai, Ram Singh, and Madni Mal. At a partition of the family inheritance among these last, the taaluq above fell to the share of Ram Singh and Madni Mal, whose latest representative survives in the person of the taaluqdar heading this memoir. From Dula Ram come taaluqdars Nos. 46, 124, 134, 135, and 169.

Estate, 27 villages and 22 *pattis* in zila Gonda. Government revenue, Rs. 29,435. The *gaddi* custom holds in this family.

No. 34.

RANI SALTANAT KUNWAR (*widow of Raja Prithipal Singh*), *Baisain, Taaluqdar of Mankapur.*

THIS is one of the oldest estates in Oudh and was once owned by Newal Sah of the Bandalgoti caste. His descendant Raja Chandra Sen died without issue, and the widow, Rani Bhagwani, adopted one Azmat Singh, son of Raja Dat Singh of Gonda. Azmat Singh succeeded to the estate in the year 1681 fasli, and since then it has remained in the family. Raja Prithipal Singh (latest representative) died in 1873 and his widow, Rani Saltanat Kunwar succeeded him.

Estate, 160 villages and 13 *pattis* in zila Gonda. Government revenue, Rs. 28,650-0-6. The *gaddi* custom holds in this family.

No. 35.

RAJA CHHATPAL SINGH, *Sombansi, Taaluqdar of Nurpur (Chatpalgarh). Title of "Raja" hereditary.*

Vide No. 11. The present taaluqdar is a lineal descendant of Lakhan Sibti, after whose death this estate was established separately. For some time after his death it remained escheated to the Nawabi Raj owing to the recusancy of some of his successors, but it was in 1250 fasli restored to a member of the family, one Meherban Singh, on whom at the same time was bestowed the title of "Babu" by the then Government of Oudh. The title of "Raja" was subsequently conferred.

Estate, 15 villages in zila Partabgarh. Government revenue, Rs. 5,980. Succession to this house is governed by the law of primogeniture.

No. 36.

RAJA MAHESH BAKHSH SINGH, *Thakur, Kanpuria, Taaluqdar of Khetauli. Title of "Raja" hereditary.*

Vide No. 12. This branch of Kanpuria house comes from Sahas, a descendant of Raja Manik.

Estate, 30 villages in zila Partabgarh. Government revenue, Rs. 16,099. The *gaddi* custom is prevalent in this family.

No. 37.

RAJA INDAR BIKRAMA SAH, *Rajput, Pahari (Surajbuns), Taaluqdar of Khairisadh, Kafura, Majhra, and Dabela.*

TAALUQ KHAIRISADH, along with Kanchanpur and others, was received as a marriage gift by Raja Trilokipal from Raja Sichapal, a Himalayan chief, whose daughter was married to Trilokipal in sambat 472. The estate remained in undisturbed possession of Trilokipal's heirs up to 922 sambat, and passing subsequently into the hands of the *Banjaras*, it was in possession of the latter for a period of about 30 years, after which it reverted to Raja Ganga Ram (a descendant of the said Trilokipal), whose proprietary right received the recognition of a *sanad* from the *Shahi* Government of Oudh. The title of "Sah" was the Emperor Akbar's gift to the family. At the settlement made by the British Government the *sanad* of estate was conferred on Raja Ramdhij Sah, father of the present nobleman.

The population of this taaluq consists largely of *Tharus* and *Bots*, who originally emigrated to the province of Oudh from Chitorgarh. At Khairagarh the ruins are still to be seen of an old fort built in sambat 1402 by Emperor Ala-ud-din Shah Ghori.

Estate, 107 villages in zila Kheri. Government revenue, Rs. 37,633. The *gaddi* custom is prevalent in this family.

No. 38.

RAJA NARPAT SINGH, *Thakur, Janwar, Taaluqdar of Khamra and Saukhra. Title of "Raja" hereditary.*

HALDEO SAH, a Chauhan nobleman from Jaipur, was deputed by Emperor Humayan to recover the affairs of this estate from the great confusion and disorder which prevailed while they were in the possession of Raja Mehma Singh. He met with considerable opposition at the outset, but after a protracted quarrel and occasional fighting for about thirteen years successfully accomplished the work of his mission. Soon after the completion of this work followed his marriage with a daughter of the said Raja Mehma Sah, who, having no male heir, sought permission of the Emperor to make over his *ilaqa* to Haldeo Sah, but the latter dying before such permission was obtained, the Raja conferred the inheritance on Udip Sah, son of the said Haldeo Sah, in sambat 1590, having previously received imperial sanction to the measure.

Several generations after and during the possession of Ajab Singh the estate passed into the hands of Nawab Sadr Jahan, on whom it was bestowed in *jagir* by the Emperor Jahangir ; but this arrangement was of short duration, for not long after Nawab Saadat Ali Khan resumed the grant and retained it in *kham tahsil*.

About a century ago, the estate reverted to the family in the person of the said Ajab Sah on his return from Jaipur, where he had gone after being dispossessed of it. Having no heir of his own, he during his lifetime gave away the possession to his cousin, Jodha Singh.

Nobleman above comes in succession to the said Jodha Singh.

Estate, 35 villages and 4 *pattis* in zila Kheri. Government revenue, Rs. 26,375. The *gaddi* custom holds in this family.

No. 39.

BEGAM AMANAT FATIMA, *widow of Nawab Husain Ali Khan, Pathan, Taaluqdar of Basitnagar. Title hereditary.*

THIS estate originally consisted of the gift of a *jagir* bestowed by Emperor Alamgir on Nawab Dilar Khan, but during the possession of his heirs was brought under the conditions of a zamindari holding by Nawab Saadat Ali Khan. The Government *sanad* of this taaluq was granted to Nawab Dost Ali Khan, who was succeeded by Nawab Husain Ali Khan. After the latter's death the present Begam inherited the property.

Estate, 29 villages and 2 *pattis* in zila Hardoi. Government revenue, Rs. 21,036. The *gaddi* custom holds in this family.

No. 40.

RAJA JAGAT BAHADUR SINGH, *Bilkharia, Taaluqdar of Amri. Title of "Raja" hereditary.*

Vide No. 7. Raja Bariar Singh, being compelled to leave his native land of Chittorgarh from fear of Emperor Ala-ud-din Shah Ghori, came to Allahabad, and taking service under Raja Ram Deo of Bilkharia, was appointed commander of his troops. On the accession of the Raja's son, Dalip Singh, to power, the new commander showed his base ingratitude by putting to death the son of his patron, annexing his *raj*, and marrying his daughter. In course of time the estate thus acquired became divided and sub-divided among the descendants of this union, and these several divisions, and subdivisions are comprised in Nos. 59, 60, 69, 70, 78, 126, 127 194, 208, 215, and 220.

Estate, 9 villages in zila Partabgarh. Government revenue, Rs. 3,600. The *gaddi* custom holds in this family.

No. 41.

RAJA MANESHAR BAKHSH SINGH, *Raikwar, Taaluqdar of Malanpur, composed of Firozabad, Malanpur, and Bikipur. Title of " Raja" hereditary.*

THIS *ilaqa* (originally a gift of Emperor Jalal-ud-din Akbar to Shahzada Firoz Shah) in A.D. 1707 came into the possession of one Madan Shah during the reign of Emperor Aurangzeb. The recipient, however, was soon after dispossessed and put to death by Raomal Kurmi, a taaluqdar of notoriety as a dacoit. As a consequence of this fatal reverse the wife of Madan Singh fled for protection to her father at Bahraich, where, about three months after, a son was born to her, whom she called Ratan Singh. This son in after years, with the help of his grandfather, recovered his possessions from Raonal Kurmi, whom he put to death. In his ninth generation Rao Basti Singh (in fasli year 1182) obtained the recognition of his title to the heritage from Nawab Saadat Ali Khan, and since then it has been in his family, the present representative holding a Government *sanad* of title.

Estate, 128 villages and 9 *pattis* in zilas Kheri, Sitapur, and Bahraich. Government revenue, Rs. 63,675. The *gaddi* custom holds in this family.

No. 42.

RAJA CHANDAR SIKHAR, *Brahmin, Taaluqdar of Sisendi, Cheolaha, and Dadalha.*

THIS is a taaluq of comparatively modern institution. Sisendi was originally obtained in *theka* (1226 fasli) by Amrit Lal, Pathak, Nazim of Baiswara, and in fasli 1231 it was bestowed in absolute right on his grandson, Shankar Prasad, by Rani Basant Kunwar, widow of Raja Digpal Singh. This was on the occasion of Shankar Prasad's investiture with the sacred Brahminical thread. The estate continued as the inheritance of Shankar's descendant up to fasli 1262. In the year following that it came into the hands of Raja Kashi Prasad, son-in-law of Mohan Lal, and son of the above-mentioned Amrit Lal.

Raja Kashi Prasad distinguished himself by loyal services to Government during the mutiny, and received as his reward the taaluqs of Cheolaha and Dadalha.

This forms one of the five "loyal taaluqs" and the component of 28 villages and 4 *pattis*, which make up its hereditary possession, and enjoy the benefits of a permanent settlement.

The present nobleman has nominated Raja Kashi Prasad as heir and successor of the estate.

Estate, 53 villages and 7 *pattis* in zilas Unao, Rae Bareli, and Lucknow. Government revenue, Rs. 57,042-10-0. The law of primogeniture governs inheritance in this family.

No. 43.

RAJA SARABJIT SINGH, *Raikwar, Taaluqdar of Ramnagar. Title of "Raja" hereditary.*

Vide No. 19. About two centuries ago, one Ram Singh, descended from Sal Deo, founded in his own name taaluq Ramnagar Dhamari, an *ilaqa* originally called Dharm Mandi, and obtained from the Court of Delhi the title of "Raja." In descent from him came Gharib Singh, who built a large tank and a temple with buildings attached at Mahadeva, near Bairamghat, and dedicated the latter to the Hindu god *Mahdeva*, distinguished by the name of "Lodheswar."

Besides this tank and temple various other places of trade, resorts for travellers, &c., in different localities, stand as monuments to the present day of the charity and munificence of successive generations of the family now represented by the subject of this memoir.

Estate, 195 villages and 72 *pattis* in zila Bara Banki. Government revenue, Rs. 1,24,287-3-4. The *guddi* custom holds in this family.

No. 44.

RAJA SHAMSHIR BAHADUR, *Mogul, Taaluqdar of Sadatnagar and Julalpur Deoria. Title of "Raja" personal.*

A HUNDRED and thirty years ago, one Muhammad Ali Beg, a *Resaldar* in the service of the Emperor of Delhi, came to Oudh and founded this taaluq. At a partition of the estate, effected in the fasli year 1223, between his two sons, Bandeh Ali Beg and Akbar Beg, taaluq Deoria Tarnagar fell to the share of the former and taaluq Sadatnagar to that of the latter. On Akbar Beg was, for the first time in 1263 fasli, conferred the present family title of "Raja" by the then Nawab of Oudh. After death he was succeeded by his son, the present taaluqdar.

Estate, 33 villages and 4 *pattis* in zilas Sitapur and Hardoi. Government revenue, Rs. 17,790. The *gaddi* custom holds in this family.

No. 45.

RAJA MUMTAZ ALI KHAN, *Pathan, Taaluqdar of Bilaspur (Atrauli). Title of " Raja" hereditary.*

IN the year 1551, when Emperor Jalal-ud-din Akbar sat on the throne of Delhi, Ali Jan with a number of followers came down from the hills and committed a raid on Atrauli, which at the time was owned by Utra Kunwar of the *Bhar* clan. The invader established his authority over the estate and declared himself Raja. The Emperor, enraged at this unauthorized assumption of power and title, expressed a desire to have this intruder chastised. This desire becoming known to Shajan Khan and Ghalib Khan (sons of Ali Jan), they cut off their father's head, and, in hopes of ingratiating themselves with the Emperor and continuing in possession of the property, carried it as a present to Delhi. The Emperor was greatly pleased, and as a mark of his pleasure gave away the estate to the assassins. Ghalib Khan afterwards returned to his own native country, and Shajan Khan returned to Atrauli, where he took up his residence. Since then the estate has formed the inheritance of his descendants.

Estate, 70 villages and three *pattis* in zila Gonda. Government revenue, Rs. 27,335-12-3. The *gaddi* custom holds in this family.

No. 46.

RAJA SHER BAHADUR SINGH, *Kalans, Taaluqdar of Deoli, Burauli, and Kamiar. Title of " Raja" personal.*

Vide No. 33. This is a branch of the Paraspur taaluq, and it was founded by Dula Rai, from whom comes the nobleman noted above. Taaluq No. 114 forms a branch of this.

Estate, 59½ villages and 11 *pattis* in zilas Bahraich and Bara Banki. Government revenue, Rs. 34,833-9-1. The *gaddi* custom holds in this family.

No. 47.

RANI SITAR-UN-NISA *(widow of Raja Nawab Ali Khan), Sayyid, Taaluqdar of Salempur and Adampur-Bhatpurwa. Title of " Raja" personal.*

SHAIKH ABDUL HUSAIN (Sunni) of Medina, with a number of his own clansmen and other followers, came to Delhi, and for successfully reducing to order the refractory *Amethias*, obtained from the

Emperor gift of Amethi (which forms the nucleus of this estate) and of the title of "Shaikh-ul-Islam." His descendant, Shaikh Salim, the founder of Salimabad, had two sons, Shaikh Adam and Shaikh Kasim, the former of whom gave his name to Adampur above, and the latter to Kasimpur, a village.

In the tenth descendant from Shaikh Abul Husain, a daughter of the family was married to one Hidayat Ali, a *Shia* resident of Kakori. From this marriage were born two sons, Sadat Ali and Mansur Ali, who inherited the estate of their maternal grandfather and went to reside at Salimpur. At a later period Nawab Ali came to the estate as grandson of Sadat Ali, and the Rani, the subject of this memoir, now owns it as the widow of the former.

Estate, 30 villages and 2 *pattis* in zilas Lucknow and Bara Banki. Government revenue, Rs. 38,980-8-0. The *guddi* custom holds in this family.

No. 48.

RAJA AJIT SINGH, *Sombansi, Taaluqdar of Tiraul, Chamiani, Harauli, Katabnagar, and Aurangabad. Title of " Raja" personal.*

Vide No. 11, of which this is a branch. The Raja deserved well for his loyal services during the late sepoy rebellion, and was honoured with the gift of *ilaqas* out of the estate of the rebel taaluqdar Gulab Singh, forfeited to Government.

Estate, 185 villages in zilas Partabgarh, Unao, Hardoi, and Kheri. Government revenue, Rs. 72,307-13-7. The *guddi* custom holds in this family.

No. 49.

RAJA DAYA SHANKAR, *Dikhit (Brahmin), Taaluqdar of Parenda. Title of " Raja" hereditary.*

ABOUT four hundred years ago one Panna Mal, the first of this family, came from Raniapur and founded the village of Parenda, from which the present taaluq derives its name. This Raja is the recognized head of his own caste.

Estate, 9 villages in zila Unao. Government revenue, Rs. 6,061. The law of primogeniture rules inheritance in this family.

No. 50.

RAJA SUKH MANGAL SINGH, *Thakur, Kanpuria, Taaluqdar of Shahman and Dhanipur. Title of " Raja" personal.*

Vide No. 12. This is a branch of the Tiloi house derived from Balbhaddar Shah, a descendant of Raja Manik.

Estate, 30 villages in zilas Rae Bareli and Sultanpur. Government revenue, Rs. 27,229-0-8. Inheritance in this family is governed by its own established custom in the event of the owner dying without making any distinct disposition of his estate.

No. 51.

THAKUR BALBHADDAR SINGH, *Janwar, Taaluqdar of Mahewa and Jahangirabad.*

THIS estate has been in existence from the fasli year 1175 and forms a branch of the house of Oel (No. 24). The present taaluqdar is a lineal descendant of Pitam Singh, mentioned in No. 24, and is second in succession from Gajraj Singh, on whom was bestowed the Government *sanad* of the *ilaqa.*

Estate, 133 villages and 10 *pattis* in zilas Kheri and Sitapur. Government revenue, Rs. 79,155. The *gaddi* custom of inheritance is prevalent in this family.

No. 52.

BABU RAM SAHAI, *Khetri, Taaluqdar of Maurawan, Jabrauli, and Banthra.*

THE original ancestor of this house was a famous shroff (sahukar), who held the office of chakladar under the Government of Oudh. His descendant, Chandan Lal, purchased this taaluq, and the latter was succeeded in its possession by his second son, Gauri Shankar, on whom the title of " Raja " was conferred for faithful services rendered during the mutiny, as also a *sanad* of the estate by the Government of India. This is one of the five taaluqs honourably mentioned in the Government rolls, and the portion of property which comprises the hereditary estate enjoys immunity from future enhancement of revenue. Up to the *régime* of Kanhya Lal, fourth son of Chandan Lal, the family property continued joint and undivided; but after his death, disputes arising among the descendants of Chandan Lal and other rightful heirs in the family, a partition of it was effected. The present taaluqdar comes lineally from Ganga Prasad, a younger brother of the said Chandan Lal.

Estate, 83 villages and 11 *pattis* in zilas Lucknow and Unao. Government revenue, Rs. 75,457-0-6. Inheritance governed by custom in the family in default of distinct disposition of the estate by the owner.

The subdivisions of this house consists of the taaluqdars of—

(1) Behta and Thalendi, now owned by Ram Charan, Shiu Prasad, and Bisheshar Prasad. Estate, 15½ villages in zilas Unao and Rae Bareli. Government revenue, Rs. 14,325-4-3.

(2) Daraita and Amawan, now owned by Madho Prasad and Debi Dayal. Estate, 24½ villages, and 1 *patti* in zilas Unao and Rae Bareli. Government revenue, Rs. 16,227.

(3) Deomi and Kandawan, now owned by Shia Dyal. Estate, 14½ villages in zila Rae Bareli. Government revenue, Rs. 14,535-9-7.

(4) Lowa Singhan Khera, Tauli, &c., and Ranbhi, now owned by Ram Narayan. Estate, 14½ villages and 1 *patti* in zilas Unao, Rae Bareli, and Bara Banki. Government revenue, Rs. 14,514-1-4.

(5) Atwat, &c., and Bachhrawan, now owned by Balmukand, Kalka Prasad, and Chandika Prasad. Estate, 5½ and ¼th villages in zilas Unao and Rae Bareli. Government revenue, Rs. 7,492-12-10.

(6) Asrenda, &c., and Haunsera, now owned by Mohan Lal and five others. Estate, 2¼ and ½ villages in zilas Unao and Rae Bareli. Government revenue, Rs. 3,249-2-5.

(7) Barwa Kalan and Talenda, now owned by Beni Prasad. Estate, 4½ villages in zilas Unao and Rae Bareli. Government revenue, Rs. 3,686-5-0.

No. 53.

Ewaz Ali Khan, *Bhale Sultan, Khanzada, Taaluqdar of Mahona.*

About four centuries ago Raja Narwand Singh, *alias* Rao Barhar, came from Baiswara and attacked and defeated the Bhars and took possession of parganah Jasauli. Several generations after came Pahan Deo, who went to Delhi and embracing the faith of the Prophet was honoured with the title of " Raja." About two centuries after, his descendant, Raja Aladad Khan, acquired the proprietary right of *ilaqa* originally made up of possessions comprised in this and separate taaluqs, Nos. 145 and 213, derived from it. The taaluqdar above is descended lineally from the said Raja Aladad Khan, and he is the recognized chief of his own clan.

Estate, 25 villages and 2 *pattis* in zila Sultanpur. Government revenue, Rs. 22,145-11-7. Inheritance governed by *guddi* custom.

No. 54.

Babu Mahpal Singh, *Baralia, Taaluqdar of Surajpur.*

In Hijri 964, Raja Bali Ram Singh came to Oudh from Kanauj as an Imperial Resaldar. His son Bhikham Singh, under orders from Emperor Jalal-ud-din Akbar Shah, put to death Zor Khan, the owner of taaluq Surajpur Barala, and in reward for his services obtained the gift of seventy-one villages, inclusive of Surajpur, which gives its name to the present estate. This gift has since formed the inheritance of Bhikham Singh's descendants, the latest of whom is Babu Mahpal Singh, who also is the recognized chief of the Baralia clan.

Estate, 61 villages and 7 *pattis* in zila Bara Banki. Government revenue, Rs. 58,963-10-0. *Guddi* custom holds in this estate.

No. 55.

Thakur Ranjit Singh, *Jangre, Rajput, Taaluqdar of Ishanagar, Amethi, Doriana, Mangauria, and Madhwapur.*

In the time of Emperor Jahangir, one Akhraj Singh (of the Sangadha Chauhan clan) left Ajmere and went to Oudh, under orders from the Emperor, to introduce a reformation in its government. At a subsequent period his grandson (by daughter), Chatarbhuj Das, was deputed by the same Emperor for an invasion of the Dekhan. Returning to Delhi after the successful execution of his mission, Chatarbhuj found his Imperial patron dead and his son Shah Jahan on the throne. His services, however, did not go unrewarded, for the reigning king bestowed on him the gift of certain *ilaqas*, as also of the title of " Raja Changez-Khakani." Jaungra, the name by which the clan to which this house belongs is known, is a subsequent gradual corruption of the said titular epithet " Changez."

Chatarbhuj Das had five sons, from the second of whom, Shamalji, comes lineally the present taaluqdar, whose title has the recognition of a *sanad* from the Government of India.

Estate, 60 villages in zilas Sitapur, Kheri, and Bahraich. Government revenue, Rs. 39,206. *Guddi* custom governs inheritance in this estate.

No. 56.

Makrind Singh, *Bais, Taaluqdar of Rampur, Bichhauli (Nandhauli), Kaithauli.*

About seven hundred years ago, Dudu Rai, an inhabitant of Mainpuri, while passing through the then *Bhar* possession of this taaluq at the head of a bridal party destined for Itaunja Mohana, was attacked, and a cart loaded with goods belonging to the procession was plundered by the robbers, and some of their party were severely wounded. He returned to his own country after the marriage, and subsequently marching with an armed gathering to the scene of the outrage, avenged himself on the aggressive *Bhars* by overthrowing their power and taking possession of their property.

In the fasli year 1253 this taaluq passed into the hands of Raja Sabbha Singh as repayment of a loan advanced by him on its mortgage to the descendants of Dudu Rai. Its present owner is a nephew of Raja Sabbha Singh.

Estate, 16 villages and 2 *pattis* in zilas Lucknow and Unao. Government revenue, Rs. 10,203-9-7. Law of primogeniture governs inheritance in this family.

No. 57.

Kunwar Harnam Singh, *Sikh, Manager of Taaluq Boundi.*

Vide No. 1. The Kunwar is a descendant of the Kapurthala house.

No. 58.

Captain Gulab Singh, Sirdar Avatar Singh, *and* Sirdar Narayan Singh, *Sikh, Taaluqdars of Bhiragobindpur, Khorepatti, and Bayla-bahayla.*

These are descended from a distinguished branch of the Panjab nobility, and the property originally owned by Rana Beni Baksh and forfeited to Government for his conduct during the mutiny of 1857 was bestowed on them in recognition of the exemplary loyalty displayed by them in those trying times.

Estate, 32 villages in zila Rae Bareli. Government revenue, Rs. 28,474.

No. 59.

Rai Jagmohan Singh *and* Rai Bisheshar Baksh, *Bachgoti, Taaluqdars of Raipur-bichor. Title of " Rai" personal.*

These are descendants of Chakr Singh (*vide* Nos. 7 and 40). Several generations after Chakr Singh came Prithipal Singh, who obtained from Government a *sanad* of this estate, of which during his lifetime he made a disposition in favour of his two sons, Drigbijai Singh and Rai Bisheshar Baksh. After his death, a partition of the property was effected between the two brothers. Rai Jagmohan Singh now holds by right of inheritance from the said Drigbijai Singh, and Bisheshar Baksh holds by his own right.

Estate, 56 villages in zila Partabgarh. Government revenue, Rs. 33,283-5-1. *Gaddi* custom holds in this estate.

No. 60.

RAI MADHO PRASAD SINGH, *Bachgoti, Taaluqdar of Adharganj, Dillippur. Title of " Rai" personal.*

Vide Nos. 7 and 40. This taaluqdar is also a descendant of Chakr Singh. Property No. 208 comes from this *ilaqa.*

Estate, 127 villages in zila Partabgarh. Government revenue, Rs. 50,699-1-7. *Gaddi* custom holds in this estate.

No. 61.

MAHANT HARCHARAN DAS, *Nanakshahi, Taaluqdar of Maswasi, Heawaj, Anji, Basantipur, Ranipur, Akbarpur, and Kakrai.*

THIS taaluqdar succeeded to the *gaddi* of his predecessor, Mahant Gur Narayan, a follower of the great Nanak and the founder of the estate, which by his will he bequeathed to the present owner. The estate during his minority was under the guardianship of the Court of Wards and received an English education in Canning College.

Estate, 187 villages and 36 *pattis* in zilas Unao, Lucknow Gonda, Bahraich, Hardoi, Sitapur, and Kheri. Government revenue, Rs. 78,433-3-8. *Gaddi* custom holds in this estate.

No. 62.

RAI SARABJIT SINGH, *Bisain, Taaluqdar of Bhadri.*

Vide No. 5. This nobleman is a lineal descendant of Rai Homepal, founder of the *Bisain* clan of Thakurs.

Estate, 96 villages in zila Partabgarh. Government revenue, Rs. 75,393-2-7. *Gaddi* custom holds in this estate.

No. 63.

CHAUDHRI MURTAZA HUSAIN *and* BECH-UN-NISA, *Shaikh, Taaluqdars of Bhilwar and Sikandarpur.*

BHILWAR, according to tradition, is called after one Bahela, a *Pasi,* who obtained possession of its site from the *Bhars* about 700 years ago. It was originally one of forty-two villages given in reward for good services rendered by Malik Adam, founder of the family, in bringing to order the refractory Bhars, of whose insubordination and enmity to the government of the country in days of Muhammadan rule mention has been made in previous memoirs. Several generations after Malik Adam came Chaudhri Lutf-ullah, who was succeeded by Chaudhri Sarfaraz Ahmad, his son-in-law. (The chaudhri had a distinguished place among the taaluqdars of Oudh). On the latter's death the estate, after protracted litigation between the present owners (the first of whom is younger brother, and the second, surviving widow of Chaudhri Sarfaraz Ahmad), was divided among them. The share of the widow, however, constitutes a life estate, as by a will made by the said Chaudhri Sarfaraz Ahmad, the succession to it was bequeathed to his grandson (by daughter), Rafi-ul-zama, whose portrait is given in its proper place. Chaudhri Murtaza Husain, the younger brother of Sarfaraz Ahmad, for his favouring the British cause during the period of the mutiny, was taken and retained a prisoner at Bounai by the mutineers. But when order was restored, his severe sufferings and faithful services found compensation in the gift to him, by the British, of the taaluq of Sikandarpur, consisting of seven villages, yielding an annual revenue of Rs. 4821.

Estate, 42 villages and 8 *pattis* in zilas Bara Banki and Rae Bareli, including the villages awarded by Government. Government revenue, Rs. 59,646-8-0. *Gaddi* custom holds in this estate.

No. 64.

THAKURAIN SHEOPAL KUNWAR (*widow of Thakur Juggannath Baksh*) *Nabatha Bais, Taaluqdar of Simri and Patnadasi.*

Vide No. 4. Mansuk Rai, separating from taaluq No. 26, founded the original village of Simri (on site formerly overgrown with jungle) and raised on it the present taaluq bearing that name. The present taaluqdar is his descendant in the ninth generation.

Estate, 39 villages and 1 chak in zilas Rae Bareli and Unao. Government revenue, Rs. 32,438-8-0. *Gaddi* custom holds in this estate.

No. 65.

THAKURAIN DARYA KUNWAR (*widow of Thakur Basant Singh*), *Bais, Taaluqdar of Simarpaha.*

Vide Nos. 4 and 14. The site of Simarpaha, after which this taaluq is called, consisted originally of waste land allotted to Rudh Sah (second son of Saukat Singh) on his separation from Khajurgaon. Makund Sai (his co-sharer of a moiety), who improved the waste, introduced sites in it and eventually became master of the newly-formed estate. To the inheritance of this estate subsequently came Prithiraj, one of his two grandsons; the other, Hindu Singh, going to Hamermau Kola, No. 139.

In the ninth generation from Prithiraj was born Lalji Singh, whose name is associated with the establishment of a large bazar in the vicinity of Simarpaha. He had two sons, Vikramjit and Fateh Bahadur, both of whom died childless.

In the fasli year 1242 the widow of Vikramjit adopted Raja Basant Singh, who succeeded to the estate, and after him came the subject of this memoir.

She has adopted Shomeswar Bahadur for her son and heir, but at present she retains the possession and management of the *ilaqa* in her own hands.

Estate, 43 villages in zila Rae Bareli. Government revenue, Rs. 37,962. *Gaddi* custom holds in this estate.

No. 66.

CHANDARPAL SINGH, *Bais, Taaluqdar of Korihar station.*

Vide Nos. 4 and 14. About three centuries ago, Pahar Singh (descended from one Alain Singh) received this estate as his own personal possession on leaving the joint family, and since then it has formed the inheritance of succeeding generations in his house.

Estate, 52 villages in zila Rae Bareli. Government revenue, Rs. 30,453. *Gaddi* custom prevails in this estate.

No. 67.

THAKURAIN ACHAL KUNWAR (*widow of Shiupal Singh*), *Bais, Taaluqdar of Gaura Kasaiti.*

Vide Nos. 4 and 14. In the fasli year 1097 this estate was founded by Dula Rai (a descendant of Rana Daman Deo) when he separated from the joint house of Khajurgaon. Sixth from him in succession was Ram Baksh. After several generations came Thakur Shiupal Singh, the deceased husband of the present Thakurain, who holds the property by her right as his widow. No. 137 is a branch of this taaluq.

Estate, 45 villages in zila Rai Bareli. Government revenue, Rs. 31,388. *Gaddi* custom holds in this estate.

No. 68.

THAKUR PRATAB RUDR SINGH, *Raikwar, Taaluqdar of Rampur, Mathra, and Bhikhampur.*

Vide No. 19. Daswant Singh, a descendant of Shakdeo, received this possession at a partition of the family inheritance. Several generations after him came Kirat Singh. In consequence of the latter's death without issue, his widow, in the fasli year 1221, adopted one Madho Singh. Madho Singh was succeeded by Goman Singh, whose title received the recognition of *sanad* from Government. On his death the present taaluqdar came into the property.

Estate, 56 villages and 6 *pattis* in zilas Sitapur and Bara Banki. Government revenue, Rs. 34,728. *Guddi* custom holds in this estate.

No. 69.

RAN BIJAI BAHADUR SINGH, *Bachgoti, Taaluqdar of Patti Saifabad ($\frac{11}{20}$th share). Title of "Diwan" hereditary.*

Vide Nos. 7 and 40. This taaluqdar is descended from Chakr Singh, the original founder of the Bachgoti house.

In later days came in succession Omar Singh, who, however, after remaining in possession for some time, made over the hereditary estate to his younger brother, Zabar Singh, and himself retired from the management of it. On the death of both the brothers, Surbdiwan Singh, son of Omar Singh, came to the *guddi*. Surbdiwan Singh dying without issue, disputes arose between Thakurain Gulab Kunwar and Thakurain Bilas Kunwar, surviving widows of the said Omar Singh and Zabar Singh, and their disputes did not terminate until a partition of taaluq Saifabad (which had hitherto continued one joint undivided estate) was effected among them in proportion of $\frac{11}{20}$th and $\frac{9}{20}$th shares. The two widows adopted Ranjit Singh and Randhir Singh respectively, and made them heirs to their own respective possessions. Ran Bijai Bahadur, the now taaluqdar, holds the inheritance from the said Ranjit Singh, and the subject of the following notice (No. 70) is the widow and heiress of the other adopted son, Randhir Singh.

Estate, 170 villages in zila Partabgarh. Government revenue, Rs. 59,352. Succession governed by law of primogeniture.

No. 70.

THAKURAIN AJIT KUNWAR (*widow of Diwan Randhir Singh*), *Thakur, Bachgoti, Taaluqdar of Patti Saijabad ($\frac{9}{20}$th share.)*

Vide Nos. 7 and 40. Full account of this taaluqdar and her inheritance is given in the preceding No. 69.

Estate, 116 villages in zila Partabgarh. Government revenue, Rs. 51,768-5-4. Succession is governed by law of primogeniture.

No. 71.

THAKURAIN JANKI KUNWAR, *Biscin*, *Taaluqdar of Pawans* (*Dhigwas*).

Vide No. 5. Thakurain comes in succession to her mother, Kailas Kunwar, who received Government *sanad* of the estate, and now occupies the *gaddi* in this branch of Rai Homepal's descendants.

Estate, 94 villages in zila Partabgarh. Government revenue, Rs. 43,487-13-6. *Gaddi* custom holds in this estate.

No. 72.

RAJA MILOP SINGH, *Rajput*, *Jangre*, *Taaluqdar of Shahpur and Majgami*. *Title of "Raja" hereditary.*

THE ancestry of this taaluqdar can be traced to one Manj, who with his brother Bhanji (both descended from Akhraj Singh, mentioned in No. 55), received a gift of the *ilaqa* from Emperor Shah Jahan for effectually suppressing and expelling from their possessions the refractory *Bachils*. The gift has formed the inheritance of the said recipient's family ever since, and latterly their title received the recognition of Government *sanad* during the ownership of Raja Ganga Singh, Sadhu Singh, Bariar Singh, Ahlad Singh. After their death the estate was divided into four equal shares, the taaluqdar Milop Singh inheriting one of them, consisting of—

Estate, 38 villages and 4 *pattis* in zila Kheri. Government revenue, Rs. 21,063. Inheritance governed by custom in the family in default of testamentary disposition of estate.

The other three shares comprise the following:—

(1) Guman Singh, Jangre Rajput, taaluqdar of Ramnagar and Daulatpur, consisting of estate, 24 villages and 3 *pattis* in zila Kheri. Government revenue, Rs. 15,987. Inheritance as above.

(2) Gobardhan Singh, Jangre Rajput, taaluqdar of Bigna and Nighasan, consisting of estate, 28 villages and 5 *pattis* in zila Kheri. Government revenue, Rs. 14,898. Inheritance as above.

(3) Dilipat Singh, Jangre Rajput, taaluqdar of Bijauria and Jagdeopur, consisting of estate, 37 villages and 4 *pattis* in zila Kheri. Government revenue, Rs. 18,303. Inheritance as above.

No. 73.

BABUS UDRES SINGH *and* CHANDRES SINGH, *Rajkumar*, *Taaluqdars of Maopur Dhaurua* (*and Mundayra.*)

THE history of the Rajkumar family is fully recorded in No. 7. From their ancestor, Bariar Singh, came Ishri Singh, from whom descended Dul Singh. Among the grandsons of this last were

Sangram Singh and Pahlwan Singh, who, about 80 years ago, came to a share of the family inheritance. Sangram Singh had two sons—Ranjit Singh and Sarbdawan Singh. From the former comes the two taaluqdars above, and from the latter the subject of the next following No. 74. Houses Nos. 95 and 155 are descendants of the said Pahlwan Singh.

Estate, 109 villages and 109 *pattis* in zilas Fyzabad and Sultanpur. Government revenue, Rs. 58,301-11-0. Inheritance according to law of primogeniture.

No. 74.

Babu Amrts Singh, *Rajkumar, Taaluqdar of Muopur Baragaon.*

Vide preceding No. 73. This nobleman is a descendant of Sarbdawan Singh, one of the two sons of Sangram Singh in the above family.

Estate, 15 villages and 30 *pattis* in zilas Sultanpur and Fyzabad, Government revenue, Rs. 11,301. Inheritance by law of primogeniture.

No. 75.

Mir Ghazaffar Husain *and* Mir Baqar Husain, *Sayyids, Taaluqdars of Pirpur.*

About a century and a half ago, during the reign of Nawab Suraj-ud-daula, one Mirza Muhammad Ali Beg came from Khorasan to Fyzabad, and afterwards, while employed under Nawab Asafadaula, purchased the villages of Pirpur, &c., which shortly after was formed into a taaluq. About this time one Chaudhri Muhammad Hafiz, taaluqdar of Saidawan, died, leaving no heir to his property, except a grandson (by daughter), named Mir Kasim, only four years old. The Chaudhri's widow gave away the estate to Mirza Muhammad Ali Beg, and with the estate she gave him in adoption the infant Kasim Ali. The Mirza formed the whole of his estate (both original and acquired by gift referred to) into one taaluq, and after remaining in possession of it for some time died and was succeeded by Kasim Ali. On the latter's death in fasli 1224, his widow entrusted the management of the estate to her son-in-law, Mir Kalb Husain, who continued in charge up to 1260 fasli. The following year found the subjects of this memoir in possession of the estate. The first is also a son-in-law of Kasim Ali, the second is a son of Mir Kalb Husain.

Estate, 176 villages and 78 *pattis* in zilas Sultanpur and Fyzabad. Government revenue, Rs. 12,001-10-0. Inheritance governed by law of primogeniture.

No. 76.

BABU UGARDAT SINGH, *Thakur, Bachgoti, Taaluqdar of Bhiti and Benaikpur.*

Vide No. 7. This taaluqdar is a descendant of the house noticed in No. 13. A century ago, Babu Bal Sah, one of the ancestors of the estate, separated from the family and received the present taaluq for his support. Additions to it were subsequently made.

Estate, 57 villages and 74 *pattis* in zilas Sultanpur and Fyzabad. Government revenue, Rs. 34,872-4-0. Law of primogeniture governs inheritance in this family.

No. 77.

RUDR PRATAB SINGH, *Thakur, Kanpuria, Taaluqdar of Sconi (Siwan).*

Vide No. 12. In A. D. 1364 Raja Madan Singh by force of arms obtained possession of this taaluq from its original owners of the Bais and Raghbansi castes. After him came Mandhata Singh and Jaswant Singh, between whom a partition of the estate was made. The former was ancestor of the Chandapur family, and the latter of the subject of the present memoir.

Estate, 16 villages in zila Rae Bareli. Government revenue, Rs. 15,117-6-0. The *gaddi* custom is prevalent in this family.

No. 78.

SITALA BAKHSH, LAL BAHADUR SINGH, KALKA BAKHSH SINGH, UDAT NARAIN SINGH, NAGESHAR BAKHSH SINGH, *and* CHAUHARJA BAKHSH SINGH, *Bachgoti, Taaluqdars of Madhpur.*

Vide Nos. 7 and 40. This is a *patti* of taaluq Saifabad. After Debi Singh's death his brother Dhana Singh divided his *ilaqa* among his six sons named above, but the possession continues joint and undivided.

Estate, 83 villages in zila Partabgarh. Government revenue, Rs. 25,794. Family custom governs inheritance in default of testamentary disposition.

No. 79.

BABU HARDAT SINGH, *Thakur, Bachgoti, Taaluqdar of Simratpur, Chakmarriya, and Simratpur.*

Vide No. 7. This is a branch of taaluq Kurwar in No. 13 mentioned, and was founded by a descendant of Chakr Singh.

Estate, 37 villages and 19 *pattis* in zilas Sultanpur and Fyzabad. Government revenue, Rs. 22,828-12-0. Inheritance governed by law of primogeniture.

No. 80.

GANESH KUNWAR (*widow of Jagarnath Baksh*), *Kanpuria, Taaluqdar of Jamu.*

Vide No. 12. This taaluq was constituted by Raj Sah, youngest and fourth son of Balbhaddar Sah, and was handed down from generation to generation till it came into the possession of Jagarnath Baksh, whose widow now holds it. Taaluq No. 164 is a branch of this.

Estate, 17 villages in zila Sultanpur. Government revenue, Rs. 14,966-4-0. The *gaddi* custom holds in this family.

No. 81.

THAKUR SHANKAR BAKHSH, *Bais, Taaluqdar of Pahan and Gularya.*

Vide Nos. 4 and 14. This taaluqdar is a descendant of Mitrjit (third son of Rana Duma Rai), who founded the estate on his separation from the rest of his family about eight centuries ago. The present owner inherited it from his father, Bhup Singh (coming lineally from the founder), in whose name the summary settlement was made.

Estate, 13 villages in zilas Unao and Rae Bareli. Government revenue, Rs. 23,820-8-0. The *gaddi* custom holds in this family.

No. 82.

MALIK HIDAYAT HUSAIN, *Shaikh, Taaluqdar of Samanpur.*

THE possession of this estate can be traced to one Ahmad Katal, who is said to have founded it about five centuries ago. Several generations after him came one Tafazzul Husain, in whose name the Government *sanad* was granted at the settlement. Tafazzul Husain died without issue, and was succeeded by his younger brother, taaluqdar Hidayat Husain, Shaikh.

Estate, 181 villages and 26 *pattis* in zila Fyzabad. Government revenue, Rs. 86,243. The *gaddi* custom holds in this family.

No. 83.

BIKARMAJIT SINGH *and* ANANT PRASAD, *Bachgoti, Taaluqdars of Rainpur, Mukundpur, and Sadipur Kotwa.*

Vide No. 7.   About 250 years ago, one Amar Singh, separating himself from the rest of his family, founded this estate, which since then has been in the possession of his descendants. The Government *sanad* was granted to Kalka Bakhsh, who was succeeded by the present owner.

Estate, 42 villages and 32 *pattis* in zilas Sultanpur and Rae Bareli. Government revenue, Rs. 17,477. Inheritance according to family custom in the event of the estate being left intestate.

No. 84.

NAU NIHAL SINGH, *son of Gopal Singh, Butan, Taaluqdar of Muhammadabad (Gopalkhera).*

THIS is one of the oldest estates in Oudh, and its former owners (ancestors of the present taaluqdar) held the distinguished position of *kanungos* and *chaudhris* under the Native Government. Muhammadabad, after which the taaluq is called, was subsequently purchased by Mohkan Singh from some Pathan proprietors. In later descent, one Chaudhri Gopal Singh received the highly valued appointment of Honorary Magistrate of the 1st class and Assistant Collector in his own *ilaqa;* he also obtained the Government *sanad.* His son and successor, who now holds the estate, also has jurisdiction as an Honorary Magistrate and Assistant Collector within the limit of his own property.

Estate, 22 villages in zila Unao. Government revenue, Rs. 14,582. Law of primogeniture governs succession.

No. 85.

BABU MAHINDRADAT SINGH, *Bachgoti, Taaluqdar of Khajurahat.*

Vide No. 7. This is another branch of taaluq No. 13. One Shankar Singh, separating himself from the Kurwar house, received as his share certain villages which, with subsequent acquisitions, he consolidated into the present taaluq. His descendants have been in undisturbed possession of it to the present day.

Estate, 38 villages and 35 *pattis* in zila Fyzabad. Government revenue, Rs. 16,429. Law of primogeniture governs succession.

No. 86.

CHAUDHRI KHASLAT HUSAIN, *Shaikh, Taaluqdar of Kakrali, Arwi Rahmanpur Asaish, Chainu, Tikatganj, and Gundemau.*

THE original ancestor of the above nobleman came from Arabia to Fariab, and from thence accompanied Emperor Timur Shah to Sandila, of which place he was nominated Chaudhri.* His descendant, Shaikh Firoz, received the title of "Khan" from Emperor Akbar and also the rights and privileges of Chaudhri, which latter honours were continued to the family up to the beginning of the reign of Nawab Saadat Ali Khan, who converted them into a fixed annual payment of Rs. 10,000 and the absolute gift of certain villages *nankar.*

In later days the grandfather of the present taaluqdar distinguished himself among the nobility of the province by investing extensively in land and by asserting his rank as a taaluqdar of Oudh. During the mutiny of 1857, his son, Chaudhri Hashmat Ali Khan, materially helped the British Commissariat with the resources of his estates in pargana Sandila, and with his own troops took a prominent part in fighting the mutineers and stamping out the rebellion. He also used his own personal influence and prevailed on many of his brother taaluqdars, who had fled, to return on condition of the safe protection of their possessions. Many were induced by him to replace themselves under our care and Government. Besides these services, Chaudhri Hashmat Ali Khan assisted the authorities by much useful advice towards the restoration of peace and order. A magnificent and tasteful Kothi and Mahalsarai belonging to him was completely destroyed by fire by the rebel leader Ahmad-ulla Shah. To compensate for this loss, which amounted to several lacs of rupees, Government bestowed on this loyal Chaudhri the proprietary right of taaluqs Asaish and Arwi Rahmanpur, comprising 43 villages and one patti, and also a *khilat* of honour of considerable value. After him succeeded the subject of this memoir.

Chaudhri Khaslat Husain is a man of great ability, and in recognition of his talents and influence an offer was made to him of the Secretaryship of the (Oudh) Anjuman-i-Hind, which he at once accepted, inasmuch as it placed within his reach the means of promoting the interests and well-being of his brother taaluqdars in the province. He is an Honorary Magistrate and Assistant Collector in his own *ilaqa*. His son and heir, Chaudhri Muhammad Azim Sahab, has passed the pleadership examination, and is well known for his legal learning and various other accomplishments. He, too, is an Honorary Magistrate within the local limits of pargana Mallanwan, which forms a part of this taaluq.

Estate, 85 villages and 11 *pattis* in zilas Hardoi, Unao, Lucknow, and Sitapur. Government revenue, Rs. 72,610-5-3. The *gaddi* custom holds in this family.

---

* A favoured nominee entitled from Government to 1 per cent. on revenue during both *rabi* and *kharif* crops, besides 4 annas from each landholder at time of payment of revenue and nazar of the landholder.

No. 87.

THAKUR BHARAT SINGH, *Nikormi, Taaluqdar of Atwa and Nasirpur*

THE ancestor of this taaluqdar originally came from Alwar Tajara, and settled in Swajpur, *ilaqa* Sandi, among the then inhabitants of which were certain of his own relations. He released and restored to liberty the raja of the place, who about this time was living under surveillance of the troops under orders from Delhi, and as a reward for his services received from the relieved raja the grant of *ilaqa* Palia. In sambat 1755 Shiupal Singh, a later descendant, made considerable additions to the family estate, a partition of which was made by and between four brothers—Newaz Sah, Govind Rai, Gaja Singh, and Kishn Singh. In the fourth generation from Shiupal Singh came Newaz Sah and Kishn Singh, who went to settle in Barda; the remaining brothers continued to reside in Atwa. The subject of this memoir is a lineal descendant of Govind Rai. He received Nasirpur in gift from Government, in recognition of loyal services rendered during the mutiny.

Estate, 40 villages and 5 *pattis* in zila Hardoi. Government revenue, Rs. 43,160. The *gaddi* custom of succession rules in this family.

No. 88.

THAKUR SHEO BAKHSH SINGH, *Gaur, Taaluqdar of Katesar and Khanipur.*

DURING the reign of Emperor Alamgir, when revolt and disorder prevailed throughout the empire, Digpal and Tribhuban Sahi, ancestors of this taaluqdar (in 1119 Hijri), cut off the heads of certain Brahmins who then owned Chadupur and buried the bodies. They then settled on the possessions of their victims, and building a fort on the spot where the bodies were buried, gave the *ilaqa* the name of Katesar, signifying the murderous deed committed on it. From this period dates the foundation of this house and estate. Subsequently a partition of the joint possession was effected between Digpal and Tribhuban Sahi, and from the former of these, lineally, comes the subject of this notice.

Estate, 95 villages and 17 *pattis* in zilas Sitapur and Kheri. Government revenue, Rs. 77,493. The *gaddi* custom holds in this family.

No. 89.

THAKURAIN BAIJ NATH KUNWAR, CHHATARPAL SINGH, SURUJPAL SINGH *and* CHANDARPAL SINGH, *Baisani, Taaluqdars of Kundrajit.*

Vide No. 5. This estate fell to the share of the founder of this branch of Rai Homepal's house at a partition of the family inheritance among the descendants of the latter. The Government *sanad* was originally granted in the name of the Thakurain, but she of her own free will caused a division of the estate into four different shares, reserving one of these to herself and giving away the remaining three to the present co-owners (her near relatives), whose titles subsequently received State recognition.

Estate, 68 villages in zila Partabgarh. Government revenue, Rs. 43,331. Inheritance governed by family custom in default of testamentary disposition.

No. 90.

DURGA PRASAD *and* WAZIR CHAND, *Kayesth, Taaluqdars of Sarwan, Baragaon, Sirsaw-Billhara, and Tualhi-Laharu.*

THE village of Sarwan was originally built by one Thakur Sarman Singh, of the *Raikwar* clan. About a century ago, Rai Jaisukh Rai (descended from an ancestor who held a permanent appointment of *chaklodar* during the former Government of Oudh), received it along with other estates in gift from the Government of Oudh and laid the foundation of the taaluq known by that name. The other taaluqs comprised in the estate were Government grants bestowed on his descendants, Dhanpat Rai and Fateh Chand, for services rendered during the crisis of 1857. After their death the present nobleman came into possession. An amicable partition of the joint family estate was made between them some time ago. Wazir Chand is in possession of his own share, and that belonging to Durga Prasad is under the management of the Court of Wards.

Estate, 68 villages and 6 *pattis* in zilas Hardoi, Kheri, and Unao. Government revenue, Rs. 46,659. The *gaddi* custom of succession holds in this family.

No. 91.

ANAND BAHADUR SINGH, *Garghansi, Taaluqdar of Khapradih, &c.*

ABOUT a century ago, Nahal Singh and Ganga Prasad (recognized heads of their own clan), purchased the taaluqs Khapradih and Sihipur. The former made some additions to the joint acquisition, which, during the life of himself and his partner, continued undivided. After their death, taaluq Sihipur, &c. (No. 94), went to Raghnath Kunwar, widow of Nahal Singh; and Khapradih, &c., to Ramsarup, a great-grandson of Ganga Prasad. The present representative is the son and heir of Ramsarup.

Estate, 88 villages in zilas Sultanpur and Fyzabad. Government revenue, Rs. 44,561-3-6. Succession by law of primogeniture.

No. 92.

DAN BAHADURPAL SINGH, *Sombansi, Taaluqdar of Dandi-kach.*

Vide No. 11, of which this is a branch. Government *sanad* of the estate was granted to Sripat Singh, who, by his last will and testament, bequeathed it to his son-in-law, the present taaluqdar.

Estate, 31 villages in zila Partabgarh. Government revenue, Rs. 14,849. The *guddi* custom of inheritance holds in this family.

No. 93.

BABU BISHAN NATH SINGH, *Bais, Taaluqdar of Katgurh.*

Vide Nos. 4 and 14. This taaluqdar is a paternal uncle of Rana Shanker Bakhsh of Khajurgaon, and he obtained the estate (originally forming part of the forfeited *ilaqa* of the rebel taaluqdar Beni Madho Bakhsh) as reward for good services rendered during the mutiny.

Estate, 11 villages in zila Rae Bareli. Government revenue, Rs. 7,136. Law of primogeniture governs succession in the family.

No. 94.

THAKUR BISHESHAR BAKHSH SINGH, *Gargbansi, Taaluqdar of Sikipur, &c.*

Vide No. 91, of which this taaluq forms a branch. The taaluqdar above holds it in inheritance from Raghnath Kunwar, widow of Nahal Singh (*vide* No. 91 mentioned).

Estate, 100 villages and 78 *pattis* in zilas Sultanpur and Fyzabad. Government revenue, Rs. 48,312-15-11. Primogeniture governs succession.

No. 95.

BABU LALU SAH, *Thakur, Rajkumar, Taaluqdar of Mcopur Dehla Kaomi, Madhuban, one-third share (held jointly with Ishraj Singh, No. 155) of Sahrapur and Mcopur Sharukati.*

Vide Nos. 7 and 73. This nobleman is one of the sons of Pahlwan Singh, and holds a share of the ancestral estate allotted to the latter on its partition between him and his brother Sangram Singh, the other share of such allotment being held by taaluqdar No. 155.

Estate, 11 villages and 45 *pattis* in zilas Sultanpur and Fyzabad. Government revenue, Rs. 12,778-11-6. Primogeniture governs succession.

No. 96.

NIWAZISH ALI KHAN, *Kazalbash, Taaluqdar of Nawabganj (Aliabad).*

IN the days of Nadir Shah, one Sardar Ali Khan came from Turkistan and was appointed Hakim of Kandahar. His son, Sardar Hidayat Khan, left Kandahar and went to reside in Kabul during the reign of Ahmad Shah Durrani. During the first Kabul war, the sons of Hidayat Khan—Muhammad Husain Khan, Muhammad Hassan Khan, Haji Muhammad Khan, Ali Raza Khan, Muhammad Raza Khan, and Muhammad Taki Khan—afforded valuable assistance to Government, and Ali Raza Khan accompanied the British on their return to India after the close of the campaign. In recognition of his excellent services, Ali Raza Khan was granted an allowance of Rs. 800 a month from the Government of India. He (as also one of his brothers) did very good service for Government at the Kangra outbreak of 1846 and at the battle of Ferozshahr.

Muhammad Taki Khan was killed and Muhammad Raza Khan was wounded in a battle with the rebels during the mutiny at Kasganj. As compensation for his wound, the Government of India conferred on the latter a monthly pension of Rs. 200.

The services of Ali Raza Khan were rewarded by the title of "Khan" and the gift of the present taaluq, which formerly belonged to the escheated rebel estate of Charda. In succession to him came the subject of this memoir.

Estate, 51 villages in zila Bahraich. Government revenue, Rs. 28,463-15-7. Law of primogeniture governs succession.

No. 97.

BHAYA UDEPRATAB SINGH, *Bisain, Taaluqdar of Bhinga, and Deotahu.*

THIS was originally one of the oldest estates belonging to the Janwar family, and was once owned by one Lallit Singh. His sister was married to Bhawani Singh, younger brother of the Raja of Gonda. When the *Banjara* subjects of Lalit Singh proved refractory, and declaring against their chief dispossessed him of the *ilaqa*, the latter made over his right and interest in it to his brother-in-law, Bhawani Singh, who at once repaired to the scene, fought with the intruders and compelled them to fly. He then settled on the estate and became its owner. Since those days the property has been in the possession of his family, the present representative of which is the subject of this notice.

Estate, 118 villages and 4 *pattis* in zilas Gonda and Bahraich. Government revenue, Rs. 85,367-8-3. The *guddi* custom of succession holds in this family.

No. 98.

Babu Bhunranjan Mukarji, *Bengali Brahmin, Taaluqdar of Shankarpur.*

Among the grants bestowed on taaluqdars and *raieses* for loyal services rendered to Government in Oudh during the crisis of 1857 is the above gift. With it also was bestowed the title of "Raja" to Babu Dukhinaranjan Mukarji, paternal grandfather of the present owner. This taaluq originally formed part of the confiscated estate of a late rebel zamindar of the province, Rana Beni Madho Bakhsh.

Estate, 14 villages in zila Rae Bareli. Government revenue, Rs. 7,562. Succession governed by law of primogeniture.

No. 99.

Thakur Bishan Nath Bakhsh, *Bais, Taaluqdar of Hasanpur and Bahadurnagar.*

Vide No. 4. This is a branch of taaluq No. 26, and it was founded about a century and a quarter ago by Ajab Singh (from Karn Rai), who received it on his separation from the house of Kori Sadauli. In fasli 1244 Thakur Bakhsh succeeded to the property, and after him came the taaluqdar heading this notice.

Estate, 21½ villages in zila Rae Bareli. Government revenue, Rs. 9,602. The *gaddi* custom of succession holds in this family.

No. 100.

Babu Sarabjit Singh, *Kanpuria, Taaluqdar of Tikari, Bhagapur, Atcha, Pura-Jamai, and Amethi.*

Taaluq Tikari above mentioned was in the sambat year 1850 allotted to Raja Gulab Sah by the then Raja of Tiloi, and it has since then continued in the possession of the family, of which the present taaluqdar is a lineal descendant. The latter distinguished himself by loyal services to the British Government during the mutiny, and was rewarded with the grant of taaluq Bhagapur. He also in later times obtained a gift of the Amethi estate from its owner, Raja Madho Singh (*vide* memoir No. 8).

Estate, 353 villages in zilas Rae Bareli, Partabgarh, and Sultanpur. Government revenue, Rs. 2,14,840-1-3. Succession governed by law of primogeniture.

No. 101.

SITLA BAKHSH SINGH *and* SHANKAR SINGH, *Bisain, Taaluqdars of Dhangarh.*

Vide No. 5. This is part of the Dhigwas family, originally derived from one Homepal.

Estate, 45 villages in zila Partabgarh. Government revenue, Rs. 15,929-3-9. Family custom governs succession in default of testamentary disposition.

No. 102.

BABU KISHAN PARSHAD SINGH, *Panwar, Taaluqdar of Birhar (Chandipur Birhar).*

ABOUT 500 years ago, one Sukhraj Deo from Azamgarh entered service under the *Raj* of the Rajehrans. He soon acquired great influence, and gradually availing himself of the declining power and prestige of his masters, brought into his possession 302 villages belonging to them, to which he also made subsequent additions by acquisitions of territory from time to time. Several generations after came Lashkari Singh and Paltan Singh, between whom, about two centuries ago, was divided the hereditary estate comprising the said 302 villages and the several subsequent acquisitions referred to. The present taaluqdar and his kinsmen of the next following number are from the said Paltan Singh, and Nos. 104 and 106 are lineal descendants of his co-sharer, Lashkari Singh.

Estate, 30 villages and 316 *pattis* in zila Fyzabad. Government revenue, Rs. 40,455. Law of primogeniture governs succession.

No. 103.

BABU HARDAT SINGH, *Ponwar, Taaluqdar of Birhar (Chandipur Haswa).*

Vide No. 102. This nobleman comes from Paltan Singh (a descendant of Sukhraj Deo), and owns the estate allotted to the latter at the partition noted in the said No. 102 mentioned.

Estate, 24 villages and 320 *pattis* in zila Fyzabad. Government revenue, Rs. 39,982. Succession by law of primogeniture.

No. 104.

SHAMSHERE BAHADUR, BABU SHEO PRAGASH SINGH, *Ponwar, Taaluqdar of Birhar (Raji Sultanpur).*

THIS is a branch of taaluq No. 102. Nobleman above owes this property to his descent from Lashkari Singh, coming from Sukhraj Deo.

Estate, 69 villages and 200 *pattis*. Government revenue, Rs. 37,044. Succession by law of primogeniture.

No. 105.

THAKURAIN DALIL KUNWAR (*widow of Chandika Prasad*), *Bais, Taaluqdar of Lahrastpur.*

THIS estate comprises several thousand bighas of waste land originally (about two and half centuries ago) bestowed by the then Emperor of Delhi on the founder of the house. The latter cleared his grant of land of the jungle which stood on it, built Birwa, so called from the fact of large and numerous trees of *bair* (a native fruit) that once grew there. This name has since been changed to Lahrastpur. Chandika Prasad, the husband of the present owner, came eventually into the property and received from Government the recognition *sanad*. His widow now holds it by her own right.

Estate, 11 villages and 3 *pattis* in zila Hardoi. Government revenue, Rs. 15,795. The *gaddi* custom of inheritance holds in this family.

No. 106.

SHIUDAST NARAIN SINGH, *son of Babu Makhape Narain Singh, Ponwar, Taaluqdar of Birhar.*

THIS is another offshoot of taaluq No. 102. The Babu represents a collateral branch tracing from Lashkari Singh, a descendant of Sukhraj Deo. Some time ago he allotted to his five sons the major portion of possessions paying an annual Government revenue of Rs. 32,987, reserving to himself only 2 villages and 15 *pattis*.

Estate, villages in zila Fyzabad. Government revenue, Rs. 1,318. Succession governed by primogeniture.

No. 107.

MUSAMMAT GANESH KUNWAR (*widow of Arjun Singh*), *Kanpuria Taaluqdar of Rehsi.*

Vide No. 12. This house and estate are traceable from Salbahan, second son of Balbhaddar Sah.

Estate, 10 villages in zila Sultaupur. Government revenue, Rs. 6,790-14-0. The *gaddi* custom of succession holds in this family.

No. 108.

SHAIKH AHMAD HUSAIN *and* WAJID HUSAIN, *Taaluqdars of Gadi-t, Goela, and Bastuuli.*

THESE taaluqdars inherit their property from their father, Shaikh Madni Zain-ul-Abdin, who in fasli 1250 succeeded to this estate as heir to his maternal grandfather, a descendant of Qazi Ala-ud-din Ansari. This last person in the Hijri year 599, came from Medina and acquired it from the Bhars by force of arms.

These taaluqdars belong to the clan of *Qidwai*, so called from their ancestor Qazi Qidwa. The first of them (Ahmad Husain) is a tahsildar in the employ of the British Government.

Estate, 14 villages and 8 *pattis* in zilas Lucknow and Bara Banki. Government revenue, Rs. 25,225. Family custom governs inheritance in case of property being left intestate.

No. 109.

THAKUR BALDEO BAKHSH (*son of Sardar Jhabba Singh*), *Janwar, Taaluqdar of Pursaini (Akbari Gopalkhera), Pursaini Gaunaha, Chak Phura Ranipur.*

THE original founder of this house owned the small taaluq of Pursaini only, and to it was subsequently added Akbari Gopalkhera (part of the confiscated *ilaqa* of Hindpal Singh), received in grant, from the British Government, together with the title of " Sardar Bahadur," by Jhabba Singh above named for services rendered during the mutiny. This taaluq ranks among the five distinguished loyal estates of Oudh, but Pursaini alone possesses the privilege of exemption from enhancement in any further settlement. Thakur Baldeo Bakhsh is an Honorary Magistrate and Assistant Collector within the limits of his own property.

Estate, 12 villages and 1 *patti* in zilas Unao, Lucknow, and Rae Bareli. Government revenue, Rs. 18,932-11-0. Succession governed by law of primogeniture.

No. 110.

THAKUR LALTA BAKHSH, *Gaur, Taaluqdar of Khajrahra and Bahrawa.*

ABOUT eleven centuries ago, Raghunath Singh, then residing in Narkalinjar, came to the province of Oudh and was appointed amil (sub-chakladar) in the service of Raja Jai Chand of Kanauj. His son, Ekanga Singh, succeeded his father in that appointment, and under orders from the Raja expelled the refractory Thateras, who originally owned this taaluq, and himself took possession of it. Since then the estate has come down to the family in order of succession, receiving from time to time accessions to it by various mortgages and purchases. The Government *sanad* of this *ilaqa* was granted to Thakur Dal Singh, predecessor of the present representative.

Estate, 25 villages and 6 *pattis* in zilas Hardoi and Sitapur. Government revenue, Rs. 27,739. Succession governed by law of primogeniture.

No. 111.

WASI HAIDAR, *Sayyid, Taaluqdar of Bhogetapur.*

IN 614 Hijri, Muhammad Soghra, ancestor of the present owner, leaving his native country, accompanied Emperor Shamsh-ud-din to Hindustan. He defeated Raja Sri of Srinagar (now called Bilgram) and obtained an imperial gift of villages situated in that pargana. A later descendant in his family founded village Bhogetapur (having cleared the jungle originally covering its site), after which the present taaluq is named. The Government *sanad* of the estate was granted to and in the name of Sayyid Muhammad Ibrahim, in accordance with whose will his younger brother, the subject of this memoir, holds possession.

Estate, 21 villages and 1 *patti* in zila Hardoi. Government revenue, Rs. 19,458. The *gaddi* custom of succession holds in this family.

No. 112.

CHAUDHRI MUHAMMAD ASHRAF, MUHAMMAD ZAIN-UL-ABDIN, MU-HAMMAD FAZIL, *and* MUHAMMAD ABRAR, *Sayyid, Taaluq-dars of Asifpur (Asifpur, Bhagiari, Durgaganj, and Dhun-pur). Title of "Chaudhri" personal to the first of these.*

THESE taaluqdars come from the same stock as their kinsman of the preceding memoir. Asafpur, the name by which taaluq is known, was originally a village established by Sayyid Asaf, a forefather of the subject of this notice, but it has since ceased to exist. In 1227 fasli, under orders from Nawab Ghazi-ud-din Haidar, was built on its site the present village Rafatganj, called after Rafat Ali Khan (one of the sons of the Nawab) better known as Nawab Nasir-ud-din Haidar. But the taaluq of which Rafatganj forms a part still bears the name of Asafpur, the original village. For a period of about thirteen years the new village remained in the *khas* possession of Government, and in 1240 fasli a gift of it in *muafi* was made to Moulvi Qazim Husain Khan, a *safir* (vakil deputed to foreign

Courts) of the Oudh Government. Since then it has formed the inheritance of the Moulvi's descendants, among the latest of whom come the present taaluqdars. Government *sanad* of this taaluqa stands in the joint names of the owners above named, but they are in separate possession of it, as shown below :—

Chaudhri Muhammad Ashraf owns taaluq Ashrafpur, comprising 11 villages, paying an annual Government revenue of Rs. 9,697;

Muhammad Zain-ul-Abdin—taaluq Baghari, comprising 8 villages, paying to Government Rs. 4,507;

Muhammad Fazil—taaluq Durgaganj, consisting of 3 villages and 2 *pattis*, paying a Government revenue of Rs. 3,276-8-0; and

Muhammad Ibrar—taaluq Dhundpur, comprising 7 villages and 3 *pattis*, paying a Government revenue of Rs. 3,569.

For loyalty displayed during the crisis of 1857 these taaluqdars were rewarded by Government with the gift of the *ilaqa*.

The whole joint estate comprises 29 villages and 5 *pattis* in zila Hardoi. Government revenue, Rs. 21,049-8-0. Succession governed by law of primogeniture.

No. 113.

Mirza Muhammad Ali Beg, *Mogul, Taaluqdar of Aurangabad.*

Two hundred years ago, Mirza Bahadur Beg, a native of Arabia, was deputed by Emperor Aurangzeb to chastize and bring under subjection the then recusant taaluqdars of Etounja. He came to the province, and successfully accomplishing his mission, founded Aurangabad (in the name of his Imperial patron) on the site of village Garhi Balpur, which he completely destroyed. Several generations after him came Muhammad Bakhsh and Kutbi Muhammad, who came to a partition of their ancestral inheritance. The taaluqdar above is a lineal descendant of the former, and the owner of Kutubnagar (*vide* No. 121) of the latter.

Estate, 29 villages and 1 *patti* in zila Sitapur. Government revenue, Rs. 27,758. The *gaddi* custom of succession holds in this family.

No. 114.

Kazim Husain Khan, *Khanzada, Taaluqdar of Bhatwamau, Dariapur and (shares in) villages.*

In the year 905 Hijri, Shaikh Babban, original ancestor of this taaluqdar, received from Emperor Babar Shah a *jagir* of parganas Bari, Biswan, Fatehpur, and Sadarpur, and settled in Bhatwamau. His descendant in a subsequent generation (1019 *Hijri*) was honoured with the title of "Khan" during the reign of Emperor Jahangir Shah, and on Pahar Khan (a later heir in the family) was conferred the higher distinction of "Mumtaz-ul-Mulk" by the Court of Delhi. Years after, the estate descended to Imam Ali Khan, who made considerable improvements in it. The present taaluqdar and his predecessors, Tajammul Husein Khan and Hadi Husein Khan, held appointments of Nazim and Chakladar under the Oudh Government. The Government *sanad* of this taaluq was granted in the name of Badshah Husain Khan, who preceded the subject of this notice in the possession. This taaluqdar and Raja Amir Husain Khan (No. 10) are from the same stock.

Estate, 58 villages and 8 *pattis* in zilas Sitapur and Bara Banki. Government revenue, Rs. 20,978-4-9. The *gaddi* custom of succession holds in this family.

No. 115.

Thakur Hari Har Bakhsh, *Panwar, Taaluqdar of Sarawra.*

Vide No. 23. This taaluq dates from one Karn Deo, to whose share it fell at a partition of the family property noted in the number mentioned. In fasli 1165 his descendant Sahji established the village of Sarawra, after which this estate is called, and several generations after this, Ganga Bakhsh came into the property, and in his name was granted the Government *sanad*. After Ganga Bakhsh succeeded the present owner.

Estate, 30 villages and 5 *pattis* in zilas Sitapur and Bara Banki. Government revenue, Rs. 23,719-13-0. The *gaddi* custom of succession holds in this family.

No. 116.

Thakur Fazal Ali Khan, *Gaur, Taaluqdar of Akbarpur.*

Mahabali and Bakhtbali (Hindus) were formerly owners of this estate, which, for their insubordination, was escheated to the then paramount power in the province and given away in grant to Seth Dianat Rai of Biswan. Subsequently, during the reign of Nawab Shuja-ud-daula (1179 Hijri), they went to Fyzabad, and on their embracing the Moslem faith (without, however, assuming any Muhammadan names), they were restored to their former possession. Since then the taaluq has been the inheritance of their descendants. Akbarpur was built by Akbar Ali, a son of the converted Mahabali. The present owner of the property comes lineally in succession from him.

Estate, 36 villages and 10 *pattis* in zila Sitapur. Government revenue, Rs. 26,313. The *gaddi* custom of succession holds in this family.

(55)

No. 117.

THAKUR JAWAHIR SINGH, *Bais, Taaluqdar of Basidih and Barmhowli.*

Vide No. 4. In the fasli year 1243 this taaluq fell to the share of Bhawanidin Singh, father of the above, at a partition of the ancestral estate (of Newaz Shah) between him and the founder of the house of Sajaulia.

Bhawanidin Singh made great improvements in his property both by purchases and mortgages. After his death he was succeeded by Jawahir Singh, whose title received the recognition of *sanad* granted to him by the British Government. He rendered good and loyal service to the State during the mutiny, and received in return the gift of Barmhowli.

Estate, 52 villages and 63 *pottis* in zila Sitapur. Government revenue, Rs. 45,796-10-8. Succession by law of primogeniture.

No. 118.

THAKUR DURGA BAKHSH, *Panwar, Taaluqdar of Nilgaon and Jalalpur.*

Vide No. 23. About a century and a half ago, Sambha Singh, adding the large possession of Nilgaon, &c. (formerly belonging to Thakur and Kayesth proprietors) to his original possession of villages which fell to the share of his ancestor Karn Rai at the family partition in the said number mentioned, laid the foundation of the taaluq above. He also made improvements in the estate by opening up several new villages in pargana Bari. Bhawanidin, his successor, in later days distinguished himself by loyalty to the British Government during the mutiny of 1857, and received, in recognition of his services, the grant of Jalalpur and *sanad* of title. He was succeeded by the subject of this notice.

Estate, 23 villges and 2 in *pattis* in zila Sitapur. Government revenue, Rs. 17,270. The *gaddi* custom of succession holds in this family.

No. 119.

THAKUR MAHARAJ SINGH, *Bais, Taaluqdar of Kanhmau Banjaria, and Udaipur.*

Vide No. 4. This taaluqdar represents a collateral branch of the house of taaluqdar No. 117. About five centuries ago one Rana Birbhan came from Dondya-khera and settled in Paharcmau, and founded this estate, having taken possession by force of 105 villages from their *Kunjra* proprietors. His descendant Beni Singh faithfully served the British Government during the late mutiny, and his loyalty was rewarded by the accession to the taaluq of a grant comprising seven villages. After his death the present representative of the family came into the property.

Estate, 24 villages and 9 *pattis* in zilas Sitapur and Kheri. Government revenue, Rs. 15,018. The *gaddi* custom of succession holds in this family.

No. 120.

RAI IBRAM BALI, *Kayesth, Taaluqdar of Rampur. Title of " Rai" hereditary.*

IN the Hijri year 708, Rae Prithi Rao, having been appointed a kanúngo by Emperor Jalal-ud-din Miran Shah, accompanied the Subadar of Oudh to Mahmudabad, the then seat of government. His wise counsel contributed much to the suppression of the refractory *Bhars* by the ruler of the province. He was recommended for imperial recognition, and the Emperor bestowed on the Rai a gift of the present taaluq.

Thirteenth in succession from the founder of the family comes the present taaluqdar, who, within the limits of his own *ilaqa* exercises the power of an Honorary Magistrate and Assistant Collector.

Estate, 31 villages and 11 *pattis* in zila Bara Banki. Government revenue, Rs. 25,601-13-9. The *gaddi* custom of succession holds in this family.

No. 121.

MIRZA AHMAD ALI BEG, *Sayyid, Taaluqdar of Qutubnagar and Karimnagar.*

THIS is a branch of taaluq No. 113, and owes its origin to Kutbi Muhammad, to whom it was allotted in share at a partition of the Aurangabad family estate. The widow of his later descendant Sobhan Ata adopted one Ibrahim Beg, who also died without leaving an heir. His widow in her turn adopted the taaluqdar Mirza Ahmad Ali Beg.

Estate, 19 villages in zilas Sitapur and Hardoi. Government revenue, Rs. 8,114. The *gaddi* custom of succession holds in this family.

No. 122.

MAULVI FAZAL RASUL, *Sayyid, Taaluqdar of Jalalpur, Daudpur Kaikhai, Rampur, Garhawan, Sitohi, Muhammadpur, Taraana, and Victoriaganj.*

ABOUT seven centuries ago, one Makhdum Sahab (whose tomb to this day forms one of the attractions of Sandila) received from the then Government of the province a *muafi* grant of land, on the site of which his descendant Sayyid Jalal built and called after his own name the original village of Jalalpur, after which the taaluq above is called. In a later generation Chaudhri Muhammad Mokim, having no male issue of his own, gave it away (about forty-five years ago) to his grandson (by daughter), Sayyid Ghulam Ashraf. In later days Munshi Fazl Rasul came into possession, and he obtained the Government *sanad* of the estate, as also the gift of *ilaqa* Muhammadpur, &c., for loyal services rendered during the rising of 1857. After his death succeeded the present representative of the family.

Estate, 33 villages and 8 *pattis* in zilas Hardoi, Unao, Sitapur, Kheri, and Lucknow. Government revenue, Rs. 19,375-9-0. Primogeniture governs succession.

No. 123.

QAZI IKRAM AHMAD, *Shaikh, Taaluqdar of Satrikh.*

THIS is a new taaluq, comprising a few ancestral possessions together with village Satrikh proper, acquired in the fasli year 1260 by Qazi Sarfaraz Ali, who made improvements to the estate by many subsequent acquisitions, and on his death was succeeded by his son, the present owner.

Estate, 11 villages and 1 *patti* in zila Bara Banki. Government revenue, Rs. 18,725. Succession by primogeniture.

No. 124

THAKUR RAGHBIR SINGH, *Kalhans, Taaluqdar of Dhanawan and Bhundiari.*

Vide No. 33. This taaluq was first founded in the family of Dula Ram by his descendant Pragdat, from whom comes the nobleman above. No. 125 is derived from this *ilaqa*.

Estate, 48 villages and 16 *pattis* in zilas Gonda and Bahraich. Government revenue, Rs. 32,845-9-9. The custom of *yaldi* succession holds in this family.

No. 125.

THAKUR MIRTUNJA BAKHSH SINGH, *Kalhans, Taaluqdar of Shahpur and Kutka-Marolha.*

Vide No. 33. This taaluq is derived from the estate referred to in the preceding No. 124. The present taaluqdar has inherited his property from Anup Singh, who, on separating from his family, received it for maintenance from his father Pragdat, then proprietor of Dhanawan.

Estate, 40½ villages and 16 *pattis* in zilas Gonda and Bahraich. Government revenue, Rs. 26,320-5-0. The custom of *gaddi* succession holds in this family.

No. 126.

DIWAN HAR MANGAL SINGH, *Bachgoti, Taaluqdar of Aworayadi.*

Vide Nos. 7 and 40. This nobleman is a descendant of Chakr Singh, and his possession forms a section of taaluq *patti* Saifabad, Nos. 69 and 70.

Estate, 53 villages in zila Partabgarh. Government revenue, Rs. 16,535. The *gaddi* custom of succession holds in this family.

No. 127.

BHAGWANT SINGH, BISHESHAR BAKHSH SINGH, JAGMOHAN SINGH, *and* ARTH SINGH, *Bachgoti, Taaluqdars of Dariapur.*

Vide Nos. 7 and 40. This is also another branch of taaluq *patti* Saifabad, Nos. 69 and 70.

Estate, 25 villages in zila Partabgarh. Government revenue, Rs. 10,915. Succession governed by family custom in default of testamentary disposition.

No. 128.

HAKIM KARAM ALI, *Sayyid, Taaluqdar of Guthia.*

THIS taaluqdar belongs to a very old family, and the estates he now owns can be traced back to many generations. He holds the rank and exercises the powers of an Honorary Magistrate and Assistant Collector within the limits of his possessions.

Estate, 13 villages in zila Bara Banki. Government revenue, Rs. 13,465. The *gaddi* custom of succession holds in this family.

[NOTE.—This nobleman has died since this work was put in hand.]

No. 129.

BABU JADUNATH SINGH, *Panwar, Taaluqdar of Mahgaon (Makona) and Udaipur.*

Vide No. 3, of which this forms a branch. Bahlan Deo, second son of Deo Rudh Rai, (about four centuries ago) founded the present taaluq and house on the estate received by him at a family partition.

In a later generation Government *sanad* was granted to Babu Pirthipal Singh. At his death succeeded the present taaluqdar.

Estate, 27½ villages in zilas Lucknow and Bara Banki. Government revenue, Rs. 15,099. The *gaddi* custom of succession holds in this family.

No. 130.

Mahbub-ur-Rahman, Inayat-ur-Rahman, Abd-ur-Rahman, *and* Fazal-ur-Rahman, *Shaikh, Taaluqdars of Barai and Aghiari.*

In the reign of Emperor Muhammad Ibrahim Shah (845 Hijri), Khwaja Muhammad Iftkar Haruni, founder of this house, accompanied Subadar Tatar Khan to this province on an expedition for the suppression and expulsion of the Bhars. His counsel and services contributed much towards the success of the invasion; he was in consequence recommended by the Subadar to the Imperial Court for some substantial reward, and in return was presented with 23 villages. These, with additions and improvements made from time to time by purchase and mortgage, comprise the above taaluq Barai, which received its present name for the first time (in Hijri 1153) from Muhammad Azim during the reign of Nawab Abul Mansur Khan. The latest rightful heir (in Muhammad Azim's family), Mahbub-ul-Rahman above, being an infant at the time of the *sarsari* settlement, gave his consent to the *sanad* being granted in the name of his uncle, Ghulam Farid. This last subsequently and against the custom hitherto obtaining in the family, caused a partition of the estate to be made in two equal shares, reserving one to his own heirs (the 2nd, 3rd, and 4th taaluqdars heading this memoir), and making over the other to the said Mahbub-ul-Rahman, whose name also about this time was recorded in the proprietary *sanad*.

Estate, 31 villages and 22 *pattis* in zilas Fyzabad and Bara Banki. Government revenue, Rs. 31,030-5-2. Family custom governs succession in default of testamentary disposition.

No. 131.

Muhammad Nasim Khan, *Pathan, Taaluqdar of Sohlamau.*

The original village giving name to this taaluq formerly belonged to Muhammadans and Kayesths, and in 1241 fasli it was bought over from them by one Fakir Muhammad Khan, who made additions to it by subsequent acquisitions and eventually laid the foundation of the estate. He was a chakladar in the province during the reign of Nawab Ghazi-ud-din Haidar. After his death succeeded his two sons, the subject of this notice and Muhammad Ahmad Khan, and these divided their inheritance: the former retaining his present possession, and the latter receiving for his share *ilaqa* Kaswandi, No. 148.

Estate, 15½ villages in zila Lucknow. Government revenue, Rs. 16,283-14-9.

No. 132.

MIR MUHAMMAD HASAN KHAN, *Sayyid, Taaluqdar of Rajapara (Hirapur).*

THE Mir is a native of Budaun, and held the appointments of collector of forces and Nazim under the former Government of the province. He acquired large estates with means of his own, and in consequence was raised to the rank and dignity of a taaluqdar in the province. A greater portion of his possessions, however, have since been sold by auction, and he has only now the remnant of the taaluq, comprising—

Estate, 1 *patti* in zila Sitapur. Government revenue, Rs. 253. Succession by primogeniture.

No. 133.

FIDA HUSAIN KHAN, *Sayyid, Taaluqdar of Alwa Piparia, Patti Marion, and Patti Misarpur, Kota.*

Is also a native of Budaun, and a brother of the preceding No. 132. During the native *régime*, he was a captain in the army and held the appointment of chakladar. This estate originally formed part of *ilaqa* No. 31, and became a separate *taaluq* since its purchase by the present owner.

Estate, 27 villages and 2 *pattis* in zilas Kheri and Lucknow. Government revenue, Rs. 9,502-11-0. Succession governed by primogeniture.

[NOTE.—This estate has been sold by auction under a decree of the civil court.]

No. 134.

BABU SUKHRAJ SINGH, *Kalhans, Taaluqdar of Ata.*

Vide No. 33. This nobleman is a descendant of Dula Rai, and owns the *ilaqa* from that ancestor.

Estate, 14 villages and 3 *pattis* in zila Gonda. Government revenue, Rs. 12,595. The *gaddi* custom of succession holds in this family.

No. 135.

THAKURAIN IKLAS KUNWAR (*widow of Bhaia Nepal Singh*), *Kalhans, Taaluqdar of Paska and Lelar.*

Vide No. 33. This estate is also from Dula Rai, whose last representative, Nepal Singh, obtained the Government *sanad*. The Thakurain above is Nepal Singh's widow.

Estate, 14 villages and 7 *pattis* in zilas Gonda and Bara Banki. Government revenue, Rs. 14,997-5-3. The *gaddi* custom of succession holds in this family.

No. 136.

SETHS RAGHBAR DAYAL *and* SITARAM, *Khattri, Taaluqdars of Muizuddinpur, Kathgura, Alau Mahwa, Kola Darianagar, Unchakhera, and Rangwara.*

VILLAGE Muizuddinpur, which gives its name to the taaluq above, was founded about four hundred years ago by Malik Muizuddin, who cut down the *jangle* which covered the original site granted to him in muáfi by the then reigning Emperor of Delhi. Several generations after him came Khan Muhammad, from whom the estate (fasli 1229) passed into the hands of Seth Lalji. This Seth Lalji stood security (*mulzamani*) for payment of State revenue due by the former. Lalji made considerable improvements to his acquisition both by purchase and mortgage. He died in 1233 fasli and was succeeded by Murli Manohar and Sitaram. After the former's death, his son, the above Raghbar Dayal, came to his share of the family estate, Sitaram continuing to hold in his own right. The villages given in grant to Seth Raghbar Dayal by Government for loyal services during the mutiny are included in this taaluq, which has recently been divided between the present owners to extent of 9 and 7 anna shares respectively.

Estate, 37 villages and 11 *pattis* in zilas Sitapur and Kheri. Government revenue, Rs. 32,502. Law of primogeniture governs succession.

No 137.

MUSAMMAT DARIAO KUNWAR (*widow of Bishnath Bakhsh Singh*) *and* THAKUR AJUDHYA BAKHSH, *Bais, Taaluqdars of Narindpur-Charhar.*

Vide No. 4. This is a branch of taaluq Goura-Kusahaiti (No. 67) and was in sambat 1885 founded by one Bajrang Bali, who separated from Ram Bakhsh and founded the village of Charhar on what was at the time good pasture land. Hence the name of Charhar or grazing-ground. For about two centuries Charhar enjoyed the privilege of muafi possession during the Nawabi Government, but after the occupation of the province by the British it was brought under taaluqdari settlement in the names of Thakur Ajudhya Bakhsh and Bishnath Bakhsh. The former is now in possession by his own right, and the Musammat above mentioned is the surviving widow of the latter.

Estate, 30 villages in zila Rae Bareli. Government revenue, Rs. 18,830. The *gaddi* custom of succession holds in this family.

No. 138.

NAWAB ALI KHAN, *Shaikh, Kidwai, Taaluqdar of Maila Raiganj.*

THE origin of this taaluq dates from Shaikh Ghulam Amir, who, in 1270 Hijri, received from Nawab Shuja-ud-daula the villages of Maila Raiganj, Bhainsaria, Durjanpur, &c. To these additions and improvements were made by a subsequent descendant, one Haidar Ali, paternal uncle of the present owner. Haidar Ali's title obtained the recognition of Government *sanad*. This taaluqdar is an uncle of Raja Farzand Ali Khan of taaluq Jahangirabad.

Estate, 4 villages and 9 *pattis* in zila Bara Banki. Government revenue, Rs. 6,268. The *gaddi* custom of succession holds in this family.

No. 139.

THAKURAIN UDE NATH KUSWAR (*widow of Thakur Sardar Singh*), *Bais, Taaluqdar of Hamirmau-Kola.*

Vide No. 4. This is a branch of taaluq No. 65, and comprises ilaqa (more or less reclaimed from *jungle*, the site of which was originally called Bhagwantpur) founded and named by Hinda Singh when he separately established himself, giving up joint partnership with his brother Prithiraj. Latest in descent from him came the deceased Sardar Singh, who obtained the recognition of Government *sanad*. After death he was succeeded by his widow, who is now in possession.

Estate, 34 villages in zila Rae Bareli. Government revenue, Rs. 21,421. The *gaddi* custom of succession holds in this family.

No. 140.

BALBHADDAR SINGH AND DARSHAN SINGH, *Bais, Taaluqdars of Gaura Husainabad.*

Vide No. 4. Meharban Singh (several generations after the great ancestor Karan Rai), separating from the Behar house (No. 195), laid

the foundation of this taaluq on a site originally covered with *jungle*
and called it Gaura, from the fact of men of his own caste, the Gaurs,
having been prevailed upon to come and reside in it. Government
sanad of title was granted to Thakur Sitla Bakhsh, after whom succeeded the above.

Estate, 9 villages in zilas Unao and Rae Bareli. Government
revenue, Rs. 6,203. Succession by law of primogeniture.

No. 141.

RAZA HUSAIN, *Sayyid, Taaluqdar of Navauli.*

DURING the reign of Emperor Sultan Ibrahim Shah, in the
Hijri year 621, Muhammad Saleh came to the province of Oudh
as Imperial Sipahsalar, and defeating the *Bhars*, obtained as a reward the grant of 84 villages originally belonging to these refractory
people. He settled in Rudauli and there built a Jama Masjid.
On his later descendant, Sayyid Abu Muhammad, was conferred the
titles of "Chaudhri" and "Nasrat Sultan" by Emperor Jalal-ud-din
Muhammad Akbar Shah. In a subsequent generation Government
sanad of this taaluq was conferred on Chaudhri Husain Bakhsh,
whose son now represents the family.

Estate, 35 villages and 10 *puttis* in zila Bara Banki. Government
revenue, Rs. 28,232-8-0. The *gaddi* custom of inheritance holds in
this family.

No. 142.

FATEH SINGH, *alias* FATEH BAHADUR (*son of Chaudhri Gulab Singh*), *Parihar, Taaluqdar, of Sarausi.*

DURING the disorder which followed the murder of Hanwant
Singh by the Sayyids of Unao (during the reign of Emperor Humayun Shah), this estate passed into the hands of the *Dhobis*, to whom
it was given in *jagir* by the Court of Delhi. Shortly after (the Emperor being away at Persia) one Thakur Maidni Ma came to the
neighbourhood of this taaluq to celebrate the marriage of his son.
Taking advantage of the general dissatisfaction prevailing among the
Thakurs of the place, who viewed the proximity of a Dhobi possession as degrading, he entered into a league with them, and putting
to death the zemindars, himself took possession of their ilaqa. In
his seventh descent came four brothers—Salu, Asis, Mak, and Huli
Dan—and among these, about three hundred years ago, the family
inheritance was divided as follows:—The first receiving Karwan, the
second Sarausi, the third Sakrpur and others, and the fourth, Aghar.
The subject of the present memoir is a lineal descendant of Asis,
the second of the brothers.

Estate, 11 villages in zila Unao. Government revenue, Rs. 13,961. Law of primogeniture governs succession.

No 143.

THAKUR ANAND SINGH, JAGAN NATH SINGH, GANGA BAKHSH, AND HARDEO BAKHSH, *Kayesth, Taaluqdars of Rampur, Piprawan, and Wali Muhammadpur.*

ABOUT seven hundred years ago, a grant of waste land, then called Nawapur, with 15 villages (originally the possession of the *Kanjars*), was bestowed as a *jagir* on the founder of this house, Ram Das, by his patron and employer, Rai Pithaura, Raja of Delhi. The recipient converted the grant into a village and called it Rampur, by which name this taaluq has been since known. In 963 Hijri, Emperor Akbar conferred on Askarn Das, a descendant from Ram Das, the appointment of kanúngo of Biswan, and later on, one Dariao Singh (1286 Hijri), established other villages and improved the ilaqa. Dariao Singh, for faithful services rendered during the mutiny, received from Government the grant of mauza Piprawan, &c., and also of a *sanad*. After his death the present owner succeeded to the inheritance.

Estate, 31 villages and 6 *pattis* in zilas Sitapur and Bara Banki. Government revenue, Rs. 15,814-6-0. Law of primogeniture governs inheritance.

No. 144.

THAKURAIN JAIPAL KUNWAR (*widow of Indrjit Singh*), *Kalhans, Taaluqdar of Mustafabad and Chingiria, &c.*

Vide No. 33. This taaluqdar represents a branch derived from No. 46. The taaluq dates in her family from certain of its former owners, who purchased it about 60 years ago from the Sayyids of Jarwal. The settlement was made in the name of a latter descendant, Thakur Indrjit Singh, the father of the present owner.

Estate, 7 villages and 12 *pattis* in zilas Gouda and Bahraich. Government revenue, Rs. 6,556-13-10. The *guddi* custom of inheritance holds in this family.

No. 145.

BABU AZIM ALI KHAN, *Bhale Sultan, Khanzada, Taaluqdar of Deogaon and Makhdumpur.*

Vide No. 53, of which this forms a branch. The present owner succeeded to the property from Babu Jamshed Ali Khan, whose title had the sanction of a Government *sanad*.

Estate, 15 villages and 1 *patti* in zilas Fyzabad and Sultanpur. Government revenue, Rs. 9,807-12-0. The *gaddi* custom of inheritance is prevalent in this family.

No. 146.

CHAUDHRI RAM NARAIN, *Kayesth, Taaluqdar of Mubarakhpur. Title of "Chaudhri" personal.*

THIS Chaudhri represents an ancient house descended from one Bishn Singh, who originally founded the village after which this taaluq is named. He made considerable additions to the estate by subsequent investments in purchase and mortgages, and his descendants ever since have been in undisturbed possession of the property.

Estate, 6 villages and 2 *pattis* in zila Sitapur. Government revenue, Rs. 2,506. Family custom governs succession in default of testamentary disposition.

No. 147.

BABU PIRTHIPAL SINGH, *Panwar, Taaluqdar of Tighra.*

THIS taaluqdar is a descendant of Sarabjit Singh, who, in the fasli year 1220, purchased the village of Tighra from its former proprietors of the Bilwar-Mitaria clan, and adding it to his own possessions, gave the whole *ilaqa* its present name, after that of the new acquisition.

Estate, 13 villages and 17 *pattis* in zila Fyzabad. Government revenue, Rs. 8,072. Succession governed by primogeniture.

No. 148.

MUHAMMAD AHMAD KHAN, *Pathan, Taaluqdar of Kasmandi Khurd.*

THIS is a division of the taaluq and family entered in No. 131. Fakir Muhammad Khan, father of the above, purchased the village of Kasmandi in separate parts from time to time during the Hijri years 1249 and 1259, and made additions to it by subsequent acquisitions. He held the appointment of chakladar during the reign of Nawab Ghazi-ud-din Haidar, and after his death was succeeded by his two sons, the subject of this notice, and taaluqdar No. 131, who came to an amicable partition of their inheritance, and are now in separate possession of their own respective shares.

Estate, 14 villages in zila Lucknow. Government revenue, Rs. 15,547-2-4. Succession governed by primogeniture.

No. 149.

BABU MAHESH BAKHSH SINGH, *Baisain, Taaluqdar of Dhaynawan.*

Vide No. 5. This forms one of the sections into which the house and *ilaqa* founded by Rai Hompal came to be divided among his descendants. The present taaluqdar inherits the property from Shiu Dat Singh, on whom a *sanad* of title was conferred by the British Government. He is an intelligent nobleman, is a good English scholar, and has acquired much legal knowledge. All this has secured for him the position of an Assistant Commissioner in the province.

Estate, 10 villages in zila Partabgarh. Government revenue, Rs. 7,845. The *guddi* custom of inheritance holds in this family.

No. 150.

SARABJIT SINGH, *Baisain, Taaluqdar of Sheikhpur Chaurasi.*

Vide No. 5. This is another section of the house and estate founded by Rai Hompal, and forms a subdivision of the Dhigwas branch referred to in No. 71. The present taaluq comprises a share of the original inheritance, supplemented by Government grants bestowed in recognition of services rendered during the mutiny on Dhoukal Singh, who also received a *sanad* of title. Dhoukal Singh was succeeded by the present representative.

Estate, 11 villages in zila Partabgarh. Government revenue, Rs. 5,455. The *guddi* custom of inheritance holds in this family.

No. 151.

THAKUR SHIU SAHAI, *Baisain, Taaluqdar of Simrawan.*

To the original family property, consisting of 14 villages, the former holders of this taaluq made additions of their own. Thakur Ram Sahai, brother of the above, received Government *sanad* at the settlement. He left no heir, and so the latter took his place. Owing to Shiu Sahai's mismanagement, the estate fell into great confusion and disorder and became much involved in debt. As a consequence it was eventually sold, and now forms integral parts of the respective possessions of Raja Farzand Ali, Subadar Ranjit Singh, and Bisheshar Parshad.

Hence no estate and succession under this head.

No. 152.

MUSAMMAT SAHIB-UN-NISA, (*widow of Chaudhri Muhammad Husain*), *Shaikh, Taaluqdar of Kharka.*

NINE hundred years ago, the original ancestor of this family accompanied Hazrat Sahu Salar from Ghazni to the province of Oudh, and compelling its former *Bhar* proprietors to surrender, took possession of mauza Kharka, which at the time consisted of waste uncultivated land. About two centuries after, his descendant, Karm Ali, built on this site the village Kharka, after which the present *ilaqa* is called. Additions and improvements made to the estate from time to time by following generations raised the *ilaqa* ultimately to the status and importance of a taaluq in the province, the *sanad* of which was granted by Government to Karm Ali, paternal uncle of the deceased husband of this Musammat. From subsequent informations received (in fasli year 1265) however, Karm Ali being convicted of complicity in the mutiny of 1857, was superseded in favour of the nephew, in whose name a fresh settlement was made. The present owner represents the estate as the surviving widow of the said nephew, Chaudhri Muhammad Husain.

Estate, 10 villages and 7 *pattis* in zila Bara Banki. Government revenue, Rs. 11,285-1-0. Primogeniture governs succession in the family.

No. 153.

MIR BUNYAD HUSAIN, *Sayyid, Taaluqdar of Bhanmau.*

THIS is an ancient house, having been founded about seven centuries ago, and the original possessions have remained in the family from that up to the present time. The British *sanad* of title was granted in the name of Aulad Husain, who died some time ago, leaving two sons—(1) the subject of this memoir, and (2) the taaluqdar next following.

Estate, 8 villages in zila Bara Banki. Government revenue, Rs. 4,745. Primogeniture governs succession.

MIR AMJAD HUSAIN, *Sayyid, Taaluqdar of Suhaipur, who owns*

Estate, 9 villages and 1 *patti* in zila Bara Banki. Government revenue, Rs. 8,637-12-6. The *gaddi* custom of inheritance holds in this family.

No. 154.

THAKUR DEB SINGH, *Sombansi, Taaluqdar of Sewajpur and Sakrau.*

THIS taaluqdar is eighteenth in descent from Raja Santan, who on the occasion of his going from Dehli to bathe in the Ganges founded the village of Santan-khera on a plot of waste land situated in kasba Sandi (zila Hardoi), and settled there. To Santan-khera he in time added further acquisitions. Sixth in descent from him was Raja Sahaj Rai, who went to reside in Sewajpur, a village which he erected himself. Eleventh from the Raja Sahaj Rai was Raja Dariao Singh, on whose death his property went to his widow. It was in the widow's name the summary settlement was made. The present taaluqdar was adopted by this last representative of the family.

Estate, 33 villages in zila Hardoi Sitapur. Government revenue, Rs. 18,923. The *gaddi* custom governs succession in this family.

No. 155.

BABU ASHRAJ SINGH, *Rajkumar, Taaluqdar of Meopur Dihlo, two-thirds share (held jointly with Lullu Singh, No. 95) of Sahrapur, and Meopur Sharakati.*

Vide Nos. 7 and 73. This is a collateral branch of taaluq No. 95. Estate, 14 villages and 78 *pattis* in zilas Sultanpur and Fyzabad. Government revenue, Rs. 18,196-13-0. Primogeniture governs succession.

No. 156.

MUHAMMAD ZAMAN KHAN, MUHAMMAD SAID KHAN, *and* MUHAMMAD SULTAN KHAN, *Pathans, Taaluqdars of Amawan.*

NUR-UD-DIN and Mustafa Khan came to the province as followers of the celebrated Mahmud of Ghazni, and obtained the appointment of Munshi, and also the pargana of Salon, where they built two villages and called them after their respective names—Nuruddinpur and Mustafabad. During the reign of Sultan Ibrahim came in their family Muhammad Khan, who (in Hijri 603) founded a village on waste lands received by him in return for services rendered to the Emperor, and after himself called it Amawa. Hence the name of the present taaluq. This last, in addition to Amawa, comprises several other villages built or acquired by the same founder. Generations after came Abdul Hakim Khan, whose title received the recognition of Government *sanad.* To these succeeded the present representatives.

Estate, 22 villages in zila Rae Bareli. Government revenue, Rs. 13,768. Succession governed by primogeniture.

No. 157.

ZULFIQAR KHAN, KARAM ALI KHAN, ASAD ALI KHAN, *and* SHAHA-
MAT KHAN, *Pathans, Taaluqdars of Pahramau.*

ABOUT 675 years ago, Hingan Khan, who had accompanied Emperor Shahab-ud-din Ghori on a successful expedition
against the *Bhars*, obtained the imperial gift of certain grants forming the original basis of this estate, and also the title of Diwan.
His descendants, availing themselves of opportunities from time to
time, built other villages on waste lands acquired by them, and,
during the reign of Emperor Akbar, consolidated the whole into
the present taaluq, which has since been retained in the family.
The *sanad* in later days was granted by Government to the present
taaluqdars.

Estate, 17 villages in zila Bara Banki. Government revenue,
Rs. 7,271. Succession governed by primogeniture.

No. 158.

THAKUR BHAGWAN BAKHSH, *Bais, Taaluqdar of Udraira and
Kasmaura.*

Vide No. 4. This forms a branch of taaluq No. 26. It was separated from the Korisadauli estate by Raghunath Singh, founder of
this house. Government *sanad* of this taaluq was given to Thakurain
Gulab Kunwar, after whom came the present representative.

Estate, 18 villages in zilas Lucknow and Rae Bareli. Government revenue, Rs. 15,259. The *gaddi* custom governs succession in
this family.

No. 159.

MUSAMMAT MITHAN KUNWAR (*widow of Balbhaddar Singh*), *Janwar, Taaluqdar of Pahrauli and Mendauli.*

ABOUT two and a half centuries ago Ugr Sen and Nirand Sah
came from Makowna, in zila Bahraich, and were appointed
Seghedars of pargana Kheron, obtaining at the same time, under
orders from Emperor Timur Shah, the proprietary gift of villages
Mirzapur, &c., and the title of "Chaudhri." About thirty-five years
ago their descendant, Raghunath Singh, received from the Oudh
Government a grant of village Pahrauli (after which the present taaluq
is called), together with other estates and the appointment of
kanungo. The taaluqdari settlement was also subsequently made in
his favour. He was afterwards succeeded by his son, Balbhaddar
Singh, and he in his turn left the property to his widow.

Estate, 22 villages in zila Rae Bareli. Government revenue,
Rs. 17,017. Primogeniture governs succession.

No. 160.

RAI RAMDIN BAHADUR, *Kurmi, Taaluqdar of Pailu, Sukheti, Nowa-pur, and Muhammadabad. Title of " Rai" personal.*

To Rai Tularam, father of the above, for loyal services to Government during the mutiny of 1857, was granted the *ilaqa* which previously formed part of the forfeited estate of the rebel Raja Lone Singh, taaluqdar of Metauli. Since his death the present owner has been in possession.

Estate, 15 villages in zila Kheri. Government revenue, Rs. 10,180. Succession governed by primogeniture.

No. 161.

BABU SITLA BAKHSH SINGH, *Thakur, Rajkumar, Taaluqdar of Na-numau, Ramgarh, Dhandupur, Mirpur, Suraiyan, and Nanumau.*

Vide No. 7. Harkarn Deo, descended from Ishri Singh, was the founder of this possession.

Estate, 34 villages and 29 *pattis* in zilas Sultanpur and Fyzabad. Government revenue, Rs. 16,932-6-0. *Gaddi* custom governs succession.

No. 162.

JAHANGIR BAKHSH KHAN, *Bachgoti, Khanzada, Taaluqdar of Gangeo, Bahmarpur, Samdabad, and Shahpur.*

Vide No. 9. This taaluqdar has inherited the property from Wazir Khan, who was descended from Tiloke Chand, *alias* Tatar Khan, and founded this separate branch of the family.

Estate, 23 villages and 4 *pattis* in zilas Sultanpur and Fyzabad. Government revenue, Rs. 11,953-12-0. Primogeniture governs succession.

No. 163.

KAMPTA PRASAD *and* BISHUN NATH SINGH, *Rajkumar, Taaluqdars of Bhadaiyan, Fazilpur, and Deoribirapur.*

Vide No. 7. Prithi Pat, a descendant of Ishri Singh, acquired this property, and since then it has been in the possession of his family, now represented by the present owner.

Estate, 48 villages and 19 *pattis* in zila Sultanpur. Government revenue, Rs. 23,646-8-3. Primogeniture governs succession.

No. 164.

SRIPAL SINGH, *Kanpuria, Taaluqdar of Barohu.*

Vide No. 12. The separate existence of this taaluq dates from its assignment to Shiu Prasad Singh (a descendant of Raj Sah) by Barjor Singh, referred to in No. 80. The present taaluqdar comes third in descent from Shiu Prasad Singh.

Estate, 13 villages in zila Sultanpur. Government revenue, Rs. 8,545-14-0. *Gaddi* custom governs succession.

No. 165.

MUSAMMAT ILAHI KHANAM, *Bachgoti, Khanzada, Taaluqdar of Maniarpur, Maniarpur Pali and Pali, Hissa (part).*

Vide No. 9. Hyat Khan, born in the family several generations after Tiloke Chand, *alias* Tatar Khan, was the founder of this estate. In later days came Basawan Khan, who was succeeded by the Bebi Soghra, a daughter by his first wife. After her came Akbar Ali (son of her father by his second wife), whom she had adopted and whose widow above is at present in possession.

Estate, 75 villages and 6 *pattis* in zilas Sultanpur and Fyzabad. Government revenue, Rs. 37,646-4-0. *Gaddi* custom governs succession.

No. 166.

IMTIYAZ FATIMA *and* BHAGBHARI, *Shaikh, Taaluqdars of Gopamau and Garmhaula.*

SHAIKH RAHIMULLA (Siddiki Ispahani) came to Delhi during the reign of Emperor Timur Shah, and was appointed Sipahsalar and Risaldar in the army. His descendant Niamut-ulla was nominated kanungo of pargana Gopamau in the days of Emperor Humayun, and he was the founder of Siria Siddiki. The present taaluq was originally constituted out of a gift of several villages which Emperor Alamgir bestowed on Shaikh Muhammad Sayyid, lineally descended from the said Niamat-ulla.

The villages of Gopamau came into existence about eight centuries ago and was originally called Gopiman from the founder Raja Gopi Nath. The present name, Gopamau, is a mere modern corruption.

Estate, 7 villages and 3 *pattis* in zilas Hardoi and Sitapur. Government revenue, Rs. 5,387. Succession governed by primogeniture.

No. 167.

Babu Hanuman Bakhsh Singh, *Sombansi, Taaluqdar of Domaipur.*

This is an estate of 600 years' standing. A full account of its original founder, Raja Bir Sibti, is given in No. 11. The subject of this notice is a descendant of his.

Estate, 50 villages in zila Partabgarh. Government revenue, Rs. 17,797-6-3. *Gaddi* custom of succession holds in this family.

No. 168.

Babu Hardat Singh, *Sombansi, Taaluqdar of Prithiganj.*

This is also an estate of six centuries' standing. The above taaluqdar is a descendant of Raja Bir Sibti (*vide* No. 11).

Estate, 33 villages in zila Partabgarh. Government revenue, Rs. 12,660. *Gaddi* custom of succession holds in this family.

No. 169.

Ude Narain Singh, *Kalhans, Taaluqdar of Bahmnipair.*

Vide No. 33. Raj Gonda at one time formed an integral part of this possession, but subsequently it ceased to do so, and the present estate alone continued in the possession of the ancestors, from whom comes the subject of this memoir. Government *sanad* of the taaluq was granted in the name of Rani Sarfaraz Kunwar, the predecessor of the present representative.

The village of Pair proper is in possession of the descendants of *birtdars.*

Estate, 104 villages and 1 *patti* in zila Gonda. Government revenue, Rs. 21,618-12-0. *Gaddi* custom of succession holds in this family.

No. 170.

Achol Ram, *Kachwaha, Taaluqdar of Birwa.*

One Pratab Mal Singh (from zila Gorakhpur) came to the province of Oudh and settled in Gauhani, a village situated in pargana Daksar. His descendants, about a hundred and seven years ago, received this estate for their share as relatives of the owners of Raj Gonda.

The latest representative of the family, Bhaia Prithipal, died without male issue, and was succeeded by his daughter, Thakurain Brijraj Kunwar. On the death of her husband the present taaluqdar came into possession.

Estate, 84 villages and 4 *pattis* in zila Gonda. Government revenue, Rs. 31,965-12-0. *Gaddi* custom of succession holds in this family.

No. 171.

Mirza Faiaz Beg, *Mogul, Taaluqdar of Baragaon.*

The present taaluqdar holds this property under a testamentary disposition made by the late Mirza Abbas Beg, who during his life obtained the gift of this taaluq (originally forming part of the forfeited estate of the Raja of Metowli) for services rendered to Government during the mutiny. The deceased testator was an Extra Assistant Commissioner in the province, and held a somewhat distinguished position in society. Having earned and obtained his pension and also some recognition of his loyal services, Mirza Abbas Beg went to England to educate his nephews. He died some time after his return from Europe.

The surviving daughter of the late Mirza has also an interest in the profits of the ilaqa.

Estate, 7 villages in zila Sitapur. Government revenue, Rs. 6,183. Primogeniture governs succession.

No. 172.

Bijai Bahadur Singh, *Bundelgoti, Taaluqdar of Shahgarh.*

This estate is a branch of taaluq (No. 8) Garh Amethi. Raja Bikram Sahi (from whom this taaluqdar claims descent) and the ancestor, Raja Madho Singh, were brothers. On the latter separating from the family, the present taaluq was allotted to him as his share. In later days its *sanad* was granted by Government to Babu Balwant Singh, on whose death came into possession the subject of this notice.

Estate, 19 villages and 2 *pattis* in zila Saharanpur. Government revenue, Rs. 10,292-2-0. *Gaddi* custom of succession holds in this family.

No. 173.

Mir Ahmad Jan, *Pathan, Taaluqdar of Raghpur.*

This taaluq, formerly belonging to Raja Shiudas Singh of Chandapur, was forfeited to Government for the offence of concealing guns within his possession, and it was given in reward to Jafar Ali Khan, *Kamadan,* for loyalty shown to Government during the mutiny. After the latter succeeded the present taaluqdar.

Estate, 2 villages in zila Rae Bareli. Government revenue, Rs. 2,530. Primogeniture governs succession.

No. 174.

MAHIP SINGH (*son of Ranjit Singh*), *Sengar, Taaluqdar of Kantha.*

ABOUT 468 years ago (in the reign of Emperor Timur Shah), one Gopal Singh went to the province of Oudh. His descendant, Jaskarn Singh, killed in battle with the Lodhas, left behind him two widows, who were shortly after delivered of three posthumous sons, Askarn, Garbhu Singh, and Asaram. These in later days recovered possession of their ancestral estate from the Lodhas, and since then it has remained with the family.

Other separate co-sharers of the estate in the family proving disloyal during the mutiny were punished with the forfeiture of their possessions, which in turn were given as reward to Ranjit Singh for faithful services rendered to Government at that critical time. Ranjit Singh also received the taaluqdari *sanad.* He was succeeded by the present owner, his son.

Estate, 5 villages and 6 *pattis* in zila Unao. Government revenue, Rs. 7,609-14-0. Primogeniture governs succession.

No. 175.

SULTAN SINGH, *Chandel, Taaluqdar of Galgalha, Mazra Piparkhera.*

UMRAO SINGH, father of the above, was a co-sharer in this ancient estate, which belonged to the Thakur Chandels. The other shares became forfeited to Government owing to the part taken by their owners during the mutiny, and were subsequently granted, in recognition of loyalty displayed by him in those days, to the said Umrao Singh, who became owner of the whole *ilaqa.* He was succeeded by the present taaluqdar.

Estate 6½ villages and 26 *pattis* in zila Unao. Government revenue, Rs. 12,513-10-3. Succession governed by primogeniture.

No. 176.

NEWAZISH ALI, *Shaikh, Taaluqdar of Ambhapur and Partabganj.*

ABOUT five hundred years ago Makhdum Kazi Kidwa came from Constantinople, and by the Emperor of Delhi was nominated the Qazi in the province of Oudh. He received an imperial grant of 52 villages comprised in the well-known Kidwara estate in zila Bara Banki. His eighth descendant, Shaikh Amir-ulla, married a daughter of Ali Muhammad (kanungo of pargana Hisampur), and from the latter obtained the taaluq above. The present owner is descended from Amir-ulla.

Estate, 36 villages and 24 *pattis* in zilas Bahraich and Bara Banki. Government revenue, Rs. 18,024-7-7. *Gaddi* custom of succession holds in this family.

No. 177.

PANDE SARABJIT SINGH, *Brahmin, Taaluqdar of Aschanau.*

THIS taaluq originally belonged to Thakurs of the Bisen clan, and about 43 years ago was purchased by Man Singh, paternal grand-father of the above. The said Man Singh and his son, Pande Baha-dur Singh, held appointments of *chakladars* in Oudh. The present owner holds possession as son-and-heir of the said Bahadur Singh.

Estate, 14 villages and 11 *pattis* in zila Bara Banki. Government revenue, Rs. 11,087-2-7. *Gaddi* custom of succession holds in this family.

No. 178.

SHEKH INAYAT-UL-LAH, INAM-UL-LAH, *and* IKRAM ALI, *Taaluqdars of Saidanpur.*

IN 836 Hijri, during the reign of Emperor Jalal-ud-din Ghori, this *ilaqa* was bestowed on Sayyid Muhammad Ibrahim in recogni-tion of services rendered by him in the expulsion of the *Bhars*. His descendants continued to hold the estate, the Government *sanad* of which was afterwards granted to Shaikh Latafat-ullah and Shaikh Vijahat-ullah, brothers, predecessors of the present owners.

After the death of these taaluqdars and in the seventeenth gene-ration from Muhammad Ibrahim, Shaikh Inayat-ullah succeeded Shaikh Vijahat-ullah and Imam-ullah and Ikram Ali succeeded Shaikh Latafat Ali in possession of the estate.

Estate, 13 villages and 3 *pattis* in zila Bara Banki. Government revenue, Rs. 2,590-2-6. Custom in the family regulates succession in default of testamentary disposition.

No. 179.

MIR FAKHR-UL-HUSAIN, *Sayyid, Taaluqdar of Banoukrah.*

ABOUT seven centuries ago, Makhdum Shah Adil Malik accom-panied Shah Ibrahim and Shah Husain (sons of Emperor Sultan Ibrahim Shurki) from Jaunpur to Rae Bareli, and for help rendered by him in a successful expedition against the *Bhars*, as also for founding the village Bareli, where formerly was a *jungle*, was re-warded by the Emperor of Delhi with the gift of 12 villages, Bibipur, Mubarikpur, &c., in muafi, and his son Sayyid Akbar-ud-din was granted the appointment and dignity of a Qazi. At a change of succession to the Delhi throne the muafi was resumed, but subse-quently Mir Haidar Husain and Mir Karamat Husain of this family, who for some time had held the appointment of Nizam under the imperial *régime*, acquired from it proprietary right of this estate.

The present ilaqa dates from the said acquisition. Ultimately the Government settlement was made in the name of the present proprietor.

Estate, 9 villages in zila Rae Bareli. Government revenue, Rs. 5,499. Succession governed by the law of primogeniture.

No. 180.

Subhan Ahmad, *Newati, Taaluqdar of Azizabad.*

Shaikh Muhammad Bachu, who was by birth a Hindu *Kayesth*, became a convert to the religion of the Prophet in 1117 fasli, and in the same year he bought the village of Kamalpur from Sayyid Miran Saiad. About six years afterwards he also acquired by purchase village Azizabad, and gradually made many additions and improvements to his property.

Estate, 18 villages in zila Rae Bareli. Government revenue, Rs. 7,010. Succession regulated by primogeniture.

No. 181.

Mir Zafar Mehdi, *Sayyid, Taaluqdar of Alinagar.*

Sayyid Muhammad Zakaria, founder of this house, obtained from Emperor Muhammad Toghlak a gift of the entire estate comprised in taaluq Jarwal, originally belonging to its refractory Raja. To this acquisition Ali Taki, the eighth in descent, subsequently added Alinagar. Third in generation from Ali Taki came the present owner of the property.

Estate, 18 villages and 17 *pattis* in zila Bahraich. Government revenue, Rs. 8,359-11-4. Primogeniture governs succession.

No. 182.

Mir Kazim Husain, *Sayyid, Taaluqdar of Werakazi.*

Several generations after Sayyid Mahmud Shah came Sayyid Safdar Husain, who married a daughter of Ahmad Ali Khan, taaluqdar of Jarwal. In 1236 fasli he received the possession above from the estate of the latter, and from him is descended the subject of the present notice.

Estate, 16 villages and 18 *pattis* in zila Bahraich. Government revenue, Rs. 10,201-5-8. Succession regulated by primogeniture.

No. 183.

SAYYID RAMZAN ALI, *Taaluqdar of Unao.*

ABOUT 750 years ago, Thakur Unwant Singh, of the Bisen clan, resident of Kunauj, was sent by the ruler of Kunauj to this province. He founded Unao village and took up his residence there; he founded other villages, and thus gradually became possessor of the whole pargana Unao. Baha-ud-din, a descendant of Sayyid Abul Krash, a native of city Wasti, however, killed Unwant Singh in revenge for the death of his father, which occurred by the hands of Unwant Singh in a battle at Kanauj. For this act the King of Delhi bestowed Unao (by which the whole taaluqa is known) and other villages on Baha-ud-din as a jagir. This taaluqa dates from this time. The ancestors of the present taaluqdar improved the estate by founding fresh villages and purchasing others. The English Government conferred a *sanad* in 1264 fasli on Chaudhri Dost Ali, the late proprietor, with whom also the settlement was effected. On Dost Ali's death Sayyid Ramzan Ali was declared heir by a Court of justice.

Estate, 4 villages and 4 *pattis* in zila Unao. Government revenue, Rs. 8,556-8-0. Primogeniture governs succession.

No. 184.

BABU BAJRANG BAHADUR SINGH, *Sombansi, Taaluqdar of Buispur.*

THIS taaluq is of six centuries' standing. The original founder of the family was Bir Sibti, whose account is set forth in No. 11, and from whom descends the present nobleman.

Estate, 29 villages in zila Partabgarh. Government revenue, Rs. 14,915. *Gaddi* custom governs succession.

No. 185.

GIRDHARI SINGH (*younger brother of Kunwar Bhagwant Singh*), *Kayesth, Taaluqdar of Gokulpur, Aseni, and Bhaisoura.*

THIS taaluq is called after village Aseni, originally built by a Brahman named Askaran. Askaran's descendant, Chaudhri Bhagwan Das, sold it to Kunwar Bahadur Singh, a predecessor of the present taaluqdar, and since then the estate has been in the possession of the family.

Estate, 10 villages and 5 *pattis* in zilas Lucknow and Bara Banki. Government revenue, Rs. 9,201-0-9. Succession regulated by primogeniture.

No. 186.

MANSAB ALI, *Sheikh, Taaluqdar of Saidaha.*

THIS taaluq originally formed part of the ancient mauza of Dewa, and the ancestors of the present taaluqdar were formerly known as the taaluqdars of Dewa. In course of time it subsequently passed into the hands of the Hindu Bais clan, whose last representatives in the possession were Thakurs Kirat Singh, &c. From these, in fasli 1257, Saidahar taaluq, with certain other villages, reverted to this Shaikh family in the person of Bu Ali, from whom lineally comes the present owner. The said Bu Ali was a descendant of the female portion of the family, and obtained possession under order from Colonel Sleeman. Taaluqs Nos. 199 and 237 are from this estate.

Estate, 4 villages and 2 *pattis* in zila Bara Banki. Government revenue, Rs. 2,919-12-0. Succession governed by primogeniture.

[*Note.*—This taaluq has since been sold.]

No. 187.

SITA RAM, *Khattri, Taaluqdar of Bhagupur (Bissaindih) and Tikar Tikur.*

ZEMINDARI BHAGUPUR was mortgaged in fasli 1244 to Kanahia Lal, father of the above taaluqdar, who for loyal services rendered during the mutiny received from Government the gift of ilaqa Tikra Tikur. Bhagupur has since been redeemed by the mortgagors, leaving to the present taaluq the property of Bissaindih (an old possession of the family) and Tikra Tikur only.

Estate, 9 villages and 9 *pattis* in zila Sitapur. Government revenue, Rs. 7,456-13-0. Succession governed by primogeniture.

No. 188.

MIR MUHAMMAD ABID, *Sayyid, Taaluqdar of Purai.*

IN the Hijri year 588 (during the reign of Emperor Sultan Shahab-ud-din Ghori) Sayyid Muhammad Saleh came from city of Kirman to Jaunpur and had an audience of the Emperor. He obtained a subsistence gift of village Bhuli. On his death, his son, Sayyid Muhammad, applied to and obtained from the Emperor eight villages, with the title of Khan. After several generations, about three hundred years ago, Muhammad Mah purchased Purai *Khas,* by which name the taaluqa was established. Since then the taaluq has descended in the possession of the predecessors of the taaluqdar, who is now its owner and manager.

Estate, 6 villages and 8 *pattis* in zila Bara Banki.　Government revenue, Rs. 8,067.　Primogeniture governs succession.

No. 189.

MUHAMMAD AMIR *and* GULAM ABBAS, *Shaikh, Ansari, Taaluqdar of Shahabpur.*

THIS is an estate of seventy years' standing.　The ancestors of the present taaluqdar, by purchase and mortgage, came to the possession of villages Faizullaganj, Shahabpur, and Fattei Sarai, from Raja Razak Bakhsh, proprietor of taaluq Jahangirabad, whose present representative is Raja Farzand Ali Khan, and they incorporated these acquisitions with the taaluq.

Estate, 5 villages and 3 *pattis* in zila Bara Banki.　Government revenue, Rs. 8,163-13-0.　Primogeniture governs succession.

No. 190.

GULAM KASIM KHAN, *Bisain (Khanzada), Taaluqdar of Usmanpur.*

ABOUT four hundred years ago Kaunsal Singh, in the reign of Emperor Humayun, received the gift of pargana Sidhaur for services rendered in subduing the *Bhars.*　He was at the time childless.　Seeing no prospect of having an heir to his possessions, he one day consulted a *fakir*, who blessed him and assured him of the birth of two sons, one of whom should be made over to the faith of the Prophet.　In the fulfilment of this promise were born to him in course of time two sons, Lakhan Singh and Bhajan Singh, the former of whom became a Muhammadan and was renamed Lakhu Khan.　His descendants, about a century and half afterwards, were Himmat Khan and Ghazaffar Khan, and among these a partition of the taaluq was made.　Ghazaffar Khan received as his share Usmanpur.　In later days Munawar Khan succeeded to the taaluq, and on his death his widow, Zahur-ul-nisa.　After the latter succeeded Roshan Zama Khan, who, however, by a Home decision in appeal, was dispossessed, the case being adjudged in favour of Ali Bahadur Khan, nephew of Munawar Khan.　Ali Bahadur, after his death, was succeeded by Ghulam Kasim Khan, who also has died since this memoir was written.　His son, Muhammad Ibrahim Khan, (aged about ten years) and his widow, Musammat Rasul-ul-nisa, are now owners of this taaluq, three-fourths of which, however, are in possession of Raja Farzand Ali Khan by right of transfer or assignment.

Estate, 21 villages and 4 *pattis* in zila Bara Banki. Government revenue, Rs. 16,105. *Gaddi* custom governs succession.

No. 191.

Insan Rasul (*son of Chavdhri Inayat Rasul,*) Shaikh, Taaluqdar of Amirpur.

During the reign of Sultan Muhammad of Ghazni (421 Hijri) Sayyid Hassan Raza accompanied Sayyid Salar Masud Ghazi to this province in an expedition against the *Bhars*, and obtained in gift the *Bhar* possessions of village Amirpur and others, which was the foundation of the present estate. Subsequently the title of "Chaudhri" was conferred on this family by the Emperor of Delhi. Taaluqdari *sanad* from Government was granted in he name of Inayat Rasul, father of the present owner.

Estate, 6 villages and 8 *pattis* in zila Bara Banki. Government revenue, Rs. 7,018-14-0. Primogeniture governs succession.

No. 192.

Nazir Husain, *Sayyid. Taaluqdar of Ahmamau and Garhi Chatana.*

Taaluq Ahmamau, after which this estate is named, was formerly in the possession of Darogha Wajid Ali under *ticca* (lease), and its proprietorship was confirmed to him by the British Government in recognition of loyal services rendered during 1857. Subsequently, with the money received by him in gift from Government, he acquired the other possessions now included in the taaluq. After the Darogha's death the present owner came to the inheritance.

Estate, 10 villages and 3 *pattis* in zilas Lucknow and Bara Banki. Government revenue, Rs. 10,513-13-7. Primogeniture governs succession.

No. 193.

Babu Balbhaddar Singh, *Sombansi, Taaluqdar of Sujakhor.*

This estate is about six centuries old, and the founder of the family, to which belongs the taaluqdar above, was Bir Sibti, whose history is given in full in No. 11.

Estate, 48 villages in zila Partabgarh. Government revenue, Rs. 12,065. *Gaddi* custom governs succession.

No. 194.

UMED SINGH, *Bachgoti, Taaluqdar of Iasanpur.*

Vide Nos. 7 and 40. This taaluqdar is a descendant of Chakr Singh.

Estate, 15 villages in zila Partabgarh. Government revenue, Rs. 4,185. Primogeniture governs succession.

No. 195.

THAKUR ARJUN SINGH and MAHESH BAKHSH, *Bais, Taaluqdars of Patan-Bihar.*

Vide No. 4. This taaluqdar by regular succession represents Bakht Bahadur (descended from Karn Rai), who received the taaluq above as his share of an ancestral estate at a family partition of it.

Estate, 25 villages and 1 *patti* in zila Unao. Government revenue, Rs. 14,820. Succession by family custom in default of testamentary disposition.

No. 196.

BABU MADHO SINGH, *Kanpuria, Taaluqdar of Nuruddinpur.*

THE family history of this taaluqdar will be found in No. 12. Five centuries ago Bahadur Singh adopted one Jorawan Singh, youngest son of Raja Kalyan Singh, and put the latter in possession of his estate. Jorawan Singh made improvements to the ilaqa and went to reside at Nuruddinpur. Sixth in descent from him came Babu Dhan Singh, who, having no issue, adopted his own nephew, Jageshar Bakhsh. After his death succeeded his widow, Thakurain Kadam Kunwar. From her eventually came to the inheritance the subject of the present notice.

Estate, 21 villages in zila Rae Bareli. Government revenue, Rs. 12,103. *Gaddi* custom of succession holds in this estate.

No. 197.

BHAYA AUTAR SINGH, *Surajbans, taaluqdar of Ranimau.*

Vide No. 25, of which this is a branch. The present taaluqdar is descended from the family of Gulal Shah, who about two centuries ago founded this separate estate. His title received the recognition of Government at the settlement.

Estate, 11 villages and 5 *pattis* in zila Bara Banki. Government revenue, Rs. 7,994-4-0. *Gaddi* custom of succession prevails.

No. 198.

Bhaya Har Ratan Singh, *Bisoin, Taaluqdar of Majhgawan and Aurah Dih.*

Vide No. 5. This taaluqdar, who had been a small zemindar for some time past, obtained the proprietorship of the present taaluq for his good and loyal services to the State during the mutiny, and was raised to the status and position of a taaluqdar in the province.

Estate, 22 villages and 17 *pattis* in zila Gonda. Government revenue, Rs. 4,712. Family custom regulates succession in default of testamentary disposition.

No. 199.

Riasat Ali, *Shaikh, Taaluqdar of Shaikhpar, zila Bara Banki.*

This is a branch of taaluq No. 186, where a full account of its history will be found. The greater part of the property has since been sold, and the present taaluqdar has only a small remnant of it for his support.

Estate, *nil.*

No. 200.

Musammat Kutub-un-nisa, *Shaikh, Taaluqdar of Gauriya Kalan.*

Shah Rafi-ud-din came from Medina and settled in Dehli. During the reign of Emperor Babar Shah, in response to a call made on him by the Shaikh Ansaris, he went to Oudh. In the year 1063 A.D. he contracted a marriage in the family of Malik Yusuf, commanding the troops of Sayyid Massaud. In descent from him came Shaikh Nizam and Shaikh Tahir, the former of whom founded Nizampur and the latter Tahirpur. On Shaikh Tahir's appointment as a pargana kanungo he acquired the proprietary right of village Gauraia, and by adding it to the property he had then, he laid the foundation of the taaluq which comprises the present estate. The Musammat above now holds it by inheritance from her deceased husband, Jahangir Baksh.

Estate, 4 villages in zila Lucknow. Government revenue, Rs. 3,270. Primogeniture governs succession.

No. 201.

Nisar Ali Khan, *Bhatti, Taaluqdar of Neora, pargana Bassaudhi.*

During the reign of Emperor Ala-ud-din Ghori (588 fasli), Imam Zabar Khan and Mustafa Khan, formerly residents of Bhutmar, accompanied Subahdar Tatar Khan to taaluq Bassandhi on an expedition for the chastisement of the *Bhars*. The success of the mission was followed by the gift of pargana Bassandhi and Mowai to Zabar Khan, whose descendants, Munna Jan and Kale Khan, subsequently succeeded to the inheritance of Mowai and Bassandhi respectively. Government *sanad* of this taaluq was granted in the name of Sher Khan, paternal uncle and predecessor of the present taaluqdar, who comes from the said Kale Khan. The taaluqdar No. 240 comes from this family.

Estate, 1 village and 13 *pattis* in zila Bara Banki. Government revenue, Rs. 4,711-4-0. *Gaddi* custom governs succession.

No. 202.

THAKURAIN DARYAO KUNWAR, *Thakur, Rajkumar, Taaluqdar of Garahpur.*

Vide No. 7. This taaluq dates from Garab Deo, a descendant of Ishri Singh, and its present owner comes in lineal descent from the former.

Estate, 30 villages and 7 *pattis* in zila Sultanpur. Government revenue, Rs. 8,406-8-6. Primogeniture governs succession.

No. 203.

DAYA SHANKAR, *Brahmin (Bajpai), Taaluqdar of Kardahu Lahraman.*

THE ancestor of this taaluqdar, who enjoyed the favour of the provincial Government of his time, held during the life the appointments of Nazim and Chakladar, and the present estate was purchased by the predecessors of the present representative. He also received accession to his property in consequence of one of his co-sharers dying without issue. Government *sanad* was granted in the name of the present taaluqdar.

Estate, 6 villages and 5 *pattis* in zila Unao. Government revenue, Rs. 8,345. Succession by custom in the family in default of testamentary disposition.

No. 204.

JAGESAR BAKHSH, *Kampuria, Taaluqdar of Bhowan-Sahpur.*

Vide No. 12. Bhowan Sah (descended from Rahas) established the original village of Bhowansahpur and laid the foundation of the taaluq bearing that name. In 1226 fasli Majhgawan was added to the estate as a " blood compensation" granted by the Oudh Government for the death of Babu Driguj Singh, a descendant of his. In later days Government *sanad* was issued in the name of Sitla Baksh, after whom came into possession the subject of this memoir.

Estate, 12 villages in zila Sultanpur. Government revenue, Rs. 5,913-0-11. *Gaddi* custom governs succession.

No. 205.

THAKUR FATEH MUHAMMAD, *Shaikh, Kairati, Taaluqdar of Tipraha.*

LONG ago Mianji from Egypt obtained the appointment of tahsildar of pargana Bahraich under a former Subahdar of Oudh, and for distinguished services rendered by him the village of Tipraha, formerly belonging to a Brahman zemindar named Chaturbhuj, was granted to his son, Shaikh Sahi. Salar Baksh, a subsequent descendant, made improvements to the estate, which has been in the family ever since.

Estate, 1½ villages and 1 *patti* in zila Bahraich. Government revenue, Rs. 6,010. *Gaddi* custom governs succession.

No. 206.

THAKUR NIRMAN SINGH, *Gaur, Taaluqdar of Inchapur, Omri, and Simra.*

INCHAPUR, from which the taaluqa takes its name, originally belonged to the Sayyids of Jarwal. In 1248 fasli, Zafar Mehndi and others, who were the Sayyids of Jarwal, sold it to Sarabjit Singh, the father of the present taaluqdar, with other villages. This taaluqa, therefore, is of a recent date.

Estate, 6 villages and 3 *pattis* in zilas Gonda and Bahraich. Government revenue, Rs. 5,633-11-4. *Gaddi* custom governs succession.

No. 207.

FATEH BAHADUR KHAN, *Bharthawan, Khanzada, Taaluqdar of Bahowa.*

THIS nobleman is from Raja Karn, who traced his descent from Raja Bikramaditya, and the taaluq forms part of an estate which was bestowed in *damadi* (portion of a son-in-law) by the said Raja Karn about seven centuries ago. The descendants of Raja Karn are called Gadewah Thakurs, but the branch of his house coming from his later generation, Awotaz Singh (who, repairing to Delhi, embraced the Moslem faith and assumed the name of Khan Azim Khan) are known as Pathans, and this taaluqdar comes from this family.

Estate, 11 villages in zila Rae Bareli. Government revenue, Rs. 10,374. *Gaddi* custom governs succession.

No 208.

SAGU NATH KUNWAR *and* KHARAK KUNWAR, *Bachgoti, Taaluqdars of Dasarathpur.*

Vide Nos. 7 and 40. This taaluq is derived from No. 60.

Estate, 13 villages in zila Partabgarh. Government revenue, Rs. 8,285. *Gaddi* custom governs succession.

No 209.

KALKA BAKSH *and* WIDOW *of Ganga Baksh Janwar, Taaluqdars of Ramkoti and Hajipur.*

DURING the reign of Emperor Alamgir, pargana Ramkoti (after which this estate is called) passed on lease into the hands of Kalyan Mal, ancestor of the taaluqdars heading this notice, but it subsequently ceased to be in the possession of his family. At a later period the said ilaqa reverted to his descendants in the person of his great-grandson, Fauji Singh, who, as adopted son of Sobha Rai (a Gaur and an after-lessee of same), succeeded the latter in possession. Fauji Singh acquired the right by granting kabuliat to the Oudh Government of the time, and after death was succeeded by his son, Hardeo Bakhsh, during the reign of Nawab Saadat Ali Khan. Hardeo Bakhsh, being childless, adopted Kalka Bakhsh, but after this adoption his son, Ganga Bakhsh, deceased, named in the heading, was born. In consequence of the then minority of the said Ganga Bakhsh, Government taaluqdari *sanad* was granted in the name of Kalka Bakhsh alone. In the late thirty years' settlement, however, the title of Ganga Baksh as a co-sharer received recognition. He has since died, and his widow is now in possession of his share of the inheritance. The photograph of Kalka Bakhsh alone is given in the present collection.

Estate, 15 villages and 5 *pattis* in zila Sitapur. Government revenue, Rs. 13,726-8-0. Family custom governs inheritance in default of testamentary disposition.

No. 210.

THAKUR JAGMOHAN SINGH, *Bais, Taaluqdar of Deogana (Girdharpur).*

Vide No. 4. Ahlad Shah (descendant of Harhar Deo), relinquishing his share of inheritance in estate Gaura Kasaiti,

No. 67, came to and settled in village Keratpur, which had been a muafi in the days of the Nawabi. His successor, Mardan Singh, (grandfather of the present owner) made considerable improvements to the property and raised his possessions to the status of a taaluq. Since then the ilaqa has remained in the family.

Estate, 12 villages in zila Rai Bareli. Government revenue, Rs. 6,531. Primogeniture governs succession.

No. 211.

JUGRAJ KUNWAR (*widow of Gauri Shankar*), *Kayesth, Taaluq-dar of Hardaspur.*

ABOUT six centuries ago one Hardas (ancestor) founded Hardaspur (after which this estate is called) on a site at the time covered with *jungle*. The present taaluq represents a gradual development of that small village. Tenth in descent from Hardas came Baijnath, on whom was conferred the Government *sanad*. After the latter succeeded his son, Gauri Shankar, whose widow, heading this notice, is now in possession.

Estate, 9 villages in zila Rai Bareli. Government revenue, Rs. 8,853-4-0. Succession governed by law of primogeniture.

No. 212.

MAHPAL SINGH, *Thakur, Gautam, Taaluqdar of Parah.*

FOURTEEN generations ago, the founder of this house, Rai Sikandar Singh, during the imperial rule of Muhammad Ibrahim, came to the province of Oudh on an expedition against the *Bhars*, whom he defeated and subdued, and from whom he subsequently took possession of their estate. He then built a new village called, after his own name, Sikandarpur, and resided in it. Third in descent, Rai Khiyal Singh, removed the family residence to Parah, from which the present taaluq is formed.

Estate, 8 villages in zila Rae Bareli. Government revenue, Rs. 7,707. Family custom governs succession in default of testamentary disposition.

No. 213.

DARGAHI KHAN, *Bhale Sultan, Khanzada, Taaluqdar of Unchgaon, Bhadour, and Chak Doma.*

THIS is a branch of estate No. 53, and the present owner succeeded to it after the death of his predecessor, Nabi Bakhsh Khan, on whom was conferred the Government *sanad*.

Estate, 6 villages in zila Sultanpur and Rae Bareli. Government revenue, Rs. 5,675-4-0. Primogeniture governs succession.

No. 214.

GAYADIN SINGH *and* SAHAJIT SINGH, *Rajkumar, Taaluqdars of Mudera.*

Vide No. 7. About six centuries ago, Jndr Sah, ancestor, established the village of Mudera on a site originally covered with *jungle.* The taaluq bearing that name fell to the share of his descendant, Ganga Das, at an amicable partition of the family estate, and the Government *sanad* of it in later times was granted to Thakurain Brij Kunwar, after whom came the present taaluqdar.

Estate, 15 villages and 7 *puttis* in zila Fyzabad. Government revenue, Rs. 7,390. Primogeniture governs succession.

No. 215.

BABU SARABDUN SINGH, *Bilkherie, Taaluqdar of Aulu and Amrupur.*

Vide Nos. 7 and 40. This taaluq is a branch of the number last named.

Estate, 5 villages in zilas Partabgarh and Sultanpur. Government revenue, Rs. 3,796. *Gaddi* custom governs succession.

No. 216.

FARZAND ALI KHAN, *Sayyad, Taaluqdar of Khalwara.*

THIS nobleman, formerly of Kora Jahanabad, was in command of a regiment during the Nawabi. At the siege of Baillie Guard he rendered valuable service to the British Government, and was rewarded with the gift of the taaluq above, which before formed part of the confiscated estate of Rana Beni Madho Singh. The recipient of the grant, however, has since caused the taaluq to be transferred to the name of his own son, Sayyid Ali.

Estate, 4 villages in zila Rae Bareli. Government revenue, Rs. 4,161. Succession governed by primogeniture.

No. 217.

BAKSHHI HAR PRASHAD, *Kayesth, Saksena, Taaluqdar of Lilauli.*

THIS taaluq, coming to the possession of Chattar Sen by purchase in the Hijri year 1214, gradually received accessions of possession and prosperity, and the ancestral predecessors of the nobleman above were marked favourites with the late Nawabs, under whose *régime* they also held the appointment of paymasters in the army. Chattar Sen adopted his nephew, who came in possession of the estate on the former's death, and who attained the Government *sanad* of title of the estate.

Estate, 8 villages and 3 *pattis* in zila Bara Banki. Primogeniture governs succession. Government revenue, Rs. 3,280.

No. 218.

SHIU RATAN SINGH, *Gamauha, Taaluqdar of Pinhona.*

THE family represented by this taaluqdar (and known to fame by the title of Rowths) comprises a section of the Thakur Bais stock and his estate is one of the oldest in the province. Bhyro Das is a descendant of Behar Sahi, the founder of the house, and the present taaluqdar comes from that family. This taaluq in former days comprised extensive possessions, but in consequence of various partitions from time to time has been reduced to its present limits.

Estate, 8 villages in zila Rae Bareli. Government revenue, Rs. 5,362-8-0. *Guddi* custom of succession holds in this family.

No. 219.

DAN BAHADUR SINGH, *Raikwar, Taaluqdar of Muhammadpur.*

Vide No. 43. This is a branch of taaluq Ramnagar-Dhamari. About four centuries ago Ram Das separated from the main house, and in a later generation Mardan Singh founded the village of Muhammadpur, after which this estate is called, in commemoration of the name of Muhammad Shah, a fakir. The ilaqa has been in the family's possession in order of succession ever since.

Estate, 3 villages and 23 *pattis* in zila Bara Banki. Government revenue, Rs. 6,301-10-0. Primogeniture governs succession.

No. 220.

DRIG BIJAI SINGH, *Bachgoti, Taaluqdar of Athgawan.*

THIS is a branch of the Bachgoti family and estate, full account of which is given in Nos. 7 and 40.

Estate, 7 villages in zila Partabgarh. Government revenue, Rs. 2,140. Law of primogeniture regulates succession.

No. 221.

FAZAL HUSAIN (*adopted son of Chand Bibi*), *Ahban Muhammadan, Taaluqdar of Kotwara and Rampur Gokal.*

FULL account of the house to which belongs the above is set forth in the following No. 262, of which it is a part. In 1234 fasli this taaluqa came in possession of Madar Bakhsh Khan and is called after the village Kotwara. Government *sanad* was granted to Chand Bibi, who adopted her grandson (daughter's son), heading this notice, and declared him heir.

Estate, 24 villages in zila Kheri. Government revenue, Rs. 8,590. *Gaddi* custom of succession holds in this family.

No. 222.

MUHAMMAD SHER KHAN, *Ahban Muhammadan, Taaluqdar of Raipur and Piparia.*

AN account of this taaluqa is also given in No. 262, of which it is a part. Mauza Raipur (by which name this taaluqa is known) came in possession of Jalal-ud-din in 1209 fasli, and since then has been in possession of his heirs.

Estate, 15 villages in zila Kheri. Government revenue, Rs. 6,470. Succession governed by primogeniture.

No. 223.

MAHPAL SINGH, *Kanpuria, Taaluqdar of Umrar.*

Vide No. 12. This taaluqdar comes in lineal descent from Sahas, a descendant of Raja Manik.

Estate, 6 villages in zila Partabgarh. Government revenue, Rs. 6,065. Primogeniture regulates succession.

No. 224.

MIR ASHRAF HUSAIN, *Sayyad, Taaluqdar of Kataria.*

ABOUT two years ago an ancestor of this taaluqdar purchased this estate, the Government *sanad* of which, in a later generation, was conferred on Mir Karamat Husain, whom the present owner succeeded.

Estate, 7 villages and 7 *pattis* in zila Fyzabad. Government revenue, Rs. 46,622. Primogeniture governs succession.

No. 225.

WASI-UZ-ZAMAN, *Sheikh, Taaluqdar of Mionganj.*

THIS *ganj* was established originally by Mian Elmas (Khoja Sarai), and after his death became Government nazul during the former administration of the province. In 1234 fasli, after British annexation, it was bestowed in gift on Bhawani Bakhsh, a Kayesth. Subsequent to the mutiny, the *ganj* became the property of one Moulvi Habib-ul-Rahman in return for his loyal services to the British Government in 1857. The Moulvi largely improved the gift. After his death the subject of the present memoir came into possession.

Estate, 7 villages and 8 *pattis* in zila Unao. Government revenue, Rs. 6,117-2-6. Primogeniture governs succession.

No. 226.

SHEO AMBAR SINGH, *Kanpuria, Taaluqdar of Rajpur.*

Vide No. 12. This taaluqdar is a lineal descendant of Sahas, who came from Raja Manik.

Estate, 9 villages in zila Partabgarh. Government revenue, Rs. 6,199. Succession governed by primogeniture.

No. 227.

SARDAR HIRA SINGH, *Sikh, Taaluqdar of Jamdan.*

THIS estate formed originally a part of the confiscated taaluq Chardah, and it was given to Sardar Jai Singh (a Khatri rais of the Panjab) in recognition of good and faithful services rendered during 1857. After his death succeeded the above.

Estate, 21 villages and 1 *patti* in zila Bahraich. Government revenue, Rs. 13,834-12-3. Primogeniture regulates succession.

No. 228.

SARDAR BAGHHALE SINGH, *Sikh, Taaluqdar of Bhangaha.*

THIS was originally a *Bonjara* possession, but subsequently becoming a Janwar, property was amalgmated with the taaluq Bhinga. Later on it was confiscated by the British Government owing to the discovery of some guns that were concealed; it was afterwards conferred on Sardar Sher Singh (from whom comes the taaluqdar above) in reward for loyalty shown during the mutiny. Sardar Baghhale Singh came in succession to Sardar Sher Singh.

Estate, 5 villages and 2 *pattis* in zila Bahraich. Government revenue, Rs. 5,128-8-10. Succession regulated by primogeniture.

No. 229.

SARDAR ALI, *Sayyid, Taaluqdar of Sissai Salon (Ajitapur).*

SAYYAD MUHAMMAD SHAH, father of the above, was a commandant in the Oudh army, and he received a reward of this ilaqa in return for his services during the mutiny. At his death the present owner succeeded him. Since coming into possession, however, he has sold the taaluq of Lissai Salon to Sardar Hira Singh.

Estate, 5 villages and 2 *pattis* in zila Bahraich. Government revenue, Rs. 1,321. Primogeniture governs succession.

No. 230.

MUHAMMAD ALI KHAN *and* HUSAIN ALI KHAN, *Sayyad, Taaluqdars of Unchgaon.*

THIS is quite a modern taaluq created out of possessions held in inheritance by the predecessors of the present taaluqdar from a great number of years past. *Sanad* of it was granted by Government to Omad Ali, father of the present owner.

Estate, 5 villages in zila Unao. Government revenue, Rs. 3,250. Succession governed by law of primogeniture.

No. 231.

SHAMS-UN-NISSA, *Shaikh, Taaluqdar of Jasmara, Malikpur and Sarai Shaikh.*

THIS taaluq formerly belonged to Jaswant Rai and Daulat Rai, Chaudhris of Lucknow, and in 1258 fasli the mauza of Jaswarah after which this ilaqa is called, was purchased by Mozuffar Ali, the husband of the above, after whose death she came to the property.

Estate, 6 villages and 10 *pattis* in zilas Lucknow and Bara Banki. Government revenue, Rs, 5,724-8-9. Primogeniture regulates succession.

No. 232.

MUHAMMAD HUSAIN, *Shaikh, Siddiki, Taaluqdar of Ghazipur, Ganowra, and Gubri Khurd.*

THIS taaluq was the ancestral property of Ahmad Bakhsh, who came to Lucknow in the reign of Emperor Humayun Shah. It was granted as a dowry to Shaikh Kamyab (an employé under Muhammad Shah), who married a sister of Shaikh Abul Kasim of Lucknow, by whom the gift was made. The present taaluqdar is a descendant of the said Shaikh Kamyab.

Estate, 11 villages and 1 *patti* in zilas Lucknow and Bara Banki. Government revenue, Rs. 7,009. Succession governed by primogeniture.

No. 233.

MIRZA JAFAR ALI KHAN, *Shaikh, Taaluqdar of Behta and Dhaurahra.*

THIS member of the Oudh aristocracy comes from the same stock to which also belonged Hakim Mehdi Ali Khan and Nawab Munawar-ud-daula, former Viziers to the Nawabs of the province. Khoja Shaffi Kasmiri Amir, who held appointment under Asafud-daula and fifth Nawab of Oudh, died leaving two sons—the said Hakim Mehdi and Hadi Ali. The former died without issue, and to the latter was born Ahmad Ali, afterwards called Nawab Munawar-ud-daula, the grandfather of the subject of this notice. Mirza Jafir Ali acquired an estate comprising two villages in zila Bijnor, one of which, Behta, gives its name to the taaluq above.

Estate, 12 villages in zila Lucknow. Government revenue, Rs. 10,755. Family custom governs succession in default of testamentary disposition.

No. 234.

SHAIKH TALIB ALI (*son of Chaudhri Musahib Ali*) *and* KARIM BAKHSH, *Taaluqdars of Dinpana.*

A HINDU Thakur *Bais* came to mauza Saila, then belonging to the Janwars, and in view to the acquirement of zemindari property, became a convert to the religion of the Prophet, and obtained the villages of Khandsara, &c. He then subsequently raised on a neglected part of the acquired estate the village of Dinpana called after himself, which gives the above taaluqa its name. The present owners came from the Chaudhris of Kursi. This estate is being gradually disintregated and reduced by sale and mortgage.

Estate, 5 villages and 1 patti in zila Bara Banki. Government revenue, Rs. 7,350. Primogeniture governs succession.

No. 235.

MAHPAL SINGH (*son of Dina Singh*), *Bais, Taaluqdar of Malauna.*

Vide No. 4. Bhimma Sah, third in generation from Kam Rai, founded the village of Malauna, and the taaluq (formed on its *basis*) has been the family inheritance ever since. Government *sanad* was granted to the said Dina Singh, after whom came his son, the present owner.

Estate 5 villages and 1 *patti* in zila Unao. Government revenue, Rs. 3,744-6-0. Family custom governs succession in default of testamentary disposition.

No. 236.

RUKMIN KUNWAR (*widow of Thakur Singh, Tribvedi*), *Brahmin, Taaluqdar of Tribediganj, Shikurabad, Tribedpur, and Saidpur Bakela.*

THE first of the above taaluqs was the acquisition of the Kunwar's husband, who was a distinguished officer under the Nawabs of Oudh. The other estates heading this notice were obtained in gift by him from Government for services rendered during the mutiny. His widow now owns them under his will.

Estate, 7 villages and 1 *patti* in zilas Unao, Bara Banki, and Rae Bareli. Government revenue, Rs. 3,412. Primogeniture governs succession.

No. 237.

MUHAMMAD NASIR-UD-DIN, *Shaikh, Taaluqdar of Mirpur.*

THIS estate and its present holder come from taaluq and house No. 186.

Estate, 6 villages and 7 *pattis* in zila Bara Banki. Government revenue, Rs. 5,840-6-8. Family custom governs succession in default of testamentary disposition.

No. 238.

PIRTHIPAL SINGH, *Amethia, Taaluqdar of Ramnagar.*

Vide No. 21. Deo Rai (fourth in descent from Raja Ram Singh), leaving Pokhra Unsari joint house, founded this separate taaluq, the Government *sanad* of which was granted to Babu Chandi Bakhsh, uncle of the present taaluqdar, who comes in lineal descent from the said Deo Rai, and who succeeded his uncle to the family inheritance.

Estate, 8 villages and 1 *patti* in zila Bara Banki. Government revenue, Rs. 8,234-8-0. Primogeniture governs succession.

No. 239.

BABU LAL BAHADUR *Amethia, Taaluqdar of Akhiapur.*

Vide No. 21. This is another taaluq brought into separate existence from the main ilaqa of Pokhra Unsari. In later days *sanad* of it was granted to Bhikhan Sah, predecessor of the present owner.

Estate, 3 villages in zila Bara Banki. Government revenue, Rs. 2,325. Primogeniture governs succession.

No. 240.

WAZIR ALI KHAN, *Bhatte, Taaluqdar of Barauli, pargana Basandhi.*

THIS taaluqa is a part of No. 201, and particulars regarding it are given under that number. Among the descendants of Zaber Khan, Munna Jan obtained possession of pargana Mowai from No. 201, and since then it has been in possession of this family.

Estate, 5 villages and 37 *pattis* in zila Bara Banki. Government revenue, Rs. 8,557-9-4. *Gaddi* custom of succession is prevalent in this family.

No. 241.

BABU KISHUN DATT, *Bais, Taaluqdar of Pali.*

FOR about five centuries past this estate in point of extent and other matters has been in the same condition as it is now. The ancestors of the present owner always during the native *régime* enjoyed the position of taaluqdars. The British Government settlement was made in the present taaluqdar's name.

Estate, 1 village in zila Bara Banki. Government revenue, Rs. 2,100. Primogeniture governs succession.

No. 242.

DIWAN KISHUN KUNWAR, *Khattri Sikh, Taaluqdar of Yakubganj.*

THIS estate during the Nawabi belonged to Yakub Ali Khan Khoja Sarai, but it afterwards became Government nazul, and was eventually conferred on Diwan Hakim Rai, who was principal minister in the court of Maharaja Ranjit Singh of Lahore. His successor is the taaluqdar above.

Estate, 1 village in zila Bara Banki. Government revenue, Rs. 2,795. Primogeniture governs succession.

No. 243.

MAULVI MAZHAR ALI, *Shaikh, Taaluqdar of Mahewa.*

THIS ilaqa, which formed originally part of the confiscated estate of Raja Lone Singh (the refractory taaluqdar of Metouli), represents proprietary possession bestowed on the present owner by the Government of India for loyal service during 1857.

Estate, 2 villages in zila Sitapur. Government revenue, Rs. 2,095. Succession regulated by the law of primogeniture.

No. 244.

KALKA BAKHSH, *Gaur, Taaluqdar of Jar Sadatnagar.*

THE subject of this notice holds the present taaluq in succession to Raghu Nath Singh, who received it from the Government in recognition of service rendered during the mutiny.

Estate, 12 villages and 5 *pattas* in zila Sitapur. Government revenue, Rs. 6,827-0-4. Primogeniture governs succession.

No. 245.

THAKUR RAGHURAJ SINGH, *Bais, Taaluqdar of Rajpur.*

Vide No. 4. This taaluqdar is son of Rana Beni Madho, the rebel taaluqdar of Shankarpur. After the confiscation referred to in the foregoing number the British Government conferred this taaluq (formerly part of the escheated estate of the Raja of Chahlari) on its present owner.

Estate, 18 villages in zila Sitapur. Government revenue, Rs. 8,157. Succession governed by primogeniture.

No. 246.

THAKUR SARABJIT SINGH (*Tilokchandi*), *Bais, Taaluqdar of Puwayan and Bahrora.*

Vide No. 18. This taaluqdar is descended from Athsukh, son of Ram Chand. During the reign of Nawab Mansur Ali Khan Pawayan was known by the name of Mansurgarh.

Estate, 10 villages in zilas Hardoi and Lucknow. Government revenue, Rs. 5,183. Succession governed by primogeniture.

No. 247.

SAFDAR HUSAIN KHAN, *Pathan, Taaluqdar of Bhanapur.*

Is Subordinate Judge of Rae Bareli. In January, 1868, the grant of this taaluq was bestowed on him in reward for good and loyal service done in the mutiny (*vide* docket No. 154, dated 14th January, 1868).

Estate, 2 villages in zila Hardoi. Government revenue, Rs. 1,816. Family custom governs inheritance in default of testamentary disposition.

No. 248.

LALA ANANT RAM, *Kayesth, Taaluqdar of Rasulpur.*

THIS estate originally comprised a gift of six villages, made out of the confiscated possessions of the rebel Raja Abbas Ali of Tanda, to the present taaluqdar for his loyal services during the mutiny. To this gift the recipient has made additions and improvements, and the result is the present taaluq.

Estate, 10 villages and 3 *pattis* in zila Fyzabad. Government revenue, Rs. 1,759. Primogeniture governs succession.

No. 249.

SHEO RAJ KUNWAR, *Thakur, Rajkumar, Taaluqdar of Sultanpur (Damodra) and Amarthun Dauria.*

Vide No. 7. This taaluq represents a mutiny grant (for loyalty and good services done) bestowed by Government on Rao Baryar Singh, who was succeeded in possession by the present owner.

Estate, 20 villages and 3 *pattis* in zila Sultanpur. Government revenue, Rs. 4,670-2-0. Primogeniture regulates succession.

No. 250.

PANDE HAR NARAIN RAM, *Brahmin, Taaluqdar of Akbarpur (Nerora.)*

THIS taaluqdar is from the same stock as Raja Kishn Dat Ram of Singha Chanda, a full account of whom, both as regards family and estate, is given in No. 32. In 1216 fasli, Bahadur Ram Pande purchased from Raja Guman Singh (*Bisain*, taaluqdar of Gonda) the proprietary possession of Akbarpur, after which this taaluq is called.

Estate, 8 villages and 4 *pattis* in zila Gonda. Government revenue, Rs. 4,857. Primogeniture governs succession.

No. 251.

BABUAIN ANAND KUNWAR, *Amethia, Taaluqdar of Usa.*

Vide No. 21. This is a branch of taaluq Kumhrawan, No. 22. It was founded about 400 years ago by one Babu Man Singh, who, on leaving the joint family, received for his share the villages of estate Usa, where he went and settled. Babu Sewamber Singh latterly succeeded to the inheritance, and it is his widow who is now in possession.

Estate, 6 villages in zila Rae Bareli. Government revenue, Rs. 6,139. *Gaddi* custom governs succession.

No. 252.

MAHARAJ BAKHSH, *Bais, Taaluqdar of Pilkaha.*

Vide No. 4. Tirbhawan Sah (fourth son of Raja Doman Deo), separating from the main house of Khajurgaon, went to reside in Jagatpur. Eighth in descent from him came Mohan Singh, who cleared a *pilu jungle*, and built on its site a village called Pilkaha, which gives its name to the taaluq under notice. Government sanad of the estate was granted in the name of the present taaluqdar, whose interest in it, however, is shared by other partners.

Estate, 4 villages in zila Rae Bareli. Government revenue, Rs. 1,496-11-0. Family custom governs inheritance in default of testamentary disposition.

No. 253.

SITA RAM, *Kurmi, Taaluqdar of Sehgaon and Pachhimgaon.*

THE history of this house can be traced to Benaik Ram and Palji Ram, who, taking service under Emperor Akbar, came to Pachhimgaon. A descendant from them, Kachan Singh (in 980 fasli), built the village of Binaikpur and (in 995 fasli) that of Pallia after the names of the above ancestors. By the gradual acquisition of mauzas Khanpur and Purbgaon and of much improvements in Pachhimgaon itself, he brought the whole into one taaluq, and to this amalgamation he gave the name of Sehgaon, *i. e.*, three villages. Government *sanad* was granted in a later generation to Thakur Singh, who distinguished himself by loyalty to the British during the siege of the Baillie guard. After him succeeded the present owner. This taaluq has other co-sharers, with their respective rights defined.

Estate, 3 villages in zila Rae Bareli. Government revenue, Rs. 4,164. Primogeniture governs succession.

No. 254.

BALBHADDAR SINGH, *Bais, Taaluqdar of Khajuri.*

Vide No. 4. Bikramaditiya, on his separation from the house described in No. 63, received (from its then head, Lal Sah) as his share the taaluq above, which has ever since been the property of his descendants.

Estate, 4 villages in zila Rae Bareli. Government revenue, Rs. 2,821-13-3. Primogeniture governs succession.

No. 255.

THAKUR BAKHSH, *Bais, Taaluqdar of Kusarua.*

Vide No. 4. This taaluq came into existence about a century ago, when Kalandar Singh and Pratap Singh separated from the main stock (Gaura) and received it for their support from Bhupat Singh, then head of the Gaura house. The estate has been in possession of their descendants ever since.

Estates, 4 villages in zila Rae Bareli. Government revenue, Rs. 1,990. Primogeniture governs succession.

No. 256.

BABU BAKHTAWAR SINGH, *Amethia, Taaluqdar of Dehli.*

Vide No. 21. This is another branch derived from taaluq No. 22. It represents an allotment, assigned about seventy years ago, to his younger brother, Bijai Singh by Araru Singh (taaluqdar of Kamhrawan), on the separation of the former from the joint house. Since then this property has remained in the family of Bijai Singh's descendants, of whom the latest is the present taaluqdar.

Estate, 3 villages in zila Rae Bareli. Government revenue, Rs. 3,044. Primogeniture governs succession.

No. 257.

GANGA BISHUN, *Brahmin, Taaluqdar of Maniahar Kutra.*

In 1268 fasli, Shiuraj Bali (son of Raja Hira Lal Misr, Nazim, of Dalmau and Bareli) purchased this taaluq from Raja Meharban Singh.

Estate, 1 village in zila Rae Bareli. Government revenue, Rs. 1291. Family custom governs succession in default of testamentary disposition.

No. 258.

MUHAMMAD MOHSIN *and* MUHAMMAD SHAFI *Sayyad, Taaluqdar of Alipur Chakai.*

THIS taaluq (formerly belonging to the confiscated estate of the rebel Rana Beni Madho Bakhsh) was bestowed for loyalty during the mutiny on Sayyid Abdul Hakim. Abdul Hakim was also an Extra Assistant Commissioner in Oudh, and died in receipt of pension for these valued services. The taaluqdars heading this notice are his sons. The second, Muhammad Shafi, is a Deputy Sherishtadar in zila Bara Banki.

Estate, 5 villages and 2 pattis in zila Rae Bareli. Government revenue, Rs. 3,711. Family custom governs succession in default of testamentary disposition.

No. 259.

BENI PRASHAD, *Chattri, Taaluqdar of Mahgawan, Mojgaon, and Hardoi.*

THIS taaluqdar inherited this estate from his father, Gajraj Singh, on whom it was bestowed by Government in recognition of his loyalty during the mutiny. The taaluq originally formed part of the confiscated possession of the rebel Raja Beni Madho Bakhsh.

Estate, 1 village in zila Rae Bareli. Government revenue, Rs. 714. Family custom governs succession in default of testamentary disposition.

No. 260.

SHIU SHANKAR SINGH *and* ARJUN SINGH, *Rajwar, Taaluqdars of Partabpar and (a moiety of) Sadipur Kutwa.*

Vide No. 7. Several generations after Khokai Singh came Mohan Sahi, to whom, at partition of the family inheritance, was allotted as his share in it the taaluq above, which to the present day has been in the possession of his descendants, now represented by this nobleman.

Estate, 2 villages and 25 pattis in zilas Rae Bareli and Sultanpur Government revenue, Rs. 7,845-3-0. In default of testamentary disposition, succession is governed in the family.

No. 261.

SHIU GOBIND, *Tewari Brahmin, Taaluqdar of Behta Bhawani.*

THIS taaluqdar is descended from Hira Lal, who, thirty years ago (from Gosain Khera), came to and settled in the taaluq above. In consequence of relationship with its former owner, Chaudhri Gharib Singh, Ishridin, son of the latter, made a gift of this property to Brahmadin (predecessor of the above) on the occasion of his investiture with the sacred Brahminical thread, and since then the estate became vested in the family of the said Hira Lal, which is now represented by the subject of this memoir.

Estate, 7 villages and 2 pattis in zila Unao. Government revenue, Rs. 4,513-8-0. Primogeniture governs succession.

No. 262.

Widow of Niamat-ul-lah Khan, Ahban Musalman, Taaluqdar of Mirzapur and Jalalpur.

Kuli and Suli came from Deccan to this province, and by force of arms established this taaluq. In this family were Nursingh Deo and Rao Jey Bhan Sah, two brothers. The former took possession of the Mitouli *gaddi*. Raja Lone Singh, who rebelled and forfeited his taaluq, is descended from this branch of the family. Rao Jey Bhan Sah fixed his residence at Kutwari and took forcible possession of 989 neighbouring villages and called the whole taaluqa Bhurwara.

In the third generation of Rao Jey Bhan Sah was Jam-i-Jahan Sah, and he had two sons, Mull and Ghasi. These men (Mull and Ghasi) embraced the Muhammadan religion in 1445 sambat in the reign of Tamerlane and obtained a *sanad* for the possession of the 989 villages. Ghasi died without issue. All the Ahban Musalmans are the descendants of Mull. This estate went out of the hands of this family in 1002 fasli, in the reign of Jahangir Shah. In 1211 fasli, however, a few villages were given to the family of the officers of the Emperor in muafi. Since then they improved the estate and it has been in their possession, but having to be divided among a number of heirs, the estate grew into several taaluqas belonging to this family. Nos. 221 and 222 and the estate under description are branches of the one estate referred to. The Government *sanad* was given in the name of Niamat-ulla Khan.

Estate, 13 villages in zila Kheri. Government revenue, Rs. 6,825. *Gaddi* custom governs succession.

Nawab Muhammad Baqar Ali Khan, Moghul, Taaluqdar of Kunwa Khera. Title of " Nawab" hereditary.

This taaluq (comprising acquisitions both by purchase and mortgage) was founded by Nawab Munawar-ud-daula, grandson of Khoja Shafi, a Kashmiri nobleman, who held service under Nawab Asaf-ud-daula of Oudh. Nawab Amjad Ali Khan, son of the said Nawab Munawar-ud-daula (for a long time Vizier of Oudh), made many improvements to the property. After him succeeded the present representative.

Estate, 52 villages and 13 *pattis* in zila Sitapur. Government revenue, Rs. 31,605-12-0. *Gaddi* custom governs succession.

Major A. P., Orr, European, Taaluqdar of Lodhwari.

Major Orr was, previous to the mutiny, Deputy Commissioner of Rae Bareli. He obtained this taaluq from Government in recognition of services rendered in those days. This ilaqa is called Lodhwari owing to the preponderance of people of the *Lodha* caste among its inhabitants.

Estate, 10 villages in zila Rae Bareli. Government revenue, Rs. 17,111. Succession governed by family custom in default of testamentary disposition.

L. D. HEARSEY, *European, Taaluqdar of Kaima Buzurg, Govindpur, Karana Timra, Mamri, and grant Sitalpur.*

THIS taaluq was received in gift from Government by Mr. William Hearsey. It formerly belonged to the estate of Raja Lone Singh of Metauli, forfeited to Government by the disloyal conduct of its owner.

Estate, 23 villages and 2 *pattis* in zila Kheri. Government revenue, Rs. 13,629. Primogeniture governs succession.

SHAHZADA SHAHDEO SINGH, *Sikh, Taaluqdar of Pandri Ganeshpur, Doenta, and Gokalpur.*

THIS Shahzada is in the Darbar list of the ex-royal family.

The first of the above taaluqs, called after its founder (Brahmin), Ganesh Tiwari, originally formed part of the confiscated estate of the rebel Rana Beni Madho Bakhsh Singh, and was given in grant by Government to the Shahzada above, who is a grandson of Maharaja Ranjit Singh of the Panjab.

Estate, 18 villages and 3 *pattis* in zila Rae Bareli. Government revenue, Rs. 13,325. Primogeniture governs succession.

ALEXANDER DOUGLAS ORR, *European, Taaluqdar of Aira.*

THIS and taaluqs Nagra and Tirabhaji, confiscated rebel estates represent mutiny gifts to Messrs. Orr and Rose for good services rendered by them to Government during 1857. Aira is now Mr. Orr's sole property.

Estate, 24 villages in zila Kheri. Government revenue, Rs. 7,515. Primogeniture governs succession.

The rest of this taaluq is distributed as below:—

Pauline Annie Orr owns Nagra, which comprises—

Estate, 14 villages in zila Kheri; Government revenue, Rs. 5,800 ; and

Louisa Fanny Orr holds Jarabhaji, consisting of—

Estate, 1 village in zila Kheri ; Government revenue, Rs. 150.

RAJA JAGAR NATH, BAKHSH SINGH, *Gaur, Taaluqdar of Wazir-nagar. Title of "Raja" hereditary.*

THIS taaluq has been sold, but the Raja holds property in the district of Shahjahanpur, North-Western Provinces.

RAJA SHIU NATH SINGH, *Brahmin (Kashmiri), Taaluqdar of Bethar. Title of "Raja" personal.*

THE former proprietor of this taaluq was Chandika Bakhsh, who, being convicted of rebellion, was sentenced to transportation for life. His confiscated possessions were disposed of by gift as follows : To Raja Gauri Shankar a portion (*vide* No. 52), to Baldeo Singh, Resaldar, one village, and Bethar to the Raja heading this notice.

Estate, 2 villages in zila Unao. Government revenue, Rs. 4,195. Primogeniture governs succession.

SARDAR JAGJOT SINGH *and* LACHMAN KUNWAR, *Sikh, Taaluqdars of Chahlari and Sikraura.*

THE Sardar is in the list of the ex-royal family.

These are descendants from the house of Maharaja Ranjit Singh of Lahore, and they came to the ownership of this property in succession to Sardars Fateh Singh and Jagat Singh, to whom it was given by the British Government.

Estate, 28 villages in zilas Gonda and Bahraich. Government revenue, Rs. 12,320. Primogeniture governs succession.

BENI MADHO BAKHSH SINGH, *Bais, Taaluqdar of Akbarpur (zila Unao).*

THIS estate has been broken up in consequence of sale or mortgage, and has ceased to exist as a separate taaluq, a remnant of 44 bighas only being assigned to the present taaluqdar for his support.

MAHPAL SINGH, *Chandel, Taaluqdar of Jojmau, zila (Unao).*

ALL the rights of this taaluqdar have been sold by a decree of the civil court to the Land Mortgage Bank of Lucknow. Mahpal Singh now only holds 85 bighas of sir land, which he cultivates himself.

The Hon'ble SIR GEORGE E. W. COUPER, BART, C.B., K.C.S.I., C.I.E.,
Lieutenant-Governor of the North-Western Provinces and Chief Commissioner of
Oudh.

1—Raja Rajgan Jagat Jit Singh Bahadur Maharaja
Kapurthala Boundi

2—H. H. the H Sir Pertap Raju Singh Bahadur
K. C. S. I. Maharaja Balrampur and Tulsipur

3 Lal Pratab Narain Singh Taulluqdar of Mihelaana

4 Raja Sheopal Singh Taulluqdar of Murar Mau

4—Raja Hanwant Singh Taaluqdar of Kalakankar

...ngal Singh, Taaluqdar of Rampur Dharupur

6 Raja Tilak Singh Taaluqdar of Kalyani

7—Raja Rudr Partab Sah Taaluqdar of Dihra

8—Raja Lal Madho Singh Taâluqdar of Amethi

9—Raja Muhammad Ali Khan Taâluqdar of Hasanpur

10—Raja Muhammad Amir Hasan Khan Taâluqdar of Mahmudabad

11—Raja Bijai Bahadur Singh Taâluqdar of Bhinga

12 Raja Narpat Singh Taalluqdar of Tiloi

13 Rani Kishan Nath Kunwar widow of Madho Prasad Singh Taalluqdar of Kurwar

14 Rana Shankar Baksh Singh Taalluqdar of Bhulai Khajurganw

15 — Rani Dharm Raj Kunwar Taalluqdar of Parhat

16—Raja Lazzool Ali Khan, Taaluqdar of
Jahangirabad

17. Raja Jang Bahadur Khan, Taaluqdar of Nanpara

18—Raja Raodhar Singh, Taaluqdar of Bharawan

19—Son of Raghu Nath Singh, Taaluqdar of Kilwa

20—Raja Muhammad Kazim Husain Khan
Taallaqdar of Paitepur

21—Raja Bhagwan Bakash taaluqdar of Pachra
Amari

22—Rai Girdhar Bakash Son of R[...] gaadhan
[...] taaluqdar of Hunsinjpore

23—Raja Jagnarian Singh Taallaqdar of Raipur
Yakoariya

24—Raja ... Singh Taalluqdar of Och

25—Raja Narindar Bahadur Singh Taalluqdar of Utrera

26—Raja Rampal Singh Taalluqdar of Kori Sudauli

27—Raja Sitla Bakhsh Singh Talluqdar of Gangol

28 Raja Sukhmun Takawa Singh Taulukdar
of Fayzapur

29 Raja Jagmohan Singh Taulukdar of Atra
Chatakapur

30 Ram Har Nath Kunwar Talukdar of Katari

31—Raja Sahib Jan widow of Musharraf Ali Khan
Taulukdar of Itara Off Sagar

...aml's Dat Ram, Officiating of Raja Kishn Dat Ram Taalluqdar of Surhin Chanda.

32 - Rani Jack Kunwar Taalluqdar of Pachotar

34 — Rani Saltanat Kunwar Taalluqdar of Mankapur

35 - Raja Chhatpal Singh Taalluqdar of Nurpur

36   Raja Mahesh Bah'adur Singh Taalluqdar of
Kuwarsa

37.—Raja Inder Bikrama Sah Taalluqdar of
Kham Gadh

38   Raja Narpat Singh Taalluqdar of Khamra

39.—Begam Amanat Fatima of Basti Nagar

40   Raja Jagat Bahadur Taalluqdar of Amri

41—Raja Manoehar Bakhsh Singh Taalluqdar
of Mailsapur

42—Raja Chandar Sikher Taalluqdar of Siseudi

43—Raja Sarabjit Singh Taalluqdar of Kaunagar

44.—Raja Sher ... Bahadur Taalluqdar of Sandwa ...ar

45.—Raja Mumtaz Ali Khan Taalluqdar of Bilaspur

46.—Raja Sher Bahadur Singh Taalluqdar of Deoli

47.—Rani Sitar-un-Nisa Taalluqdar of Salempur

48—[illegible] Raja Ajit Singh [illegible] Talukdar of [illegible]

49—Raja Deyo Singh [illegible] Talukdar of [illegible]

50—Raja Sukh Mal [illegible] Singh [illegible] Talukdar of
Bhan Mau

51—Thakur [illegible] Singh Talukdar of
Maini[illegible]

52—Babu Ram Sahai Taalluqdar of Mahmawan

54 Har Prashad Taalluqdar of Mutura...

52— Ram Charan Taalluqdar of Bihta

55— ... Taalluqdar of Thulendi

52 - Mathoo Prashad Taalluqdar of Daretha

5. - Debi Dayal Taaluqdar of Amawan

52—Shro Dayal Taalluqdar of Dewni Kanlawan

52 Ram Narain Taalluqdar of Izzatnughan Khera

5.   Lu makund Tashildar of Aiwat

52   Kalka ramshad Tashildar o. Balbawan

32   Chandar Prasan tashildar of Behirava

5.   M... L. Bateman Tashildar of Aanda

52   Beni Prasad Taluqdar of Hawa Kasan
Baraula

53   Iwaz Ali Khan Taaluqdar of Mahona

54   Babu Mahipal Singh Taaluqdar of Sonagpur

56— Makhrod Singh Tahsildar of Rampur

57 Kunwar Harnam Singh Manager of Boundi

58 Captain Gulab Singh Bhagoolsurpur

59 Sardar Atta Singh Tahsildar of Basti

58—Sardar Narain Singh Taelluqdar of Bela Bhela

59— Rai Jagmohan Singh Taelluqdar of Raipur
Bichsur

60 Bisheshar Bhat... Taelluqdar of Isaipur
Bichsur

61 Rai Mardan Pr... Singh Taelluqdar of
Atisafganj

61   Ma... Hy...... Dev Raulraphai   Maswasi

62   Lal Sarabjit Singh Taallrqdar of Bhadri

63   Chaudhri Murti A........ Tassildpost of
Ithawa

64   Hafeez..... an Officials Beeham-Nisa Taalluqdar of Sensindarpur

64 Thakurain Bhoopal Kunwar Taalluqdar of
Samti

65 Thakurain Parvu Kunwar Taalluqdar of
Nimarpaha

66—Thakur Chandarpal Singh Taalluqdar of
Keribaraitiwan

67 Thakurain Arka' Kunwar Taalluqdar of
Gauraaartai

68—Thakur Pratab Gudr Singh Taalluqdar of
Kampur

69—Diwan Rao Bijai Bahadur Singh Taalluqdar
of Patti Saifabad

70—Thakurain Ajit Kunwar Partner of Patti
Saifabad

71—Thakurain Jasbr Kunwar Taalluqdar of
Pawaran Dhagos

74   Raj Milap Singh Taalluqdar of Shahpur
Majhgain

Guman Singh Taalluqdar of Ramnagar Daulatpur

Gobhar Dhan Singh Taalluqdar of Dichhawanighasan

Dalip Singh Taalluqdar of Dichhawanyan Jaghupur

72.- Babu Udree Narpt Taalliopdar of Me pur Ishirwa

73.- Babu Chandree Rin I Taalliopdar of Mengur Ihurwa

74. Babu Amree Singh Taalluqdar of Mengur Barngaum

75. Seyad Gazaffur Hussin Taalluqdar of Pirpur

75 — Rajah Syed Baqar Husain Taaluqdar of ...pur

76 — Babu Ugardat Singh Taaluqdar of Bihti

77 — Rudr Prateb Singh Taaluqdar of Soomi Siwan

78 — Nawab Bakhsh Taaluqdar of Me...

77—Lal Bahadur Singh Taulluqdar of Madhpur

78—Kalka Bakhsh Singh Taulluqdar of Madhpur

76—Udat Narain Singh Taulluqdar of Madhpur

78—Nageshar Bakhsh Singh Taulluqdar of Madhpur

78—Chaudharja Bakhsh Singh Taalluqdar of Madhpur

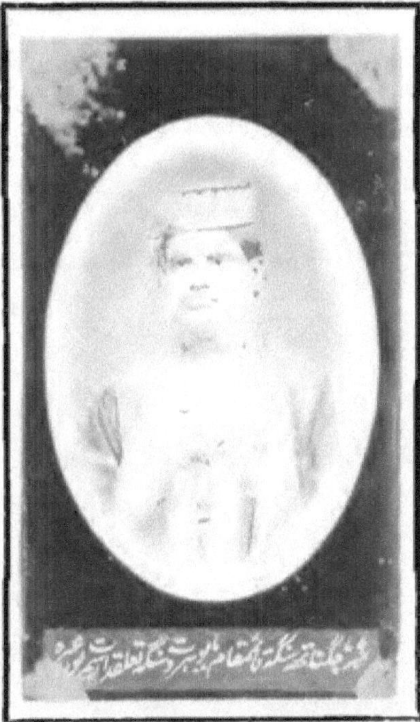

79—Jagan Nath Singh offg of Babu Hardat Singh Taalluqdar of Shiwratpur

80—Ganesh Kunwar widow of Jagar Nath Baksh Taalluqdar of Jamau

81—Thakur Shankar Bakhsh Taalluqdar of Pahu Gulariya

82   Ali & Hingat Hossain Tahsildar of Samastipur

83   Mulat Prasad Thanedar of Ranipur

Bhawani Ajit Singh Tahsildar of Ranipur

55 Babu Mahipal Lal Singh Taulluqdar of Manimau.

56 Khaslat Husen, Taulluqdar of Kakrali.

57 Thakur Bharat Singh Taulluqdar of Atwa

58 Thakur Faro Husen Taulluqdar of Katora.

89— ... ...th Kunwar Taalluqdar of ...

88—Lal Chhatarpal Singh Taalluqdar of Kandrajit

69—Lal Surajpal Singh Taalluqdar of Kandrajit

59— Chandarpal Singh Taalluqdar of Kandrajit

90—Wazir Chand Taalluqdar of Sarun Bara Ganw

93—Durga Prashad Taalluqdar of Sarun Bara Ganw

91—Thakar Anand Bahadur Singh Taalluqdar of
Kampradih

92—Dan Bahadur ... Taalluqdar of
Daundik ...

... Singh, Taaluqdar of Katyudh

94— Thakur Bisheswar Bakhsh Singh Taaluqdar of Sautpur

95— Babu Lalu Sah Taaluqdar of Meopur Dihla

96— Nawazish Ali Khan Taaluqdar of Nawabganj Aliyabad

97—Bhaya Udepratab Singh Taalluqdar of Bhinga

98—Babu Bhunrunjan Mukarji Taalluqdar of
Shankarpur

99—Thakur Bishan Nath Bukhsh Taalluqdar of
Hasanpur

100—Babu Sarabjit Singh Taalluqdar of Tikari

104—Sithi Bakhsh Singh Taalluqdar of Dhangadh

101—Shankar Singh Taalluqdar of Dhangadh

102—Lachmi Narain Son of Babu Kishan Parshad
Taalluqdar of Barhar Jalalpur

103—Babu Hardat Singh Taalluqdar of Barhar
Chandapur Haswa

104—Shamsher Bahadur Son of Babu Shiv pargash
Singh, Taalluqdar of Bahraj Suchat pur.

105—Thakurain Dalil Kunwar Taalluqdar of
Lohrasatpur

106—Shamsher Bahadur Singh Son of Babu M. bhajan
Narain Singh Taalluqdar of Bahraj.

107—Ganesh Kunwar widow of Arjan Singh
Taalluqdar of Behsa

105—Shekh Ahmad Husain Taalluqdar of Gadya

106—Shekh Wajid Husain Taalluqdar of Gadya

109—Thakur Baldeo Bakhsh Taalluqdar of Pursaini

110—Thakur Lalta Bakhsh Taalluqdar of Khajrahra

111—Saiyud Wari Haidar Taalluqdar of
Bhivatyapur

112—Cawaihri Muhammad Ashraf Taalluqdar of
Asifpur

112—Muhammad Zain-ul-Abidin Taalluqdar of
Bhagyari

112—Muhammad Fazil Taalluqdar of Daryabad

1. — Sayyid Muhammad Akbar Taalluqdar of
Dhanaalipur

113 - Mirza Muhammad Ali Beg Taalluqdar of
Aurangabad

114—Kazim Husain Khan Taalluqdar of
Bhatwa Mau

115—Thakur Hari Har Bakhsh Taalluqdar of
Saraura

116—Thakur Fazal Ali Khan Taalluqdar of Akbarpur

117—Thakur Jawahir Singh Taalluqdar of Uasi Dih

118—Thakur Durga Bakhsh Taalluqdar of Nil Ganw

119—Thakur Maharaj Singh Taalluqdar of Kanh Mau

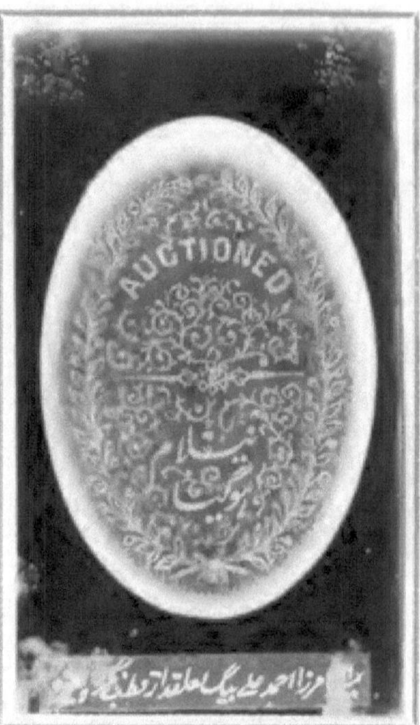

120—...Ram Bux Taalluqdar of Rampur

121—Mirza Ahmad Ali Beg Taalluqdar of Qutub Nagar

122—Maulvi Fazal Rasul Taalluqdar of Jalalpur

123—Qazi Ikram Ahmad Taalluqdar of Satrikh

124—Thakur Raghbir Singh Taalluqdar of Dhanawan

125—Thakur Mirtunja Bakhsh Singh Taalluqdar of Shahpur

126—Har Mangal Singh Taalluqdar of Utiya Dih

127—Bhagwant Singh Taalluqdar of Daryapur

... Singh Taalluqdar of Daryapur

Bisheshar Bakhsh Singh Taalluqdar of Daryapur

Arth Singh Taalluqdar of Daryapur

146—Hakim Karam Ali Taalluqdar of Gotya

129   Babu Jwal Nath Singh Taalluqdar of Mahganw

130   Shekh Mahb..oor Rahman T..llu..dar of Barra

Shekh Inayat-ur-Rahman Taalluqdar of Barra

Shekh Ab.. ...

Sheikh Fazal-ur-Rahman Taalluqdar of Barai

131—Muhammad Nasim Khan Taalluqdar of
Sohla Mau

132   Mir Muhammad Hasan Khan Taalluqdar of
Rajapara

133—Sayad Fida Husain Khan Taalluqdar of
Alwapurya

134—Babu Sukhraj Singh Taalluqdar of Ata

135—Thakurain Iklas Kunwar Taalluqdar of Paska

136—Seth Raghbar Dayal Taalluqdar of
Muna-ud-Dinpur

136—Seth Sita Ram Taalluqdar of Muna-ud-Dinpur

137— Thakur ... ... Bakhsh Taaluqdar of
Narindpur Charhar

137— Musammat Daryao Kunwar widow of Bishan
Nath Singh Taaluqdar of Narindpur Charhar

139— Shekh Nawab Ali Khan Taaluqdar of
Hulas Ha ganj

139— Thakurain Ude Nath Kunwar Taaluqdar of
Mamir Mau Kola

140—Balbhaddar Singh Taallu[q]dar [o]f Goara

140—Darshan Singh Taalluqdar of Hussainabad

141—Saiyad Razá Hussin Taalluqdar of Narauli

142—Fatuh Singh Ali [illegible]

143—Thakur Anand Singh Taalluqdar of Rampur

Thakur Jagan Nath Singh Taalluqdar of Rampur

Thakur Hardeo Bakhsh Taalluqdar of Rampur

Thakur Ganga Bakhsh Taalluqdar of Rampur

144—Thakurain Jaipal Kunwar Taaluqdar of
Mustafabad

145—Babu Azim Ali Khan Taulluqdar of Deoganw

146—Chaudhri Ram Narain Taalluqdar of
Mubarakpur

147—Babu Firthipal Singh Taalluqdar of Tigra

148—M... Ahmad Khan Taalluqdar of Rae Bareli

149—Babu Mahesh Bakhsh Singh Taalluqdar of Dhoyanwan

150—Sarabjit Singh Taalluqdar of Sookhej

151—Hanwant Sing Sahai Taalluqdar of Sanerawan

152—Saiadat-un-Nisa Taluqdar of Kharka

153—Mir B... Taluqdar of Lucknow

155—Mir Amjad Hussain Taluqdar of Sultanpur

154—D. Su... Taluqdar ...

... Singh Taalluqdar of Meerpur
Libia

153—Muhammad Zaman Khan Taalluqdar of
Amawan

Muhammad Said Khan Taalluqdar of Amawan

Muhammad Sultan Khan Taalluqdar of Amawan

157—Zulfiqar Khan Taslluqdar of Pahra Mau

157—Kerem Ali Khan Taslluqdar of Pahra Mau

157—Shahamat Khan Taslluqdar of Pahra Mau

157—Asad Ali Khan Taslluqdar of Pahra Mau

158.— Thakur Bhawani ... ah Taulluqdar of Gondah

159.— Million Kunwar widow of Deo Moulkdar Singh Taulluqdar of Bhartaul

160.— Rai Ram Pershad Bahadur Taulluqdar of Pera...

161.— Babu Sita Bakhsh Taulluqdar of Nasa Mau

162—Jehangir Bakhsh, Talukdar of Gonzoo

163 Lachman Prashad Laali, Talukdar of Bhumian

165 Lachman Nath Singh, Talukdar of Bhainga

164 Lachman Singh, Talukdar of Bhainga

105—Bibi Khanam Taaluqdar of Maniyarpur

106—Imtiyaz Fatima Taaluqdar of Gopa Mau

Baaghbari Taaluqdar of Barambhola

107—Babu Hanuman Bakhsh Singh Taaluqdar of Dunepur

168—Babu Hardat Singh Taalukdar of Pirthiganj

169—Udo Narain Singh Taalukdar of Bhumnipair

170—Lal Achal Raro Husband of Brij Raj Kunwar Taalukdar of Birwa

171—Mirza Abbas Beg Taalukdar of Baraganw

172—Raja Bahadur Singh Taalluqdar of Shahpadh

173—Mir Ahmad Jan Taalluqdar of Raghupaur

174—Mahip Singh Taalluqdar of Kerahia

175—Sultan Singh Taalluqdar of Galgalha

176—Sheikh Niwazi Ali Taalluqdar of Anabhapur

177—Pande Sarabjit Singh Tev... ...dar of Asadaman

175—Shekh Inayat-ul-lah Taalluqdar of Saidaupur

178—Shekh Ikram Ali Taal' ...dar of Saichapur

S. …Sh…am-ul-Lah Taalluqdar of Sailanpur

179- Mir Fakhr-ul-Husain Taalluqdar of Banaulra

180—Subhan Ahmad Taalluqdar of Azizabad

181—Mir Zafar Mahdi Taalluqdar of Ali Nagar

182—Saiyad Kazim Husain Taalluqdar of Dera Qazi

183—Saiyad Ramzan Ali Taalluqdar of Unao

184—Babu Bajrang Bahadur Singh Taalluqdar of
Baispur

185—Girdhari Singh Taalluqdar of Gokulpurasem

... Mu... ab Ali Taalluqdar ... ...anpur

167—Sita Ram Khattari Taalluqdar of Bhagupur

156 Saiyad Muhammad Abid Taalluqdar of Pural

185 Shekh Muhammad Amir Taalluqdar of
Shahabpur

16.—Shekh Gulam Abbas Taalluqdar of Shahabpur

190—Gulam Qasim Khan Taalluqdar of Umarpur

191—Shekh Ihsan Rasul Taalluqdar of Amirpur

192—Saiyad Nasir Husain Taalluqdar of Ahmadpur

193—Babu Bakhshiar Singh Taalluqdar of
Sujakhar

194—Umed Singh Taalluqdar of Asanpar

195—Mahesh Bakhsh Taalluqdar of Patanbihar

196—Arjun Singh Taalluqdar of Patanbihar

196—Babu Madho Singh Taalluqdar of
Nur-ud-Dinpur

197—Bhaya Autar Singh Taalluqdar of Ranimau

198—Bhaya Har Ratan Singh Taalluqdar of
Majhgawan

199—Shekh Rayazat Ali Taalluqdar of Shekhpur

200. Qutb-un-Nisa Taalluqdar of Gauriya Kalan

201—Muhammad Husain Khan Father of Nisar
Ali Khan dead Taalluqdar of Banaara

202—Thakurain Daryao Kunwar Taalluqdar of
Garabpur

203—Daya Shankar Ikajjai Taalluqdar of Kardaha

204—Jagesar Baklish Singh Taalluqdar of Bhawan
Shahpur

205—Thakur Fateh Muhammad Taalluqdar of
Tigeaha

206—Thakur Nirman Singh Taalluqdar of
Amchapar

207—Fateh Bahadur Khan Taalluqdar of Bahwa

204—Thakurain Sagu Nath Kunwar Taalluqdar of
Dasrathpur

205—Thakurain Kharak Kunwar Taalluqdar of
Dasrathpur

206—Thakur Ganga Bakhsh Taalluqdar of Ramkot
and Hajipur

207—Thakur Kalka Bakhsh Taalluqdar of Ramkot
and Hajipur

210—Thakur Jagmohan Singh Taalluqdar of
Dongarapur Gur-Harpur

211—Jugraj Kunwar P. Haqdar of Hardaspur

212—Mahpal Singh Taalluqdar of Bara

213—Dargahi Khan Taalluqdar of Unch Ganw

211—Gaya Din Singh Taalluqdar of Mudera

Subhjit Singh Taalluqdar of Mudera

215—Babu Samb Dun Singh Taalluqdar of
Utawamarupar

216—Saiyad Farzand Ali Khan Taalluqdar of
Kathwara

217—Har Prashad Taalluqdar of Libali

218—Sheo Ratan Singh Taalluqdar of Pinhauna

219—Dan Bahadur Singh Taalluqdar of Muhammadpur

220—Drig Bijai Singh Taalluqdar of Athganwan

221—Chand Bibi Taalluqdar of Katwara

222—Muhammad Sher Khan Taalluqdar of Raipur

223—Mahpal Singh Taalluqdar of Atur

224—Mir Ashraf Hussin Taalluqdar of Katariya

225—Shekh Wasi-uz-Zaman Taalluqdar of Miyanganj

226—Sheo Ambar Singh Taalluqdar of Rajpur

227—Sardar Hira Singh Taalluqdar of Jamadan

228—Bir. Sahib Singh son of the Taalluqdar of Isauli

229—Saiyad Sardár Ali Taalluqdar of Sissi Salon

230—Saiyad Muhammad Ali Khan Taalluqdar of Uchgaaw

Saiyad Husain Ali Khan Taalluqdar of Uchgaaw

231—Shams-un-Nisa Taalluqdar of Jismora Malikpur

232—Muhammad Husain Taalluqdar of Gazipur

233—Mirza Jafar Ali Khan Taalluqdar of Bilta

234—Sheikh Talib Ali Taalluqdar of Dinpanah

234—Sheikh Karim Bakhsh Taalluqdar of Dinpanah

235—Mahpal Singh Taalluqdar of Malauna

236—Rukman Kunwar Taalluqdar of Tirbediganj

237—Shaikh Muhammad Nasir-ud-Din Taalluqdar of Mirpur

238—Thakur Pirthipal Singh Taalluqdar of Ramnagar

239—Babu Lal Bahadur Taalluqdar of Akhyapur

240—Wazir Ali Khan Taalluqdar of Barauli

241—Baba Kishun Datt Taalluqdar of Pali

242—Diwan Kishun Kunwar Taalluqdar of Yaqubganj

213—Maulvi Mazhar Ali Taalluqdar of Mahawa

241—Thakur Kalka Bakhsh Taalluqdar of Jar Saadatnagar

243—Thakur Raghuraj Singh Taalluqdar of Rajpur

244—Thakur Sarabjit Singh Taalluqdar of Pawayan

247—Safdar Hussin Khan Taalluqdar of Bhanapur

248—Lala Anant Ram Taalluqdar of Rusulpur

249—Shoo Raj Kunwar Taalluqdar of Sultanpur

250—Pande Har Narain Ram Taalluqdar of
Akbarpar

251—Bobwain Anand Kunwar Taalluqdar of Ausa

252—Maharaj Bakheh Taalluqdar of Palkha

253—Sita Ram Taalluqdar of Sihganw

254—Balbhaddar Singh Taalluqdar of Khajuri

255—Thakur Bakhsh Taalluqdar of Kimarwa

256—Babu Bakhtawar Singh Taalluqdar of Dihla

257—Ganga Bishun Taalluqdar of Mahanaur Khera

258—Saiyud Muhammad Muhsin Taalluqdar of
Alipur Chakai

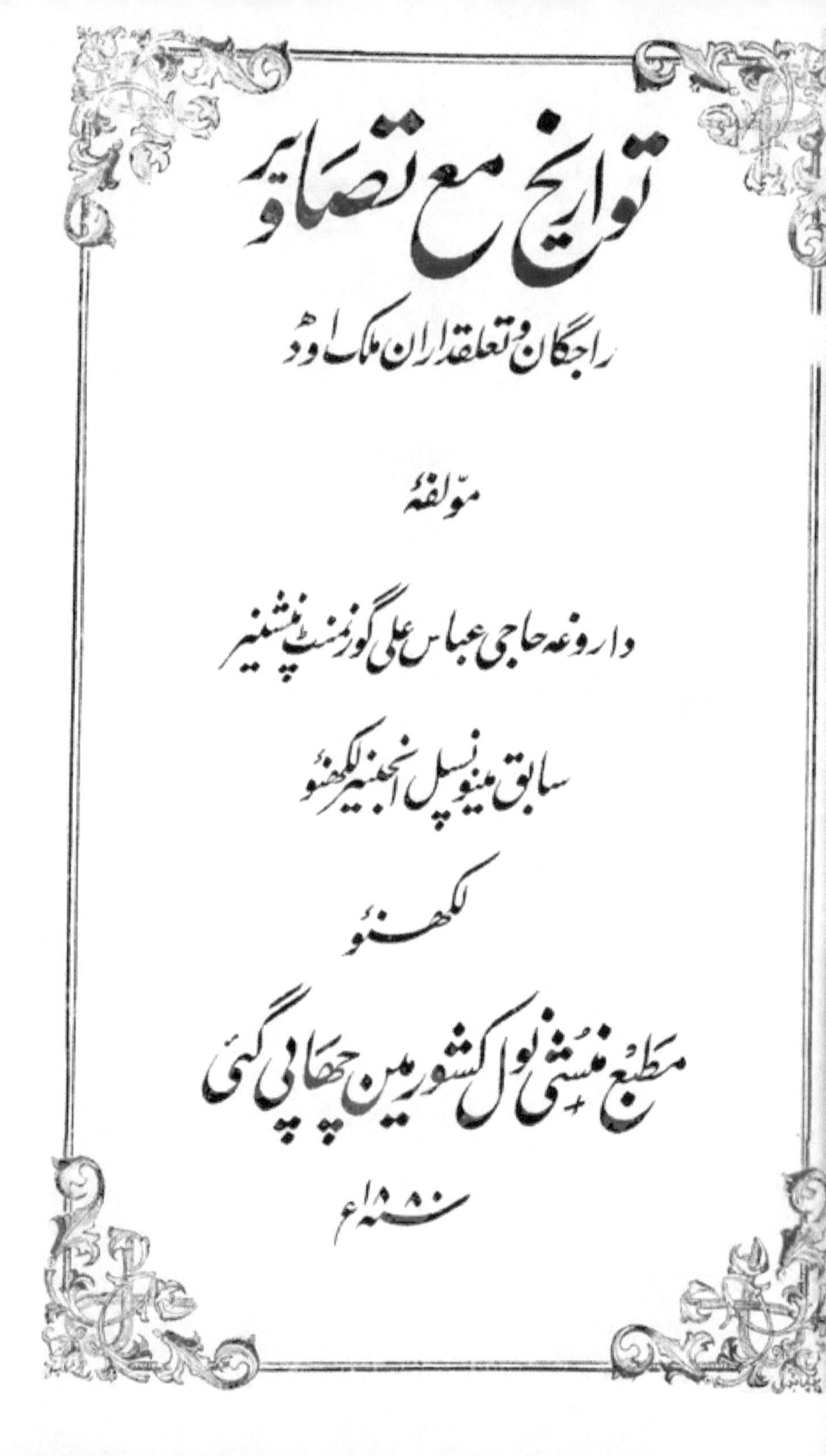

تواریخ مع تصاویر

راجگان و تعلقداران ملک اودھ

مؤلفہ

داروغہ حاجی عباس علی گورنمنٹ پنشنیر

سابق میونسپل انجنیر لکھنؤ

لکھنؤ

مطبع منشی نول کشور میں چھاپی گئی

سنہ ۱۸۸۰ء

بخدمت جناب ہائی لیول سر جارج ابی نیزرالسن کورپریو

کی سی ایس آئی ۔ سی بی ۔ سی آئی ای

لفٹننٹ گورنر ممالک مغربی و شمالی وحیف کمشنر اودھ کہ جنبکی مستحکم و حا

حکمت عملی ہو واسطے استحکام و مدد کر زو وفاداران روشندلان تعلقداران اودھ

حسب اجازت یہ تواریخ ساتھہ عاجزی و زور مانبرداری کہ عباس علی نے

تالیف کی

فہرست مضامین

فہرست تعلقداران ملک اودھ ضلعوار

دایاں حصہ

نام تعلقہ	نام تعلقدار	تعداد	نمبر	ضلع
نمامی پورہ وغیرہ	محمد حسین	۴۵	۲۳۲	لکھنؤ
سمسٹند نبی وغیرہ	راجہ چندر سکسر	۱۱	۴۳	
گوریہ کلان	قطب النسا	۶۶	۳۰۰	
سیلم پورہ وغیرہ	رانی ستارہ النسا	۱۲	۴۲	
راسے پورہ وغیرہ	راجہ مگبہ من سنگہ	۶	۲۳	
منگانورہ وغیرہ	بابو جوبیا تھ سنگہ	۳۲	۱۳۹	
کمشنری خرد	محمد احمد خان	۵۰	۱۸۰	
سہلامکو	محمد نسیم خان	۳۳	۱۳۱	
مہتاب وغیرہ	مرزا جعفر علی خان	۴۵	۲۳۳	
اہیا مسعود وغیرہ	نظیر حسین	۶۳	۱۹۲	
پرسینی وغیرہ	ٹھاکر بلدیو بخش	۳۶	۱۰۹	اناؤ
رام پورہ وغیرہ	کمتا پرشاد سنگہ	۱۸	۵۷	
بونٹھی	کنور مرزا مان سنگہ نیر	//	۵۴	
اوتیج گاؤں	سید محمد علی خان	۴۳	۲۳۰	
//	سید حسین علی خان	//	۰	
کانتہ	نمبت سنگہ	۵۸	۱۴۴	
مورا نواں	مہر پرشاد	۱۸	۵۲	
حفتارہ بابیہ وغیرہ	رام دین	//	//	
تہملمندی	انبیشر پرشاد	//	//	
مرتیا وغیرہ	مادھو پرشاد	۱۵	//	
اماواں	دیبی دیال	//	//	

بایاں حصہ

نام تعلقہ	نام تعلقدار	تعداد	نمبر	ضلع
دیوی می کنڈلایون	شیو دیال	۱۵	۵۲	اناؤ
لوہنگکھان کھیری وغیرہ	رام نراین	//	//	
آنوش و وغیرہ	بال کند	۱۶	//	
بکچھاون می وغیرہ	کالکا پرشاد	//	//	
//	چندکا پرشاد	//	//	
آسرغریا وغیرہ	مومن لال	//	//	
برو اکلان تیلندہ	بینی پرشاد	۱۴	//	
مولسی وغیرہ	مونت سرجو دیال	۳۰	۶۱	
سروسی	فتح بہادر	۴۴	۱۴۲	
محمودآباد وغیرہ	نونہال سنگہ	۲۸	۸۴	
گورا	بلبھدر سنگہ	۴۳	۱۴۰	
حسین آباد	درشن سنگہ	//	//	
ملونہ	دیپال سنگہ	۴۶	۲۳۵	
گالگاہا وغیرہ	سلطان سنگہ	۵۸	۱۴۵	
اودھ	سید رمضان علی	۶۱	۱۸۳	
پربندا	راجہ باٹنکر دیت	۱۳	۴۶	
کریا وغیرہ	ڈیہا شنکر بابجی	۲۶	۲۰۳	
اکبر پور	بینی مادھو بخش	۸۲	۰	
پائن بہار	معیش بخش	۶۴	۱۹۵	
//	ارجن سنگہ	//	//	
بانتھر وغیرہ	بابو رام سہائے	۱۴	۵۲	

دायاں حصہ

نام تعلقہ	نام تعلقدار	نمبر شمار	نمبر	نام تپہ
میان گنج	شیخ شیخ الرحمٰن	۴۳	۲۲۵	اوناؤ
جا جاموئہ	میاں سنگھ	۸۶	۰	
بتیہر	شیخ زادہ تھ سنگھ	۸۴	۰	
بیشہ مجوانی نجیب	شیو گوبند تواری	۸۳	۲۶۱	
گوکل پور ساہنی	گروہ حارتی سنگھ	۶۱	۱۸۵	بارہ بنکی
جہارا لکان پور وغیرہ	شمس العلما	۷۴	۲۳۱	
دین سپاہ	شیخ طالب علی	۷۵	۲۳۴	
//	شیخ کریم بخش	//	//	
سید اپار	شیخ منصب علی	۶۲	۱۸۶	
شہاب پور	شیخ محمد امیر	//	۱۸۹	
//	شیخ غلام عباس	۷۳	//	
کھرگا	صاحب النسا	۱۵	۱۵۲	
جہانگیر آباد وغیرہ	راجہ فرزند علی خان	۵	۱۴	
شترکھہ	قاضی اکرام احمد	۴۴	۱۲۳	
گوشیا	حکیم کریم علی	۴۲	۱۲۸	
اسلام پور	پانڈی بھگوت سنگھ	۵۹	۱۴۴	
بھجان پور	بنیا حسین	۵۱	۱۵۳	
سمیل پور	میر احمد حسین	//	//	
سمرادیوان	ٹھاکر شیو سہائے	۵۰	۱۵۱	
گدیہ وغیرہ	شیخ احمد حسین	۳۶	۱۰۸	
//	شیخ داؤد حسین	//	//	
تبیدی کی گنج وغیرہ	رکمن کنور	۴۷	۲۲۳	
سیدن پور	شیخ غنایت اللہ	۵۹	۱۶۸	

بایاں حصہ

نام تعلقہ	نام تعلقدار	نمبر شمار	نمبر	نام تپہ
سیدن پور	شیخ اکرام علی	۵۹	۱۶۸	بارہ بنکی
//	شیخ انعام اللہ بیگ	۶۰	//	
میلا رائے گنج	شیخ نواب علی خان	۴۲	۱۳۰	
بھگوا امنڈو وغیرہ	کاظم حسین خان	۳۸	۱۱۴	
رام نگر	لالہ بہادر بخت سنگھ	۱۱	۴۳	
محمد پور	دیوان مبادر سنگھ	۶۱	۲۱۹	
لیلونی	ہیر پرشاد	//	۲۱۴	
میر پوریہ	شیخ محمد نصیر الدین	۴۷	۲۳۴	
شیخ پور	شیخ ریاست علی	۶۵	۱۹۹	
پہلوان پور وغیرہ	چودھری تقی حسین	۲۰	۶۳	
سکندر پور	رفیع الزمان خان	//	//	
شیو راج پور	بابو بسیال سنگھ	۱۶	۵۴	
ٹھیبا	راجہ بندر بہادر سنگھ	۶	۲۵	
رام پور بریا بیہ	راؤ ابراہیم علی	۴۰	۱۲۰	
برکی وغیرہ	شیخ محبوب الرحمٰن	۴۳	۱۳۰	
//	شیخ عنایت الحسن	//	//	
//	شیخ عبد الرحمٰن	//	//	
//	شیخ فضل الرحمٰن	۴۴	//	
ترولی	سید رضا حسین	۳۴	۱۴۱	
پوسئی	سید محمد عابد	۹۳	۱۸۸	
امیریہ	شیخ احسان رسول	۶۳	۱۹۱	
لوکرا انسا بی	راجہ بھگوان بخش	۶	۲۱	
رام نگر	ٹھاکر تیجھا آنگل	۴۷	۲۳۸	

نام ضلع	نمبر فہرست	[illegible]	نام تعلقدار	نام تعلقہ
بارہ بنکی	۲۳۹	۷۷	بابو برلال بہادر	رکھیا پور
	۱۹۰	۶۳	غلام قاسم خان	عثمان پور
	۱۹۷	۶۵	بھیا اوتار سنگھ	رانی مئو
	۲۰۱	۶۶	محمد حسین	نیورا
	۲۴۰	۷۷	وزیر علی خان	برولی
	۲۴۱	//	بابو کشن دت	پالی
	۲۴۲	//	دیوان کشن کنور	یعقوب گنج
سیتاپور	۱۸۷	۶۲	سیتا رام کھتری	بھاگو پور وغیرہ
	۱۱۷	۳۹	ٹھاکر دوارکا سنگھ	بسیڈو ڈیہہ وغیرہ
	۱۱۹	//	ٹھاکر مہاراج سنگھ	کانھ مئو وغیرہ
	۱۲۱	۴۸	مرزا احمد علی بیگ	قطب نگر وغیرہ
	۱۱۸	۳۹	ٹھاکر درگا بخش	تیلگانون وغیرہ
	۱۱۳	۳۸	مرزا محمد علی بیگ	اورنگ آباد
	۱۳۶	۴۵	سیٹھ رگھبر دیال	سفر الدین پور وغیرہ
	//	//	سیٹھ سیتا رام	//
	۶۸	۲۲	ٹھاکر تربھون سنگھ	رامپور وغیرہ
	۱۱۶	۳۹	ٹھاکر فضل علی خان	اکبر پور
	۰	۸۳	نواب محمد باقر علی خان	کنوا کھیرہ
	۴۴	۱۲	راجہ شمشیر بہادر	سعادت نگر
	۸۸	۲۹	ٹھاکر شیو بخش سنگھ	کمیسر وغیرہ
	۱۴۳	۴۸	اننت سنگھ	رام پور وغیرہ
	//	//	جگناتھ سنگھ	//
	۱۴۳	۴۸	مردن بخش	//

نام ضلع	نمبر فہرست	[illegible]	نام تعلقدار	نام تعلقہ
سیتاپور	۱۴۳	۴۸	گنگا بخش	رام پور وغیرہ
	۱۱۵	۳۸	ٹھاکر ہری ہر بخش	سرورا
	۱۰	۳	راجہ محمد امیر حسن خان	محمود آباد وغیرہ
	۲۰	۶	راجہ محمد کاظم حسین خان	بینتی پور وغیرہ
	۲۰۹	۶۸	ٹھاکر گنگا بخش	رام کوٹ وغیرہ
	//	//	ٹھاکر کالکا بخش	//
	۰	۸۴	راجہ جگناتھ سنگھ	وزیر نگر
	۱۴۶	۴۹	چودھری رام نرائن	مبارکپور
	۱۳۲	۴۴	میر محمد حسن خان	بارہ وغیرہ
	۱۷۱	۵۷	مرزا عباس بیگ	ڈبرا گانون
	۲۴۳	۷۸	مولوی مظہر علی	میسوا
	۲۴۴	//	ٹھاکر کالکا بخش	سعادت نگر
	۱۴۵	//	ٹھاکر رگھوراج سنگھ	راج پور
ہردوئی	۶	۲	راجہ تلک سنگھ	کٹیاری وغیرہ
	۱۸	۵	راجہ رندھیر سنگھ	بھراون وغیرہ
	۸۶	۲۹	چودھری حشمت حسین	گکرائی وغیرہ
	۸۷	//	ٹھاکر بھارتھ سنگھ	اٹوا وغیرہ
	۱۱۱	۳۷	سید وصیع حیدر	بہوکتیا پور
	۱۱۲	//	چودھری محمد اشرف	آصف پور وغیرہ
	//	//	سید محمد زین العابدین	بہکیاری
	//	//	سید محمد فاضل	درگا گنج
	//	۳۸	سید محمد ابرار	دھوندھر پور
	۱۲۲	۴۰	مولوی فضل رسول	جلال پور وغیرہ

پرگنه	نمبر	تعداد دیهات	نام تعلقدار	نام تعلقه	پرگنه	نمبر	تعداد دیهات	نام تعلقدار	نام تعلقه
برہولی	۱۰۵	۳۵	تھاکر این لال کنور	لوہ رست پور	کهیری	۱۷۱	۱۱	رانی جیشری بختہ نگہ	سلطان پور وغیرہ
	۱۵۴	۵۱	ودیپ سنگه	سوج پور بکران		۳۶	۱۰	راجه بلند رکاب راسنا	کهیری گمدہ نگر
	۱۱۰	۳۶	تھاکر للتا بخش	کهجریہ وغیرہ		۱۶۰	۵۴	رای رامدین سہائ	چیلیا وغیرہ
	۳۹	۱۰	بیگم لال ناتہ	سبعیت نگر		۰	۸۵	الکزندر ڈگلاس ارجنا	امیا وغیرہ
	۹۰	۳۱	وزیر حسین	سرون طاب کانو		ٗٗ	ٗٗ	پولین ابنی آر	لکهم امرا پ وغیرہ
	ٗٗ	ٗٗ	درگا پرشاد	ٗٗ		ٗٗ	ٗٗ	پولین فینی آر	جبر اوجی لہ رابینی
	۲۶۲	۸۰	تھاکر حربخش سنگه	بودایان وغیرہ		ٗٗ	۸۴	ایل ٹی ہی ترسی صاحب	کیمان بنگ مہ وغیرہ
	۱۶۶	۳۲	اقتیاز فاطمه	گویا مئو	نصیرآباد	۳	۱	لال ٹهاک پائی چمن	تمدر وزہ وغیرہ
	۰	ٗٗ	سجاگ کهری	بریم بولا		۶۳	۲۴	بابو ادری سنگه	سیب پور زہ مور را
	۲۴۰	۴۹	صفدر حسین خان	بہنا مئو پور		ٗٗ	ٗٗ	بابو ہند رتیس سنگه	ٗٗ
کهیری	۳۱	۸	رانی حسن جان	سبا و نگر وغیرہ		۲۱۴	۶۰	گیا دین سنگه	موہ پور را
	۱۳۳	۴۴	سید غلام حسین خان	اٹوا پیرہ وغیرہ		ٗٗ	ٗٗ	بهاگ جیت سنگه	ٗٗ
	۲۲۲	۶۲	محمد شیر خان	راجی پور وغیرہ		۶۵	۲۴	سید غفنظر حسین	پیر پور پہ
	۶۲	۲۳	راج ملا سنگه	شاہ پور وغیرہ		۰	۲۵	سید باقر حسین	ٗٗ
	ٗٗ	ٗٗ	گمان سنگه	رانی ورزہ کیت پور		۲۲۴	۶۲	میر شہروت حسین	کتاریہ
	ٗٗ	ٗٗ	گو بہ بخشن سنگه	کجہرا نگلہ ماسن		۶۶	۲۵	بابو اوکار دوت سنگه	سہبی وغیرہ
	ٗٗ	ٗٗ	دلیپ سنگه	سیپور یا جگدم پور پہ		۱۵	۲۹	بابو مندر را دوت	کهجراوت
	۲۳۱	۶۲	فضل حسین	کروٹ دوارہ وغیرہ		۹۴	۳۲	تھاکر بیشن شیر بخش سنگه	سہبی پور
	۲۲۲	۸۳	مرزا نعمت قدر خان	مرزا پور وغیرہ		۹۱	۳۱	تھاکر لانت جبا بہادر	کهجرا وسہہ
	۲۴	۸	راجکند سنگه	اویل وغیرہ		۱۴۵	۳۹	بابر اعظم علی خان	دیوکانون وغیرہ
	۱۵	۱۳	تھاکر بہادر سنگه	مسیہ وغیرہ		۱۰۲	۳۴	کهہبی نراین	بہہ جانہدی پور
	۳۸	۱۰	راجه نربت سنگه	کهمرا وغیرہ					
	۵۵	۱۷	تھاکر نجبت سنگه	علمی نگر وغیرہ					

جدول اول (دائیں)

نام تعلقدار	نام تعلقہ	نمبر شمار	نمبر	ضلع
بابو بشمبر پرکاش سنگھ	چوہریک سلطان پور	۳۵	۱۰۵	نصف آباد بار
بابو مہربت سنگھ	مہر چھاؤنی لہسوا	۳۴	۱۰۳	
شیو دت سنگھ	نیر	۳۵	۱۰۶	
بابو پرتھی پال سنگھ	جگیر اسلام پور	۴۹	۱۸۶	
ملک بدایت علی خاں	پرتاب اکبر پور	۲۸	۸۲	
لالہ اننت رام	رسول پور ماندہ	۴۹	۲۴۸	
راجہ اسکندر پرتاب سنگھ	پیاگ پور	۸	۲۸	نبھاپچ
راجہ دگبنگا بہادر خاں	نانپارہ	۵	۱۶	
راجہ بستیا نین سنگھ	گنگول	۶	۲۴	
پسر گھو ناتھ سنگھ	رہوا	۵	۱۹	
بھیا اودے پرتاپ	بھگنگا وغیرہ	۳۳	۹۷	
ٹھاکر فتح محمد	پچپیرا	۹۶	۳۰۵	
ٹھاکر زبان	انجھا پور وغیرہ	۹۷	۳۰۶	
ٹھاکر این جہان کنور	مصطفی آباد وغیرہ	۳۹	۱۸۲	
شیخ نور پرشاد علی	انبہا پور وغیرہ	۵۹	۱۶۴	
میر ناظر مہدی	علی نگر	۶۰	۱۸۱	
سید باقر حسین	دیرہ آرامی	۶۱	۱۸۴	
نوازش علی خاں	نواب گنج علیا آباد	۳۲	۹۷	
سرداس سنگھ	جہمدان	۶۵	۲۲۰	
سید سردار علی	سسائی سلطان پور وغیرہ	۶۴	۲۲۹	
سردار بجائے لال سنگھ	نبینگا	۶۳	۲۲۸	
سردار جگت پرکاش سنگھ	چہلاری وغیرہ	۸۵	بلا نمبر	
گوبند کنور	[illegible]	۹۶	۱۱	

جدول دوم (بائیں)

نام تعلقدار	نام تعلقہ	نمبر شمار	نمبر	ضلع
راجہ جگت پرشاد سنگھ	بوشتی وغیرہ	۱	۱	گوندہ
مہاراجہ دگبجے سنگھ بہادر	بلرام پور وغیرہ	۱	۲	
شیو دت رام	شنکا چندہ	۹	۳۱	
رانی سلطنت کنور	شنکا پور	۹	۳۸	
رانی جانکی کنور	پرانس پور	۹	۳۳	
راجہ بشیر بہادر سنگھ	دیویلی وغیرہ	۱۳	۱۶	
ٹھاکر جھوبخش سنگھ	ساہ پور وغیرہ	۱۳	۱۲۵	
ٹھاکر گھور سنگھ	درنہانوان وغیرہ	۴۱	۱۸۰	
ٹھاکر گیلا دین کنور	پسکا وغیرہ	۴۵	۱۳۵	
بابو سکھراج سنگھ	انا	۴۵	۱۳۳	
بھیا برتن سنگھ	مجھگاؤں وغیرہ	۷۰	۱۹۱	
پانچ پیر این	اکبر پور وغیرہ	۶۹	۴۵۰	
اودھو نراین سنگھ	بیر	۵۷	۱۶۹	
راجہ متنا بیلیخان	بلا سید پور وغیرہ	۱۲	۴۵	
لال اجلال رام	بیرو	۵۷	۱۶۰	
راجہ بشیو پال سنگھ	مراد شو وغیرہ	۱	۴	رائے بریلی
راجہ سرجوال سنگھ	تلوئی وغیرہ	۴	۱۲	
رانا شنکر بخش سنگھ	سہجا گور کاؤون	۴	۱۵۳	
بابو بشناتھ سنگھ	کاش گدہ	۳۳	۹۳	
رام لسیر بخش	نرشنگ پور وغیرہ	۶	۲۶	
راجہ رام پال سنگھ	گوری سودرہی	۸	۲۶	
راجہ جگدیو سنگھ	اوراجا نورپور وغیرہ	۸	۲۹	
ٹھاکر بشیو پال کنور	سمری وغیرہ	۳۱	۶۴	

راستہ بریلی

سمت راست

بجنس	نمبر شمار	نمبر	نام تعلقدار	نام تعلقہ
راستہ بریلی	۱۵	۳۱	ٹھیکدار این با کنور	سمرپہا
	۶۶	۳۱	ٹھاکر بندی سہائے سنگھ	گوریا بسارن
	۹۶	۳۱	ٹھاکر امان کنور	گوری کسیتی
	۸۱	۲۶	ٹھاکر دیسا بخش	یاہو گلریا
	۹۹	۳۳	ٹھاکر ریسا بخش	نانا پور وغیرہ
	۸	۳	راجہ اودھو سنگھ	امیٹھی
	۱۰۰	۳۴	بابو مہربت سنگھ	سیکاری وغیرہ
	۱۳۴	۳۴	مسماۃ دریا کنور حرپرہ	نیبیلد پور حرپرہ
	؍؍؍	؍؍؍	ٹھاکر احمد قیاس سنگھ	بنی سنگ
	۱۳۹	؍؍؍	ٹھاکر این ذیا تکنور	حمیر پو کہولی
	۱۵۶	۵۲	محمد زمان خان	اماوان
	؍؍؍	؍؍؍	محمد سعید خان	؍؍؍
	؍؍؍	؍؍؍	محمد سلطان خان	؍؍؍
	۱۵۷	۵۳	ذوالفقار خان	بہرامؤ
	؍؍؍	؍؍؍	کریم علی خان	؍؍؍
	؍؍؍	؍؍؍	شہامت علیخان	؍؍؍
	؍؍؍	؍؍؍	اسد علیخان	؍؍؍
	۱۵۸	۵۴	ٹھاکر بھگوان بخش	اودہرہ وغیرہ
	۱۵۹	؍؍؍	مستہان کنور	سیروی وغیرہ
	۱۶۹	۶۰	میر محمد الحسین	بی نوسرپا
	۲۱۰	۶۹	ٹھاکر حکم این سنگھ	ریوگار حرموا
	۲۱۱	؍؍؍	جگ راج کنور	ہر آس پور
	۲۵۱	۸۰	بجبا این انند کنور	اوسا
	۲۵۲	۸۰	تورائے بخش	ملکہا

سمت چپ

بجنس	نمبر شمار	نمبر	نام تعلقدار	نام تعلقہ
راستہ بریلی	۲۵۳	۸۰	سیتا رام	سنگانوں غیرہ
	۲۵۴	؍؍؍	بلبھدر سنگھ	کھجری
	۲۵۵	۸۱	ٹھاکر نخش	کمیسرہ
	۲۵۲	؍؍؍	بابو نخباد بخش	دہلی
	۲۵۶	؍؍؍	گنگا لچھن	منہیار کھیرہ
	۳۰۴	۷۴	فتح مہادر خان	بیوا
	۵۰	۱۳	راج لکھن سنگل سنگ	شاہ مئو وغیرہ
	۲۱۸	۶۱	شیوترن سنگھ	ننہنی
	۱۹۶	۶۵	بابو یار دھو سنگھ	نورالدین پور
	۲۱۲	۶۹	مہیال سنگھ	بابرہ
	۶۶	۲۵	رودر پرتاپ سنگھ	سیولی سیدن
	۱۸۰	۶۰	سبحان احمد	عزیزآباد
	۰	۸۸	شہزادہ شمشیر سنگھ	پیندری گنیش پور بہ
	۵۸	۱۸	کپتان گلاب سنگھ	بھیرا گوبند پور
	؍؍؍	؍؍؍	اودھمار سنگھ	کھوربی
	؍؍؍	۱۹	نذامین سنگھ	بیلا بہلا
	۹۸	۳۳	بابو سپور نجن تکریمی	مشنکر پور
	۱۶۳	۵۸	میر احمد خان	ارگھور پور
	۲۱۶	۶۰	فرزند علیخان	کھشورا
	۰	۸۳	میواۃ پنے ارباب صاحب	لودھواری
	۲۵۸	۸۱	سید محمد محسن	علی پور دکابی
	؍؍؍	۸۲	سید محمد شفیع	؍؍؍
	۲۵۹	؍؍؍	بینی پرشاد	سنگانوں غیرہ

پرگنہ	نمبر	تعداد	نام تعلقدار	نام تعلقہ
سلطانپور	۱۵۵	۵۲	بابو بشیراج سنگھ	سیمپور دبلا وغیرہ
	۳۴۹	۴۹	شیوراج کنور	سلطانپور وغیرہ
	۹	۳	راجہ محمد علی خان	حسن پور وغیرہ
	۱۳	۸	رانی کشن باتھہ کنور	گوڑہ واں وغیرہ
	۱۷۵	۵۲	آمی خانم	غیار پور وغیرہ
	۱۶۳	۵۵	لچھمن پرشاد	بہمریان وغیرہ
	//	//	بسنت ناتھہ سنگھ	//
	۲۰۲	۶۶	ٹھکرائن بایو کنور	گرسہ پور
	۲۷۰	۸۳	شیو شنکر سنگھ	پرتاب پور وغیرہ
	//	//	ارجن سنگھ	//
	۸۲	۲۸	انست پرشاد	نام پور وغیرہ
	//	//	کنبھا اجیت سنگھ	//
	۶	۲	راجہ اور پرتاب ساہی	دمرہ وغیرہ
	۱۴۲	[illegible]	[illegible] بابو سنگھ	شاہ پور گڑھ
	۳۵۰	۱۶	[illegible] خان	معہندہ
	۳۱۳	۶۹	درگاہی جمان ایچ گاؤں وغیرہ	[illegible]
	۳۰	۸	رانی [illegible] ناتھہ کنور	کشاری
	۹۰	۲۴	گنیش کنور	جامو
	۱۷۴	۵۵	سری پال سنگھ	بردلیا
	۲۰۴	۶۴	[illegible] سنگھ	سہجورن ساہ پیا [illegible]
	۱۰۴	۳۵	گنیش کنور	رسہی
	۴۹	۲۴	جگنناتھہ سنگھ	سمرتہ پور وغیرہ
	۱۶۲	۵۵	جہانگیر بخش	گنگلو وغیرہ

پرگنہ	نمبر	تعداد	نام تعلقدار	نام تعلقہ
سلطانپور	۹۵	۳۴	بابو الہ داد ساہ	سیمپور دبلا وغیرہ
	۱۶۱	۵۴	بابو بستلا بخش	نانا شیر وغیرہ
	۴۸	۲۴	بابو اولس سنگھ	سیمپور شیو آگا نت
پرتاپ گڑھ	۵	۲	راجہ بھون سنگھ	کالا کا نگر
	//	//	رام پال سنگھ	رام پور باروپور
	۱۱	۳	راجہ جوبہادر سنگھ	سہبول پور
	۱۵	۴	رانی دھرماج کنور	برہمنھ وغیرہ
	۳۶	۱۰	راجہ منش نجس سنگھ	کیتھولا
	۴۸	۱۳	راجہ حبیب سنگھ	بمرول وغیرہ
	۵۹	۱۹	راجہ جگموہن سنگھ	رائے پور وغیرہ
	//	//	بیسیر بخش	//
	۷۰	//	رام بہادر پرشاد [illegible] گنج وغیرہ	اودا گنج وغیرہ
	۶۲	۲۰	لال سرجیت سنگھ	بھجاری
	۶۹	۲۲	دیوان الہ [illegible] سنگھ	نبی سیف آباد
	۶۰	//	ٹھکرائن [illegible] کنور	[illegible]
	۶۱	//	ٹھکرائن میاکی کنور	میراسی وغیرہ
	۶۸	۱۵	سیتلا بخش	مدہو پور
	//	۲۶	لال مبارک سنگھ	//
	//	//	کالکا نتھ سنگھ	//
	//	//	اودتا نرائن	//
	//	//	کمیش نجرس سنگھ	//
	//	۲۶	جوبا نرائن سنگھ	//
	۸۹	۳۰	ٹھکرائن جہان ناتھہ کنور	رکن راجپوت

نام تعلقہ	نام تعلقدار	شمار	نمبر شمار		نام تعلقہ	نام تعلقدار	شمار	نمبر شمار	نمبر
جمیس پور	بابو جگن ناتھ سہادت سنگھ	۲۱	۱۸۳		کندرجہبیت	چھتر بال سنگھ	۳	۱۹	نیتاپ کٹرہ
سوجا کھر	بابو بلبیر سنگھ	۲۸۳	۱۹۳		//	سورج بال سنگھ	///	///	
اسمان پیر	امید سنگھ	//	۱۹۸		//	خیدر بال سنگھ	///	///	
درتعہ پور	ٹھاکر این سنگھ ناکینور دہہ	۶۸	۳۰۸		راہ مدنی حصہ	ووان بہادر بال سنگھ	۳۱	۹۲	
//	کھمگ کنور	///	///		اودنیا ڈہیمہ	ہر منگل سنگھ	۴۱	۱۲۶	
الوامرہ پور	بابو سرجیون سنگھ	۴۰	۲۱۵		دریا پور	بھگاوت سنگھ	///	۱۲۷	
اتہاہ گانون	دیگجے سنگھ	۴۱	۲۲۰		//	جگموہن سنگھ	۴۲	///	
اعرار	میہاں سنگھ	۴۲	۲۲۳		//	نبی بخش بخش	///	///	
زربوہ وغیرہ	راجہ چھتیال سنگھ	۹	۳۵		//	ازتحہ سنگھ	///	///	
دہنگلدہ	سیتلا بخش سنگھ	۳۸۳	۱۰۱		نبیا نوان	بابو مہیشیر نتھ سنگھ	۵۰	۱۴۹	
//	شنکر بخش	///	///		شیخ پور دوبہ اس	سرجیت سنگھ	///	۱۵۰	
راج پور	سیوا امبر سنگھ	۴۳	۲۲۲		دورمی پور	بابو نربہان بخش	۵۱	۱۶۴	
امری	راجہ جگت بہادر	۱۱	۸۴		پرتھی گنج	بابو پردت سنگھ	۵۷	۱۶۸	

ديباچہ

ان اوراق کے مولف نے دو غرض سے اس رسالہ کو تالیف کیا ہے ۔ ایک یہ کہ ہر ایک تعلقہ دار اودھ کے تاریخی حال اور اپنے آبا و اجداد کی مفصل کیفیت معلوم ہو ۔ دوسرے یہ کہ گزشتہ زمانے کے وہ مختلف انقلابات جو اس صوبے میں موجودہ ترقی کے باعث ہوئے اور جنکے سبب خود تعلقہ داروں نے موجودہ مرتبہ و عزت اس ملک میں حاصل کی ۔ لہذا اس رسالے کو دو حصوں میں تقسیم کیا ۔ ایک میں عام طور پر تاریخ اودھ درج ہے ۔ دوسرے میں خاص معزز مالکان اراضی یعنے تعلقہ داروں کا ذکر خیر ہے ۔ تعلقہ داروں کے خاندانی حالات سے اس صوبہ کی تاریخ سلسلہ کا ملانا محال تھا ۔ کل تعلقہ داروں نے ایک ہی طور پر یہ عزت نہیں حاصل کی بلکہ سب کے حالات میں اختلاف ہے ۔ اونہیں سے اکثر تعلقہ داروں کے آبا و اجداد ہندوستان کے اور حصوں سے آئے اکثروں نے یہ تعلقے خریدے ۔ یا اس جلدی میں پائے کہ غدر کے دنوں میں انہوں نے خیر خواہی کی تھی ۔ ہیئت مجموعی، ہم کہہ سکتے ہیں کہ ان اودھ میں لوگوں کی نسل سے ہیں وہ ایسے کوئی رئیس یا والی ملک نہ تھے جہاں کہ ذکر اس ملک کی تاریخ سلف میں ہوا ہو جن سے پایا جاوے کہ وہ طرحے مرتب کے لوگ تھے ۔ اسی سبب سے مناسب معلوم ہوا کہ صوبے کا حال اور مالکان اراضی کا ذکر علیحدہ علیحدہ قلمبند کیا جاوے اور اس رسالے کے دو مختلف حصوں میں دونوں کا پورا تذکرہ ہو ۔

مناسب ہے کہ جو فوٹو گراف اس کتاب میں شامل ہیں اور کی نسبت اس مقام پر اختصار کے ساتھ صرف اتنا
عرض کیا جائے کہ بہت وقت اور محنت اور روپیہ صرف کر کے اس صوبے کے ہر ایک تعلقہ دار کی تصویر اتاری گئی
اور ان فوٹو گراف کی تصویروں پر کسی قسم کی تصویروں کو لحاظ مناسبت ہیئت اصلی ترجیح بنین وہی گئی
نے ان ڈاکش فوٹو گرافون کو اس درجہ سے شامل کیا کہ اولاً جن صاحبوں کا اس کتاب میں ذکر ہے وہ نے غرا
واحباب اسکی قدر کر سینگے ۔ زمانہ آئندہ میں اونکے اٹکے والے اپنے ان بزرگوں کی دیکھکر طفیل میں انھوں نے دولت
اور مرتبت حاصل کی ۔ صاف تصویریں دیکھکر خوش ہوینگے ۔ آمین املا تشک بنین کہ اس قسم کی تصویروں سے
صرف خوشی ہی بنین حاصل ہوتی بلکہ اپنے اولادکو اپنے بزرگوں کے چال چلن کے حالات دریافت کرنے کا بھی اچھا
موقع ملتا ہے ۔

یہ مقدمہ لکھکر اب ہم بہت اختصار کے ساتھ اودھ کی تاریخ زبان پاستان معرض بیان میں لائینگے ۔ اور اسکے بعد
زمانہ گذشتہ سے علمداری برٹش تک سابقہ دربار شاہون نے حکمرانی کی انکاحال مختصر طور پر درج کرینگے ۔ پھر تفصیل
ملک اودھ اور غدر اور ان واقعات کو بیان کرینگے جنکے سبب سے ملک کی حالت موجودہ پیدا ہوئی ۔

باب اول

اودھ کی تاریخ قدیم

زمانِ پاستان میں یعنی ذی عنائی ہزار برس کا عرصہ ہوا ملک اودھ کوشالا کے نام سے مشہور تھا ۔ اور جو دھ چیلا اسکا دارالسلطنت تھا ۔ تعجب کا مقام ہے کہ اس کوشالا اور کوتھم کا مخرج قریب قریب ایک ہے ۔ کوتھم مشہور و معروف شہر قنوج کا پُرانا نام ہے ۔ اسمیں اصلا شک نہیں کہ قنوج کے حکمرانوں کا اگلے زمانے میں صوبہ اودھ میں بڑا رعب تھا ۔ لیکن یورپ کے السنہ میں حکمرانان قنوج اور اقوام کا اسقدر کم حال ترجمہ ہوا ہے کہ اس ملک کی پرانی تاریخ سے ہمیں چنداں واقفیت نہیں ۔

اسمیں شبہ نہیں کہ اودھ میں کوئی ایسی تاریخ نہیں ہے جس سے صوبہ اودھ کا اور صوبون سے علیحدہ ہو نیکی حالت میں کچھ حال معلوم ہو سکے ۔ شہر اودھ جسکو اودھیا کہتے ہیں بڑا پُرانا مقام ہے ۔ راجمندر کی نسبت جو باتیں مشہور ہیں انسے یقدر پایا جاتا ہے کہ کون کون قوم وقتاً فوقتاً اس حصہ ملک پر قابض تھی ۔ ظاہرا معلوم ہوتا ہے کہ قوم آریا بہت عرصہ دراز سے قابض تھی اور اسکے قبل قوم بھار کا قبضہ تھا ۔ لیکن بھار کی قوم کا حال بہت ہی کم معلوم ہے ۔ صرف اسقدر معلوم ہے کہ وہ لوگ شایستہ تھے ۔ اور چودہ صدی کے اوائل میں سلمانون سے انگو نکال دیا تھا ۔ انکا دارالسلطنت سلطانپور تھا ۔ جب علاءالدین سلطان دہلی نے یا شاید انکے کسی جنرل سنے اسپر قبضہ کیا تب سلطانپور نام رکھا ۔ بشیر کمپہ اور نام تھا ۔

اُس زمانے میں پاسیر بھی ایک بڑی قوم تھی جسمیں سے بہت سے خاندان اب بھی اودھ میں بودوباش کرتے ہیں ۔ انکا بائی پہشیہ ڈکیتی ہے ۔ لوگ کہتے ہیں کہ جب کبھی ملک میں بدنظمی ہوئی تو بلاتنخواہ فوکری کر ایسے وہ آمادہ ہوگئے ۔ اس طمع سے کہ لوٹ مار سے فائدہ کثیر اٹھائیں گے ۔ اِنہین سے اکثرون کو لوگ راجپوت کہنے لگے ۔ خاصکر اسوجہ سے کہ انکے پاس دولت زیادہ ہے ۔ اور انکی لڑکیان اچھی اچھی عالیشان اذان لبیب بیا ۔ لیگئے ان راجپوتون میں قوم کا غرور اسدرجہ تھا کہ چھے گھر میں شادی نہ ملنے کے خوف سے اکثر آدمی دختر کشی کے مرتکب ہوستے تھے ۔ ابھی تھوڑا ہی زمانہ ہوا کہ اودھ اسکے لیے اسقدر بدنام تھا کہ شاید کوئی اور ملک اتنا بدنام نہ ہو ۔

نشاہ عرب سے عہد سعادت علیخان تک ہمیں صوبہ اودھ کا حال قریب قریب کچھ بھی نہیں معلوم ہم ان صرف اسقدر جاتے ہیں کہ محمود غزنوی جو مشہور سردار تھے شنہ عرب میں قنوج کو فتح کیا تھا ۔ شنہ لاہ میں سابق شہنشاہ دہلی قطب الدین ایبک کے ایک جنرل نے قریب قریب کل اودھ کو فتح کر لیا تھا ۔ شنہ لاہ میں بابر بشکر لیکر آیا اور اپنے کل شمیون کو اسی صوبے سے نکال دیا ۔ لیکن افغان سردار بابر نے سنے آخرکار اس ملک میں حملہ داری قائم کر لیا اور لکمہ فتح کر لیا ۔ جب بابر نے وفات پائی بابر نے کوشش کی کہ اودھ

میں غدر کرادیئے۔ شہزادہ ہمایوں نے فوراً غدر فرو کردیا فتنہ عمیں جو نیوپور اور دواب پر قبضہ کر لیا اور اودھ زیر نگیں ہوگیا۔

اس وقت سے اس وقت تک جبکہ سعادت علیخان نے اس صوبے کی گورنمنٹ لی کوئی مشہور تاریخی بات قابل یقین۔

باب دوم

نواب سعادت خان برہان الملک جنگ بہادر

وزیر ممالک

یہ رئیس زادہ مرزا نعیم سید شمس الدین نیشاپوری حسینی موسوی کا لڑکا تھا۔ اسکا باپ مرزا کی نظم کی نسل سے تھا شیعہ عمیں اسکا باپ بنگال گیا اور اپنے ہمراہ اسکے ایک دوسرے لڑکے میر محمد باقر کو لایا۔ دونوں عظیم آباد میں جا کر لگے اور شجاع الدولہ سابق ناظم بنگال کے زیر حفاظت رہے۔ اسکے بعد نیشاپوری میں میر محمد امین (یہ نام نواب سعادت خان کا وقت ولادت رکھا گیا تھا) بھی عظیم آباد کی طرف روانہ ہوئے کہ اپنے باپ کو دیکھیں مگر آنکے باپ نے انکے داخل ہونیکے قبل ہی وفات پائی۔ بعد وفات والد اپنے بھائی کو لیکر وہ شاہجہان آباد گئے اور یہاں بھی اس سے کارنمایاں شروع ہوے۔ مشہور ہے کہ وہ بہادر اور جری آدمی تھا۔ سید عبداللہ خان قطب الملک نے مہربانی سے اسکو مدد دی۔ اور اپنی ذاتی سرگرمی اور لیاقت سے وہ چھوٹے چھوٹے عہدوں سے نیشاپور میں مقابات ہندستان ودکھن کا صوبہ دار مقرر ہوا اور آخر کار محمد شاہ نے اسکو سعادت خان برہان الملک کا خطاب دیا۔ پہلے وہ اہل تشیعہ کے سرخہ تھے مگر آخر میں سنیوں کی طرف ہو کر اہل تشیعہ کے قتل میں شریک ہوئے۔

اس زمانے میں سید وں کی شہنشاہ ہون کے دربار میں بڑی بڑی منزلتیں تھی۔ پس پرانے ارکین سلطنت آنکے دشمن تھے۔ خصوصاً نظام الملک محمد امیر خان اور اعتماد الملک۔ یہ ارادہ سمجھتے تھے کہ اگر سید عبداللہ خان اور سید حسین علی استقدر بڑھ نیگے تو وایرانیوں اور ورانیوں کو پھر کوئی نہ پوچھیگا۔ اعتماد الملک تاک میں تھے کہ اگر سید سینی علی کو کہیں علاحدہ پا جائیں تو قتل کر دالیں مگر اس قتل سکے لیے آنکو کوئی معتبر دوست نہیں ملتا تھا۔ آخر کار سعادت خان اور میر حیدر خان کاشغری نے کہا کہ ہم دونوں قاتل ہونا چاہتے ہیں جبکے نام جیچی نکلے۔ جیچی میر حیدر خان کے نام نکلی اور انصون نے سید کو قتل کر دالا۔ ۳۰ نومبر ۱۷۲ء مطابق ۱۱۳۵ہجری محمد شاہ کی فوج نے عبداللہ خان کو شکست دی اور اس فتح کی خوشی میں خطاب بہادر جنگ منجلہ اور خطابوں سکے سعادت خان سکے نام کے ساتھہ بخشا یا گیا اور صوبہ دار آگرہ مقرر کیے گئے۔ سید وں کا ولی دوست راجہ رجپت سنگھہ گورنر گجرات واجہ تھا اس لیے اور شہنشاہ وقت میں جنگ چھڑ گئی سعادت خان بلواے گئے کہ فوج کی کمان کرین خوب کوشش ہوئی کہ جنگ ایسی طرح سے ہو۔ لیکن باہمی اختلاف راے کے سبب سے کوئی اور تیاری نہوی۔

کچھ عرصے کے بعد سعادت خان نے اپنی صوبہ داری آگرہ کے علاوہ اودھ کی صوبہ داری بھی لی اور اودھ
میں آگر چار جریا ایک وقت سے اور دہ ایک جدا گانہ صوبہ قائم ہوا تو اس وقت ایک حادثہ ایسا ہوا کہ سعادت خان
شاید اپنی رائے بدل دے۔ جب وہ آگرے سے چلے کہ اودھ میں آگر بہان کے امور دیکھیں اور صوبہ داری کو کسی
تو اپنی جگہ پر پرانے نائب کنٹھ کو بطور نائب مقرر کر آئے۔ اسکو ایک جاٹ نے گولی سے مار ڈالا۔ جبکہ وہ سوار
ہوکر کہیں جا رہا تھا۔ سعادت خان کو اس پر اسدرجہ غصہ آیا کہ انہوں نے سنتے ہی فوراً آگرے سے اپنے استینے یعنی
نائب کے قتل کا عوض لینے۔ لیکن اودھ کی خوش نصیبی سے آنگورا جہ سنگھ سے سوائی دستیاب ہوگئے۔ یہ جانب
کے جانی دشمن تھے۔ آنکو اپنا نائب مقرر کر دیا تاکہ جاٹون سے بدلہ بھی لیں اور انتظام بھی اچھا کریں۔ یہ سعادت خان
اپنے عہدہ پر بدستور رہ گئی۔ لیکن بہت دن تک وہ صوبہ دار اودھ نہین رہے تھے کہ مصیبت نے اپنی
مہیب صورت دکھائی۔ مرہٹہ سردار باجو راؤ اس زمانے میں دہلی کی طرف اپنے مقبوضات اور اپنی طاقت
بدریج بڑھاتا جا تا تھا۔ ان جگڑون میں ملہر راؤ اسکا سپہ سالار مقامات سید آباد وجلیہ سہتک بڑھ آیا۔ اور لوٹ
شروع کی۔ اس وقت سعادت خان دورہ کرتا تھا اور لشکر بھی اسکے ساتھ تھا۔ جب اسنے یہ خبر سنی تو قصد کیا
کہ اس شہزادہ سے کورو سکے۔ بڑی سخت جنگ ہوئی اور نتیجہ یہ ہوا کہ مرہٹہ شکست پاکر ملک سے منتشر ہوگئے
اسکا اثر اسقدر پڑا اور زیادہ ہوا کہ کل تمام دکن کی طرف فوراً بھاگا دیے گئے۔ جب باجی راؤ نے اپنے لشکر
منتشر ہو نیکا حال سنا تو انہوں نے بڑی سی تیاری کی کہ شاہ دہلی سے لڑیں۔ سعادت خان نے خبر پائی کہ
باجی راؤ کی فوج غالباً دہول پور میں داخل ہوگئی۔ وہ ان فوراً چلا گیا کہ جنگ کرے۔ مگر مان نہ باجی راؤ
تھے نہ انکا لشکر۔ اسکے بعد انہوں نے تیاری کی کہ چیل عبور کرکے غنیم کے اس حصہ ملک میں لڑین
تیاری کر بھی رہے تھے کہ انہوں نے خان دوران خان کو ضرور حکم دیا کہ جبتک ہم آندین تب تک کوئی کارروائی
نہ کرو۔ ہمارا اور تمہارا الشکر ملکر حملہ آور ہوگا۔ خان دوران خان سکے آتنے اور دعوت وغیرہ میں کچھ توقف ہوا
لہذا باجی راؤ دبل کو چ کرتا ہوا مقام کا لکاتک جو دہلی سے متصل ہے آگیا اور کسی سے اسکو نہ روکا۔ کچھ عرصہ
کے بعد سعادت خان دہلی میں داخل ہوا اور باجی راؤ دکن واپس گیا۔

جب نادر شاہ اور محمد شاہ کی لڑائی پانی پت کے میدانوں میں تھی سعادت خان لشکر لیکر میدان میں آگیا۔
اسکے پاس تو بہانہ نہایت عمدہ تھا جس سے لوگ از بس خائف ہوسے اور عش عش کرنے لگے۔ لیکن
فوج میں کھٹ پٹ ہوگئی نادر کی فوج سعادت خان کے لشکر سے ملکر رہی نہایں پسندکرتی تھی نتیجہ یہ
سبب سے آپسمیں مقابلہ ہوگیا۔ چند روز کے بعد نادر شاہ اور سعادت خان میں دوستی ہوگئی اور سعادت خان
کی وفات تک نادر شاہ اسکا ثناخوان رہا۔ اوکرور روپیہ دیکر سعادت خان نے عہدہ وزارت دہلی کا جبکہ وہ بہت

شایق تھا یا یہ کہ مگر اس آرزو کے برآنے سے اسکا نقصان ہوا اور اسنے ظلم و تعدی پر کمر باندھی۔ نادر شاہ کو جو اسنے اصلاح فضول دی اس سے نادر نے دہلی کو غارت کر دیا اور سخت بدنام ہوا۔ شاہی خزانہ اور جواہرات سے لے لیے گئے اور جس شخص نے اپنا رویہ چھپایا وہ بڑی بیرحمی سے سزایاب ہوا۔ سعادت خان اسمیں نہ شریک تھے مگر ایک پھوڑا اپنے پھپھے پر نکلا جب اس سے وہ مر گئے۔ اور بعض کی رائے ہے کہ زہر کھایا یا بعض کہتے ہیں کہ نادر اول ہی اسکے دشمن تھے۔ انھوں نے ظلم کا عوض لیا اس طرح پر سعادت خان مرے جو اس نے عہد سے سے اپنی لیاقت اور جوانمردی کے سبب سے اد و کے بانی ہوے۔ انکی جرات ضرب المثل ہے اور فنون جنگ میں لیاقت تام حاصل تھی۔ اسکے ہند و غنیم تک کہتے ہیں کہ بگوبت سنگ کو اسنے بڑی جوانمردی سے قتل کیا۔ اور اسکے لشکر نے ایک بار شکست کھا کر بھی اپنی سفید دڑھی والے سردار کی سرکردگی میں آخر کو فتح حاصل کی لی اور دو میں سعادت خان کا جانشین ابوالمنصور خان عہدا۔ جو صفدر جنگ کے نام سے تاریخ میں مشہور ہیں۔

باب سوم
ابوالمنصور خان صفدر جنگ

صفدر جنگ برہان الملک کا بھانجا اور داماد تھا۔ اس سے پیشتر کا اسکا حال معلوم نہیں ہو سکتا۔ جب نادر شاہ بادل سرہند میں محمد شاہ سے لڑنے آیا ہے۔ تو میرزا احمد کے ہمراہ صفدر جنگ بھی گئے تھے اور وہ ان اس شاہزادہ کے ساتھہ بڑے سے کارنامے اپنے توپ خانہ سے دکھانے تھے اس کے سبب سے شاہ سے شاہ ابدالی کو تین دفعہ شکست ہوئی تھی۔ جب محمد شاہ کا انتقال ہوا تو یہ شاہزادہ راہ میں تھا۔ وہ اپنے باپ کا جانشین ہوا۔ جب وہ خود بادشاہ ہوا۔ تو اس نے صفدر جنگ کو منصب وزارت عطا کیا اور پھر یہ منصب اس خاندان کا لقب ہی ہو گیا وزیر مقرر ہونے کے بعد صفدر جنگ اپنے افعال سے ایک مصیبت میں پھنس گیا اس زمانہ میں یہ باتیں بہت ہوتی تھیں۔ جب محمد خان بنگش وال روہیلکنڈ مر گیا تو اسنے قائم خان پسر محمد خان بنگش وال فرخ آباد کو لکھا کہ اسکے بیٹھنے تخت پر نہ بیٹھنے پائیں قائم خان جب ارشاد اور ملک کی طمع میں اگر سعدالہ خان پسر علی محمد خان لشکر چڑھا کر لے گیا۔ اور اسکو مرادیوں کے قلعہ میں جا کر گھیر لیا۔ ہر چند اس سنے عاجزی کی اس سے ایک نیتنی اگر کو مراٹ کیا تباہ ہو اندر سے لشکر لیکر نکلا اور اس نے قائم خان کو شکست دے دی۔ اس کی جان بھی لی۔ جب یہ واقعہ وقوع میں آیا تو صفدر جنگ سنے فرخ آباد میں اگر قائم خان اسکے سارے ملک پر قبضہ کر لیا۔ فقط فرخ آباد اور چند مواضعات اسکے مان اور بیوی کی سب کچھ ضبط کر لیا۔ نول رائے اپنے نائب کو جو ملک اور دو میں تھا یہ سارا ملک لیا ہوا سپرد کر دیا۔ اس نائب نے قنوج کو اپنا صدر مقام بنایا۔ قائم خان کا بھائی احمد خان صفدر جنگ کی خدمت میں رہتا تھا۔ جب اس سنے یوں دیکھا کہ بھائی اور باپ کا ملک چھین گیا تو اس نے اپنی

وزیر کی رفاقت چھوڑ دی اور رجب میں عین نول رائے پر لشکر کشی کی اور اسکو مار ڈالا۔ جب یہ سانحہ پیش آیا تو یار علی خاں نے صفدر جنگ سے نئے سرے سے پٹھانوں سے لڑنا شروع کیا اور ایسی شکست پائی اور زخمی ہوا۔ یہ شکست پا کر جو دلی میں گیا تو وزارت میں خلل پڑا مگر اس کارواں کو رشوت دے کر پھر وزارت کی بنیاد پختہ کر لی۔ احمد خاں نے اپنے ان فتوح کے بعد اودھ اور الہ آباد پر ہاتھ صاف کیا۔ جب صفدر جنگ نے روہیلوں سے مقابلہ کیا لیکن اٹھائیں تو اس نے اپنی بدنامی کے دھبہ کو اس طرح دعویٰ کیا کہ وہ اور روہیلے گیا دینے اس سے مرہٹوں کو اپنی امداد پر مستعد کیا اور انگلی اعانت سے جنوری میں حسین پور پر لڑائی ہوئی۔ دس بارہ ہزار افغان مارے گئے اور اس فتح سے سرحد کوئل اور جالیسر سے لیکر کوہ ہمالیہ کے سب پہاڑیوں تک مرہٹوں کا قبضہ ہو گیا۔

جب افغان ان مرہٹوں اور صفدر جنگ کے ہاتھ سے تنگ آنے تب حالت نومیدی میں ان سے صلح کر لی۔ اسکے بعد شہنشاہ سے کبھی بنی کبھی بگڑی۔ پہلے تو باہم ملاقاتیں اور قول و قرار ہوے اس نے منہ پھیر کے خواجہ سرا کی دعوت کر کے اسکو قتل کیا۔ شہنشاہ اس سے ناراض ہو گئے آخر کار صفدر جنگ کو یہ حکم ہوا کہ اودھ اور الہ آباد چلا جاؤ ولیکن اس نے پس و پیش کیا اودھ اور عر بچہ تیار ہوا آخر کار سو چکا جا تا ہو تو ظلم سہوں گا بلکہ موت نصیب ہوگی۔ لہٰذا اُن لی کہ مقابلہ کر دون جن جن سرداروں کو بلانا تھا بلایا اور لڑائی شروع ہوگئی اس میں ایران اور توران کا پرانا جھگڑا شیعوں اور سنیوں کی عداوت کا شروع کا ہوا۔ فوج کی خود کمان کی اور روہیلہ کے پاس پیغام بھیجا کہ شہنشاہ سے لڑ جاؤ اور صفدر جنگ کے لشکر میں پیغام بھیجا کہ نیکی جنبہ کو نتیجہ یہ ہوا کہ کل پٹھان شہنشاہ کی طرف ہو گئے۔ یہ کہنا تھا کہ اول لشکر افغانوں کا اس سے ساتھ ہو گیا۔ غازی الدین خاں نے ہو لکر کو اپنی اعانت کے لیے بلایا۔ انھوں نے اپنے ہم مذہب بلایا اور پرانے دوست صفدر جنگ پر حملہ کرنے میں تامل کیا۔ غرض جو ق جوق جو چہ مہینے تک ہزار خم ہری کڑائی توپ بندوق دارالخلافتہ کے اندر باہر ہوتی رہی۔ آخر کار صلح ہوگئی اور صفدر جنگ نے اس بات پر قناعت کی کہ اودھ اور الہ آباد کی صوبہ داری پر چلا جائے جمادی الاول میں ہجری پیغام اجل پہونچا۔ شجاع الدولہ اس کا نیا جانشین ہوا۔

باب چہارم

نواب شجاع الدولہ

اس نواب میں باپ دادا کی ساری ساری لیاقتیں موجود تھیں۔ فن سپہ گری سے خاص کر خوب واقف تھا۔ انتظام ملکی سے بھی خوب ماہر تھا۔ احمد شاہ ابدالی نے نجیب الدولہ وزیر شاہ دلی کو اس کے پاس بھیجا کہ بلایا تو وہ دس ہزار سوار لیکر اس پاس آیا۔ مرہٹوں سے بھی خط و کتابت جاری رہی۔ غرض ایک واسطے بیچ کا مرہٹوں اور ابدالیوں کے معاملہ میں بنا رہا۔ احمد شاہ فتحیاب ہوا۔ علی گوہر شہنشاہ ہند ہوا۔ اور

شجاع الدولہ اُن کے وزیر پہونچے ۔ یہ اوائل اشتہ ۱۷۶۳ء کا ذکر ہے ۔ شجاع الدولہ اودھ والا روانہ ہوکر اور اور
مہانسی میں شکست دیکر الہ آباد پہونچے ۔ جب میر قاسم نواب بنگالہ نے انگریزوں سے شکست کھائی اور پینتھ میں گیلا
تب شجاع الدولہ راستہ امانت کا طالب ہوا ۔ شجاع الدولہ اور میر قاسم نواب کی نہایت دلجوئی کی اور رجا کہ پینتھ وہیں
سے مگر اسمیں اُس سے بڑی بری نزک پائی ۔ پھر چند روز تک باہوسے وغیرہ کے سبب سے جنگ نہیں ہوئی ۔ اسکے
بعد انگریزی فوج سے لیسہ کردگی میر منزو اور دو کی سپاہ سے بیٹام کہ بہ مقابلہ کیا اور غنیم کو بڑی شکست دی ۔
مگر خود بھی نقصان اُٹھایا ۔ اس شکست کے بعد شجاع الدولہ نے کوشش کی کہ صلح کر بھیجیے ۔ انگریزوں کو اس پر
اصرار تھا کہ میر قاسم و غیرہ کو انگریزوں کے حوالہ کریں ۔ اور شجاع الدولہ کو اسپہ اصرار تھا کہ میر جعفر کو ۔ لہذا پھر جنگ
شروع ہوئی ۔ بادشاہ نے انگریزوں کی مدد حاصل کرنے کے لیے انگریزوں کی اکثر شرطیں منظور کر لیں ۔
غازی ہی پور ۔ دیدیا ۔ انگریزوں نے سنے وعدہ کیا کہ ہم شجاع الدولہ کا ملک دید بھیگے ۔ انگریزی لشکر سے اور دھ کی طرف
کوچ کیا ۔ شجاع الدولہ تخرہ اور متعلقین کو لیکر بریلی چلا گیا ۔ اسکے بعد صلح کی کوشش پھر فوراً کی گئی ۔ مگر اس بات
پر شجاع الدولہ راضی نہ ہوسکے کہ میر قاسم کو انگریزوں کے حوالہ کر دیں ۔ حالانکہ میر منزو ۔ اور کپتان اسمبلس
کے ذریعہ سے بھی صلح کی بات چیت ہوئی مرتیوں اور افاغنہ سے اُنہوں نے مدد مانگی ۔ افاغنہ نے اقرار
کیا ۔ مگر مدد نہیں دی ۔ مرہٹا افسر مارہ نے کچھ مدد دی ۔ لیکن تاہم برٹش کا مقابلہ شجاع الدولہ نکر سکا ۔
۴ مئی اشتہ ۱۷۶۵ء کو جنرل کارناگ سے انگو مقام کوڑا واقع اودھ میں شکست دی ۔ اور آخر کار عالم پور میں شکست
دی ۔ شجاع الدولہ شکست کھاکر فرخ آباد میں احمد بخش خان کی یہاں روپوش ہوا ۔ اور انگی صلاح سے ان
شہر انتظہ پر عہد نامہ ہوا ۔ ——

۱ ۔ کوڑا اور الہ آباد بادشاہ کو دیا گیا باقی کل ملک شجاع الدولہ کے حوالے کیا گیا ۔

۲ ۔ جنگ کے اخراجات کا ایک حصہ اُس سے لیا گیا ۔

۳ ۔ قلعہ چنار اُن سے لے لیا گیا ۔

۴ ۔ ایسٹ انڈیا کمپنی کا جو اسباب اُسکے ملک کی طرف جاے محصول معاف رہے ۔

۵ ۔ میر قاسم اور اُسکے کسی عزیز کو نوکر نہ رکھیں ۔

۶ ۔ لیونٹ سنکیہ سے ، جو برٹش کے دوستوں میں کسی امرین مواخذہ نکرے ۔

شجاع الدولہ کی طاقت سے برٹش گورنمنٹ کو غبطہ پیدا ہوا کہ اس سے کل قرضہ ادا کر دیا ۔ مال سکے کام
میں بہت لائق تھا ۔ لشکر بہت اچھا جمع کیا ۔ یہاں تک کہ ایک نئے عہد نامہ کے ذریعہ سے برٹش کو مجبور ہوکر
انکی فوج کم کرنے نہیں دی ۔ اُس کے پاس ۳۵ ہزار آدمی تھے سپلے انگو برٹش کی دست اندازی بھی

نہ معلوم ہوئی۔ مگر تین چار سال کے بعد انگریزوں سے اس نے ایسی مدد دی کہ وہ مشکور ہوا۔

سنہ ۱۷۶۲ء میں ایک زبردست لشکر مرہٹہ سنے اس کے پرانے دوست احمد بخش خان والی روہیل کھنڈ پہ حملہ کیا اور اس کا ملک چھین لیا۔ روہیلہ سنے شجاع الدولہ سے یہ مدد مانگی کہ برٹش کی فوج اُنکا جتھہ کرے۔ اگر ایسا ہو تو ہمیں زرِ کثیر دوں۔ مدد دلگیر مرہٹہ بھاگے۔ مگر روہیلہ سنے وعدے کے خلاف کیا۔ شجاع الدولہ سنے اُنکی سزا دی۔ برٹش سنے الٰہ آباد اور کڑا بھی اُسکے حوالے کر دیے۔ فتح روہیل کھنڈ کے بعد وہ روہیلہ سے بری طرح پیش آیا۔ کرنل چیپمین کی رپورٹ سے اسکی تعدی ظاہر ہے۔ برٹش کی مدد بھی اس سنے پائی۔

اور شاہ عالم: بادشاہ کی بھی۔ شجاع الدولہ کے بندران پر پھوڑا نکلا اور ایسا بڑھا کہ جب وہ فیض آباد میں آیا تو سنہ ۱۷۷۵ء میں ۴۸ برس کے سن میں ہزاروں حسرت و ارمان کے ساتھ دارِ آخرت کو سدھار گیا اور اس کی جگہ آصف الدولہ معروف مرزا امانی جانشین ہوا۔

باب پنجم

نواب آصف الدولہ عرف مرزا امانی

آصف الدولہ کا چال چلن اُنکے اسلاف سے ہر طرح مختلف تھا۔ وہ سپاہی آدمی تھے یہ امن اور عیش کے خواہاں وارن ہیسٹنگز نے اسکی بزدلی سے اسکی بزدلی سے بڑا فائدہ اٹھایا یا اس درجہ بزدل تھا کہ جہلہ اور جو کہنا اسکو قبول کر لیا تھا۔ اس زمانے میں ذرہ بھی برٹش کا حوصلہ فتح کم نہ ہوا۔ نواب شجاع الدولہ کے مرتے ہی یہ امر فیصل ہوا کہ شجاع الدولہ کے ذمہ جو روپیہ واجب الادا ہے اُسکو بہت جلد دینے سے وصول کرنا چاہیے اور یہ کہنا چاہیے کہ جو عہد و پیمان اُسکے باپ کے ساتھ سرکار کمپنی کے ٹھہرے تھے وہ سب اُسکے ساتھ قبر میں گئے۔ اور کوئی اُن میں سے اب باقی زندہ نہیں اب جو ہم سے نیا سودا اعداد و اعانت کا معاملہ کرے تو اسکی قیمت از سرِ نو ٹھہرائی جاوے گی۔ پُرانے بھاؤ پر نہیں۔ درجانگی اُن سکے باپ کی وفات کے چھہ مہینے بھی نہیں ہوے تھے کہ آصف الدولہ سنے ایک سندھ پر دستخط کر دی جسکے ذریعہ سے جو نیپور اور بنارس اور غازی پور اور راجہ چیت سنگھ کا علاقہ برٹش کو دیا گیا۔ اور ہر برگذیدہ سپاہ کے خرچ کے واسطے دو لاکھ یا اسی ہزار روپیہ مہینہ دینا پڑ گیا۔ اور الٰہ آباد اور کڑا اسکے اضلاع جو اسکے باپ کے ہاتھ فروخت کیے گئے تھے اسکو عطا ہو سکے۔ اس عہد نامہ کے موافق آصف الدولہ پر سرکار کی بقایا یا بمتہ رہنے لگی۔ اس روپیہ کے لیے اُسنے اپنی ماں اور دادی کو ستانا شروع کیا۔ اسکی ماں کا نام بہو بیگم تھا۔ چھتیس لاکھ روپیہ تو اُن سے جھپٹ لیا۔ اسی لیے بہو بیگم نے سرکار کمپنی سے فریاد کی تو آصف الدولہ اور بہو بیگم کے درمیان سرکار کمپنی سنے اپنی ذمہ داری کر کے عہد نامہ لکھا دیا کہ بیگم صاحبہ آئندہ اپنی جاگیر اور دولت پر بدستور فرین

آصف الدولہ دست اندازی نہیں کرنے پائیگا۔ سپاہ انگریزی اور تعلقات انگریزی بدست نواب مسر کار کمپنی کا بڑا وقت فدا ہوگیا۔ اس نے گورنر جنرل کے روبرو فریاد کی کہ خدا کے واسطے اس خرچ کو میری گردن سے اتارا جاوے میں اسکے تلے دب کر مرا جاتا ہوں اور میں وہ میں تین برس میں میری ہی ساری یو ملک کی آ ۔نی کہا گئے ۔اس سبب سے نواب کا اور وارث پیٹنگٹر صاحب گورنر جنرل کی ملاقات مٹ ۱۸۰۱ع میں جناب گذر حریں موسیٰ اور یہ فیصلہ ہوا کہ سوا سے

اُس بریگیڈ سکے جبکہ خرچ شجاع الدولہ کے زمانہ میں بھی لیا گیا تھا۔اور اس ایک لپٹین کے جو رزیدنٹ کی حفاظت کرے باقی تمام سپاہ کے خرچ نواب کے ذمہ سے ہٹا لیے گئے ۔اور نواب کو یہ اختیار دیا گیا کہ وہ اپنے ملک میں جسکی چاہے جاگیر ضبط کرلے۔ مگر جب جاگیر دار کی سرکار کمپنی دستگیری کرے اسکی نہیں نقل سوا فق محاصل جاگیر نواب مقرر کرے ۔تیسرے یہ شرط ٹھہری کہ نواب وقت مناسب پر فیض اللہ خان کی جاگیر ضبط کرلے اور اسکو پنشن مقرر کردے ۔اب سرکار کو یہ دشواری پیش آئی کہ اگر ۱۸۰۱ع کے عہد نامہ کے موافق ملک اودھ سے سپاہ بلا لیجتی تو ملک میں اندھیر مچ جاتا ۔میدان خالی دیکھ کر اس پاس کے دشمن اور دور یہ بھی پڑوستے خصوص صاحب بیٹھے ہوئے اسی تاک میں بیٹھے ہوئے تھے دو ضرور ملک پر چڑھ آتے اور پامال کرڈالتے

آصف الدولہ نے فیض اللہ خان سے پانچ ہزار سوار اپنی خدمت کے ا لیے مانگے کہ انگریزی سپاہ کو اس وقت اسکے ملک سے فرانسیسوں سے لڑنے کے لیے جانا ضرور تھا ۔غرض جب اس سپاہ کا انصرام فیض اللہ سے نہ ہو سکا تو اسکی جاگیر آصف الدولہ نے ضبط کرنی چاہی ۔مگر سرکار کمپنی نے بیچ میں پڑ کر اس جاگیر کو بچایا اور فیض اللہ خان کی نسل میں یہ جاگیر نسلاً بعد نسل ہوگئی ۔آصف الدولہ کا حال روز بروز بد تر ہوتا جاتا تھا گورنمنٹ انگریزی کا رز موعود قرض سے ادا ہوتا تھا اگر کوئی تیرا نا قرض ادا ہوتا تو نیا قرض لیا جاتا تھا آمد نی ملک سے نہیں ادا ہوتا تھا ۔مٹ ۱۸۰۱ع سے جبکہ عہد نامہ جاری ہوا تھا اسکی وفات ۱۷۹۹ع تک اس بہری پڑتی گئی لارڈ کارن والس نے انیں کچھ مدد وی مگر خرابیاں بالکل دور نہ ہوئیں پھر جان لوز کی آخری کاروائی سے اور بھی زیادہ سختی ہوئی ۔یہ نواب بڑا عیش دوست تھا ۔اسکے عہد میں ایک کا رنمایاں یہ ہوا کہ شہر لکھنؤ میں جو ہندوستان کے نہایت عمدہ شہروں میں سے قائم ہوا ورنہ پہلے لکھنؤ ایک گاوں تھا اسنے عمارت اور پل اور مسجد اور را امام باڑے نبوائے سے یہ نواب بہت بڑا فیاض تھا ۔اسی کی شان میں یہ کہا جاتا تھا کہ جسکو نہ دے مولا۔ اسکو دے آصف الدولہ ۔اسکی بخشش و عطا خط و خطا سے خالی نہ تھی ۔

غریب رعایا سے جبر و ظلم سے لینا ۔یہ وزیر دہلی بھی مقرر ہوا سے اڑوے کی شادی میں بہت روپیہ صرف کیا

باب ششم

نواب مرزا علی عرف وزیر علی خان

مرزا علی نے بہت تھوڑے دن حکومت کی اور خوش نہ رہا مشہور ہوا کہ آصف الدولہ کا بیٹا ہے لہذا
تخت کا وارث ہے۔ اسکی جانشینی پر یہ اعتراض سعادت علی خان نے کیا کہ آصف الدولہ کا کوئی بیٹا نہیں
اور جو یہ بیٹے اسکے مشہور ہیں وہ اسکے نطفے سے نہیں۔ اسلیے میرا استحقاق جانشینی کا ہے۔ یہ جھگڑا چکے
کیوا سلے گورنر جنرل ثالث الخیر نہہرے۔ نواب آصف الدولہ کی ماں اور بیگم کی بھی مرضی تھی کہ وہ تخت نشین
ہو۔ سارے دارالسلطنت کے آدمی اسکے نواب ہونے سے خوش تھے۔ غرض مرزا علی مسند آرائے
سلطنت ہوا۔ اور انگریز وزیر نے۔ اسکی جانشینی کو تسلیم کر لیا۔ اس نوجوان سے بہت دفعان سلطنت
کے مزے نہ اوزرے تھے کہ گورنر جنرل کے پاس اسکے چال چلن کی اور اسکے ناحق جانشینی کی خبریں
پہونچنے لگیں۔ اسلیے گورنر جنرل کو برسر موقع آنے کی ضرورت ہوئی جب گورنر جنرل لکھنؤ گئے تو نواب
کے چھچک نکلی تھی گورنر کو سازش کا خوب موقع ملا تھا۔ سر جان شور ان امور سے بڑی وقت میں تھے
اب ایک قوی شہادت اسپر گذری کہ مرزا علی نواب کا بیٹا نہیں ہے۔ نواب کا بڑا معتمد خواجہ سرا تھا اسی
یہ افسانہ سنایا کہ وزیر علی کی ماں کا خاوند موجود ہے وہ نواب کے یہاں ماماتی۔ اور خاوند کے پاس
وہ آتی جاتی تھی۔ جب وزیر علی اسکے یہاں پیدا ہوا ہے تو اس سے پانچ سو روپیہ کو نواب نے مول لیا
نواب کی عادت تھی کہ وہ حاملہ عورتوں کو مول لیتا تھا۔ اور اسکے جب بچے پیدا ہوتے تھے تو اسکو اپنا
بنایا کرتا تھا۔ اور انکی پرورش اولاد کی طرح کیا کرتا تھا۔ غرض جب سر جان شور کے نزدیک وزیر علی کا
نطفہ ناتحقیق ہونا ثابت ہو گیا تو سعادت علی خان کے نواب بنانے کی تجویز ہوئی۔ مرزا علی کے لیے
دیڑھ لاکھ کی سالانہ پنشن قرار پائی۔ اور وزیر علی بنارس بھیجے گئے مگر وہان چیری صاحب رزیڈنٹ کو مارڈالا
اور کھلا غدر کیا لہذا قید کرکے کلکتہ بھیجا گیا۔ اور وہین مر گیا۔ مرزا علی کے چال چلن کا اور کچھ حال
نہیں معلوم ہوا۔ سوا اسکے کہ بدمزاج تھا۔

<h2 style="text-align:center">باب ہفتم</h2>

نواب سعادت علی خان

جب نواب سعادت علی خان تخت نشین ہوا تو حسب دستور عہدنامہ جدید ان سے ہوا اور برٹش نے
فائدہ اٹھایا عہدنامہ ہوا کہ نواب چھتیس لاکھ روپیہ سالانہ انگریز بزون کو دیا کرے۔ قلعہ آباد حوالہ کرے۔
انگریزی سپاہ اکثر ود ہمین دس ہزار رہا کرے گی۔ مرزا علی کو پنشن دین اور اسکے اعزہ کی بھی خبرگیری کیں
اسکے عوض میں برٹش گورنمنٹ نے وعدہ کیا کہ سعادت علی خان کو دشمنوں کے حملے سے بچائیں گے۔
اور اگر عاملی میں بدنظمی ہوگی تو بلوہ فرو کر دینگے سعادت علی خان ان شرائط پر تخت چھوڑنے کو تھا لارڈ ویلزلی

سنے ایسا ہونے دیا۔ پھر لارڈ ولزلی نے سعادت علی خان کو لکھا کہ نواب کو اس سے اطلاع دو کہ جانباز شاہ
دریائے سندھ پار آگیا ہے وہ ضرور اودھ پر حملہ کر بیگا۔ اور اطلاع دی کہ یہ حملہ آسان ہے کیونکہ رہیلے
سعادت علی خان کے خلاف تھے ۔اور سپاہ کے کارخانوں کے خرابیوں سے نواب خود مقرر تھا۔ ایک
طویل طویل خط کتابت اس باب میں سعادت علی خان اور گورنر جنرل کے درمیان ہوتی رہی جس سے
مدبر نواب کی لیاقت ظاہر ہوتی ہے ۔نواب نے کہا کہ میں تارک دنیا ہوکر حج اور زیارات کو جاتا ہوں
مگر انتظام ملک درست رہے آخر کو عہدنامہ جدیدہ موافق دو باب کا استقرار ملک جس کی آمدنی
ایک لاکھ روپیہ سے زیادہ تھی عوض خرچ سپاہ اور حفاظت ملک دینا پڑا اور اپنی سپاہ کو گھٹانا پڑا۔ اور
عہدنامہ میں یہ بھی داخل ہوا کہ دریائے گنگا اور اودھ دریاؤن میں جو سرحد اودھ میں واقع ہیں انگریزی
مرکب رانی بلا فرماحمت ہوا کرے ۔

۱۰ نومبر ۱۸۰۱ میں عہدنامہ پر دستخط ہوے تھے اس کی وفات تک جو ۱۱ جولائی ۱۸۱۴ کو
ہوئی کوئی قابل ذکر نہیں نواب کے چال چلن کی بابت رائے مختلف ہے ۔یہ نواب ہندوستان میں
بڑا دانشمند اور کفایت شعار مشہور ہے ۔اور بعض کی رائے کہ ظالم تھا رعایا سے سختی و تعدی پیش
آتی تھی یورپین مورخ کہتے ہیں کہ تیرہ برس تک سعادت علی خان نے عاقبت اندیشی اور لیاقت سے
حکومت کی اُن کا انتظام بے نظیر تھا ۔اودھ اس کے وقت میں گلزار سرا پا بہار تھا ۔

باب ہشتم

نواب غازی الدین حیدر

بعد وفات نواب سعادت علی خان اُن کا بڑا بیٹا نواب غازی الدین حیدر تخت سلطنت پر بیٹھا ۔بروقت اس کے
جانشینی سے سرکار کمپنی سے یہ عہدنامہ ہوا کہ جو پہلے نواب سعادت علی خان کے عہد میں عہد نامے لکھے گئے
ہیں اُن کی شرائط پر طرفین سے پوری تعمیل ہوگی ۔الگ عہد خاص کار اسلیے مشہور ہے کہ انگریزوں کو زر خطیر قرض
دیا۔اودھ مختلف صوبہ ہوا اور غازی الدین حیدر اور اس کے جانشین بادشاہ کہلانے لگے ۔لارڈ ولزلی نے
کہ جس نے اودھ آکو ایک کرور روپیہ دولگا ۔مگر انہوں نے کہا مفت نہیں ہم چھے روپیہ سیکڑا سود دینگے ۔

۱۸۱۴ میں لارڈ منیرا کو اور روپیہ کی ضرورت ہوئی کہ جنگ نیپال کے اخراجات کے لیے کانی ہو نواب نے
روپیہ دیا اور اس کے عوض میں ترائی سکے جنگل بابتے اس سے نواب کا فائدہ ہوا بلکہ باغی اور ڈاکوان دین
میں چھپنے لگے اور طرح کا خطر کا بیج ہوا ۔اس قرض اور مدد کانی سکے عوض میں آخر کار سلسلہ میں نواب کو
خطاب بادشاہی دیا گیا اور اس ۔یہ بھی منشا تھا کہ دہلی اور لکھنو کے والیوں میں رنجش ہو جاے ۔

اور سنہ ۱۸۲۵ء میں دو کرور روپیہ اور قرض لیا اسکے سال بھر بعد باپ لاکھ اور لیا اور اسوقت کہا گیا کہ صرف دو سال کے لیے یہ قرض لیتے ہیں ۔ —

اکتوبر سنہ ۱۸۲۷ء میں غازی الدین حیدر نے انتقال کیا ۔ اسنے برٹش کو بہت کچھ روپیہ قرض دیا تھا ۔ یہ شائستہ اور ہر دلعزیز بادشاہ تھا اگر چہ اسکے ارکین خراب نہ ہوتے خصوصاً آغا میر وزیر تو اسکا عہد اور بھی قابل تعریف ہوتا ۔

باب نہم

نصیر الدین حیدر

نصیر الدین حیدر عرف سلیمان جاہ غازی الدین حیدر کے فرزند اکبر تھے ۔ تخت پر جب متمکن ہوے تو کل امور بحسب دلخواہ پاسکے ۔ خزانہ عامرہ پر تھا راہ نوجوان نواب کی دلی خواہش تھی کہ روپیہ کو عمدہ امور میں صرف کریں ۔ انکی پہلی درخواست یہ تھی کہ جو روپیہ غازی الدین حیدر نے قرض دیا اسکا سود اور بارہ لاکھ جو دیے گئے تھے اور اسکا سود انکی بیگیات اور مخدرات خاندان کو بطریق پنشن ملا کرے مگر منظور نہ ہوئی ۔ آغا میر سے کہا کہ جو روپیہ غازی الدین حیدر کے یو قتین لے لیا تھا وہ واپس دو ۔ مگر اسمیں بھی برٹش گورنمنٹ نے اسکی راے سے اتفاق نہ کیا اور جب آغا میر کا پنور کا گئے تو آ اسنے مواخذہ نہ کیا ۔ —

دس برس حکومت کر کے نصیر الدین حیدر نے انتقال کیا پہلے لوگ سمجھتے تھے کہ اسکا حال ایڈ این اچھا ہوگا مگر اسکے برعکس نکلا رزیڈنٹ کسی امر میں صلاح نہیں دیتے تھے ارکین سب انتہا کے کمینے تھے ۔ نواب عیاش ہو سگئے اور جن امور کی اصلاح کا خیال تھا کہ اسکے عہد میں عمل میں آئیگی آنیں اصلاح نہ ہوئی ۔ — وہ دوسرے سعادت علیخان ہوسکتے مگر ان لوگوں نے انکو غارت کر دیا ۔ —

باب دہم

محمد علی شاہ

محمد علی شاہ آسانی تخت نشین ہوے ۔ یہ نصیر الدین حیدر کے چچا اور سعادت علیخان کے بھائی تھی ۔ اہل اسلام کے قواعد سے موافق وہ تخت و تاج کے وارث تھے مگر نواب مرحوم کی بیوہ بادشاہ بیگم نے جھگڑا الگا یا نصیر الدین کے ایک لڑکا تھا منا جان ۔ یہ افضل محل کے بطن سے پیدا ہوے تھے مگر بادشاہ نے انکو عاق کر دیا تھا جب محمد علی شاہ تخت نشین ہوے تو بادشاہ بیگم محل میں گئیں سلح آدمیوں کی جتھا ساتھہ تھی ۔ جا کر منا جان کو تخت پر بٹھا دیا کر نیل نور رزیڈنٹ نے بڑی مستعدی اس معاملے میں کی ۔ — تھوڑی سی سپاہ لیکر منا جان کو گرفتار کر لیا اور چار بجیدر پا ایک سو آدمی اس جھگڑے میں کام آئے ۔ — محمد علی شاہ کے عہد میں کوئی بات قابل تاریخ نہ تھی ۔ اقرار کیا تھا کہ عہد نامہ سابق کے مطابق

کارروائی کردی لگا مگر وعدہ پورا نہ کیا۔ کمپنی نے ان سے ایک اور عہد نامہ کیا۔ جسکی روسے وہ اپنا لشکر معین
قائم رکھ سکتے تھے یورپین آٹھ دو رجٹین سواروں کی اور پانچ رجمنٹ پیادوں کی رکھ سکتے تھے۔ اور اسکے عوض
سالانہ وہ برٹش کو دین۔ اس عہد نامے کو محمد علی شاہ نے نہایت حسرت کے ساتھ منظور کیا۔ یہی عرصہ میں
انتقال کیا۔ وہ عاقبت اندیش آدمی تھا۔ اسکے علاوہ اور کوئی صفت نہ تھی۔ ایسی بری بھی۔

باب یازدہم

امجد علی شاہ

محمد علی شاہ کے بعد اسکا دوسرا بیٹا امجد علی شاہ تخت نشین ہوا۔ انکے عہد میں کوئی اچھی بری بات قابل
تاریخ نہیں ہوئی۔ گو انکی جانشینی کے وقت سے انکی سلطنت اچھی تھی۔ لیکن بد انتظامی کی بڑی ترقی تھی۔
کل صوبے میں ایک قسم کی طوائف الملوکی تھی۔ صرف پانچ برس کی حکومت کے بعد فروری میں انتقال کیا۔ اسکے بعد واجد علی شاہ آخری شاہ اودھ تخت پر بیٹھے۔

باب دوازدہم

واجد علی شاہ

واجد علی شاہ کے عہد میں خاص بات یاد رکھنے کے قابل یہ ہے کہ صوبہ اودھ ضبط ہوگیا۔ انکے انتظام
خراب سے برٹش گورنمنٹ نے مجبور ہوکر ایسا کیا۔ واجد علی شاہ کی نسبت لوگ سکتے ہیں کہ تربیت یافتہ بین لیکن طرز تمدن اور کاروبار ملکی سے محض ناواقف۔ تخت نشینی کے وقت تعلقہ داروں کو بہت زور تھا مگر وہ
انکے زور کو گھٹانے سکے یہاں تک کہ مطالبہ جائز بھی نہ لے سکے۔ وہ یوں ہے کہ ہر تعلقہ دار اپنے تعلقے کا بادشاہ تھا
اپنی حفاظت کے لیے گزہیان اور تلعہ بناتے کیوں اسلے رعایا کو لوٹ لیتا تھا۔ بادشاہ کے خوف کے بغیر جو بن
پایا ہو وہ کیا۔ نہ قانون نہ آئین ان سب امور سے ضبطی کی ضرورت لازم آئی جسکی نسبت یہ بات درج ذیل ہے۔

باب سیزدہم

ضبطی ملک اودھ

لارڈ ڈارہنگ کے عہد سے اودھ جدا کا نہ ہندوستانی صوبہ نہ میں رہا جب واجد علی شاہ تخت پر بیٹھے تب لارڈ ڈارہنگ
ہی گورنر جنرل ہندوستان تھے۔ لارڈ موصوف نے بڑی کوشش کی کہ ترقی کریں۔ خود لکھنؤ جاکر بادشاہ سے
مشورہ کیا انکی بد انتظامیوں کے کل حالات بیان کیے اور کہا کہ اگر اسکا انسداد نہ کیجے گا تو آپکے حق میں برا ہوگا۔
دو برس کے عرصہ میں ضروری امور کی اصلاح ہونی چاہیے یہ وقت دیا جاتا ہے۔ دو برس کے بعد لارڈ ڈلہوزی
گورنر جنرل ہند مقرر ہوکر آئے۔ انہوں نے کرنل سلیمین کو حکم دیا کہ صوبہ اودھ میں دورہ کرے اور بعد ازان

ان حالات کی نسبت رپورٹ کامل بھیجو کہ لارڈ ڈارڈنگ کی رائے کی اصلاح ہوتی یا نہیں۔ کرنل موصوف کی رپورٹ بہت ہی خراب تھی۔ انہوں نے لکھا کہ بادشاہ دیوانہ اور کم طاقت ہے۔ خواجہ سراؤں اور دُھاڑیوں اور نالائق وزرا کے بس میں ہے۔ اور لکھا کہ رعایا سے اودھ کی خواہش یہ ہے کہ برٹش گورنمنٹ دائمی حکومت اودھ اپنے تعلق کرے۔ اور اسکی اشد ضرورت ہے مگر تاہم کرنل سلیمین نے یہ خواہش نہیں ظاہر کی کہ الحاق ہو جائے مگر صرف استقرار چاہا کہ جو ہندوستانی عہدہ دار بدنظمی کے باعث ہیں اُنکی یورپین افسروں کے ذریعہ سے نگرانی کیجائے۔

سنہ ۱۸۵۵ء میں کرنل سلیمین نے علالت کی وجہ سے رخصت لی اور کرنل اُٹرم اُنکے قائم مقام مقرر ہوے۔ کل اُمور کو گورنر نے بدستور پایا۔ صاحب گورنر جنرل نے اِنکو بھی حکم دیا کہ کامل تحقیقات کریکے فوراً اطلاع دو۔ چار مہینے کے بعد انہوں نے بڑی طویل رپورٹ بھیجی۔ اور کل امور جو دیکھے تھے سب لکھے اور افسر اُنکے قبل بھیجے گئے تھے اُنکے کاغذات سے بھی مصالح جمع کیا۔ لکھا کہ کرنل سلیمین کیوقت سے جو اب حالت خراب ہے، سات برس ہوے لارڈ ڈارڈنگ نے جو باتیں لکھیں تھیں اُنکی طرف ذرا توجہ بادشاہ نے نہیں کی سب مجبور ہوکر مجکو اپنی خاص حکمت عملی سے جو ہندوستانی ریاستوں کی نسبت سب خلاف ہوکر لکھنا پڑتا ہے کہ بہت سختی سے اب پیش آنا چاہیے تاکہ پچاس لاکھ رعایا کی جان و مال کی حفاظت ہو۔

اسکے علاوہ کرنل لومبر کونسل گورنر جنرل نے بھی ایسا ہی لکھا۔ یہ اودھ سے خوب واقف تھے کرنل لو نے لکھا دو برس کا اقرار نامہ دورہ ختم ہوگیا۔ مگر مہینہ ور روز اول ہے اب گورنمنٹ کو سختی سے پیش آنا چاہیے۔

یہ کاغذات لارڈ ڈلہوزی نے سب کورٹ آف ڈائرکٹرس کے پاس بھیج دیے اور سنہ ۱۸۵۵ء میں اودھ ملحق ہوگیا کرنل اوٹرم سے تعلق یہ کام کیا گیا فوجی تیاریاں ہوئیں۔ ۳۰ جولائی ۱۸۵۵ء کو وزیر اعظم کو صاف صاف لکھا گیا کہ گورنمنٹ ہند صوبہ اودھ کو ضبط کرنا چاہتی ہے تین دن کی مہلت دیگی کہ اسکے بعد گورنمنٹ اودھ ایسٹ انڈیا کمپنی کے تعلق ہو جائیگی بادشاہ کا خطاب عزت مرتبت اور عظمت بدستور رہیگی اور اپنے محل اور اپنے گھر پر اُنکو کامل اختیار رہیگا۔ تین دن گذرنیکے بعد واجد علی شاہ نے عہد نامہ پر دستخط نہ کیے لہذا کرنل اوٹرم کو تعمیل حکم کرنیکی فروری ۱۸۵۶ء کو اشتہار دیا کہ برٹش گورنمنٹ نے اودھ کو ہمیشہ کے لیے ضبط کر لیا اور یہ باسانی عمل میں آیا۔

کل قسمتوں اور رعایا صلاح کے لیے سول افسر مقرر ہوے ہر صیغہ میں نیا انتظام کیا گیا کرنل اوٹرم ادنیٰ سی بات پر بھی کمال توجہ کرتے تھے بادشاہ کی فضول خرچی اور غلطی سے جن لوگوں کا فائدہ تھا وہ بہت ناخوش ہوے لیکن کرنل اوٹرم کی کارگذاری ہر آئینہ قابل توصیف ہے۔

باب چہاردہم

تاریخ ضبطی سے تاریخ غدر تک کا حال

جب امور پنجاب میں کامیابی حاصل ہوئی انہیں قواعد کے موجب برٹش گورنمنٹ نے اودھ میں بھی انتظام شروع کیا جو ڈوئشل اور فنانشل کمشنر دہلی کشمیر اسٹنٹ واکہ اسٹنٹ کمشنر مقرر ہوئے کرنیل ایڈن کا عہدہ ریذیڈنٹ سے اب چیف کمشنر اودھ ہوا اور چیف گورنر خبرل ہوا کہ بادشاہی عمارتوں پر قبضہ کرلیا گیا پولیس مقرر کیا گیا جیلخانے اور ہسپتال و محصہ تعمیر عدالت فوجداری و دیوانی قائم کی گئی یہ تجویز ہوئی کہ بندوبست زمین لوگوں کے ساتھ کیا جائے جو قابض اراضی ہیں تین تین سال کے لیے یہ کیا گیا کہ قابض اراضی اپنے کاٹنوں کے زریعہ اروں کے ساتھ بندوبست کیا گیا تعلق اردن سنہ کو یہ دراست بادشاہ کی نسبت یہ ہوا کہ جند شرطین کی گئیں اگر انہوں سے عہدنامہ پر دستخط کیے ہوتے تو شرطین انکے حق میں زیادہ مفید ہوتیں انکار کرنے سے انہوں سے اپنی آزادی کا حق کھو دیا لارڈ ڈلہوسی سے وعدہ نہیں کیا کہ انیسا ہی خطا سوروٹی ہو گا اسکے علاوہ گورنمنٹ سے اور باوجود میں واجد علی شاہ کے ساتھ بڑی فیاضی سے برتاؤ کیا بارہ لاکھ روپیہ سالانہ مقرر ہوا سابق شاہان اودھ کے اعزاز کے لیے یہ وثیقہ مقرر کیا گیا اور کہا گیا کہ اسکے معین حیات انکا اعزاز مثل بادشاہ کیا جائے گا لوگ برٹش گورنمنٹ سے خوش ہوے مگر بیکار رہی سے ناخوش ہوکر علاوہ ان لوگوں کے جو بذریعہ معاشی سے ذریعے سے بہت کچھ پیدا کر لیتے تھے بہت سے کاریگر اور سپاہی اور اہلکار بیکار ہو گئے جس کام سے لیے بہتر ترین سونتظم مقرر رہتے وہ اب بارہ دہی کمشنر کرتے تھے اسلیے لوگ ہیں علاوہ بریں تعلق اران کارعب اور روپیہ پیدا کر سکتے ویلے بھی کم ہو گئے جس سے وہ خوش نہیں لوگوں کی اور اکثر مستعصب آدمیوں کی بھی راس سے کراس حالے میں گورنمنٹ سے غلطی کی مگر خیر غدر سے اس غلطی کی اصلاح ہو گئی ۔

باب پانزدہم

ملک اودھ کا غدر

مضمون غدر خصوصاً نئے فتح کیے ہوے صوبہ اودھ کے غدر کی نسبت اہل الرائے نے اسقدر لکھا ہے کہ ہم ذیل میں اس واقعے کو جو تاریخ ہندوستان میں سب سے بڑا واقعہ ہے صرف سرسری طور پر عرض بیان کریں گے مارچ عشرہ عین سرہنری لارنس چیف کمشنر اودھ مقرر ہوے ۔ ایک مہینے کے بعد ملک میں جو طرفہ ان کا توصف نسبت افواہیں اور سنے لگیں جو ہندوستانی فوج کو دیے گئے تھے اس صوبے کی خوش قسمتی تھی کہ سرہنری لارنس سالاری ایک ہیرہ مبارک وقت میں اعلیٰ حکمران صوبہ تھا ۔ انکو معلوم ہوا کہ لوگ سب ناخوش ہیں اور اکثر مقامات پر قریب قریب بلوہ ہونیوالا ہے تعلقہ دار برٹش گورنمنٹ کے دشمن ہو رہے تھے ۔ ہزارہا بادشاہ غزدل کے سپاہی سے روزگار شہرین بجرس ہوے سے تھے ۔ ہزاروں اہلکار شاہی اور اہل حرفہ و پیشہ

جو اس انقلاب کو اپنی معاش کے لیے نا مبارک سمجھے تھے چالیس ہزار باغی سپاہیوں کے اہلی و عیال
اسی ملک میں رہتے تھے ۔ اکثر ہی پیادہ دوں کی رتبہ ت، سب سے پہلے گبڑی اور اُؤ سے ازنالیس کی پیدل پلٹن
اور دو بنگال رسالے کو بلایا ۔ رفتہ رفتہ سب برٹش کی حکومت کے دشمن ہوگئے مگر بعض جن آخر تک خیر خواہ
رہے ۔ چو طرفہ سے اور یہی درد ناک خبریں سر مہری لارنس کے پاس اُنکے خاص صوبے اور ہندوستان
کے مختلف حصوں سے آنے لگیں لازم آیا کہ فوراً حفاظت کی جگہ ذخیرہ ثابین اور اسقدر گولی بارود اور رسد
جمع کرلیں کہ اگر زیادہ مدت تک گھرے رہے تو کانی ہو ۔ پہلے خیال کیا گیا تھا کہ مچھی بھوں اور رزبڑ نسی دو توں
میں فوج محفوظ رہ سکتی ہے بلکہ آخر کار مچھی بھوں کی نسبت خیال ہوا کہ اُن ہیں فوج نہیں رہ سکتی اندا چھوڑ دیا
کیونکہ اسکی دیواریں توپوں کو نہیں روک سکتی تھیں اور اسمیں ہہ بھی خوف تھا کہ نغیم خندق کی راہ سے سرنگ
نہ لگا دے ۔ اسکے بعد وہ واقعہ خوفناک ہوا ۔ عام غدار کشت خون ۔ بھگدر ۔ حبیث کی مصیبت ۔ باقی اندہ نگر خواہ
کو ایک مقام پر جمع ہونا ۔ نیک اور اولوالعزم سر مہری لارنس کی وفات درد انگیز آنگی سپاہ کو جو رزبڑ نسی میں
کتنی بُرے خطرے اور تردد میں تھی کہ اتنے میں جنرل ہیولیٹ اور جنرل اور نرم باہر سے مدد لیکر آئے لیکن
دو تین مہینے تک وہ فوج اپنی ہی مدد پر رزبڑ نسی کے اندر رہی آخر کار نومبر میں سر کالن کیمبل نے آنکو مدد دیکر
بچایا یا اسپہر نغیم کی فوج بھاگ غالباً تاریخ میں ایسی اعلیٰ درجے کی فوجی لیاقت درستی اور شایستگی فوجی کا
یکا اس خوبی اور خوش اسلوبی سے برتاؤ کیا کہ کل سپاہ مردا اور عورتیں اور بچے ناف شہر لکھنؤ سے
کے باہر آ گئے مگر نغیم نے دق کیا اوصرف نغیم ہی نے نہیں بلکہ تنخنیًا اور پچاس ہزار آدمی نمی بایقین
مردوں کی کیو نا کہ وہ جانتے تھے کہ انگریزی فوج نکلی جاتی ہے ۔

اسکے بعد یہ رائے قرار پائی کہ اگرچہ انگریزی فوج تمام لکھنؤ پر قبضہ کر سکتی قابل نہیں ہے تاہم اگر کل فوج نہیں
دو ہ سے پہلی گئی تو اسوقت اسکا نتیجہ خراب ہوگا لہذا عالم باغ پر قبضہ کیا گیا اور سر کردگی سرجیمیں اور نرم
تھوڑی سی فوج ویان رہی تاکہ شہر میں بلوہ نہ ہونے پائے سر کالن کیمبل اور خاص فوج کانپور کو بچ کر گئی تیلیا
تین مہینے سے زیادہ عرصے تک نغیم کے ساتھہ بر سر مقابلہ رہا اور جسقدر علطا اسپہر نرم سے اُن سب میں بایقین
حاصل کی آخر کار مارچ ۱۸۵۸ء میں سر کالن بڑا لشکر لیکر کانپور میں داخل ہوئے تاکہ عالم باغ
کی فوج کو مدد دیں اور شہر لکھنؤ پر قبضہ کر لیں یہ بات اس مادہ کے اختتام کے قبل بخوبی حاصل ہوگئی اور
آدمی بھی بہت کم ضائع ہوئے اب چونکہ ہندوستان کے سب سے حصہ کا سب سے مضبوط مقام برٹش کے
قبضے میں آگیا لہذا تھوڑے ہی عرصہ میں بہت سی خفیت لڑایاں ہوکر صوبے کو باغیوں سے
صاف کر دیا اور ملک سکے اس سرے سے اس سرے تک لواتے صورت انگلشیہ نصب کر دیئے گئے

دو برس سے کم عرصے میں کل پلٹوفان غدر و بغاوت کا جو دفعۃً اودھ میں اگیا تھا بالکل صاف کر دیا گیا اور امن و امان کا ڈنکا سابق کی نسبت بھی زیادہ دھڑلے سے سارے صوبے کے ہر مکان اور موضع میں بجنے لگا

باب شانزدہم

غدر سے الحاق تک کا حال

جب لکھنؤ پر برٹش سے قبضہ کیا تو انگریزی گورنمنٹ کو لازم آیا کہ بذریعہ لارڈ کلنگ گورنر جزل کے اس حکمت عملی سے عوام کو اطلاع دے کہ جو گورنمنٹ موصوف اس صوبے کے آئندہ طرز تمدن کی نسبت اختیار کرنا چاہتی ہے لارڈ کلنگ نے فورا اشتہار اودھ میں جو مشہور ہے اپنے خیالات ظاہر کیے کہ غالبا گورنمنٹ کی اور کسی کاروائی پر جو غدر کے ایام میں کی گئی اس قدر توجہ عوام نہیں ہوئی جس قدر اس کاروائی پر ہوئی اشتہار مذکور میں اس بات سے کم و بیش اور کچھ نہ تھا کہ اودھ کی کل اراضی ضبط کر لی گئی ۔ یہ استثنا سے ان ریاستوں کو جو سرداران ذیل کے قبضے میں تعین ۔

راجہ سردب گجے سنگہ ۔ بلرام پور

راجہ کالونت سنگہ ۔ پدروالا

راو ہردیو بخش ۔ تعلقہ دار کنیاری

راو کاشی پرشاد ۔ تھاکھر سکیندری

لہور سنگہ ۔ زمیندار گوپال کھیری

چندن لال ۔ زمیندار مرادا

یہ بھی آئین میں درج تھا کہ جو تعلقہ دار اپنے الآت حرب صاحب چیف کمشنر کے پاس بھیج دیں گے اور باغی نہ فوجی کنارہ کشی اختیار کر دیں گے وہ معاف کیے جائیں گے بشرطیکہ انہوں نے کسی یوربین کے قتل میں مدد نہ دی ہو اودھ کے حکام سنے بری سے اس اشتہار کو پڑھا خصوصاً سر جیمس اثرم نے جن کے خیالات پر ارا کین انگلستان کو اس معاملے میں بڑا اعتبار اور خیال تھا ۔ انجام یہ ہوا کہ اشتہار مذکور میں بورڈ آف کنٹرول زجنگے پریسیڈنٹ لارڈ المیورا اس زمانے میں تھے کچھ ترمیم کی ۔ اور صاحب گورنر جزل نے اشتہار نافذ فرمایا ۔ اسکے نافذ ہوتے ہی پہلے تو بڑی کھل بل مچ گئی ۔ لیکن بعد ازاں جب لوگون نے غور کیا تو سمجھے کہ اشتہار کو انہوں نے صرف اپنی گھبراہٹ سے سب سے برا کہا تھا ۔ اور یہ کہ اسکے نتائج اس قدر سخت نہ تھے جس قدر وہ لوگ سمجھے بیٹھے تھے ۔ اس عرصے میں سر جیمس اثرم نے اپنے عہدے سے چارج سر رابرٹ ماںکمری کو دے دیا اور جون ١٨٥٨ء میں تعلقہ دار لکھنؤ میں بلائے گئے اور انسے صاف کہہ دیا گیا کہ جو اراضی قبل

خبطی اُنکے قبضے میں تھی اسپر دہ فلاں فلاں طور پر قابض رہ سکتے ہیں ۔ نتیجہ یہ ہوا کہ وہ ہیں تعلقہ داروں
نے اطاعت برٹش گورنمنٹ کی اور آخرکار صوبے کی کل آمدنی اُنکے ذریعے سے خزانہ میں آئی ۔ سرابرٹ مانٹگمری
کے بعد مسٹر ونیک فیلڈ مقرر ہوئے جنہوں نے گورنمنٹ کی پالیسی کا اور بھی زیادہ سرگرمی سے بتبا و
کیا ۔ اُنکے وقت میں صوبہ اودھ کا کامل انتظام ہو گیا اور رعایا کے ہتھیار چھین لیے گئے ۔ پولیس کو سیقعدر تعلیم
ہوئی اور رفتہ رفتہ اودھ جو ایک جنگل صوبہ تھا ہندوستان سکے اور صلح جو اور تابع صوبوں کیطرح صلح جو ہو گیا
مشہور ہے کہ کوئی ۲ ۱۵ جنگل کاٹ ڈالے گئے اور ۲۰ نومبر اور ۷ ۱۹۲۳ بندوقیں اور ۲ بندوقیں وغیرہ
اور ۴ ۹ ۵ ۷ ۵ تلوارہیں اور ۴ ۹۴ اور قسم کے کل ۴۹ ۴ ۷ ۷ ۔ آلات حرب توڑ ڈالے گئے ۔ اسوقت
سے تعلقہ داران اودھ کی عزت و توقیر کہیں زیادہ ہوتی گئی ۔ پیشتر کیطرح وہ اب رعایا کے سخت دشمن
نہیں ہیں ۔ نہ حکام سرکاری سکے موہب نعیم ہیں ۔ نہ اپنے پروسیوں یا سرکاری عاملوں سے لڑتے ہیں
بلکہ اب حکمران اور رعایا کے درمیان میں ترقی اتحاد کے باعث ہیں اور سلطنت انگلستان کے خیر خواہ صلح
جو والعزم رعایا ۔ یہ تعلقہ دار کوئی تین چار سو ہیں اور لارڈ ڈکنیک کے دربار میں جو ۱۸۴۷ء میں منعقد ہوا اتحا کوئی
۲ ۷ تعلقہ دار حاضر تھے ۔ انہیں سے اکثر اب آنریری مجسٹریٹ اور بعض اسسٹنٹ کمشنر ہیں اپس تمدن ملک میں
اسطرح شریک ہیں ۔ آخرکار لارڈ لارنس کے زمانے میں کوشش کی گئی تھی کہ کاشتکاروں کے مفید چند اصول
میں تجویز واقع ہوں لیکن جسطرح پر لارڈ ڈکنیک نے تعلقہ داروں کے حقوق کو تسلیم کیا اتھا قریب قریب
ویسی ہی عایت اب بھی کی گئی ۔

اب اودھ میں قریب ۲۲ ۷ ۵ موضع ہیں ۔ اور ہر موضع کی اوسط ایک میل مربع ۔ ان موضعوں میں سے
۳ ۵ ۵ ۱ موضعوں سکے چار سو دس قابض و مالک ہیں ۔ اور ان میں سے ہر ایک مطالبہ سرکاری کم سکے کم
پانچ ہزار روپیہ یا اس سے زیادہ ادا کرتا ہے ۔ باقی ۲۹۰ ۱۰ موضعوں سکے مالک و قابض ۷۵۰ حصہ دار ہیں
یہ زمیندار تعلقہ دار اپنے حصہ اراضی پر قابض ہیں اکثر اموردیں اودھ نے بہت ترقی کی ہے ۔ سول اور فوجداری
قوربوں سنے بڑا فائدہ پہنچا اور ڈصیخون کا بھی ابھا اور مستقل اثر ہوا لیکن اور کسی امر میں اسقدر
تبدل نہوا ہوگا جسقدر صیغہ تعلیم میں ہوا ۔ اب صوبے میں جابجا بیشمار مدارس میں جبکہ ضرورت ہو
تعلیم پا سکتا ہے ۔ کیننگ کالج سے کبھی فوائد کثیر حاصل ہوے اور منشی نو لکشور کے مطبع نے لوگوں میں
اعلی اور عمدہ لیاقت کی اشاعت میں بہت کچھ مددی ہے ان باتوں سے علاوہ تعلقہ داروں نے
ایک خاص طبقہ قائم کیا ہے ۔ جس سے وہ خود بڑا فائدہ اٹھا پاتے ہیں ۔ اور گورنمنٹ بھی صوبہ اودھ کے
طبقہ معزز کے لوگ یعنے تعلقہ دار اپنے خیالات اور اپنی اپنی رائے سال میں ایک بار ایکسے ذریعہ سے ظاہر کر ہیں

باب ہفتدہم

ملک اودھ کا ممالک مغربی کی گورنمنٹ کے ساتھ شامل ہونا

کچھ دن سے افواہ تھی کہ اودھ کے ممالک مغربی و شمالی مین شامل کرنے کا گورنمنٹ نے قصد کیا ہے اور جنوری ۱۸۷۷ع مین ملک اودھ ممالک مغربی کی گورنمنٹ کے ساتھ واقعی شامل ہو گیا۔ موقع بھی بہت تھا کیونکہ سرجارج کوپر صاحب بہادر چیف کمشنر اودھ اس وقت مین قائم مقام لفٹننٹ گورنر ممالک مغربی و شمالی مقرر ہوے۔ اس تبدیل سے خاص صرف سررشتون اور حکمون مین ہوا۔ قوانین اودھ اور حقوق و مدارج رعایا اس الحاق سے بدستور قائم رہے۔ گورنمنٹ انڈیا نے یہ فیصلہ بھی کر دیا کہ گو دارالحکومت اودھ کا الہ آباد مین منتقل ہونا تجویج دیا گیا مگر ہر سال صاحب لفٹننٹ گورنر تین مہینے لکھنؤ مین بھی قیام فرمایا کرینگے۔ پہلے یہ خیال کیا گیا تھا کہ اودھ کے تعلقہ داروں کے الحاق ملک سے حق تلفی ہو گی مگر خوشی کی بات ہے کہ لارڈ لٹن صاحب نے خود ماہ مارچ ۱۸۷۷ع کے دربار مین ان خیالات کی تردید کی اور رئیسون کا اطمینان کر دیا کہ وہ کسی طرح حکام سے ان شامل کر دینے سے نہ ڈرین۔ بہت کچھ اطمینان ان اس بات سے تعلقہ داروں کا کر دیا گیا کہ اس تغیر سے اُنکے حقوق مین کسی طرح فتور نہیں آئیگا اور جو آئین و قوانین بیان کے ہین وہ بدستور قائم رہینگے۔

باب ہیژدہم

خاتمہ

اب ہم اس دیباچہ کو ختم کرتے ہین اور اس صوبے کو ہم مبارک باد دیتے ہین کہ برٹش گورنمنٹ کے زیر نگین ہے اور گورنمنٹ بڑی توجہ کرتی ہے۔ سابق مین گورنمنٹ سنے اودھ کے معاملات مین دست اندازی کرنا مناسب سمجھا اور تجربہ سے ظاہر ہو گیا کہ گورنمنٹ کا منشا ملک کے فائدے کے لیے تھا۔ قبل علمداری برٹش یہان کی رعایا کے حالات سے ہم خوب واقف ہین۔ غنیم کے حملے سے حفاظت محال تھی۔ ظالم سرداروں سے بچنا دشوار تھا۔ پردیسیون اور آدمیون کی سازش سے بھی بچنا مشکل تھا۔ اسلیع مجبور ہو کر ہل جوتتے تھے اور رات کو ڈرتے کانپتے اپنے گھر جاتے تھے۔ اب قضیہ اسکے برعکس ہے۔ گورنمنٹ تعلقہ داروں پر بڑی مہربانی کرتی ہے اور دیہ کسانون پر مہربان ہین۔ ظلم کا فور ہو گیا۔ ذرا شکایت ہو دیوانی یا فوجداری عدالت مین چارہ جوئی کی۔ پچیس برس ہوے کہ ہندوستان کے سب صوبون سے بدنظمی اور خوف جان و مال یہان زیادہ تھا۔ اب غالباً اس خوبی سے اور ملک کی رعایا نہ بڑھتی ہو گی۔

خلاصہ حالاتِ تواریخی

تعلقہ داران ملک اور وہ کہ جن کی تصویرات بھی اسی میں نصب ہیں

(نمبر ۱) راجہ راجگان سرکت جیت سنگھ والی کپورتھلہ قوم سکھ تعلقہ دار بوندھی و پرسولی و بنولی

حضور والا ریاست کپورتھلہ ضلع جالندھر ملک پنجاب کے حکمران ہیں جنکے خاندان کی خیر خواہی اور جیں وفاداری کا بار ہا گورنمنٹ انگلشیہ سے اظہار شکر ہو چکا ہے اسی راہ و رسم رئیسانہ کے برتاؤ سے آپ کے جد امجد مہاراجہ رندھیر سنگھ صاحب بہادر (جی سی ایس آئی) فرمین شباب غدر میں اپنی موجودگی ذات خاص و نیز افواج ریاست سے اول ضلع ہوشیارپور ملک پنجاب میں کرنیل بہادر ڈپٹی کشنر ہوشیارپور کو انسداد بلوہ میں مددگار اور پھر یہ تحریک صاحب ممدوح و جناب رابرٹ منٹگمری صاحب چیف کشنر سابق ملک اور رئیس موصوف مع اپنی فوج کثیر کے بہادرانہ دلی ہو کر اور وہیں چھدری گورنمنٹ سے سرکوبی باغیان میں سرگرم رہے اور فوج مہاراجہ صاحب نے متعدد و موقعوں پر عمدہ عمدہ کارنمایاں کیا اور مفسدان کو زک فاش دی اس حالت شرکت معرکہ میں مہاراجہ صاحب بہادر نہ صرف مددزبانی اور فوج کی بہیں دی بلکہ کل بار اصراف اپنی فوج اپنے ذمہ رکھ کر کمال شجاعت و بہادری سے بنفس نفیس اپنے وقت معرکہ میں جنرل فوج رہ پر کپتان فرمائی بعد فرو غدریہ ریاست جن کی آمدنی ۵ لاکھ ہے اضلاع ہرانج و گونڈہ و کہیری میں مالکانہ مہاراجہ صاحب ممدوح الشان کو مرحمت ہوئی بعد چند حضور موصوف بالابزم سیر ولایت جہاز پر تشریف لیے جاتے تھے عدن میں پہونچ کر قضا کی آکو بعد مہاراجہ کھرگ سنگھ صاحب بہادر رونق بخش مسند ریاست ہو ہی بعد انکے حضور مہاراجہ صاحب سرکجت سنگھ بہادر مسند نشین ریاست ہیں اور اس علاقہ میں جناب کنور بہزام سنگھ صاحب بہادر حقیقی چچا حضور کے منیجر علاقہ ہیں ۔

(نمبر ۲) نہرائینس آنربل سردار گجو سنگھ بہادر کے ۔ سی ۔ ایس ۔ آئی ۔ مہاراجہ لبرام پور ولمسی پور وغیرہ ۔

مہارا میں سکھ دیو مورثِ اعلیٰ ریاست دارجا پانیہ منصف وطن صوبہ گجرات تھو انکے پسر ششم پریا ساہی ثبت ۱۳۳۲ میں وطن مالوفہ سے اگرہ دلی میں بلا ریاست شاہ وجہاء تاج الدین شاہ اشرف بوی و بہراہی شاہ براہی سیر و تشکار ضلع ہرانج پرگنہ کوئین تشریف لائا اور واسطے سرکوبی مفسدان مامور ہو کر قلعہ وقع سرکشان پرگنہ کرکے از سرنواآباد کیا اور وہیں اقامت اختیار کی انکی ہفتی پشت میں سے راجہ ماد ہو سنگھ نے رام گذ و گوری میں دارالریاست قرار دیا اور کو نگنیش سنگھ انچوبائی کو دریا بلراچ پسر دوم انکے بزرگ نامی راجہ ہو ہو چکے نام سے رام گذ و ملقب لبرام پور ملقب ہوا انکی پانجوین پشت میں راجہ نول سنگھ مالک ریاست ہوے مضمون سنے باین فرائیون میں راجگان نوا کو شکست قوت دی انکے راجہ ارجن سنگھ و ما بعد راجہ زراں سنگھ وشتثت میں مہاراجہ صاحب حال رونق افروز ریاست باجاہ و جلال ہوے ابتدا سے جلوس میں آپ فرا راجگان جنگا وائرہ و تلمسی پور کو مستوار لڑائیوں میں ہیں پاکیا و حسب الحکم سرکار شاہی دایا سے صاحب رزیڈنٹ بہادر بہراہی فوج ہزار راجہ درگ نراین سنگھ تعلقہ دار تلمسی پور کو جنسے اپنے باپ سے راج چھین لیا تھا محاصرہ کرکے بھگا دیا اور

سے صدہا ہاتھی دروازہ پر بجو ستے ہیں جنگلی جانور درندہ کہروں میں گھو ستے میں ہر علم و ہنر کا درباریں پر چاہ
ایجاد و دو شکاری اور شعر و سخن کی قدر ہو فی زمانہ ہر فن کے موجد کا اس ریاست میں بڑا گذر بہ بلند ہو حاصلگی
رئیسانہ سے ایک عجائب خانہ ریاست میں بنوایا ہاہر مجلس انجمن ہند میں آپ ہی کی ذات با برکات سے قائم
و باعث ترقی تعلقداران اور وہ چو آپ کی ریاست میں لا بعطہ مواضع اور تین بتی جمی صہ لاکھ للعظمہ طا بلغیم
۱۴، ۵ پائی

اضلاع گونڈہ و بہرائج و لکھنو میں واقع ہیں رسم گدی نشینی اس خاندان میں ہو

نمبر ۴۸۸ لال پرتاب نرائن سنگھ قوم برہمن تعلقدار مہدونہ و اہیار واد میرا و کلشی پورہ و مہدونہ
و شیمبر پور خطاب لال ۔ آپ قوم برہمن شکلد یب سے آغاز تعلقہ کا راجہ نجتا و رسنگہ سے ہوا اور وہ کو نواب
سعادت علینہان کے وقت میں سلطنت اودہ سے خطاب راجگی ملا اور سکے چھوٹے بھائی راجہ در رشن سنگھ
صاحب ہمیشہ عہدہ نظامت پر حکمران رہے سہ مہارا جہ مان سنگھ صاحب قائم جنگ اور ایام قدر رعہ اللہ
میں جانبازی کا برتا و گورنمنٹ انگلشیہ سے فرمایا اور مستعد دار ہیں یورپ سکے محافظ جان ہوسے اور سکے جلد و
میں خطاب مہا راجہ جلی و (کے سی آئی) اور نیتہ نائب کما نذر آف اشتراف انڈیا کا و ملکیت تعلقہ لسیمبرپور
کی گورنمنٹ انگلشیہ سے راجہ مانسنگھ صاحب کو مرحمت ہوئی اور مہارا جہ صاحب موصوف معززین و مدبرین
تعلقداران اودہ سے دہ سے تصور ہوتا تھی جب مہارا جہ صاحب سنے وفات پائی تو مہارانی سوبھا کنور صاحبہ
اونکی زوجہ منتظم و قابض ریاست ہوئیں مہارانی صاحبہ سنے لال ترلوکی ناتہہ سنگھ خلف راجہ رگھوبر دیال سنگھ
بہرادر مہارا جہ مانسنگھ صاحب کو ریاست لکھدی تھی لیکن بحکم پروی کونسل اب لال پرتاب نرائن سنگھ
صاحب نواسہ مہارا جہ صاحب وارث ریاست مقرر ہوئے اور کنور صاحب اکثر عبادات و خصائل میں ہے مرحوم
مہارا جہ صاحب میں اور تہذیب علوی و فکری میں مہارا جہ صاحب کے نمونہ ہیں امید ہو کہ بہت تھوڑ
عرصہ میں برٹش گورنمنٹ کے ساتھ اپنی متانت رائے سے با سلوب شایستہ اپنے ارادت و نیاز کو
نبا ہر کر سکے کامل ناموری حاصل کریں گے تعلقہ میں سا بعطہ موضع مالعطیہ بنی معہ عطیہ جمعی
اضلاع فیض آباد و گونڈہ و بارہ بنکی و لکھنو و سلطانپور میں واقع ہیں رسم گدی نشینی اس خاندان میں جاری
۱۰، ۶ پائی

(نمبر ۴) راجہ شیو پیال سنگھ قوم میں تعلقدار مرائو و اراضی دریا برآمدہ سنگرام پور خطاب راجہ موروٹی ۔
آغاز قوم بیسو نکارا جہ سابا ہن سے ہو اود یس سو سال ہوسے راجہ سابا ہن قوم چھتری سے راجہ
بکرا جیت سنے قوم نیوار سے جنگ عظیم کرکے اونکو شکست دی اس وجہ سے راجہ بکرا جیت
سنے اپنی دختہ کی شادی راجہ سابا ہن سے کردی بعد شادی راجہ سابا ہن سنے ساتھ لا
بکرا جیت معلوم کرکے ساتھ لا سابا ہن اپنے نام سے جاری کیا اور سیالکوٹ و مونگلی میں واقع

ملک پنجاب آباد کیا اوسکی بیسویں پشت میں راجہ ابجو چند و پرتھی چند یہ قصہ داستان گنگ کی بمقام شیوراج
واقعہ ضلع فتحپور معہ فوج کے آئے اور رانی راجہ ارکل ضلع فتحپور بھی اسی کے قریب سے اوس مقام پر
آ ئی تھی صوبہ دار تسینہ پراگ نے بہ نیت فساد اوسکو محاصرہ کرکے مجبور کر رکھا تھا حسب استدعائے
رانی ان ہر دو برادران نے صوبہ دار سے لڑائی کی پرتھی چند قتل ہوا ابجے چند نے فتحیاب ہوکر رانی کو
پاس راجہ ارکل کو بعزاز تمام پہنچایا راجہ نے خوش ہوکر اپنی دختر کی شادی ابجو چند کے ساتھہ کردی اور ریاست
جہیر میں دی ابجے چند معہ فوج شیوراج پور میں آکر مقیم ہوے اور قوم بہدرلگا قلع و قمع کرکے اوسکی علاقیات
پر بھی قابض ہوے جب سے آغاز ریاست بیسوارہ کا ہوا چونکہ بیسویں پشت میں سابا ہیں سکے راجہ ابجو چند
نے اپنا تسلط کیا تھا اس وجہ یہ ملک بیسوارہ مشہور ہوا ابجے چند کی دسویں پشت میں راجہ تلوک چند ہوے سے
اوسکے دو لڑکے تھے ہر ہردیو اور راجہ پرتھی چند جب تلوک چند بیمار ہوے اوسوقت بعدم موجود گی ہر ہردیو کرہل
میں تھے پرتھی چند کو مالک ریاست کر دیا جب ہر ہردیو سے نسبی میں آباد ہوے تو وجہ سکونت سے بھی اوسکی
اولاد سے نسبی میں کہلائی اوسکے خاندان سے تعلقدار ان نمبری ذیل میں نمبر ۱۸ و ۵ و ۶ و ۷ و ۱۳ و ۲۱ و ۲۵ و ۲
اور ہر ہردیو دہلی سے واپس اگر مالک ریاست بھی ہوے سے جبکہ ذکر نمبر ۱۸ میں درج ہوا اور اس سے موضع نسبی
سے ایک شخص کرن را و اولاد ہر ہردیو سے موضع نمبہ میں جاکر آباد ہوا اوسکی اولاد نمبہ نسبی میں مشہور ہوئی اور
خاندان نسبی تعلقدار ان ذیل میں نمبر ۱ و ۲ و ۳ و ۹ و ۹ و ۱۸ و ۱۹ و ۲۲ و راجہ پرتھی چند کی پانچویں پشت میں راجہ رنگ دیو نے
جنگل کٹوا کر مرار و آباد کیا اور خود سکونت پذیر ہوے سے رنگ دیو کی دوسری پشت میں راجہ درگنج سنگہ نے اس ریاست
پر قبضہ پایا اور بسلہ خیر خواہی ایام غدر ۱۸۵۷ء گورنمنٹ انگلشیہ سے علاقہ و خطاب راجگی واپسی میں آئی
حاصل کیا بعد اوسکے یہ رئیس قابض ریاست ہیں اور سنجلہ پانچ تعلقداران خیر خواہ یہ ریاست سے اور
موروثی علاقہ کا بندوبست استمراری ہو تعلقہ میں معہ ملکیت عطیہ مالعوضہ موضع عبی ضلع
اودنام ور اسے بریلی میں واقع میں رسم گدی نشینی اس خاندان میں ہوے—

(نمبر ۵) ۱ راجہ ہنونت سنگہ ۲ راجہ رام پال سنگہ قوم نسین تعلقداران رامپور و معار و پور
دکالاکانکرو ایاجنیا خطاب راجہ موروثی

بچہ سو برس سے ہوے رائے ہوم پال برادر خورد سبے چند راجہ قنوج قوم چھتری گوت میں موریہ علی
مقام مجھولی ضلع گور کھہ پور سے بتقریب استنان پراگ جمی میں آے اور مانک پور میں راجہ مانک
کے ہمراہ اگر اوسکی دختر سے شادی کرکے ریاست حاصل کی اوسکی اولاد اقوام ٹھاکر نسین کہلا و ین
اوسکے وقتاً فوقتاً تقسیم ہوتے ہوے بہت حصہ اس ریاست سکے ہوگئے تعلقدار ان نمبری ذیل

نمبر ۶ و ۷ و ۸ و ۹ و ۱۰ و ۱۴ و ۱۵ اس خاندان سے ہیں راجہ ہنونت سنگھ ایام نذر مین خیرخواہ سرکار رہے بجلد دوسرے اوسکے گورنمنٹ انگلشیہ سے تعلقہ عطیہ حاصل کیا اسند عطیہ باسند عاسے راجہ ہنونت سنگھ نبام راجہ رام پال سنگھ اوسکے نواسے کے گورنمنٹ سے مرحمت ہوئی راجہ رام پال سنگھ صاحب علم انگریزی سے فیضیاب ہیں اور عرصہ تک لندن میں تفریحًا قیام کرسکے تہذیب اہالیان یورپ سے گرہ تعلقداران مین ایک نامور نوجوان شخص ہیں، منجملہ علاقہ عطیہ تعلقہ بھاگل واقع ضلع بہرائچ فروخت کر ڈالا اب اس تعلقہ مین عطیہ ما بقیہ موضع جمی ۱ اضلاع پرتاب گڈھ وراے بریلی مین واقع ہین رسم گدی نشینی اس خاندان مین سہے۔

(نمبر ۷) راجہ تلک سنگھ قوم کنیار تعلقدار کنساری مُجودولت پور در وان و فتح پور اپلے اس ملکیت مین زمیندار ی اقوام دھانک اور منہار کی تھی اور سہر دو اقوام مین تنازعات با ہمی بربابا رہتی تھی دیورام دت قوم نسا کر تو نمبر مورث قوم کنیار جانب نواح تو نبر کنسار علاقہ گوالیار سے مقام سنگی رام پورواقع ضلع فرخ آباد تقریب اشنان گنگا جی بہ جماعت کثیر آنے اور اقوام منہاروں سے جوکہ زبردست تھے ساز ش کرکے اقوام دھانک کو قتل کیا بعدہ اقوام منہار وکو بھی تہ تیغ کرکے بالکل بچراع کر دیا اور اپ سہر دور یاست پر قابض ومالک ہو گئے اوسوقت سے آغاز اس ریاست کا ہؤا اور قبضہ مورثان برابر چلا آیا آخرالامر راجہ سہر دیونش مالک ریاست ہوسے انہون نے بصلا خیرخواہی ایام غدر ۱۸۵۷ء تعلقہ دولت پور وغیرہ گورنمنٹ سے عطیہ حاصل کرکے افزونی ریاست کی اور خطاب (سی ایس آئی) پایا بعد وفات راجہ سہر دیونش ان کے بھائی اوسکے قابض ریاست مین اور اپنی قوم مین آپ سرگروہ مین اور اس علاقہ کا نبدولبت استمرار ہی ہر اور منجملہ پانچ تعلقداران خیرخواہ آپ بھی ہین۔

(نمبر ۸) راجہ رو در پرتاب ساہ قوم را جکمار تعلقدار دیرہ و امہٹ دو نبا وڈ یہ و مدن پور پنیر و رام نگر وکشن پور کوائی و پورا سی خطاب راجہ موروثی۔ عرصہ یا نبے سو برس کا ہوا راجہ بربار سنگھ مورث اسلے سمبل مراد آبا دسے اول بہد بیان نمبری ۱۶۳ مین آنئے اور بعد قتل اقوام بھرد وکی موضع بہد بیان خاص و نیز دیگر موضعات ضلع سلطانپور پر قابض ہوسے اوکی چار اولاد تھین رسال سنگھ کھوکھی سنگھ گلاتم دیو راج ہبوت سنگھ چونکہ لقب بربار سنگھ سابق مین چوہان تھا اور اقوام چوہان حاکم دلی سے جب علارالدین غوزی تخت نشین دہلی ہوسے اورچاہا کہ بنیاد چوہانیت ونامود کر دیدین اوسوقت اولاد بربار سنگھ نے لقب اپنا چوہان کا تبدیل کر ڈالا کھوکھی سنگھ رجہ ازمشہور ہوسے اوسکے خاندان مین نمبر ۶ و ۷ کے تعلقدار ہین رسال سنگھ وگلاتم دیو وراج ہبوت سنگھ بمجبوتی کھلاسے راج ہبوت سنگھ کے تین سر کہ موتور راجہ چوہ پنکھ

راجہ جگر سنگھ راجہ ایشری سنگھ نمبر او سکے خاندان سے تعلقداران نمبری فیل ہیں نمبر ۱۳ و ۳۰ و ۹ و ۲٦ و ۷۹ د ۸۰ و ۲٦ و ۷۹ و ۸۴ و ۸۵ و ۸۶ و ۱۲۱ و ۱۴۹ و ۱٦۹ و ۲۰۰ و ۱۵۲ ہیں اولاد راجہ ایشری سنگھ کے راجکی مشہور ہوئے اوس خاندان سے تعلقداران نمبری فیل ہیں ۳۰ و ۴۸ و ۹ و ۴۳ و ۱۵ و ۱٦۱ و ۱٦۳ و ۲۰۲ و ۲۴۹ سنبھا اولاد راجہ ایشری سنگھ جا اور اسے مورث سے بہدئیان سے علیحدہ ہوکر جنگل کٹوایا اور آبادی کیا کے دہرہ نام سے موسوم کیا اور افزونی ریاست کرکے تعلقہ باسم دہرہ قائم کیا آخر الامر راجہ رستم ساہی سنے بصلہ خیر خواہی ایام نذر ۱۸۵۷ء ما سنگ موضع تعلقہ امہٹ وغیرہ گورنمنٹ انگلشیہ سے عطیہ حاصل کرکے شامل تعلقہ کیے بعد وفات اوسکے آپ قابض ریاست ہیں اس تعلقہ میں معہ ملکیت عطیہ ما علقہ موضع و مالیہ

نبی ممبی ایک و ایک لاکھ ۔۔۔ اضلاع سلطانپور و فیض آباد و راس بریلی میں واقع ہیں رسم گدی نشینی اس خاندان میں

 راجہ مادھو سنگھ قوم نندل گوتی تعلقدار امیٹھی خطاب راجہ موروثی ۔

سنہ ۱۳۲۲ء میں بہ عہد جلال الدین اکبر بادشاہ مورث اعلی انکو بنظر قلع و قمع اقوام بھر اس ملک میں آئے تھے اور بہت وسیع ملکیت اقوام بہرو کی اضلاع گونڈہ وغیرہ میں اوسکے قبضہ میں رہی اوسی خاندان میں تین سو سال سے یہ راج قائم تھا اب ان رئیس سنے اپنی ریاست بابو سرجیت سنگھ تعلقدار نیکا ری تذکرہ نمبر ۱۰۰ کو سپرد کردی ہو جسمیں ما سنگ موضع اور اس سے نئی ممبی ایک لاکھ ۔۔۔ کی واقع ہیں اور اس ریاست سے تعلقہ نمبری ۲۷۱ علیحدہ قائم ہے ۔

 راجہ محمد علی خان قوم بجگوتی خانزادہ تعلقدار حسن پور و جوس نگر پور و سنگرہ و پلیا پرتاب خطاب راجہ موروثی ۔ اولاد پیار سنگھ مورث اعلی متذکرہ نمبر ۷ میں ہند شتوں کی بعد تلوک چند فرزند پہ عہد بابر شاہ بادشاہ دہلی بوجہ باقیداری مالگذاری مذہب اسلام قبول کیا تھا اور تتار خان موسوم ہوئے اوسکے دو بیٹے بازید خان جلال خان تھے نمبر اسکے لڑکے حسن خان ہوئے منجھون سنے پہ عہد بابر شاہ دہلی خطاب راجگی و نیزیہ منصب کر حبکی بحصول نذرانہ و ڈیکا لگا دین لقب راجہ مشہور ہوئے حاصل کیا اونہون سنے اس قصبہ کو آباد کرکے نبا مرد اپنے حسن پور موسوم کیا اسنخان کی بار میں بثبت میں یہ تعلقہ دار قابض تعلقہ ہیں اور اس خاندان سے تعلقداران نمبری فیل ہیں نمبر ۹ و ۵۷ و ۱٦۱ اس تعلقہ میں مالعہ موضع معہ نئی ممبی ۔۔۔ اضلاع سلطانپور و فیض آباد میں واقع ہیں رسم گدی نشینی اس خاندان میں ہے ۔

 امیر الدولہ سعید الملک راجہ محمد ایس حسن خان بہادر ممتاز جنگ انزری اسسٹنٹ کشنہ محمود آباد

تعلقدار محمود آباد و ضلع سیتاپور و بسہا ضلع لکھنو و متولی ضلع کھیری کو انڈہ ضلع نوا گنج و ۲۰۳ رجب ۱۸٦۹ بہری مقام ملہرہ ضلع نوا گنج میں ولادت پائی فہ رمضان ۱۲۸۵ھ کو اوسکے والد مقیم الدولہ راجہ نواب علی خان

قیامِ جنگ سے مقام بیبونہ انتقال فرمایا اور امیرالدولہ بہادر عمر و سالگی سند ریاست پر متمکن ہوئے علاقہ
اہ۔ مارچ سنہ ۱۹۲۰ عرتک بوجہ ناباغی کورٹ آف وارڈس رہا مدرسہ سیتاپور و بنارس کالج و کینگ کالج لکھنؤ مین
تعلیم پائی سولہ برس سے سن مین انجمن ہند سکے ممبر مقرر ہوئے ہمیشہ عمین بجائے مہاراجہ مانکنگہ سکے
ولیں پریذیڈنٹ انجمن ہند مقرر ہوئے اور سوقت سے جو مباحث متعلق قوانین و امور انتظامی صوبہ اور ہر کچھ
وسین پیرو کار رہے بعوض ان خدمات کے سالانہ رپورٹ ۱۹۲۳ عمین لوکل گورنمنٹ نے آپ کی تعریف اور تشکریہ ادا کیا اور بطور
ایک تحسین کے نواب نزر جنرل بہادر لارڈ ڈلارنس صاحب نے خلعت مین تمشیر ولایتی دربار مین عطا فرمائی اور بعد ازیں ۱۹۲۵
چیفی نمبری ۶ مہ مورخہ ۵ فروری ۱۹۲۵ عمہری ڈویس صاحب سابق کشنر بہادر ملک اودھ نے بعضو نواب بہادر
بہادر سفارش فرمائی کہ القاب امیرالدولہ سعیدالملک ممتاز جنگ کا لکھا جاوے گورنمنٹ ہند نے اس سفارش
کو منظور فرما کر حکم منظوری القاب مذکورہ یانسبت اوس فیاضی سکے جو راجہ صاحب نے زمانہ محلا
۱۹۲۵ عمین فرمائی صاحب ڈپٹی کشنر ضلع سیتاپور نے یہ عبارت تحریر فرمائی ہے کہ مین نے اپنے
زمانہ دورہ مین اس بات کا اطمینان کر لیا ہے کہ راجہ امیر حسن خان نے اسراف کے ساتھ رعایا
کی تکلیف کم کر نیک وصرف کیا ہے جناب بعلی القاب سر جارج کو پر صاحب لفٹنٹ گورنر بہادر در
مغربی و شمالی و چیف کشنر بہادر در اودھ نے بہراہ قدردانی دربار عام مین راجہ صاحب ممدوح کو خلعت
سے ممتاز فرمایا یا حالات نسبی راجہ صاحب ممدوح سکے ذیل مین تحریر ہوتے ہین ۔
یہ خاندان شیخ صدیقی اولاد خلیفہ اول پیغمبر علیہ السلام کی ہین راجہ صاحب سکے بزرگ بغداد سے زمانہ
سلطنت سلاطین غوریہ مین ہندوستان مین وارد ہوے اور شہر امروہہ مین سکونت گزین ہوے جاے
پشت تک عہدہ قضا شہر امروہہ کا اس خاندان سے متعلق رہا قریب ۱۳۳۲ عمین قاضی نصرۃ اللہ غرف
یہ شیخ تمن ہمراہ لشکر ظفر پیکر ملک ناصرالدین سکے اوسکے مشہور حملہ اودہ مین وارد صوبہ اودہ
ہوے اور استیصال اقوام بجہ بہادر بعت مین سے سرگرم رہے بجلد وسے ان کارپاسے نایان سکے
وہ دیہات جواب جزو تعلقہ جات محمود آباد و لمہرہ و عیشوا مؤ و بیتی پور وزمیندداری ہاے نشبن پور
محمد پور اچیجہ منور رال بہاری بہوری کنوری سدرایوان بابو پور نعمت پور سروی مشہور مین حاصل
کیے اور راے الآن اوسنگے اولاد کے قبض و دخل مین موجود ہین قاضی نصرۃ اللہ صاحب نے
بمقام لمہرہ انتقال کیا اور وہین مدفون ہین بعد اوسکے شیخ نظام اور بعد ازان شیخ غلام مصطفیٰ
اوسکے بیٹے بعد اوسکے بیٹے شیخ محمد داؤد ہوے جو لشکر اکبر بادشاہ مین عہدہ جابیلہ پر ممتاز
تھے اور جنگو خطاب خان بہادری کا اکبر بادشاہ سے دیاتھا یہ نہایت جرأت سکے ساتھ قلعہ رنتبور سکے

پیچھے پر معین دحاوہ میں مار سے سکے محمود خان اورنگ بیٹھے تھے اونہوں نے اپنے نام سے محمود آباد
آباد دکیا انکا انتقال بحالت فوجداری جونپور کے جونپور میں ہوا بعد اونکے بیٹھے اونکے بیٹھے اونکے نواب بایزید خان
قائم مقام ریاست ہوئے اور کل ریاست کو اپنے انعام و اپنے پراسٹور سے تقسیم کیا کہ بھجوایا پہاڑ خان کو
اور بہتی پور سعید خان کو دیا اور محمود آباد و بلہرہ اپنے قبضہ میں رکھا یہ بھی عمدہ ہو اسے جلیلہ پر عہد
جہانگیر بادشاہ میں ممتاز رہے اور جہانگیر بادشاہ نے خطاب عمدۃ الملک خضر الدولہ بایزید خان بہادر
مظفر جنگ عطا فرمایا اور اپنی خاص کرکی تلوار جسمیں نام جہانگیر بادشاہ کا لکھا ہے اور حربی کی صورت
سنقوش ہے عطا فرمائی جواب تک قبضہ میں راجہ صاحب محمود آباد کے موجود ہے بایزید خان کے
تین بیٹھے تھے عنایت خان، ہدایت خان فتح خان ان تینوں میں تقسیم ہوئی عنایت خان کو بلہرہ
فتح خان کو سدرا وان ہدایت خان کو محمود آباد ملا یہاں اونہوں نے رہنا اختیار کیا اور خدا گنج آباد کیا
یہ شکار دوست اور عمدہ شہسوار تھے گھوڑ سے پر سے گر پڑے اور مر گئے محمود آباد میں مدفون ہوئے
انکے ایک بیٹھے خلیل الرحمٰن خان تھے وہ متمکن مسند ریاست ہوئے اون کے بعد ہدایت اللہ خان
صاحب اکلوتے بیٹھے رئیس محمود آباد ہوئے یہ ہمعصر نواب معز الدین خان بہادر کے تھے جو ایک
رئیس خاندان شیوخ لکھنؤ میں سے تھے اور جیسے کہ ہدایت اللہ خان صاحب سے قرابت بھی تھی ہدایت اللہ خان
صاحب اوس جنگ میں جو نواب معز الدین خان صاحب بہادر اور افاغنہ کے بکس سے ہوئی تھی شریک تھے اور
نواب صاحب بہادر کی جنگ بھجولہ لما گھاٹ میں بھی شریک تھے جبکہ حال اود ہر گزیرہ و عماد السعادت اور
سیر المتاخرین اور سلطان التواریخ وغیرہ میں مندرج ہے ہدایت اللہ خان صاحب کے کوئی اولاد زرینہ
نہ تھی اون کے داماد محمد اکرام خان ریاست محمود آباد پر بعد اونکے قابض ہوئے محمد اکرام خان صاحب
کے دو بیٹھے تھے سرفراز علی خان صاحب و مصاحب علی خان صاحب سرفراز علی خان صاحب بعد محمد اکرام
صاحب ریاست محمود آباد پر قابض ہوئے اور گوندہ اور بہرائچ اور سندیلہ اور بانگر مؤ وغیرہ کی نظامت
پر عہد آصف الدولہ بہادر میں مامور ہوئے اور جنگ روہیلہ میں ہمراہ لشکر وزارت تھے بعد اونکے
انتقال کے مصاحب علی خان صاحب بھجو سگے بھائی اونکے مسند ریاست محمود آباد پر متمکن ہوئے اور اونہوں
نے خدمات جانکاہ زمانہ نواب سعادت علی خان میں کیں اور نواب سعادت علی خان صاحب کو اپنا بھائی
کیا اور بڑے سے عظیم و شان سے دعوت کی جمع و لشکر وزارت سے تمام چھاونی محمود آباد کے پانی نے
آکنھانڈی اور کنویں خشک ہو گئے مگر ایک کنواں ولتمن جواب تک موجود ہے اونکا یہ پانی نہیں ہوا
سکا یہ پانی کم ہوا صاحب علی خان صاحب کی اس عالی حوصلگی اور سیر چشمی کے صلہ میں کہ اتنے بڑے سے تمام لشکر کو

طعام نفیس دیا اور بعوض دیگر خدمات کے نواب سعادت علیخان صاحب بہادر نے محال فیلیانہ خطاب کیا
صاحب علیخان صاحب کی فیاضی اور دسترخوان اور مہمان نوازی سنے بڑی شہرت پائی ان کی رعایا
ان کو بہت عزیز رکھتی تھی اور اب تک ان کو ایک نہایت متقدس شخص جانتے ہیں مصاحب علیخان سنے
لاولد انتقال کیا ان کے بعد ان کی بیوہ و انکی قابض ریاست محمود آباد ہو ئین جو قریب ورثاء سے مصاحب علیخان
صاحب میں تھی بیوہ مصاحب علیخان صاحب سنے ان کو اپنا وارث اور جانشین اپنی حیات میں
مقرر کیا اپنے مقیم الدولہ راجہ نوابعلیخان بہادر قیام جنگ کو جو بھتیجے مصاحب علیخان صاحب کے تھو
ان کو اپنا جانشین کیا راجہ نواب علیخان والد راجہ صاحب محمود آباد عالم اور شاعر جرار قدم بقدم
صاحب علیخان صاحب کی فیاضی اور سیر جشمی میں تھے ان کا کلیات نظر سے چھپ گیا نہایت عمدہ
شاعر تھے یہ ہمیشہ حاضر دربار شاہی رہے اور اکثر ایسے احکام شاہی ان کے نام صادر ہو ا کیے جیسے میں
عہدہ داران شاہی ہو بون معاونت ان کے ناکا میاب رہتے تھے چنانچہ ان سے بہت کارہائے
نمایاں ہو سے جنہا سے سرور اور سنتا سے قاسم گنج رام پور متھرا بوندی چپلا رہی علیہ نگرانی پارہ متولی
بہنگا کسگا ان وہل وکمیٹہ ومتولی وجنگ مولوی امیر علی وتدارک فضل علی وغیرہ میں واسطے سرکوبی
باغیوں کے مامور ہو سے اور فتوحات نمایاں حاصل کیے اور راجہ نواب علیخان صاحب کی شادی ہوئی
نواب معزالدین خانصاحب بہادر رئیس خاندان شیوخ لکھنؤ سے ہو ئی جیسے راجہ امیر حسن خانصاحب
بہادر رئیس حال محمود آباد ومتولد ہو ئے جواب بتمکن ریاست محمود آباد میں ہیں ۔

(نمبر ۱۱) راجہ بجے بہادر سنگہ قوم ٹھاکر سوم نبسی تعلقدار بہاولپور خطاب راجہ موروثی ۔

چھہ سو برس ہو ئے راجہ ہیرستی مورث اعلی پرگنہ بھجونسی ضلع الہ آباد سے بخوف شیخ تقی درویش کامل
صاحبان فوج جو کہ قوم ہنود کے دشمن تھے معہ اپنی زوجہ کے بقام اور ل جو کہ اب پرتابگڈھ مشہور ہے
آئے ان کے ایک لڑکا لکھن سمبتی نامے پیدا ہوا اس لڑکے کو کچھ دفینہ دستیاب ہوا و اسنے فوج نوکر رکھی
افواج ہر سی بعد معرکہ ریاست کی اور سرکار شاہی سے خطاب سا دیا پایا بعد کو خاندان میں
علیحدگی ہو کر متعدد ریاستیں قائم ہوگئیں نمبر ہائے ذیل اسی خاندان سے ہیں نمبر ۳۵ و ۴۰ و ۹۲
و ۱۶ و ۱۶۸ و ۱۸۴ و ۱۹ ۔ اور ان تعلقدار سنے اپنا کچھ حصہ بدست راجہ اجیت سنگہ مذکرہ نمبر ۴۸ فروخت
کر ڈالا ۔ اس تعلقہ میں اب ایک لاش موضع محبی دعبد ضلع پرتاب گڈھ میں واقع ہیں رسم
گدی نشینی اس خاندان میں سے ہے ۔

(نمبر ۱۲) راجہ سری بال سنگہ قوم کنپوریہ تعلقدار تلوئی وبھوپورکنوان وصورت گڈھ درست بودو

پتر بزرگ و پیر ہی و مصطفیٰ آباد خطاب راجہ موروثی ہے ۔ راجہ مالک قوم گھروار موروث اعلیٰ اس خاندان نہیں
تھے اور اوسکی بجز ایک دختر کے کوئی وارث نہ تھا سو سات سو برس ہوے اونہوں نے اوسکی شادی ایک
برہمن سے کرکے کل ریاست اوسکو بخش دی اوسکی ایک لڑکا پیدا ہوا جسکا نام راجہ کانہہ مشہور ہوا اوسکی
اولاد کنپوریہ ٹھاکر کہلاتی ہے کانہہ کے تین لڑکے ہوے راجہس سہمش رود اَٹن رہیس کی اولاد دگا
و مدن سنگھ و مان سنگھ ہوے جو کانہہ سنگھ کے خاندان میں بلبھدر ساہ سے مترجیت ہوے چنانچہ یہ تعلقدار
نمبر ۵۰ خاندان بلبھدر ساہ سے ہیں اور مترجیت سے تعلقداران نمبر ۱۰ کا ہے بلبھدر ساہ کے چار لڑکے
ہوے پہاڑ امل و سالبان ہین و تربیون ساہی و راج ساہ پہاڑ امل سے تعلقدار نمبر ۳۰ کے ہیں
اور سالبا ہین سکے خاندان سے تعلقدار نمبر ۱۰ و تربیون ساہی کے خاندان سے تعلقدار نمبر ۲۰
راج ساہ کے خاندان سے تعلقداران نمبر ۸۰ و ۱۶ اور مدن سنگھ پسر دویم رہیس کے خاندن سے
تعلقداران نمبر ۲۹ و ۷۷ ہیں اور مان سنگھ پسر سوم رہیس کے خاندان سے نمبر ۹ اسکے تعلقدار
سمس پسر دویم راجہ کانہہ کے خاندان سے تعلقداران نمبر ۲۹ و ۲۲ و ۲۲ قائم ہیں اور رود ان پسر
سوم راجہ کانہہ کی اولاد مین زمیدار ان مفرد دیہات سکے ہین ۔ اس تعلقہ کے مالک آخر الامر راجہ جوہن سنگھ
جو تعلقدار حال ہوے اونہوں نے اس ریاست کو بہت ترقی دی بعد وفات اوکی راجہ جگ پال سنگھ
وارث ریاست ہوے اوکی وفات کے بعد اب یہ تعلقدار مالک ریاست ہین اور اس تعلقہ مین نامی موضع
جمبی حدید کالویہ اضلاع راے بریلی و سلطانپور و پرتاپ گڈہ مین واقع ہین رسم گدی نشینی اس خاندان مین نہیں

(نمبر ۱۳) کشن ناتھ کنور زوجہ راجہ مادھو پرتاپ سنگھ تعلقدار کوڑوار و مجیس و میگہات کوڑہ و ہگاوت
قوم بجگوتی خطاب رانی موروثی ۔ تذکرہ خاندانی آپ کا نمبر ۷ پر درج ہی خاندان چگر سنگھ موروث مین
سے یہ ریاست قائم ہوئی اوکی سولہوین پشت مین راجہ مادھو پرتاپ سنگھ شوہران رئیسہ کے قابض
تعلقہ کے ہوے بعد وفات اوکے یہ رئیسہ قابض ریاست ہین تعلقہ نمبری ۷ و ۹ و ۵ ہنیالخ اس
تعلقہ کے ہین ما بین موضع عنبی جمبی حدید اضلاع سلطانپور و فیض آباد مین واقع ہین
رہم گدی نشینی اس خاندان مین ہے ۔

(نمبر ۱۴) راجہ رانا شنکر سنگھ بخش سنگھ قوم سومبسی مین تعلقدار کمجور کانون و ابراہیم گنج و تمدری و کڑو ہیا
خطاب رانا موروثی ۔ آپ کا تذکرہ خاندانی نمبر یہ پر درج سے جب ہرہر دیو موروث دہلی سی واپس آئی تو
راجہ تلوکچند نے پرتمی راج اپنے چھوٹے لڑکو راج سے خارج کرکے ہرہر دیو کو مالک ریاست
کیا اور خطاب رانا کا نمبشاہ پر تمی راج مرار موین رہے ہرہر دیو نے اس مقام پر جگل کمجور کٹواکر

کھجور گانون آباد کیا اور خود سکونت پذیر ہوے اوئگی تیسری پشت میں رانا ٹھکر سنگھ ہوے اوسکے تین لڑکون
رانا دومن دیو رو دوڑہ ساہ عالم شاہ تھے مین علاقہ تقسیم ہوا نمبر اول کو کھجور گانون ملا نمبر دوم کو سمرسیا نمبری ۴
نمبر ۳ کو ہر تساون نمبر ۶ پھر رانا دومن دیو سکے بعد اوسکے آٹھوں لڑکونین ریاست موئی منبلا اونکے
اجیت مل کو تعلقہ کھجور گانون ملا اور باقی سب سنے ایک، ایک دو دو موضعات بطور گذارہ پاۓ اجیت مل
کے گیا۔ عون پشت مین اب قابض ریاست ہین اور آغاز علمداری سرکار سے آپ انریزی محبترہ تربیت
واسنٹ کلکتہ مین انتظام علاقہ اور داد گستری آپ کا مشہور ہے قحط ش۱۲ ۱۲ فصل مین آپ سنے بہار دگی
رعایا و محتاجان مین ہزار ہا روپیہ اپنا صرف کیا اور ترتیب قوانین مختص المقام ملک اود مین شہر کی
صلاح رہے اور بمنصب والیں پریذیڈنٹ انجمن ہند بہبود ہ گروہ تعلقداران مین سرگرم ہین رانا اوڑی یو
کے خاندان سے ذیل کے تعلقدار ہین نمبر ۷ و ۱۸ و ۲۵ و ۹۳ ۔اور رو دوہ ساہ کے خاندانشہ
نمبر ۳۹ و ۵۰ ۔۔۔ کے تعلقدار مین اس تعلقہ مین مانتا ۱۲ موضع جمعی یک لاکھ للعوی مابعہ۹ اصلاع
بریلی و لکھنو و راے بریلی مین واقع مین رسم گدی نشینی اس خاندان مین ہوتی ۔۔۔ منبلا و تعلقداران
کے یہ بھی دربار دہلی مین منتخب ہوے اور تمغہ قیصری عطا ہوا اور بجلد و سے پرورش بہتا جین قوتہ
لکھنو مین سار ٹیفکٹ عطا ہوا ۔

(نمبر ۱۵) رانی دھرم راج کنور زوجہ مہیش نرائن سنگھ قوم درگ بنسی تعلقدار پرہت و راے ۔۔۔
بجہپور و سنگھولی و ٹونک ۔ چار سو برس ہوے درگ ساہی قوم درگ بنس مورث اعلا اپنا تعلقہ موئی کلا
واقع جو پور بوجہ نزاع باہمی چھوڑ کر دہلی مین آئے اور بحکم شاہ وقت دہلی بھر کو جو سرکش تھی
اور اونگی ریاست پر قابض ہوے وخطاب راجگی سلطنت سے حاصل کیا صاحب سہ قبضہ اس خاندان مین
چلا آتا ہے آخر الامرا راجہ مہیش نرائن سنگھ کو بصلہ خیر خواہی ایام غدر ش۱۸۵۸ء گورنمنٹ انگلشیہ سے تعلقہ سنگھولی
حاصل ہوا بعد وفات اونکے یہ رئیسہ قابض ریاست مین ش۔۔۔ موضع جمعی ۔۔۔ معہ ملکیت علیہ
اصلاع پر ابگنڈہ و سلطانپور و راے بریلی مین واقع ہین رسم گدی نشینی اس خاندان مین ہو ۔

(نمبر ۱۶) راجہ فرزند علی خان شیخ قدوائی تعلقدار جہانگیر آباد و ہگاون و روئی و شیر اکنی خطاب راجہپور و
شیخ رزاق بخش مالک اس تعلقہ سکے تھے جنکے مورثان سنے جہانگیر بادشاہ سکے نام پر اس موضع کو
آباد کیا تھا ش۱۲ ۱۲ فصل مین بوجہ لاولدی رزاق بخش یہ ملکیت بذریعہ ہبہ ان تعلقدار کو حاصل ہوئی
اور خطاب راجگی آخری سلطنت اود سے حاصل ہوا جواب تک قائم ہے بعد ہبہ و ثبت یختہ المنون قرتلقہ
عثمانپور و مہرانوان مین بہت ملکیت حاصل کرکے ترقی ریاست کی جو سند تعلقداری سے باہر ہے تعلقہ

اور موضع واقعہ پٹی مجہی ملیہ ... اضلاع لکھنؤ نواب گنج بارہ بنکی و سیتاپور میں واقع ہیں فوج کدری نشینی اس خاندان میں ہیں ہے ۔

(نمبر ۱۷) راجہ جنگ بہادر خان قوم بھجان ملوع تعلقہ داران پارہ خطاب راجہ موروثی ۱۱۹۵ فصلی عہد سلطنت شاہجہان میں رسول خان مورث اعلیٰ انکو قلعہ دار ہوکر دہلی سے بہرائچ میں آئے اورا وزنکو بجاد وسے سرزادہی اقوام بنجارہ دیہات پرگنہ ساون کے سلطنت سے بجق دہ کیک مرحمت ہوئی ۱۲۱۸ فصلی میں مدار بخش مورث کو علاقہ گور گنج بجکم نواب سعادت علیخان مرحمت ہوا ۱۲۲۸ فصلی میں کریم خان مورث سے عہد نواب شجاع الدولہ بہادر زمان پارہ میں گدہمی ہوواکر سکونت اختیار کی وخطاب راجگی ونیز علاقہ سنگاؤ بہرائچ دکاداپور وغیرہ نواب موصوف سے بطور جاگیر حاصل کیا جب سے یہ دریا قائم سے عطہ موضع کیک پٹی نمبی کیک لاکھ ... ضلع بہرائچ میں واقع ہیں رسم گدی نشینی اس خاندان میں ہے ۔

(نمبر ۱۸) راجہ زند جہیر سنگھ تعلقہ دار بہراوان ولسبنت پور مرہاپور خطاب راجہ موروثی اس ریاست میں رامچند مورث اعلیٰ سنے اپنی شادی قوم گو رزنہ زمیندار ان اس علاقہ سے کرکے بہراون میں سکونت اختیار کی حب اقوام گورکو اسبات کا کشک از جانب رامچند پیدا ہوواکہ ایسا نہ ہواک ایسا علاقہ دخل کر یہ وس لہذا اوس قوم سے رامچند کو قتل کر ڈالا اوسکے بعد زکے تین الزکے الکنگ رتی بھجان لکھتیں سود کتے سنجلہ اوسکے نمبرا و ۳ سے دہلی میں جاکر ملازمت شاہ اختیار کی اور اپنی خدمت سے بادشاہ کو ایسا خوش کیا کہ بادشاہ سنے جاگیر ومنصب دیا چاہا اوسوقت اونھون سنے درخواست انتقام خون اپنی کی شاہ وقت سے کی چنانچہ بامداد فوج شاہی اقوام گورکواگر قتل کیا اور ریاست پر قابض ہووئے اوسوقت سے میچھ سو برس ہووسے یہ ریاست قائم سے آخرالامر راجہ مردن سنگھ بذریعہ تبنیت مالک اس تعلقہ کے ہووسے اور اونھون سنے بصلائہ خیر خواہی ایام غدر ۵۷ عرگورنمنٹ انگلشیہ سے تعلقہ مرہا پو رعطیہ حاصل کیا دسند تعلقہ داری پائی بعد وفات اوسکے آپ بیٹی اوسکے قابض ریاست میں اس تعلقہ میں معہ ملکیت عطیہ ضلعہ موضع للعہ پٹی مجہی ملعیہ ... اضلاع لکھنؤ و بہردوئی واد نام میں واقع ہیں رسم گدی نشینی اس خاندان میں ہے ۔

(نمبر ۱۹) خاندان راجہ رگوناتھہ سنگھ قوم ریکوار تعلقدار رہوہ یہ ریاست موروثی قوم ریکوار کی ہوکنتہہ مضلی میں پرتاپ ساہ ودھونندی ساہ قوم راجپوت سوج منسی ساکنان ریکہ جانب ملک کشمیر سنتاس جوار میں آئے اوکی اولاد میں سالدیو والدیو نے دریب چندر راجہ قوم بھجرکو قتل کرکے

ریاست علاقہ بہنوٹی حاصل کی اور کی اولاد میں دیدہ سوبرس بعد گجیت سنگھ کو خطاب راجکی حاصل ہوا اور اولاد رگھو ناتھ سنگھ آپ کے والد مالک ریاست ہوئے بعد وفات اونکے آپ قابض ریاست ہیں اور آپ نابالغ ہیں نمبر کسی نام سے موسوم نہیں ہوئے اور تعلقہ کا نام رہا ہو اسوجہ سے مشہور ہوا گر اس کا نو نگر زمین میں رہیو مٹی پیدا ہوتی ہے جو صفائی و ثوب لپرجہ وغیرہ میں کام آتی ہے تعلقدار ان نمبری ۳۰۱م و ۲۹۱ سی خاندان نسبی دربا موضع للعہ بٹی ممبی للع۔۔۔ ایک دہ۔۔۔ ضلع بہرائچ میں واقع ہیں رسم گدی نشینی اس خاندان میں ہے

(نمبر ۲۰) راجہ محمد کاظم حسین خان قوم خانزادہ تعلقدار نتھی پور و لبھرہ خطاب راجہ موروثی

آپ ہم خاندان تعلقدار محمود آباد متذکرہ نمبر ۱ کے ہیں مفصل تذکرہ اوسی نمبر پر درج ہے ۔ عطا خان خلف بازگیر ریاست لبھرہ پر قابض ہوئے ان کے پانچ بیٹے تھے قائم خان اصالت خان منظم خان غضنفر خان اور ساینہ اولیا خان کے اولاد میں زمینداران محمد پور میں معظم خان اور اصالت خان کی اولاد نہیں باقی ہر غضنفر خان کی اولاد ہے مگر کوئی ریاست اونکے پاس نہیں ہے قائم خان ریاست لبھرہ پر قابض ہوئے اون کے بیٹے رحمت خان تھے اور جیتے بنجما اور سنگھ عرف مکھا رنگوارسے لڑائی ہوئی اور یہ فتحیاب ہوئے مرحمت خان صاحب کے چار بیٹے اول بیدار بخت خان جنکی پشت میں زمیداران سن توار میں دوم غلام حسین عرف سایں جنکی اولاد میں زمینداران منورا اور سبوری میں سیوم میں جاہ خان جنکی اولاد دیسری میں کوئی نہیں سے چہارم محمد امام خان جو بعد تقسیم ریاست آبائی ریاست لبھرہ کے مالک و قابض ہوئے اور ہمراہ نواب معزالدین خان صاحب جنگ افاغنہ نگبتش وغیرہ میں شتریک ہوکر داد جوا مردمی او سکے دو بیٹوگو محمد اکرام خان و منظر علینان محمد اکرام خان ابد ہدایت ابد خان صاحب اپنے نسر کی ریاست محمود آباد پر قابض ہوئے اور منظر علینان اپنے باپ کی ریاست لبھرہ پر قابض ہوئے منظر علی خان صاحب کے بعد اونکے بیٹے اور علینا نصاحب قابض ریاست لبھرہ ہوئے اور ہمراہ نواب اصف الدولہ بہادر جنگ رو ہیلہ میں تھے امیر علینان صاحب کے بعد اونکے بڑے بیٹے راجہ عباد علی صاحب قابض ریاست لبھرہ اور دربار شاہی سے مخاطب بخطاب راجہ عباد علینان بہادر ہوئے اور مخلع نجماعت ہوئے راجہ عباد علینان بہادر کو ریاست نتھی پور خاد م علینان صاحب رئیس نتھی پور نے ہبہ بالعیوض کرکے قابض کیا اور خود لا ولد انتقال کیا اور محجوبے بیٹے والد راجہ صاحب محمود آباد جو رئیس محمود آباد بجائے مصاحب علی خان صاحب کے موسوب اب راجہ کاظم حسین خان بسر راجہ عباد علی خان بہادر ریاست لبھرہ پر قابض ہوئے اور یہ راجہ محمود آباد حقیقی چچا زاد اور خالہ زاد بھائی ہیں بنکی بارہ بنکی میں واقع ہیں موضع ۔۔۔ بٹی ممبی مللع۔۔۔ اضلاع سیتاپور بارہ بنکی میں واقع ہیں

رسم گدی نشینی اس خاندان مین سے ہے ۔

(نمبر ۱۳) راجہ بھگوان بخش نابالغ خلف راجہ امراو سنگہ قوم ٹھاکر امیٹھیا تعلقدار پوکھرا انصاری خطاب راجہ موروثی ۔ سات سو سال ہوئے راجہ پرتھی چند مورث اعلی شیو پوری سے نارکنجو بین اکرآباد ہوئے او ردہان سے بعد راشنان اجودھیا میا جی ایستھی ضلع لکھنؤ مین آئے او نکی اولاد مین راجہ دیگر ساہ مورث نے سپہ سالار فوج شاہ دہلی ہو کر بہروں سے معرکہ کر کے بعد فتح علاقہ بابا اوسوقت سے یہ ریاست ہوئی راجہ دیگر ساہ کے رام سنگہ بھائی تھے اونکو یہ تعلقہ پوکھرا انصاری ملا جو سابق مین بنام لاہی معروف تھا اور دوسرے بھائی دیپک رائے ودیبجی ہرا اور رام سنگہ لے گئے دیگر ساہ خود مشیو راج پورمین رہے آخر الامراو نکی گیارھویں پشت مین رام سنگہ سے راجہ امراو سنگہ والد آپ کے قابض تعلقہ ہوئے بعد وفات اونکے بوجہ نابالغی آپ کے یہ علاقہ تحت کورٹ آف وارڈس سے ہے اور تعلقہ نمبری ۲۲ و ۲۳۸ و ۲۳۹ اسی خاندان سے ہین اس تعلقہ مین موضع اللعہ بنی تبھی ضلع بارہ بنکی مین واقع ہین رسم گدی نشینی اس خاندان مین سے ہے ۔

(نمبر ۲۲) راجہ بشبیشر بخش قوم ٹھاکر امیٹھیا تعلقدار بر سنگہ پور و کھراوان و سکندر پور و حصہ شرا کتی خطاب راجہ موروثی ۔ الکا مذکرہ خاندانی نمبر ۱۳ پر درج سے ہے راجہ پرتھی چند مورث اعلی سکے خاندان این راجہ ازارو سنگہ مورث سے یہ ریاست قائم ہوئی آخر الامراو راجہ جگمو ہن سنگہ مالک اس ریاست کے ہوئے اور گورنمنٹ انگلشیہ سے سند تعلقداری حاصل کی بعد وفات اونکے یہ رئیس قابض ریاست ہین اور تعلقداران نمبری ۱ و ۲۵ و ۱۵ اسی خاندان سے ہین اس تعلقہ مین منجملہ موضع جمبی ضلعا بارہ بنکی و لکھنو و رائے بریلی مین واقع ہین رسم گدی نشینی اس خاندان مین سے ہے ۔

(نمبر ۱۴) راجہ جگمو ہن سنگہ خلف راجہ رتن سنگہ قوم نیوار تعلقدار رائے بریکیدار بہ اٹونجہ خطاب راجہ موروثی او نیس پشت گذرین رائے دیور و دہ رائے مورث دہ مار انگر تعلقہ صوبہ گوالیا رائے سے اکر شاہ دہلی سکے ملازم ہوئے اوسوقت پر او نکا بھائی اقوام کورمی مالکان ریاست مہو نہ کا ملازم تھا دیور و دہ رائے نے سبارش بھائی کے یہان اقوام کورمی نیکو ریاست سے خارج کر دیا اور آپ مالک ہو گئے او نکے تین لڑک ہوئے دنگار دیو نہلاد دیو کرن دیو اور اُن مین ملکیت تقسیم ہو کر کمی تعلقہ اس ریاست کے ہو گئے اب اولاد نکار دیو سے قابض اس ریاست کے ہین اور اولاد نہلاد دیو قابض تعلقہ نمبر ۹ و ۱۴ اسے ہین اور کرن دیو کی اولاد تعلقہ نمبری ۱۵ و ۱۱ پر قابض سے ہین اور آپ سرگردہ قوم نیوار تصور ہوتے ہین تعلقہ مین رہوان موضع کیمٹ بنی تبھی ضلع لکھنو مین واقع ہین رسم گدی نشینی اس خاندان مین سے

(نمبر ۲۴) راجہ کرشنت سنگھ قوم جنبوار تعلقدار اوبل بڈاگاؤں وجکول وبیلانی ورسول پنیا وبیافور و برو پساد کمہونیا و مہریا خطاب راجہ موروثی ۔ تین سو برس ہوے راجہ بنیاد سنگھ مورث نے موضع اوبل چکے نام سے تعلقہ مشہور پہوآ وکیا اور جہان ساہ مورث نے بوجہ لاولدی اپنی مسمی او روپ ساہ اپنو نواسہ کو بجے پور سے طلب کرکے تشبے کیا بعد اوسکے دیڑھ سو برس ہوا بوجہ فساد باہمی راجہ کشمیرہ سکے یہ ریاست اس خاندان میں رہی اور اودیب ساہ جانب تنہرا افرار ہوگیا پھر شے ۱۱ء فصلی میں سنبھلا اولاد اودیب ساہ کی پیتم سنگھ نے اوبل پر قبضہ پایا اوسکی اولاد سے تعلقدار مہیوا نمبری ۱۱ء اور یہ تعلقدار سمند تعلقہ نبام راجہ ازدہ سنگھ گورنمنٹ سے عطا ہوئی تھی بعد وفات اوسکے قابض ہین یہ رئیس اس تعلقہ میں ہا۔۔ء موضع اور دعۃ پٹی جمبی یک لاکھ سعہ سا جہء۹ ضلع کھیری وسیتاپور مین واقع ہین رسم گدی نشینی اس خاندان میں ہے

(نمبر ۲۵) راجہ نراندر بہادر سنگھ قوم سورج میں تعلقدار شہرابا خطاب راجہ موروثی ۔

شے شہ فصلی میں بہ عہد سلطنت تیمور شاہ بہرام سنگھ مورث اعلی اسنے ضمانت زر بقایا بالگذاری رئیس سابق اس علاقہ سکے عوض میں روپیہ سلطنت وقت کو ادا کرکے یہ ریاست حاصل کی اور نام اس ریاست کا دہرداہ رکھا جور فتہ رفتہ ہڑا مشہور ہوا اوسکی آنھوں پشت میں لچھی نزان سنگھ قابض ریاست ہوے اونھون سے گلال ساہ اپنے بھائی کو اس ریاست میں سے یک حصہ تقسیم کردیا جونمبر ۱۹۔ پر علیحدہ قائم ہے لچھی نزان کی نویں پشت میں یہ تعلقدار وارث ملکیت ہین تعلقہ میں ۲۵ء موضع دعۃ پٹی جمبی طلاعہ ضلع بارہ بنکی میں واقع ہین رسم گدی نشینی اس خاندان میں ہے

(نمبر ۲۶) راجہ رام پال سنگھ قوم میں سنتہ تعلقدار کوری سدولی تذکرہ خاندانی آپ کا نمبر ۲۰ء پر درج سہے کرن راے مورث اعلے کے تین لڑکون ہرنگ راے نرسنگھ راے بیرجان میں جب ریاست تقسیم ہوئی نمبر اسنتہ میں رہے اور نمبر ۲۱ء نرسنگھ پور میں گئے اور نمبر ۳ بہار نمبری ۱۹۵ میں آباد ہوے ہرسنگھ راے کی جوتھی پشت میں ابے بلٹیند سنگھ راے میں جب تقسیم ملکیت کی ہوئی ابے چند اس ریاست سکے مالک ہوے اور سنگھ تعلقہ سمری نمبر ۵۸ء کے وارث ہوے ابے چند کی جوتھی پشت میں صدیق سنگھ نے خطاب راجگی شاہ دہلی سے پایا با صدیق سنگھ کی پانچویں پشت میں یہ تعلقدار قابض ریاست ہین اور اس تعلقہ سے تعلقہ نمبر ۹ قائم سہے اس تعلقہ میں ۔۔عہ۔۔ موضع دعۃ جمبی نعہ علا علیہ ۔ ضلع راے بریلی میں واقع ہین رسم گدی نشینی اس خاندان میں سہے ۔

(نمبر ۲۷) راجہ سیتلا بخش سنگھ قوم جنوار تعلقدار گنگول و جیرام چوت خطاب راجہ موروثی۔

سمت ۱۳ مین بریار رسالہ مورث اعلی نے بعہد فیروزشاہ بادشاہ دہلی بامداد فوج شاہی اقوام بھرون کا قلع قمع کر کے راج اکونہ واقع ضلع بہرایچ ریاست بھرون پر قبضہ پایا اور پھر خطاب راجگی پاکر سینتیس سال تک راج کیا چند پشتون کے بعد بھیا پرتاب سنگھ نے ہنگام تقسیم باہمی تعلقہ گنگول پایا اونکو خطاب راجگی حاصل نہ تھا بلقب بھیا مشہور تھے اونکی چوتھی پشت مین گنیش پرشاد سنگھ ہوئے اونھون نے کسیطرح سے خطاب راجگی حاصل کیا اب چند پشت بعد یہ رئیس قابض ریاست ہوئے اور گورنمنٹ انگلشیہ سے سند تعلقداری حاصل کی تعلقہ مین للوہ موضع اور چھ پٹی جمعی ساہے اضلاع بہرایچ و گونڈہ مین واقع ہین رسم گدی نشینی اس خاندان مین ہے

(نمبر ۲۸) راجہ مہندر بہادر سنگھ قوم جنوار تعلقدار پیاگپور خطاب راجہ موروثی۔

عرصہ چار سو سال کا ہوا چودھری شیام سنگھ مورث اعلی گجرات سے دہلی مین آئے اور رسالہ دار ہوکر ہمراہ سعادتعلیخان وزیر الممالک اودھ مین بموضع بالاپور تیرہ مالکانہ مقیم ہوئے بعد شیام سنگھ پیاگ سنگھ مالک ہوئے اور اونکو پیاگپور خاص سلطنت دہلی سے مرحمت ہوا اونکی پانچوین پشت مین بخت سنگھ مالک ریاست ہوئے اور سلطنت اودھ سے اونکو خطاب راجگی عطا ہوا انکی چند پشتون کے بعد یہ رئیس قابض ریاست ہین۔ اور اس تعلقہ مین ماہ موضع للعہ پٹی جمعی ملوہ مالوے ضلع بہرایچ مین واقع ہین رسم گدی نشینی اس خاندان مین ہے۔

(نمبر ۲۹) راجہ جگموہن سنگھ قوم کنپوریہ تعلقدار اٹرا چنداپور و تیپھی کھور خطاب راجہ موروثی۔

انکا تذکرہ خاندانی نمبر ۲۱ پر درج ہے بعہد عالمگیر شاہ راجہ مدن سنگھ مورث اعلیٰ پرگنہ مانکپور ضلع پرتاب گدھ سے سمروتہ مین آئے اور اقوام بھر کو شکست دیکر ایک مکان بنام نہاد کوٹ طیار کرایا اور اس پرگنہ سمروتہ مین جنگل ایسا بکثرت تھا کہ دنکو بخوبی روشنی ظاہر نہوتی تھی اوسکو کٹوا کر بوجہ ظاہر ہونے روشنی کے بتشبیہ چاند چنداپور نام رکھا جس نام سے تعلقہ مشہور ہے جانب پچھم سمروتہ پرگنہ ہردوئی ہے جو بیالیس مشہور تھا اوسجگہہ بھی آبادی بھرون کی تھی اوس پرگنہ کو بھی اقوام بھر سے اپنے قبضہ مین لائے اور اوس جگہہ ایک مکان عظیم الشان طیار کرایا جو اٹرا مشہور ہوا اوسوقت سے علی الاتصال قبضہ مورثان چلا آتا ہے اور جو صوبہ دار دہلی سے آتا تھا انتظام ملکی مین آپ کو مورثان سے مدد لیتا تھا بجلدوے اوس خیر خواہی کے مواضع پرگنہ سمروتہ مین بطور معافی مورثان کو عطیہ حاصل ہوئے چند پشتون کے بعد راجہ جگجراج سنگھ اس خاندان مین ہوئے اونھون نے تنبیہ اقوام بھر مین صوبہ دار اودھ کو بہت مدد دی اور انتظام شاہراہ جہان پر کہ رہزنی وغیرہ ہوتی تھی بخوبی درست کیا بجلدوی اس خیر خواہی کے خلعت بیش بہا اور ملکیت ماہدیے موضع پرگنہ سمروتہ بطور مالکانہ اور پانچ موضع بطور معافی

واقع پرگنہ ہر دوئی شاہ دہلی سے حاصل کیے اور روراو سنگھ مورث کو شاہ دہلی سے ڈنکا و توپ و خلعت و تربیت

اور راجہ دکبیھ سنگھ نے محتاج خانہ جاری کیا اور مصدہ با غریب آدمیوں کی دختر کی روپیہ دیکر شادی کرا دی

جب راجہ شیو رشن سنگھ مالک ریاست ہوئے تو اوھون نے اپنے حقیقی برادر راجہ ہری شاہ دسنگھ والا تعلقدار

حال کو مالک ریاست کر دیا مگر راجہ ہری شاہ نے بہت جلد وفات پائی اور سوقت راجہ شیو رشن سنگھ نے خان تعلقدار

کو مالک ریاست کیا یہ رئیس خیر خواہ گورنمنٹ انگلشیہ ہیں دربارہائے گورنمنٹ میں لکھنؤ میں انکو خلعت فاخرہ

اور ایک ولایتی عیش تمیت مرحمت ہوئی و بنظر و فور لیاقت گورنمنٹ انگلشیہ سے اختیارات انریزری محبت شرقی و

اسسٹنٹ کلکٹری حاصل ہیں اور روربار دہلی شبائع میں منجملہ و تعلقداران کے یہ رئیس بھی منتخب فرما دئے

اور تمغہ عطا ہوا اور قانون مختص المقام او دصہ میں شریک یک کونسل ہوئے ۔ اب تعلقہ میں منتہ موضع جمعی

ضلع بریلی میں واقع ہیں اور اس خاندان میں رسم گدی نشینی ہے ۔ ایام قحط سالی شبائع

بجلاد و سے پرورش متابعین دربار لکھنؤ میں خلعت فاخرہ پایا ۔

(نمبر ۳۰) ہر ناتھہ کنور زوجہ راجہ سر نام سنگھہ قوم کنپہ ریہ تعلقدار کٹاری خطاب رانی ۔

انکا تذکرہ خاندانی وآغاز ریاست نمبر ۳۲ پہ مندرج ہر خاندان راجہ ہانک سی طلبی پرساوہ مورث کی چار اولادیں

جب تقسیم باہمی ہوئی او سوقت سے یہ ریاست علیحدہ و قائم ہوی یہ تعلق راولا دیہا اہل سے میں اس تعلقہ میں

یہ موضع جمعی میت ضلع سلطانپور میں واقع ہیں رسم گدی نشینی اس خاندان میں ہر ۔

(نمبر ۳۱) رانی صاحب جان بیوہ راجہ مشرف علیخان قوم سید تعلقہ دار رہا دنگر و نرسنگھہ پور و

احمد نگر و گلدا پور و بانکا گاؤں و منصور نگر خطاب رانی نیوروٹی ۔ شنتہ اوعہد جہانگیر شاہ بادشاہ دہلی میں نواب

حیدر جہان مورث شوہر رئیسہ کو یہ ریاست بطور جاگیر مرحمت ہوئی تھی پھر بعد شاہ اورنگ زیب بادشاہ عزیز

بعد انتقال مورث مذکور اقوام اہین ٹھاکر مالک ریاست جند عرصہ تک رہے عشاہ والفصلی میں اشرف علیخان

مورث قابض ملکیت ہوئے او سوقت سے برابر قبضہ اس خاندان میں چلا آ اہر تعلقہ میں الیہ موضع جمعی

اضلاع کھیمری و ہر دوئی میں واقع ہیں رسم گدی نشینی اس خاندان میں ہر ۔

(نمبر ۳۲) راجہ کشہندت رام قوم برہمن پانڈے چندہ تعلقدار دنگھا چندہ راجہ میں حیات

شنتہ شبائع میں بوقت آذ نادر شاہ کئی لاکھ روپیہ نواب سعادت خان برہان الملک صوبہ دارا و دہ کو بضرورت زینہ

فوازی رام مورث قرض دیا تھا بعد وفات برہان الملک بلدی رام پانڈے بیٹے اونکے پاس ابو المنصور خان

داماد برہان الملک بغرض وصول روپیہ دہلی سے آ گئے اور تعلقہ گوندہ وغیرہ بطور جر بوگ حاصل کیا پھر جہد عرصہ کے بعد

بعد نظامت معزالدین خان میں لاکھہ روپیہ راجہ شیو پرشاد و تعلقدار گوندہ بہت اور ہی مالکداری سرکار بریلی ۔

قرض دیا جب راجہ گوندہ سے روپیہ ادا نہ ہو سکا اور سوقت لبوفض روپیہ چند دیہات بطور بیع حاصل کرکے ریاست
قائم کی بعد کو مردون رام مورث فرزے بیع و نا مالک اس راس تعلقہ کو زیادہ وسعت دی اب اس تعلقہ میں سابق
موضع محلہ بی جمعی بیلہ بی لالہ کو خطہ گوندہ میں واقع ہیں ہم گدی نشینی اس خاندان میں ہے۔

(نمبر ۳۳) رانی جانکی کنور زوجہ راجہ مہیپت سنگھ قوم کلہن تعلقدار بیسپور خطاب رانی۔
نقشہ حجری میں جسکو قریب زمانہ یا نسو برس کے ہوا بہ عہد سلطنت نورالدین جہانگیر بادشاہ دہلی میں
مورث المخاندان راجہ بجرو درس مالک راج لگلا نہ فی چھبیت کثیر اپنے وطن گھو منج سے جلا وطن ہو کر
علاقہ پہ گکہ ثانسہ جواب گوندہ مشہور ہے حاصل کی اولادی اولا دیں نہال سنگھ مورث کے تین لڑکے ہوئے
دولہ راے رام سنگھ بیند فی مل اور دونیں علاقہ تقسیم ہوا رام سنگھ وبیند فی مل کو یہ تعلقہ ملا اور دولہ راے
کے خاندان سے تعلقدار ان نمبری ذیل قائم ہیں نمبر ۲۸ و ۱۲۴ و ۱۳۴ و ۱۳۵ و ۲۶۹۔ اب چند پشتان
کے بعد یہ رئیس قابض ریاست ہوئے تعلقہ میں مورث موضع محلہ بی جمعی بیلہ بی خطہ گوندہ میں واقع ہیں
ہم گدی نشینی اس خاندان میں ہے۔

(نمبر ۳۴) رانی سلطنت کنور ومیوہ راجہ پرتھی پت سنگھ قوم بیسین تعلقدار منکاپور خطاب رانی۔
یہ ریاست بہت قدیم ہے اول یہ تعلقہ نول ساہ مورث اقوام ہندل گوتی کا تھا بوجہ لا اولادی راجہ چندر بیسین
اوکی رانی بھاگ بان نے عظمت سنگھ خاندان راجہ دوت سنگھ گوندہ کے رئیس کو اپنا متبنی کیا اسنے فصل میں خط سنگھ
مالک ریاست ہوئے جب سے نسلاً بعد نسل قبضہ تعلقدار چلا آیا تھا ایک تک راجہ پرتھی پت سنگھ مالک ریاست
رہے بعد وفات اسکے یہ ریسہ ترکہ نشوہری یہ قابض ہیں تعلقہ میں مائہ موضع محلہ بی جمعی بی خطہ گوندہ
میں واقع ہیں ہم گدی نشینی اس خاندان میں ہے۔

(نمبر ۳۵) راجہ جیت پال سنگھ قوم سوم بنسی تعلقدار نور پور مجھت پال گڈہ خطاب راجہ موروثی۔
تذکرہ خاندانی و آغاز ریاست اکا نمبر اوپر درج ہے یہ تعلقہ بعد لکھن بتی کے علیحدہ و قائم ہوا تھا اور چند عرصہ تک
بجرم عدول حکمی یہ ملکیت خام تحصیل سرکار شاہی میں رہی نشستہ فصل میں بابو مہربان سنگھ مورث ذریعہ خطاب
بابو پیر اس ملکیت کو سرکار شاہی سے حاصل کیا اسوقت سے نسلاً بعد نسل قبضہ موروثان چلا آتا ہے بعد کر اس خاندان
میں خطاب راجگی حاصل ہوا۔ اس تعلقہ میں وقت موضع جمعی صد موضع پتا گڈہ میں واقع ہیں اس خاندان میں
اولا دا اکبر وارث ریاست ہوتا ہے۔

(نمبر ۳۶) راجہ دیش بخش سنگھ قوم کنپوریہ تعلقدار کٹھولہ خطاب راجہ موروثی۔
اکا تذکرہ خاندانی و آغاز ریاست نمبر اوپر درج ہے یہ تعلقہ اسی نمبر ۲۱ کا ایک شاخ ہے خاندان میں ہا مالک میں اولا د

مورث سے یہ تعلقدار قابض ریاست ہیں۔ منجملہ موضع جمبی پرگنہ ضلع پیاگڑ معین واقع ہیں رسم گدی نشینی اس خاندان میں رہی ہے

(نمبر ۴۸) راجہ اندر بکرم سیاہ قوم راجپوت پہاڑی سوج بنس تعلقدار کھیری گنڈہ و کفارہ و مجبرہ و دو بیلا خطاب راجہ موروثی ۔ ہمشتہ میں شادی راجہ ترلوکی پال کی دختر راجہ سہا پال مالک کو ہمالہ سے ہوئی تھی اور قوم علاقہ کھیری گنڈہ و کنجن پور وغیرہ راجہ ترلوکی پال کو جہیز میں ملا تھا سمت ۔۔۔۔ تک اس کی اولاد کا قبضہ چلا آیا پھر سمت ۔۔۔ سال تک انقلاب ریاست اقوام خجارہ سے رہا بعد کورو راجہ گنگا رام راجہ دیپ سیاہ سنے پنجابیگان سے علاقہ کھیری گنڈہ پر قبضہ پایا اور سرکار شاہی سے سند حاصل کی جب تو قبضہ خاندان میں برابر چلا آیا آخر الامر سمت قلمدار گورنمنٹ انگلشیہ بہری نام راجہ زند ہوج سیاہ ہوئی بعد وفات اوسکے یہ رئیس قابض ریاست ہوئے اور عہد اکبر شاہ بادشاہ میں یہ خاندان بانقسب سیاہی نامزد ہوا تھا اوسوقت ہر شخص بنام سیاہی نامزد ہوتا ہے اور اقوام بوٹ و تھارو چیور گڑھ ڈہ سے ویران ہوکر اس علاقہ میں آباد ہوئی ہے سمتہ میں علاوالدین سیاہ غری فی بقام کھیری گنڈہ ایک قلعہ بھی بنوایا تھا اوسکا نشان ہنوز موجود ہے اس تعلقہ میں ہامہ موضع جمبی موضعہ سمتہ ۔۔ فسلع کھیری میں واقع ہیں رسم گدی نشینی اس خاندان میں ہے۔

(نمبر ۴۹) راجہ نریپت سنگھ قوم چنوار تعلقدار کیمہرہ خطاب راجہ موروثی ۔ پہلے مالک اس ریاست کے مہان سیاہ قوم چنوار تھے جب علاقہ میں بدنظمی واقع ہوئی اوسوقت پیشیگاہ ہمایون سیاہ بادشاہ دہلی بالدیو سیاہ قوم تھا کر جو مہان کے رئیس جہیور نبا بدفع بدانتظامی علاقہ مامور ہوکر یہان آئے اور زیرہ پشت۔۔ بعد جنگ جدل علاقہ پر تسلط پایا اوسوقت راجہ مہان سیاہ سنے اپنی دختر کی شادی بالدیو سیاہ سے کر دی اور بوجہ لا اولاد ہی اپنی درخواست بحضور شاہ بھیجی کہ میری ملکیت حوالہ بالدیو سیاہ ہو جاوے ہو لیکن قبل صدور حکم شاہی بالدیو سیاہ سنے وفات پائی سمتہ میں اور دیت سیاہ بپسر بالدیو سیاہ بحکم شاہ دہلی مالک ریاست ہوئے اور چند پشت تک قبضہ خاندانی چلا آیا آخر الامر عجب سنگھ مورث کے عہد میں یہ ملکیت فراب بدر جہان کو بحکم شاہ جہان بادشاہ بطور جاگیر عطا ہو گئی چند عرصہ کے بعد نواب سعادت علیخان سنے ضبط کرکے خالص تحصیل کر لی اب عرصہ قریب یکصد سال کے گذرتا ہے کہ عجب سنگھ نے جہیور سے واپس آکر پھر اس ریاست پر قبضہ حاصل کیا اور بوجہ لا اولادی خود بجہین حیات اپنی جو دہا سنگھ پدر و عم زاد کو مالک ریاست کر دیا بعد وفات جو دہا سنگھ یہ تعلقدار اسکے ارثے قابض ریاست ہیں ۔ تعلقہ میں ہسب موضع للعہ پٹی جمبی مشارقے ضلع کھیری میں واقع ہیں رسم گدی نشینی اس خاندان میں ہے۔

(نمبر ۵۰) امانت فاطمہ بیگم زوجہ نواب حسین علیخان قوم شیخان تعلقدار باسطہ نگر خطاب نواب موروثی ۔ نواب دلیر خان مورث کے عہد شاہ عالمگیر میں یہ ریاست سلطنت سے بطور جاگیر ملی تھی بعد وفات اوکی عہدہ معافی تعلقی

یوسف علی جاگیر زمیندارانہ اور کی اولاد کے قبضہ میں آیا اب سرکار قبضہ موروثیان چلا آتا ہے اخرالذکر سند تعلقہ بنام دوست علی خان
گورنمنٹ انگلشیہ سے مرحمت ہوئی بعد از کے نواب حسین علی خان مشہور بریسہ قابض ہوئے بعد وفات اب نکہ اب نہ یہ
قابض یہ ریاست میں یہ اسٹیٹ موضع دروبی بھی اس ضلع ہردوئی میں واقع ہیں رسم گدی نشینی اس خاندان میں
(نمبر ۳۴) بیگ ست بہادر سنگھہ قوم بلکھہ باتعلقہ دار امیٹھی خطاب راجہ موروثی۔

راجہ جمیار سنگھہ مورث اعلیٰ متوطن جے پور گڑھہ متنکرہ دہہ بنجوف سلطان علاء الدین غوری جلا وطن ہوکر بمقام
آبا و آئے اور راجہ دیو رام بلکھہ یا کے ملازم ہوکر رسالا فوج ہوگئے بعد وفات راجہ دیو رام دیو دلیپ سنگھہ اور کے لڑکے
مارک خود مالکان ریاست ہوگئے اور راجہ کی لڑکی سے شادی کرلی اولاد پیدا ہوئی اور زمین وراثتاً فروختاً ریاست
تقسیم ہوتی گئی تعلقہ دار ان نمبری ذیل اسی خاندان سے ہیں نمبر ۵ و ۹ و ۲۰ و ۶۹ و ۷۹ و ۷۹ و ۱۲۶ و ۱۳۰ و ۱۹۴ و ۱۹
و ۲۰۸ و ۲۱ و ۲۲ اور یہ رئیس بھی اسی خاندان سے ہیں اور سردار قوم بلکھہ یا کے تصور ہوتے ہیں اس
تعلقہ میں یہ موضع بھی مسلہ ضلع پتاگڑھہ میں واقع ہیں اس خاندان میں رسم گدی نشینی ہے۔

(نمبر ۳۵) راجہ منشی بخش سنگھہ قوم ریکوار تعلقہ دار تعلقہ لمانپور فیروز آباد لمانپور دیو بہر دیو خطاب راجہ موروثی
پہلے یہ علاقہ بعہد جلال الدین اکبر بادشاہ دہلی فیروز شاہ زادہ کو عطا تھا پھر شنبئہ ام مین لہہ دا اورنگ نصیب
مدن شاہ مورث قابض علاقہ ہوا اور سکور وامل کوری تعلقہ دار نے جو پیشہ غارتگری کرتا تھا قاتل کرکے علاقہ پر
اپنا قبضہ کرلیا مدن شاہ کی زوجہ حاملہ اس وقت پر بھاگ کراپنے باپ کے گھر ضلع بہرایچ میں علی کئی تین مہینے بعد
رتن سنگھہ نامی اور کے ایک لڑکا پیدا ہوا اور سنے باعنت اپنے ننا کے راو مل کوری کو قتل کرکے اس ریاست پر
پھر قبضہ پایا رتن سنگھہ کی نویں پشت میں راو بستی سنگھہ مورث عہد الافضلی میں بعہد نواب سعادت علی خان قبول نبیا
اس علاقہ کے ہوئے جبہہ برابر قبضہ موروثیان چلا آتا ہے اب گورنمنٹ انگلشیہ سے آپ کرام نہ و بست اس علاقہ کا
ہوا اما یہ موضع لوہ بی جمی تعلقہ کھیری دیہاتپور بہرایچ میں واقع ہیں رسم گدی نشینی اس خاندان میں ہے۔

(نمبر ۳۶) راجہ چندر شیکھر قوم برہمن تعلقہ دار سیندی وجیوہ لیا ودلہا خطاب راجہ موروثی۔

یہ ریاست بہت جدید ہے امرت لال یا ٹھاکس سرکار شاہی میں ناظم علاقہ بیسوارہ تھے اور نہوں نے عہد الافصلی میں
علاقہ سیندی کو بطور رستہ جاہری حاصل کیا تھا پھر سنہ الافصلی میں رانی بسنت کنور زوجہ درگپال سنگھہ نے علاقہ
سیندی کو بتقریب انزار داری نتکنگر لال پوتہ امرت لال کے نام علاقہ مذکور یہ کردیا اور سوقت سے نہایت
سنہ الافصلی یہ ملکیت اور کی اولاد کے قبضہ میں رہی سنہ الافصلی میں راجہ کاشی پشاد وراما و موہن لال خلعت
امرت لال قابض ریاست ہوئے اور بصلہ خیر خواہی ایام غدر سنہ ۱۸۵۷ عیسوی تعلقہ دردہا وجیوہا گورنمنٹ
سے عطیہ حاصل کیا اور منجملہ پانچ تعلقہ دار ان خیر خواہ یہ تعلقہ بھی ہے راو راجہ موروثی کا بند و

استمراری ہوا اور بعد وفات راجہ کاشی پرشاد یہ تعلقہ دار قابض ریاست ہیں اور تعلقہ میں سب ملکیت عدلیہ ۔۔۔ پٹی جمعی موضع ۔۔۔ اضلاع اعظم و راست بریلی و لکھنؤ میں واقع ہیں ۔ اولاد اکبر اس خاندان میں وارث ریاست ہوتا ہے ۔

(نمبر ۳) راجہ سر بجیت سنگھ بہادر قوم پکوار تعلقہ دار رام نگر خطاب راجہ موروثی ۔

تذکرہ خاندانی و آغاز ریاست اکا نمبر ۱۹ پر درج ہو چکا ہے ۔ در عرصہ زیادہ از دو صد سال رام سنگھ مورث ۔۔۔ تھے رام نگر و ہمیری جو پہلے دھرم سندی مشہور تھا و کر سکے بنام رام نگر تعلقہ قائم کیا اور بنیاد و حل ۔۔۔ راجگی حاصل کیا اونکی اولاد میں راجہ غریب سنگھ نے ایک تالاب و عمارت پختہ مقام بہار دیوا میں تعمیر کرائی جو ایک ۔۔۔ پرستشگاہ اہل ہنود و بنا مزدوں درمیانہ سیر قریب سیر ہرام گھاٹ ہر سوا ۔۔۔ اسکے مورثان تعلقہ دار ۔۔۔ و گنج و مہانسر اور غیرہ تعمیر کرائی ۔ اب چند پشت بعد یہ رئیس قابض ہیں تا بقض ہیں تعلقہ میں را ۔۔۔ موضع اور ۔۔۔ جمعی ۔۔۔ مضلع بارہ بنکی میں واقع ہیں اِس خاندان میں بروج گدی نشینی ہے ۔

(نمبر ۴) راجہ شمشیر بہادر قوم مغل تعلقہ دار سعادت نگر و جلالپور دیوریہ خطاب راجہ حسین حیات ۔

عرصہ ایک و بیس سال کا ہوتا ہے محمد علی بیگ رسالدار نے دہلی سے اودھ میں آ کر ملکیت حاصل کر کے تعلقہ ۔۔۔ قائم کیا اور سنکے ۔۔۔ افصلی میں بندہ علی بیگ اور اکبر بیگ پسران محمد علی بیگ میں ریاست تقسیم ہوئی ۔ اکبر بیگ مورث اس تعلقہ سکے ۔۔۔ اور بندہ علی بیگ کو دیوریہ نگر ملا تا ۔۔۔ افصلی میں اکبر بیگ ریاست ۔۔۔ والد کو خطاب ۔۔۔ سلطنت اودھ سے حاصل ہوا اور بعد اونکے یہ تعلقہ دار قابض تعلقہ ہیں ۔۔۔ موضع الہ ۔۔۔ جمعی موضع ۔۔۔ اضلاع ۔۔۔ و ہردوئی میں واقع ہیں رواج گدی نشینی اس خاندان میں ہے ۔

(نمبر ۵) راجہ ممتاز علی خان قوم چھان تعلقہ دار بلاسپور اترولہ خطاب راجہ موروثی ۔

۱۵۰۔۔۔ میں بہ عہد سلطان جلال الدین اکبر بادشاہ علی جان مورث اعلیٰ نے کوہستان سے بجایت ۔۔۔ سکے مقام اترولہ جو اراری ریاست او تراکنور ۔۔۔ قوم بھر کا تھا اگر یہ شخن ملا اور رواج و ریاست پر قبضہ کر لیا و بلا حکم شاہ وقت خود راجہ مشہور ہوی جب یہ خبر بادشاہ کو ہوی کہ علی جان و اصلاح ملک کیا ۔۔۔ وقت پر سجن خان و غالب خان پسران علی جان نے بنظر خوشنودی سلطان وقت و بقا ای ریاست اپنے ۔۔۔ اپنے سرکار ۔۔۔ بادشاہ نے خوش ہو کر ریاست اترولہ کی غالب خان اپنے وطن کو بھیجے کے سجن خان ریاست پر قابض ہوئے اور سو وقت سے نسلاً بعد نسلاً قبضہ چلا آتا ہے تعلقہ میں منت موضع نے پٹی جمعی موروثی ۔۔۔ مضلع گنڈہ میں واقع ہیں رسم گدی نشینی اس خاندان میں ہے ۔

(نمبر ۶) راجہ بشیر بہادر سنگھ قوم ٹھاکر کلسن تعلقہ دار دیول بروولیا و کیار خطاب راجہ حسین حیات ۔

تذکرہ خاندانی و آغاز ریاست انکا نمبر ۳۰ م پر درج ہے یہ تعلقہ نمبر ۳۰ کی ایک شاخ موجودہ رئیس مورث نے اس ریاست کو قائم کیا تھا اوسی خاندان سے آپ ہیں اور تعلقہ دار نمبر ۴۸ بھی اسی خاندان سے ہیں۔ اس تعلقہ میں موضع لعبہ جمعی موروثہ لاولدیہ، اضلاع گونڈہ و بہرائچ و بارہ بنکی میں واقع ہیں رسم گدی نشینی اس خاندان میں ہے۔

(نمبر ۴۷) سماحۃ ستارالنسا بیوہ راجہ نواب علی خان تعلقہ دار سلیم پور دیار بھجت پور دہ خطاب پانی ہیں جناب شیخ ابوالحسن انصاری اہل سنت جماعت مورث اعلیٰ مدینہ سے مع جمعیت و قوم اپنی کے دہلی میں آئے اور بحکم شاہ دہلی بجملہ ورستہ تدارک راجہ اشھیا و دیگر اقوام مہیجا پرگنہ اینہی جو شامل سلطنت ہر تعلق سوئے لقب شیخ الاسلام حاصل کیا اور یکے خاندان میں شیخ سلیم نے سلیم پور اپنے نام پر آباد کیا یا شیخ سلیم کے دو درجے ہوئے ہیں شیخ آدم و شیخ قاسم شیخ آدم پور و شیخ قاسم نے قاسم پور دیہہ مفرود آباد کیا دسویں پشت میں مورث اعلیٰ میں ایک دختر کی شادی ہدایت ﷲ اہل شیعہ سکنہ کاکوری کے ساتھ ہوئی اوسکی اولاد میں سے سعادت علی و منصور علی ورثہ نامہال سلیم پور میں اگر قابض ریاست ہوئے سعادت علی کی دوسری پشت میں جو دوسرے نواب علی صاحب آپ کے قسو ہیں اس ملکیت پر قبضہ پایا بعد وفات اونکی اب یہ بیوہ قابض ریاست ہیں انکے تعلقہ میں بسکہ موضع و دیہی جمعی ہیں اضلاع لکھنؤ و بارہ بنکی میں واقع ہیں رسم گدی نشینان اس خاندان میں ہے۔

(نمبر ۴۸) راجہ جہیت سنگھ قوم سوم نہسی تعلقہ دار تروک دیہیانی وہ بڑی قلعہ نگر آباد وفطاب راجہ ہیں حیات۔ تذکرہ خاندانی انکا نمبر ۱۱ پر درج ہے یہ تعلقہ نمبر ۱ کا ایک شاخ ہے تعلقہ دار ایام غدر شاع میں خیر خواہ سرکار سے بجملہ ورستہ اوسکے سنبھالہ علاقہ منضبط بابو گلاب سنگھ باغی گورنمنٹ انگلشیہ سے عطیہ حاصل ہوا اب اس تعلقہ میں مع ملکیت عطیہ وارثہ موضع جمعی ہیں اضلاع پرتاب گڑھ اور نام وہر و روئی و کھیری میں واقع ہیں اور اس خاندان میں رسم گدی نشینی ہے۔

(نمبر ۴۹) راجہ دیا شنکر قوم برہمن زرکت تعلقہ دار پریندا خطاب راجہ موروثی۔ قریب چار سو سال کے گذرا کہ بنا مل مورث نے مقام بنا پور سے اگر موضع پریندا کو آباد کیا وکیا جسکے نام سے تعلقہ مشہور ہے جب سے یہ ریاست قائم ہوی یہ رئیس سردار اپنی قوم کے ہیں۔ اس تعلقہ میں مع موضع جمعی سے لے کہ بضلع اُنام میں واقع ہیں اس خاندان میں اولاد اکبر مالک ریاست ہوتا ہے۔

(نمبر ۵۰) راجہ شکر منگل سنگھ قوم نکاک کنپوریہ تعلقہ دار ساہ مؤو وہانی پور خطاب راجہ ہیں حیات۔ یہ رئیس ہم خاندان شیخ تعلقہ لوئی تذکرہ نمبر ۴۷ کے ہیں خاندان راجہ ہانک میں بلبہد راساہ مورثی یہ ریاست قائم ہر بپتر اوسی خاندان سے ہیں بت موضع جمعی موضع ابوسط اضلاع رای بریلی و سلطانپور میں واقع ہیں اس خاندان میں اگر

مورث اعلیٰ بلا وصیت فوت ہو جاوے تو بموجب آئین معمولی اشخاص ذی حق وارث ریاست ہونگے۔

(نمبر ۵۱) ٹھاکر بلبھدر سنگھ قوم جبوار تعلقہ دار میوہ و جہانگیر آباد۔

اسکا تذکرہ خاندانی و آغاز ریاست نمبر ۳۲ پر درج ہو چکا ہے تعلقہ اوسی نمبر کا ایک شاخ ہے یہ رئیس خاندان پیتم سنگھ سے ہیں سندِ تعلقہ کی گورنمنٹ انگلشیہ سے بنام گجراج سنگھ ہوئی تھی اور نکر بعد ٹھاکر گردر سنگھ اور بعد گردر سنگھ کے یہ تعلقہ دار قابض ریاست ہوکر اس تعلقہ میں آئے۔ موضع اور دیہات بھی جمعی موضعات ضلاع کھیری و سیتاپور میں واقع ہیں اور اس خاندان میں رسم گدی نشینی ہے۔

(نمبر ۵۲) بابو رام سہاے قوم کھتری تعلقہ داران موراواں جبروی وغیرہ ا۔

انکے موثان نامی سابو کاران ملک اور دعوے تھے اور عہدہ سلطنت اور دہ میں ہمیشہ عمدہ چکلہ داری پر سرفراز رہے لالہ چیدن بعلی یہ تعلقہ خرید کیا تھا بعد ازیکے گور شنکر بسرہ دوم قابض تعلقہ ہوا اور گورنمنٹ انگلشیہ سے ببہ لایہ خیر خواہی خطاب راجکی و سند تعلقداری حاصل کرکے پانچ تعلقداران خیر خواہ میں شامل ہوئے جسقدر قدیمی علاقہ اس تعلقہ میں ہر اسکا بندوبست استمراری ہوا بعد وفات اونکے کنہیا لعل پسر چہارم راجہ چیدن لعل تک ریاست کی جائی رہی پھر بوجہ نزاعات باہمی کل خاندان میں علاقہ تقسیم ہوا خاص آپ کے تعلقہ میں بموجب تقسیم جدید موضع طہ بھی موضعات ضلاع اناام و لکھنؤ میں واقع ہیں اور یہ تعلقدار خاندان گنگا بیرشاد برادر خورد راجہ چیدن لعل سے ہیں۔ اس ریاست میں اگر مورث اعلیٰ بلا وصیت فوت ہو جاوے تو بموجب آئین معمولی اشخاص ذی حق وارث ریاست ہونگے۔

ضمیمہ نمبر ۴ ھ ۔ راجچرن وشیو برشاد و بشیشر برشاد۔
تعلقداران بھٹہ و تعلنڈی می اقوام کھتری۔

یہ تعلقدار ایک شاخ اصل تعلقہ نمبر ۴ ھ کے ہیں جو تقسیم حال میں جدا تعلقہ قرار پایا تعلقہ میں و طہ موضع جمعی ہیں ضلاع اونام و راے بریلی میں واقع ہیں۔

ضمیمہ نمبر ۵ ھ۔ مادھو برشاد و روبی دیال تعلقدارانِ دریبہ و امافواں اقوام کھتری۔

یہ تعلقدار ایک شاخ اصل تعلقہ نمبر ۴ ھ کے ہیں جو تقسیم حال میں جدا تعلقہ قرار پایا تعلقہ میں و موضع ایک پٹی جمعی ہیں ضلاع اونام و راے بریلی میں واقع ہیں۔

ضمیمہ نمبر ۶ ھ۔ شیو دیال قوم کھتری۔
تعلقدارِ دیومی و کنڈہ اقوام۔

یہ تعلقدار ایک شاخ اصل تعلقہ نمبر ۴ ھ کے ہیں جو تقسیم حال میں جدا تعلقہ قرار پایا تعلقہ میں وغیرہ موضع جمعی ہیں ضلاع راے بریلی میں واقع ہیں۔

(ضمیمہ نمبر ۵۰) رام نرائن قوم کھتری تعلقدار لوا سنگن کھیرہ و تونی وغیرہ و انہی۔

یہ تعلقدار ایک شاخ اصل تعلقہ نمبر ۲ دکے میں جو تقسیم حال میں جدا تعلقہ قرار پایا یا تعلقہ میں الٹعبہ موضع کیک بٹی جھبی علاقہ اضلاع اودھ نام ورا سے بریلی ورا بدہ نبکی میں واقع ہیں۔

(ضمیمہ نمبر ۵۱) بال مکند و کالکا پرشاد وجیا کا پرشاد تعلقدار ان الثرث و بجھر اوان وغیرہ۔

یہ تعلقدار ایک شاخ اصل تعلقہ نمبر ۲ دکے میں جو تقسیم حال میں جدا تعلقہ قرار پایا یا تعلقہ میں یہ موضع جبی علاقہ اضلاع اودھ نام ورا سے بریلی میں واقع ہیں۔

(ضمیمہ نمبر ۵۲) موہن لال اقوام کھتری تعلقدار اسپر بلعہ سہوا وغیرہ۔

یہ تعلقدار ایک شاخ اصل تعلقہ نمبر ۲ دکے میں جو تقسیم حال میں جدا تعلقہ قرار پایا یا تعلقہ میں دو موضع جبی بلوطہ علاقہ اضلاع اودھ نام ورا سے بریلی میں واقع ہیں۔

(ضمیمہ نمبر ۵۳) بنی پرشاد و قوم کھتری تعلقدار اسپر و اکلان و لمنٹھہ۔

یہ تعلقدار ایک شاخ اصل تعلقہ نمبر ۲ دکے میں جو تقسیم حال میں جدا تعلقہ قرار پایا یا تعلقہ میں بلعہ موضع جبی علاقہ اضلاع اودھ نام ورا سے بریلی میں واقع ہیں۔

(نمبر ۵۴) عوض علیجان قوم بجابے سلطان خانزادہ تعلقدار مسوہ۔

حالا سو سال سوبے رام نرذ خد سنگھ عرف راو بہار سورث اعلٰی علاقہ بیسواڑہ سے پرگنہ ایسولی میں آئے اور بعبہ اخران اقوام سہبردین کے ریاست پرو نرل پایا آنکی چند استھون کے بعد یا ہیں دبو ولی میں جاکر سلمان ہوے و خطاب راجگی پایا و سو ہیں کا واقعہ گزرتا ہے کہ راجہ استد واو خان نئے قبولیت اس علاقہ کی لکھی ہے اس خاندان میں قبضہ مونان کا چلا آما آمد بعد کو تقسیم ریاست ہوکر کئی آماقہ اس ملکیت کے ہوگئے تعلقہ نمبری ۲ ۱۳ و ۱۴ اسی خاندان سے علمحدہ قائم ہیں آذر الا یہ تعلقدار تابین ریاست سوبے یہ ریس اپنی قوم میں سردار تصور ہوتے ہیں تعلقہ میں مسے موضع روہٹی جبی سلطانپور میں واقع ہیں رستم گدی انشینی اس خاندان میں ہر۔

(نمبر ۵۵) ابو مہپال سنگھ قوم بجریلیا تعلقدار سورہپور خطاب بابو۔

سوبے بجریلی میں عہد سلطنت جلال الدین اکبر بادشاہ دہلی یا بچ بلی رام بہم سنگھ سورث علاقہ قنوج سے رسالدار ہوکر اس نوک میں آئے ان جنبے راجہ بچیکم سنگھ پیسہ راوہ موصوف نبجہ بجیکم بادشاہ دہلی زور خان تعلقدار سورہپور بجر بلبہ کو قتل کیا نجر اس انتظام علاقہ کاکیا بجلد وہ اس نبیر خواہی اپنی کی یہ اعرا سوا منعات انعبہ تعلقہ سورہپور خاص راجہ بچیکم سنگھ کو سرکار کا خطاب دہلی سے مرحمت سوی ہوت آسونت ہے یہ ریاست سداو آبا اسی خاندان سے قائم ہے یہ تعلقدار ہیں اور اپنے قوم کے سردار تصور ہوتے ہیں اس تعلقہ میں ادلہ موہن چنبی جبی میکپے۔ منصب بابا بدہ نبکی میں واقع ہیں اس خاندان میں رستم گدی انشینی ہر۔

(نمبر ۵۵) شکار رنجیت سنگھ قوم جا نگڑ ۔ راجپوت قاعدہ ایسائی نکرہ و آئینی و ر دیو یانا و نگوریا و مدھوا پور ۔

...

(نمبر ۵۶) حکمہ سنگھ قوم جٹ تعلقدار رام پور چھچھولی تندوالی و کٹھیوالیا ۔

...

(نمبر ۵۷) کنور بہرام سنگھ سینچر پونڈی قوم سکھ ۔

...

(نمبر ۵۸) کپتان گلاب سنگھ سردار او ما سنگھ تعلقدار بہرائچ بند پور و کشور جی و بیلا بیلا ۔

...

(نمبر ۵۹) اشجگھوں سنگھ و راے بستیہ بخش قوم شکار جگوتی تعلقدار رام پور خطاب راے خوبن حیات ۔

...

راے مکبوں سنگھ بہوان سنگھ میں

(نمبر ۶۰) رائے مادھو پرشاد شنکر تعلقدار ادھار گنج دلیپ پور قوم ٹھاکر قومی خطاب ایس مین حیات۔

تذکرہ خاندانی الکانیہ و رسم پرداج ہے یہ رئیس خاندان ٹھاکر شنگ مورث سے قابض اس ریاست کے ہیں اور اس تعلقہ سے تعلقہ نمبری ۰۰ و قائم ہے اس تعلقہ میں نام موضع موضع جمعی سالانہ ضلع پرتابگڈھ میں واقع ہیں اس خاندان میں رسم گدی نشینی ہے۔

(نمبر ۶۱) منت ہر دیال اس قوم ناگمک شنابی خطاب منت تعلقدار سوسی و ہمراہ دلہچی دلاپ پستا پور اقر پور کلکہ پور آپ ناگمک شنابی فقیر گدی نشین منت گورنلائن صاحب کے ہیں جنہوں نے اس ریاست کو پیدا کیا تھا حسب معیت بعد وفات آنکے آپ قابض ریاست ہیں اور بایام طفولیت جب علاقہ زیر انتظام کورٹ تھا آپ نے کنک کالج میں تعلیم پائی ہے ریاست میں ۱۲ موضع ہے پٹی جمعی مینہ اطلاع او نام دلکھنؤ و گونڈہ و بہرائچ و ہردوئی و سیتا پور و کھیری میں واقع ہیں رسم گدی نشینی اس خاندان میں ہے۔

(نمبر ۶۲) رائے سر بخت سنگھ قوم بیسین تعلقدار بہیدسی خطاب رائے۔

تذکرہ خاندانی و آغاز ریاست الکانیہ پرداج ہے اولاد رائے رام پال سے آغاز خاندان قوم بیسین کا ہوا ہے آسی خاندان سے یہ رئیس قابض تعلقہ ہیں موضع موضع جمعی ضلع پرتابگڈھ میں واقع ہیں رسم گدی نشینی اس خاندان میں ہے۔

(نمبر ۶۳) چودھری مرتضیٰ حسین و بیبو النسا قوم شیخ تعلقدار بہلوال و سکندر پور۔

سرکار نجیب بہلوال نامے قوم یاہی کا ہر جنسے نمبر و عرصہ سات سو سال قوم بھرسے حاصل کیا تھا اور یہ تعلقہ پنجے حبیسکو ملک آ و م سورث نے کبلہ و سے تنبیہ اقوام بھر جو بہت شورش کرتی تھی سرکار شنابی سے بطور انعام پایا تھا آگے جنہا نیشنوں کے بعد جو دھری لطف انتہا قابض ریاست ہوے آنکے بعد جو دھری سرفراز احمد داما و آنکے وارث تعلقہ ہوے یہ رئیس معزرین تعلقداران او دوہمین تصویر یوتے تھے بعد وفات جو دھری صاحب مقدمہ دائر عدالت ہوکر تقسیم ریاست ہوئی نصف علاقہ زو جہ جو دھری صاحب او نصف علاقہ آنکے حقیقتی بھتے سمجھائی جو دھری مرتضیٰ کو ملا بعد وفات جو دھرائن صاحبہ آنکے حصہ پر رفیع الزمان نواسہ حسب وصیت جو دھری سرفراز احمد صاحب مالک ہوینگے اور جو دھری مرتضیٰ حسین صاحب بوجہ خیر خواہی گورنمنٹ انگلشیہ مصاہرہ باغیان میں بمقام میونڈی ی تعینات یانیہ لمیوس خیر خواہی و تکلیف مقیدی تعلقہ سکندر پور میں سعہ موضع جمعی لاملہ عینہ سعہ عطا ہوا اس تعلقہ میں منع ملکیت عطیہ ملکہ موضع سے پٹی جمعی لویاست۔ اطلاع باہ نکلی ورالہ آبری میں واقعہ ہیں اس خاندان میں رسم گدی نشینی ہے۔

(نمبر ۷۴) ٹھکہ این شیو پال کنور بیوہ جگنا تختہ نبخش قوم میں تعلقدار سمری و ٹبنا واسی ۔

اپ کا تذکرہ خاندانی نمبر ۷۴ پر درج ہے اور یہ تعلقہ ایک نخلاخ نمبر ۵۰ کا ہے منکھہ راسے مورث اعلیٰ تعلقہ نمبر ۵۰ سے علیحدہ ہوکے اس مقام پر آئے اور جنگل کٹوا کر موقع سمری آباد کیا ہوکیا اور تعلقہ اسی نام سے قائم کیا ۔ جیسے قبضہ موروثیان برابر چلا آتا ہے منکھہ راسے کی نوین پشت میں آپ قابض ریاست میں تعلقہ میں لوحہ موقع اور ایک جبک جمعی عبیت ۔ اطلاع راسے بریلی ولا نام میں واقع ہیں رسم گدی نشینی اس خاندان میں ہے ۔

(نمبر ۷۵) ٹھکہ این دریا وکنور بیوہ ٹھاکر بسنت سنگھ قوم میں تعلقدار سمریہا ۔

اپ کا تذکرہ خاندانی نمبر ۷۵ پر درج ہے اور یہ تعلقہ ایک نخلاخ تعلقہ نمبر ۵۰ کا ہے درا اٹ نکٹ سنگھ کی دوسری اٹکی اولاد بیا کو وقت علیحدگی کی کنجور کا ناون سے جب یہ ریاست علیٰ اس وقت آتگے آتکی مکند راسے نئے موقع سمری بچا کر ہوجہ پانچہ پریا سے دیوان پیدا تھا از سرہ فروا آباد کرکے اس نام سے تعلقہ قائم کیا آتکے دو بیوتے ہند و سنگھ و پرتی راج بیوہ سیدہ سنگھ تعلقہ نمبر ۵۰ اسکے وارث موتے پرتی راج اس ریاست پر قابض ہوئے آتکی نوین پشت میں لالہی نئے اس ریاست قبضگی اور اتہون نئے ایک بازار وسیع متصل سمری بچا یا ہ آتکے دو بیٹے بکربان جیت و فتح بہادر پیدا ہوئے دونون لا ولاد موت ہوئے سنہ ۱۸۲۷ء مفصلی میں زوجہ بکربان جیت نئے ٹھاکر بسنت سنگھ کو اس نشین کرکے مالک ریاست کیا ہ بعد وفات آتکے یہ ریسہ زوجہ آتکی قابض ریاست میں اور اتہون نئے ٹھمشیر بہادر سنگھ کو اس نشین اپنا کیا ہ مگر یہ قبضہ وزیل علاقے پر اپنا کیا ہ ولک ۔ موقع دبی موریسہ ۔ ضلع راسے بریلی میں واقع ہیں رسم گدی نشینی اس خاندان میں ہے ۔

(نمبر ۷۶) ہند پال سنگھ قوم میں تعلقدار کورہ بہرستاون ۔

اپ کا تذکرہ خاندانی نمبر ۷۶ پر درج ہے اور یہ تعلقہ ایک نخلاخ کنجور کا ناون نمبر ۵۰ کا ہے ہ بعد عہدہ تین سوہ پریس کا سہ اخاندانی عالم ساہ ساہ سورت میں بہادر سنگھ مورث نئے بوقت علیحدگی یہ ریاست ماصل کی تھی جیسے قبضہ موروثیان برابر چلا آتا ہے منکھہ موقع جمی ایلا بیٹہ ۔ ضلع راسے بریلی میں واقع ہیں رسم گدی نشینی اس خاندان میں ہے ۔

(نمبر ۷۷) ٹھکہ این اجل کنور بیوہ شیو پال سنگھ قوم میں تعلقدار گورا کسیٹی ۔

تذکرہ خاندانی اپ کا نمبر ۷۷ پر درج ہے اور یہ تعلقہ ایک نخلاخ نمبر ۵۰ کا ہے درا نادوسن دیوکی اولاد میں دولہ راسے دیوکی سہ مفصلی میں بوقت علیحدگی کی کنجور کا ناون سے اس ریاست کو قائم کیا تھا آتکی جمیٹی پشت میں سام بخش سورت لکھا ریاست سوبے آتکی جیدہ پشتوں سکے بعد آخری ریسس ٹھاکر شیو پال سنگھ تھے بعد وفات آتکے یہ ریسہ قابض ریاست بین اور تعلقہ نمبری ۱۳ اس ریاست کی ایک نخلاخ ہو وللہس ۔ موقع جمی راسلیٹہ ۔ ضلع راسے بریلی میں واقع ہیں رسم گدی نشینی اس خاندان میں ہے ۔

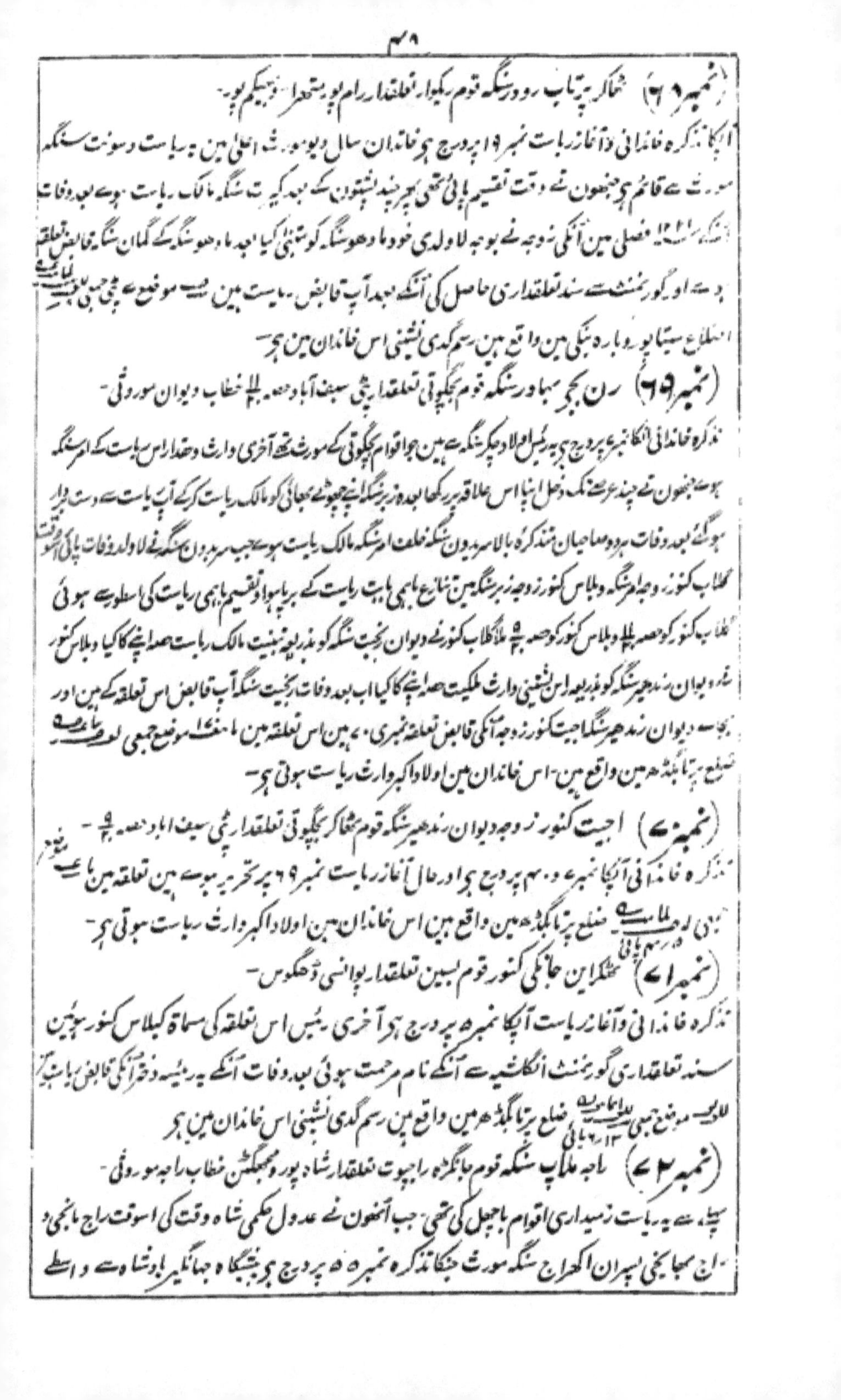

(نمبر ۹۲)

(نمبر ۶۹)

(نمبر ۷)

(نمبر ۷۱)

(نمبر ۷۲)

گرفتاری باحجلوں کے مقرر ہوئے ان لوگوں نے یہاں آکر باحجلوں کو ریاست سے خارج کرکے اپنا قبضہ کرلیا اور موضعات مجھگیین وغیرہ بیٹیگاہ شاہ ہ شاہ وقت سے آنکم حاصل ہوئی اسوقت سے آغازہ اس بابت کا ہے اور موزستان تعلقہ دارہ قابض چلے آتے ہیں اب یہ تعلقہ دار خاندان راج مائینی سے قابض تعلقہ ہیں سندہ تعلقہ داری گورنمنٹ انگلشیہ سے بنام راجہ گنگا سنگھ وسادھو سنگھ و بریار سنگھ والبا سنگھ مرمت ہوئی بھی اب بعد وفات آنکے یہ تعلقہ دار صاحبان قابض ریاست ہیں اور باہمی تقسیم ریاست کرلی جو اس تعلقہ ساہ پور مجھگیین کے یہ رئیس مالک ہیں اور تعلقہ میں سے موضع مستے پٹی جمبی لابت ضلع کہیری میں واقع ہیں ۔ اس ریاست میں اگر مورث اعلی بلا وصیت فوت ہو جاوے تو بموجب آئین معمولی انتخاص ذی حق وارث ریاست ہونگے ۔

گمان سنگھ ۔ قوم راجپوت جانگڑہ تعلقہ دار ام نگر دولت پور ۔

یہ تعلقہ دار بشاخ تعلقہ مندکرہ نمبر صدر کے ہیں تعلقہ میں لاحصہ موضع سے پٹی جمبی مطعام ضلع کہیری میں واقع ہیں ۔

گوبردھن سنگھ ۔ قوم راجپوت جانگڑہ تعلقہ دار بجوا و لکھاسن ۔

یہ تعلقہ دار بشاخ تعلقہ راجہ ملاپ سنگھ مندکرہ نمبر ۳ کے ہیں اس تعلقہ میں سے موضع صبی جمبی اللغم کے ضلع کہیری میں واقع ہیں ۔

دلیپ سنگھ ۔ قوم راجپوت جانگڑہ تعلقہ دار بجوریہ وبکد یوپور ۔

یہ تعلقہ دار بشاخ تعلقہ یا بہ ملاپ سنگھ مندکرہ نمبر ۳ کے ہیں تعلقہ میں معہ موضع اللغم پٹی جمبی سے ضلع کہیری میں واقع ہیں ۔

(نمبر ۳ع) بابو اور یس سنگھ و چندر یس سنگھ قوم راجکمار تعلقہ داران میو پور دوہ و اسندیر ۔

ذکرہ خاندانی قوم ۔ راجکمار کا نمبر ۳ بموجب ہر خاندان بریار سنگھ مورث اعلی میں ایشری سنگھ کی اولاد سے دلت سنگھ کے پوتے سکرام سنگھ و سبھوان سنگھ ہوئے ہیں قریب بیس برس کے ہوا ریاست تقسیم ہوئی سکرام سنگھ کے دو لڑکے ہوئے رنجیت سنگھ ۔ دوسرہ روٹن سنگھ رنجیت سنگھ سے آپ ہیں اور دوسرے سے نمبر سم ، کے تعلقہ دار ہیں او بہلوان سنگھ سے نمبر ۹ و ۵ و ۵۱ کے تعلقہ دار ہیں اس تعلقہ میں مالعہ موضع اور ماعہ پٹی جمبی سے ضلع فیض آباد و سلطانپور میں واقع ہیں اولاد واکبر اس خاندان میں وارث ریاست ہوتا ہے ۔

(نمبر سم ع) بابو امریس سنگھ قوم راجکمار تعلقہ دار میو پور بڑار گاؤں ۔

ذکرہ خاندانی آبکا نمبر ۳ بموجب ذکریہ تعلقہ نمبر ۳ کا ایک شاخ جو سردبدون سنگھ بیر و ام سنگھ سکرام سنگھ سے

یہ ریاست علیحدہ قائم ہوئی جبکہ قبضہ مورثان کا چلا آتا ہر تھلکہ موضع مسکرہ بٹی جمبی ہے تو سارے ۔ اضلاع
فیض آباد و سلطانپور میں واقع ہیں اولاد اکبر اس خاندان میں وارث ریاست ہوتا ہر

(نمبر ۷۵) میر غفنفر حسین و میر باقر حسین قوم سید تعلقدار پیرپور

عرصہ ودیڑھ سو سال کا سوتا ہر مرزا محمد علی بیگ خراسان سے مقام فیض آباد و بوبہ شجاع الدولہ بہادر آئے اور نواب
آصف الدولہ بہادر کی ملازمت کرکے مواضعات پیرپور وغیرہ خرید کرکے تعلقہ قائم کیا اس وقت میں سید
محمد حفیظ چودھری تعلقہ سیداون کے کوئی اولادہ نتھی جو انتظام ریاست کرتا آگی سو دیبنے مرزا محمد علی
کوا نیا جانشین کرکے مالک ریاست اپنے کا کر دیا اور میر قاسم علی اپنے لڑکا سہ عمر جار سالہ کو آگی گود میں دریا
محمد علی بیگ نے ہر دو علاقجات شامل کرکے ایک تعلقہ قائم رکھا بعہ وفات محمد علی بیگ میر قاسم علی مالک
ریاست ہوے سہ ۲۳ فصلی میں میر قاسم علی نے انتقال کیا اس وقت آگی ز وجہ بنے علاقہ سہ پر دو میر
کلب حسین اپنے داماد کے کیا سہ ۲۶ فصلی تک وہ منتظم علاقہ رہے سہ ۲۱ فصلی میں میر باقر حسین
پسر میر کلب حسین وغفنفر حسین داماد و دوم میر قاسم علی قابض ریاست ہوے اس وقت سے ایتک قبضہ چلا آتا
تعلقہ میں ماسی موضع مسکرہ بٹی جمبی علیحتہ ۔ اضلاع فیض آباد و سلطانپور میں واقع ہیں واقع میں ولا اکبر
اس خاندان میں وارث ریاست ہوتا ہر ۔

(نمبر ۷۶) بابو اگروت سنگھہ قوم ٹھاکر سکھوتی تعلقدار سیٹھی نبا ایک پور ۔

اکا نذکرہ خاندانی نمبر ۸ پر درج ہر اور یہ تعلقدار ہم خاندان ان اور شاخ تعلقہ ایا نذکرہ نمبر ۱۳ اکے میں
عرصہ ایک سو سال کا ہوا بابو بال ساہ صورت اعلی کو بر وقت علیحدگی بطور گذارہ یہ ریاست حاصل
ہوئی تتھی بعد کو واور ترقی ملکیت ہوئی ۔ تعلقہ میں موضع ماسی بٹی جمبی علیحتہ اضلاع فیض
و سلطانپور میں واقع ہیں اس خاندان میں اولاد اکبر وارث ریاست ہوتا ہر

(نمبر ۷۷) رو دور پرتاب سنگھہ قوم ٹھاکر کنپوریہ تعلقدار سیٹھی فی سیون ۔

مفصل نذکرہ خاندانی اکا نمبر ۱۲ پر درج ہر ۲۵۔۲۶۴ع میں راجہ مدن سنگھہ صورت نے اقوام مہر و گکومنشی
سے اس ریاست کو بزور تیغ حاصل کیا تھا آگی اولاد میں سے جبونت سنگھہ صورت نے و ماندھا تا سنگھہ نے
اس ریاست کو باہمی تقسیم کرلیا جبونت سنگھہ قابض جبونت اس تعلقہ کے ہوے اور ماندھا تا سنگھہ صورث تعلقدار
چند اپور نمبری ۹ کے ہوے چند نتون کے بعد یہ پرنیس قابض تعلقہ کے ہیں ۔ اس تعلقہ
میں ماسی سو موضع جمبی ماسی موضع علیحتہ ضلع راے بریلی میں واقع ہیں ۔ رسم گدی نشینی
اس خاندان میں ہر

(نمبر ۸) ۱۔ سیتلا بخش ۲۔ لال بہادر سنگھ ۳۔ کالکا بخش سنگھ ۴۔ اودت نرائن سنگھ ۵۔ مہیسر بخش سنگھ ۶۔ چودھاری جدھ بخش سنگھ۔ اقوام بجگوتی تعلقہ داران مادھوپور۔

تذکرہ خاندانی الکا نمبر ۶ پر مندرج ہے یہ تعلقہ ایک نسانخ بٹی سید آباد نمبری کا ہے سوبہ دیی سنگھ دھناشکا آنکے بجائی نے اس علاقہ کو اپنے حصہ بیٹوں کو تقسیم کر دیا چنانچہ بمشارکت سب صاحبان قابض تعلقہ ہیں تعلقہ میں سے سونع جمہی ہے۔ ضلاع پرتابگڑھ میں واقع ہیں اور اس خاندان میں اگر سو علی بلا وصیت فوت ہو جاوے تو بموجب آئین معمولی کے اشخاص ذی حق وارث ریاست ہوئینگے۔

(نمبر ۹) بابو مہردت سنگھ قوم بجگوتی تعلقہ دار سہرت پور و چک مویا و سہرت پور۔

تذکرہ خاندانی الکا نمبر ۶ پر مندرج ہے اولا دھکر سنگھ مورث اعلی اس خاندان سے یہ ریاست قائم ہوئی چونکہ اس خاندان میں جلا آتا سلادریہ تعلقدار سہ خاندان و نسانخ تعلقہ کوڑ و ارستند کرہ نمبر ۱۳ اسکے ہیں سو منع عدپٹی جمہی عنہ۔ اضلاع سلطانپور و فیض آباد میں واقعہ ہیں اس خاندان میں اولا د اکبر وارث ریاست ہوتا ہے۔

(نمبر ۸۰) گنیش کنور زوجہ جلکناتھہ بخش قوم کنپوریہ تعلقہ دار جامو۔

تذکرہ خاندانی الکا نمبر ۱۲ پر منفصل درج ہے ریاست ہردیہ ریاست راج ساہ صورت اعلی لسپر ہیپارم بایعد رساہ سے ماندہ قائم ہوئی جبکہ اس خاندان میں نسلا بعد نسل قبیضہ جلا آیا آخرالامر جلکناتھہ بخش قابض تعلقہ ہوے ابعد وفات آنکے یہ ریئسہ رو جہ آنکی قابض ہیں اور اس ریاست سے تعلقہ نمبری سہ ۱۶ مائندہ قائم ہوا اس تعلقہ میں سے سونع جمہی ہے۔ ضلاع سلطانپور میں واقع ہیں رسم گدی نشینی اس خاندان میں ہے۔

(نمبر ۸۱) شاکر شنکر بخش قوم میس تعلقدار پاہو و گولریا۔

الکا تذکرہ خاندانی نسب سہ پر درج ہردیہ تعلقہ ایک نسانخ تعلقہ کمبور کا نون نمبر ۱۱ کا ہے عرصہ اٹھہ سو سال کا ہے ا را نا ڈوس دیو کے تیسرے رشکے ترہبیت نے وقت عالمہ گی اس ریاست کو حاصل کیا تھا اس وقت سے اس خاندان میں برابر قبیضہ چلا آتا ہی بنا و لبست سہ سری بنام بجو پ سنگھ باپ تعلقدار کے ہو استعفا بعد وفات آنکے یہ تعلقدار قابض ریاست ہوے سو منع جمہی ہے۔ اضلاع بریلی واونام میں واقع ہیں رسم گدی نشینی اس خاندان میں ہے۔

(نمبر ۸۲) ملک بدایت حسین قوم شیخ تعلقہ دارسین پوہ نظاب ملک
شرعیہ باشندہ سوسال کا موزع ہو احمد تہال موریث اسلے نے اس ریاست کو پیدا کیا تھا جیسے تنبیہ موزان چلا رہا
آخر الامر زندہ پشتون کے بعد ملک افضل حسین نے اس ریاست پر قبضہ پایا اور سند تعلقہ گویمنٹ انگلشیہ سے
حاصل کی جب انخون نے لاولد وفات پائی یہ تعلقدار رجیدون چہانی انکے توابض ریاست دوسے تعلقت ہیں
غالباً موضع اور منشا ہمی جبی پریاست سے کی ۔ قصبہ فیض آباد میں واقع ہیں رسم گدی نشینی اس
خاندان میں ہے ۔

(نمبر ۸۳) بکہ جان جیت سنگہ وانت پریشاد ، قوم بجگوتی تعلقدار رام اور برہکند پوہ رساوی پوکورو
انکا مذکرہ خاندانی نمبر میں درج ہے عرصہ دوحانی سوبریس کا موزع امرسنگہ موریث اسلے نے بوقت علہدگی اپنے
خاندان سے یہ تعلقہ سلسلہ قائم کیا جیسے تنبیہ موزان بدار چلا آتا ہو گویمنٹ سے سند تعلقہ شہادہ کا رکاش
ہوئی بھی اب انکے یہ تعلقدار قابض ریاست میں صلب موضع اور بعضہ جبی بھی موضع
سلطانپور دراسے بریلی میں واقع ہیں ۔ اس ریاست میں اگر موریث اسلے بلاوصیت فوت ہوجاوے توبھی
آئین عمومی اشخاص نزدیق وارث ریاست ہوینگے ۔

(نمبر ۸۴) نونہال سنگہ خلفندگوپال سنگہ قوم باتم تعلقدار محمد آباد گوپال کھیرو
یہ ریاست قدیم ہے موریان تعلقدار سلطنت مہندرسہا ہیں عہدہ قانونگوئی وجود ورہ ریت سے ممتاز ہے
محکم سنگہ موریث نے محمد آباد وخاص افوام افغانان سے سردیاروکے بنام محمد آباد تعلقہ قائم کیا آخر الا
چودھری کی گوپال خانقابض ریاست ہوے اور گویمنٹ انگلشیہ سے سند تعلقہ را حاصل کی اسکو اختیارات
آخری مجشریف و سند کلکٹر میں اسہ صلاحت میں حاصل تھے بعد وذات اوکی یہ رئیس مالک ستے ہیں
اور انکو بھی اختیارات پیدا ہی حاصل ہیں تعلقہ میں موضع بفع جبی ملوعیات
ہمین اولاد اکبر اس خاندان میں مالک ریاست ہوتا ہو ۔

(نمبر ۸۵) بابو مہندرادت سنگہ ، قوم بجگوتی تعلقدار کھیرو ہٹ
انکا مذکرہ خاندانی نمبر میں درج ہو یہ تعلقہ اب شاخ تعلقہ نمبر ۱۳ کا ہی سنگہ موریث نے بوقت
علہندگی تعلقہ کو زوار ستے جنبہ بریہات بطور گذر رہا اپنے تھے بعد کو باندہ جبی ترقی وکی تعلقہ
قائم کیا سوقت سے اس خاندان میں یہ ریاست چلی آتی ہو ۔ اس تعلقہ میں منشہ موضع او
جنب چی ضلع فیض آباد میں ہوی ہمین اولاد اکبر اس خاندان میں وراثت
ریاست مقرا ہو ۔

(نمبر ۸۶) چودھری خصلت حسین قوم شیخ تعلقدار ککرالی ورار مدہی رحمان پور درا سایش
و کنیت گنج و گو ندا مؤ خطاب چودھری موروثی ہے ۔ پہلے مورث آپ کے عرب سے فاریاب میں آگے
تھے پھر تیمور شاہ و دہلی سے بمنصب چودھرائی سندیلہ خاص ممتاز ہوئے اور عہد اکبر شاہ میں شیخ
فیروز چودھری بخطاب خان موسوم ہوئے۔ عہد نواب سعادت علیخان میں آپ کے موٴرثان کو بجائے علاوہ
حق چودھرائی درس ہزار روپیہ سالیانہ نانکار اور نہایت معانی سلطنت اور ہر سے مقرر ہوئی آخر الامر
چودھری بمنصب علی صاحب جدامجد را سرکار اودھ سے میں زری وقار ہوکر ریاست کو بہت وسعت دی اور
تعلقدار علاقے نششتا میں آئے والد چودھری حشمت علیخان صاحب نے بمقام جوار پرگنہ سندیلہ گورنمنٹ
انگلشیہ کو امدار رسد دخیرہ و مہربانی و فروع مطیع و سرکوبی باغیان میں مع اپنے سپاہیان کے شریک ہوکر معرکہ ہوکر
اصلاح ملک میں شریک بصلاح حکام رہے ۔ اور تبالمین تلوب تعلقداران غیر حاضر کو بھی اپنے اطمینان سے
فوراً نوبر دار ی سرکار میں حاضر کرایا ایام خدر ششتہ عوض میں ایک بیش قیمت املاک محلہ رائے سے لاکھوں
روپیہ کا نقصان میہا اسکے عوض میں چودھری صاحب کو گورنمنٹ انگلشیہ سے حق مالکانہ تعلقہ اسایش
ورار مدہی رحمان پور کا نیس میں بمنصب مفتع ایک نہی ورافع میں مع خلعت فاخرہ مرحمت ہوا اُن کے بعد آپ
قابض ریاست ہیں اور نظر و فور لیاقت گروہ اعظم تعلقداران نے آپ کو منتخب فرماکر انصرام عہدہ مذکور پر انتجاب منتہد
کے واسطے آپ سے التجا کی النہا کی چونکہ سب فرقہ کا بہبود و اس سے متعلق تھا لہذا آپ بار انصرام اس عہدہ کے متحمل ہوئے اور
آپ اپنی ریاست میں آنریری مجسٹریٹ و ڈسٹرکٹ بورڈ کے ممبر ہیں اور چودھری محمد عظیم صاحب آپ کے ولی عہد ریاست
جبکی لیاقت تمام انوٴنی وہ تطاعت علمی ولیاقت رُعیانہ کا ایک معالم ثنا خوان ہیں امتحان بی وکالت میں کامیاب
ہو چکے ہیں پرگنہ علاوان حصہ ریاست میں وہ بھی آنریری مجسٹریٹ ہیں ۔ تعلقہ میں ورث موافعات ادبیات آدم لاطبی
جبھی بیت ریاست سے ۔ مع علیہ اضلاع ہر روہ کی واردام رونگ ۔ بیتسا پور میں رانو ہیں سرگم نخ نہی حاجہ نہیں

 سہجار تھہ سنگہ قدیم تحار نیکم قدیم نقدار اُٹوا نفیسر بوچہ

جنگ ساہ مورث اعلے تعلقدار کے الور تجار راسے مقام سلاج پور علاقہ سانڈی میں ہیں بوجہ رشتہ دار ہی میں آئے تھے
چونکہ راجہ دوانکا بجکر شاہ و دہلی مقبید فوج تھا اور انکے مورثان نے اوس راجہ کو کسیدھر جسے راہ لی دہ پہ بچایا و فراراً
راجہ نذکور نے علاقہ بلبا مورثان تعلقدار کو دیا اُس وقت سے ریاست قائم ہوئی پھر جبیت میں شیو بال سنگہ
مورث نے علاقہ کو ترقی دی شیو بال سنگہ کی جو تھی اینت میں نوازساہ گوبندرائے گیا جنگہ کشن سنگہ
یہ چار بھائی ہوئے سے اور انہیں ریاست قسیم ہوئی نوازساہ و کشن سنگہ پردامین گئے اور گوبند راسے

وگیا سنگھ اسی ریاست میں رہے گو نبد رائے کی اولاد میں یہ تعلقدار صاحب تھا بعض ریاست میں انہوں نے
ایام غدر کی خیر خواہی میں ملکیت تعلقہ نصیرہ لوہرمال کرکے ریاست کو ترقی دی ۔ تعلقہ میں موضع
ضلع چہبی جہبی رہے ہائے ۔ مع ملکیت عطیہ ضلع مہروی میں واقع ہیں اس خاندان میں رستم گدی نشینی ہے ۔

(نمبر ۸۸) ٹھاکر شیو بخش سنگھ تعلقدار کشمیرہ و ہائی لوہر قوم ٹھاکر گور

سن ۱۰۱۹ ہجری میں عہد عالمگیر بادشاہ و جب سلطنت میں عبدالظفی واقع ہوئی اس وقت درگیہ پال مورث جون تھی
موضع ان نے اقوام پر ہمیں ملقب چودھری مالکان جاند وید رکھ سکار اٹھائے اور آنکی نعمت مذکور میں اسی جگہ
گدھی بنوائی اور کشمیر نام رکھا جب نام سے یہ تعلقہ مشہور ہوا اور آنکی ریاست پر قبضہ کرلیا جیسے یہ ریاست
قائم ہوئی پھر باہم ہر دو مورثان میں علاقہ تقسیم ہوا اور گیہ پال کی اولاد سے یہ تعلقدار بعض ریاست میں
اور اس تعلقہ میں وقف موضع موضعک پچی نملہ سیتا پور رکھہری میں جہبی موضعات مشہور واقع ہیں اور
اس خاندان میں رسم گدی نشینی ہے ۔

(نمبر ۸۹) ۱۔ ٹھاکر این بہچنا تھہ کنور ہ ۲۔ جہبر پال سنگھ ۳۔ سورج پال سنگھ بہ بندر پال سنگھ
اقوام لسبین تعلق باران کونڈر راجیت ۔ تذکرہ خاندانی و آغاز ریاست آنکا نمبر ۵ پر درج سنہے
خاندان رامی مہوم پال مورث اعلاء میں جب ریاست تقسیم ہوئی اس وقت میں موزان تعلقدار کو یہ ریاست
علی سند تعلقداری گورنمنٹ سے بنام ٹھاکر این صاحبہ مرحمت ہوئی تھی لیکن انہوں نے اس علاقہ کو
چار حصے کرکے ایک اپنے تبضہ میں رکھا اور تین حصے نمبر ۲ و ۳ و ۴ ۔ اپنے قرابت دار و دیگر نام ہر سہ
صاحبان منسوب رج سند کرا دیے اب بمجموعی دیہات علاقہ کے مدت موضع جہبی بیسیار سالہ مع ضلع
بریاباپ گڈھ ہر میں واقع ہیں ۔ اس خاندان میں اگر مورث اعلاء بلا وصیت فوت ہوجاوے تو جو بھی
آئین بمعمولی کے اشخاص ذی حق وارث ریاست ہونگے ۔

(نمبر ۹۰) ۱۔ درگا پرشاد ۲۔ وزیر چند اقوام کا یتھہ تعلقداران سہرون بڑا گاؤں
و سہرسوا ملہرہ و تلہی لاہرو ۔ موضع سہرون جنگلے نام سے تعلقہ مشہور رہا و میں سہرون بڑا سہرون سنگھ
قوم ٹھاکر رکیوار کا آباد کیا ہوا ہے عہد سلطنت شاہی میں حاشیہ حکایہ اریان کرتے رہے عرصہ ایک سو سال کا
ہوا رای جیکے رای صاحب مورث نے موضع سہرون و نیز دیگر دیہات سرکار شاہی سے حاصل کرکے بنام سہرون
تعلقہ قائم کیا بعد کو وضیت رامی فتح چند مورثان نے بجلد روی حسن خدمات ایام خدا رسیدہ اعم گورنمنٹ
انگلشیہ سے تعلقہ سہرسوا ملہرہ و نیلہی لہرو عطیہ حاصل کیا بعد وفات آکو یہ تعلقداران تھا بعض ریاست میں ہیں
اور باہم ہر دو صاحبوں کو علاقہ منقسم بہ حصہ درگا پرشاد وزیر اہتمام گورنمنٹ یہ تعلقہ میں مع ملکیت عطیہ بیست موضع

چھپ ٹکی جمعی بلوہ ساوہ ضلع کھیری قوم روہائی واردانام ہیں واقع ہیں رسم گدی نشینی اس خاندان ہیں ہے۔

(نمبر ۹۱) اننت سہائے درسنگھ تعلقدار کھیرو نیمبہ قوم ٹھاکر گرگ نسبی تخمینًا سو برس ہوئے نہال سنگھ و گنگا پرشاد موزیان اعلٰی نے جوانائی قوم کے سردار قصور ہوتے تھے تعلقہ سہی پور کھیرو نیمبہ بذریعہ بالاشتراک پیدا کیا تھا پھر نہال سنگھ نے ہند و ریاست اپنی قوت بازو سے حاصل کیے کہ شمال تعلقہ کیے دونوں صاحب علی حیات نمک رشتہ کمجائی رہی بعد وفات ہر دو صاحبان یہ تعلقہ کھیرو نیمبہ رام سروپ پریوتہ گنگا پرشاد کو ملا اور تعلقہ سہی پور مستذکرہ نمبر بہ۹ مساۃ رگھنا تھ کنور روحبہ نہال سنگھ نے پایا بعد وفات گنگا پرشاد یہ تعلقدار ترکہ بدرسی پر قابض ہیں اور اس تعلقہ میں ہدہ سموضع سب پٹی جمعی بلوہ حارث اضلاع سلطان پور و فیض آباد میں واقع ہیں اولاد اکبر اس خاندان ہیں وارث ریاست ہوتا ہے۔

(نمبر ۹۲) دوران سہا دریال سنگھہ قوم ٹھاکر سوم نسبی تعلقدار داندئی کاچھہ یہ تعلقہ ایک شاخ نمبر ۱ کا ہی مفصل تذکرہ اسی نمبر پر درج ہی گورنمنٹ انگلشیہ سے سند تعلقداری بنام بابو سری پت سنگھ ہوئی تھی بعد وفات آنکو یہ رئیس درامد و نکو حسب وصیت قابض ریاست ہیں اس موضع جمعی بلوہ حارث لالوعیث ضلع رتاپ گڈھ میں واقع ہیں رسم گدی نشینی اس خاندان میں ہے۔

(نمبر ۹۳) بابو جسنا تھ سنگھہ قوم ٹھاکر عیس تعلقدار گنگہ تذکرہ خاندانی آپ کا نمبر بہ۳ و سہ۳ پر درج ہی آپ حقیقی چچا زاد ناشنکر جیش صاحب تعلقدار کھجور کا نون مستذکرہ نمبر ۱ کے ہیں بسلسلہ خیر خواہی ایام نفذ رنگ شدہ یہ ملکیت بابو صاحب کو گورنمنٹ انگلشیہ سے منجانبہ علاقہ منضبطہ بینی مادھو بخش سنگھہ باغی کے مرحمت ہوئی اس تعلقہ میں اعلٰی موضع جمعی ہم ماحش ضلع رائے بریلی ہیں واقع ہیں اولاد اکبر اس خاندان ہیں وارث ریاست ہوتا ہے۔

(نمبر ۹۴) بشیشر بخش سنگھہ قوم ٹھاکر گرگ نسبی تعلقدار رسمی پورہ وغیرہ ان کا مفصل تذکرہ نمبر ۹۱ پر درج ہی یہ تعلقہ ایک شاخ اسی نمبر کا ہی یہ تعلقدار بجای مساۃ رگھنا تھ کنور روحبہ نہال سنگھ کے قابض ریاست ہیں تعلقہ میں کیقندہ موضع اور ہدہ موضع پٹی جمعی مہدیہ ساوہ حارث آپا لی ضلاع فیض آبا و سلطان پور میں واقع ہیں اس خاندان میں اولاد اکبر وارث ریاست ہوتا ہے۔

(نمبر ۹۵) بابو لالو ساہ قوم راجکلار تعلقدار میو پور ڈہلا و کروری مدہو ین و ایک ثلمث حصہ جائداد شہرادا پور و میوپور وغیرہ نسبر اکت ایشراج سنگھ نمبر ۵۱۔ آپ کا تذکرہ خاندانی نمبر ۵ پر درج ہی اور حال آغاز ریاست نمبر ۵۱ پر لکھا ہی یہ ریاست پہلوان سنگھ نام اپنے بھائی سے ہنگام تقسیم حلقہ دہ حاصل کی تھی پھر آپ نے والیشوج سنگھ نے اس تعلقہ کو باہمی تقسیم کر لیا آپ اس ریاست پر قابض ہیں اور ایشوج سنگھ

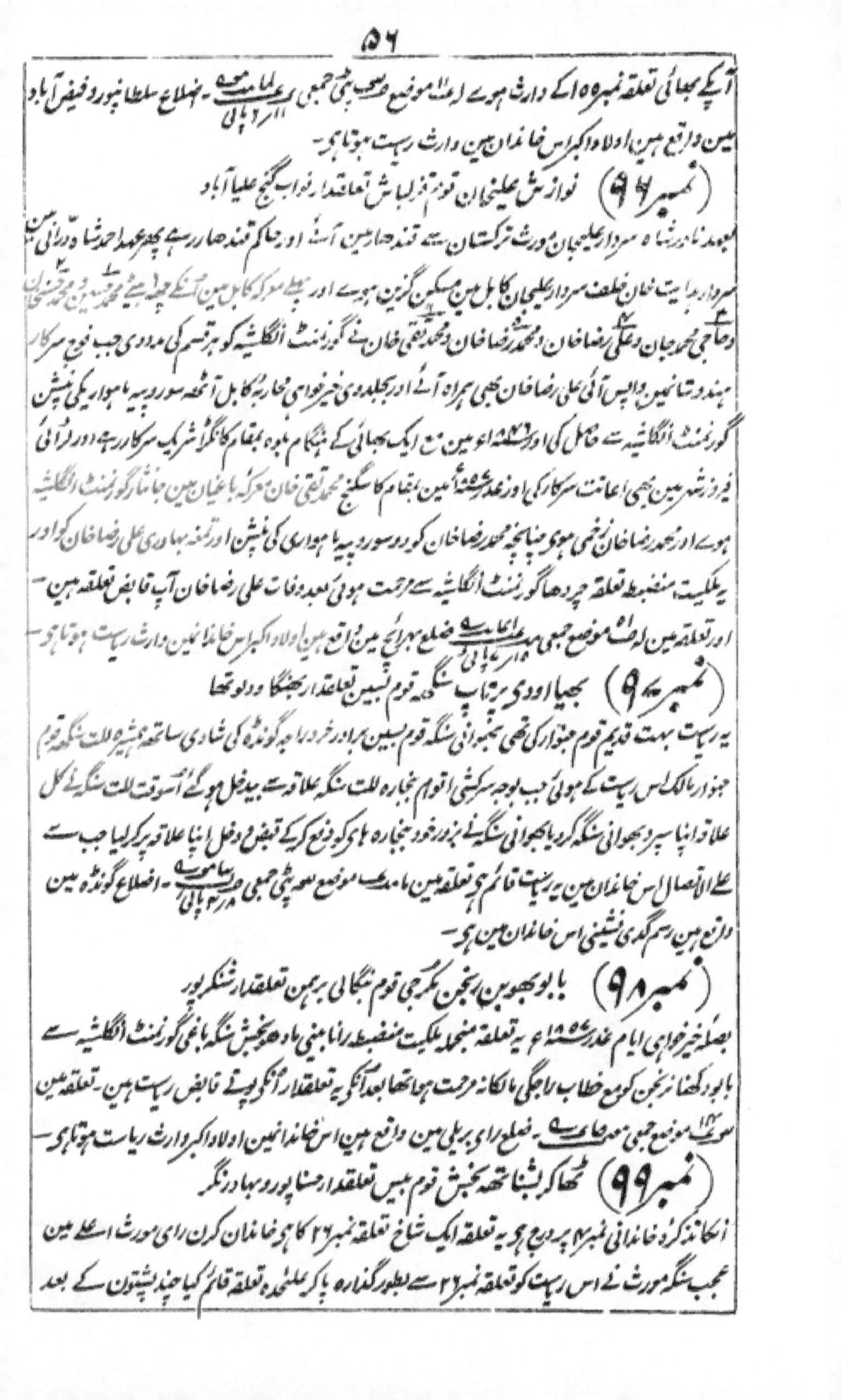

(نمبر ۹۶)

(نمبر ۹۷)

(نمبر ۹۸)

(نمبر ۹۹)

سلسلۂ افصلی میں تجھا کربخش وارث ریاست ہوید وبعد وزارت آنکی یہ تعلقدار نوابض ریاست ہیں ریاست موضع جبھی ریاست ملک ... ضلع بریلی میں واقع ہیں رسم گدی ہی نشینی اس خاندان میں ہے چو

(نمبر ۱۰۰) بابو سرجیت سنگھ تعلقدار نیکاری موبجاگو پوردا نیٹھا وغیرہ رپورہ جبھی و امیٹھی قوم تجھا کر کنپوریہ ۔۔۔ یہ تعلقدار بجنا خدان وشلاخ راجہ تلوئی مستذکرہ نمبر ۹۰ واکے ہیں سمبنث ۱۱ میں راجہ گلان سیاہ مورث اصلی کو ریاست تلوئی سے یہ تعلقہ نیکاری گذارہ ملاتھا آسوقت سے تبقہ مورثان چلا آتا ہے

اور بسبب خیر خواہی ایام غدر رشتہ ۱۸۵۷ء بابو سرجیت سنگھ نے گورنمنٹ انگلشیہ سے ریاست تعلقہ بجاگو پور وغیرہ عطیہ حاصل کیے اور راجہ ماوی موہن سنگ تعلقدار گڈہ میٹھی مستذکرہ نمبر ۸۰ نے اپنی کل جائداد بابو سرجیت سنگ کو تعلقدار حال کرکی اب سب ملکیت تعلقدار صاحب کی مع عطیہ وغیرہ با مصرف موضع اور تین پچی جبھی معہ ... ۔ اضلاح راسے بریلی وریتاب گدہ و سلطانپور میں واقع ہیں اولاد واکبر اس خاندان میں مالک و ریاست ہوتا ہے

(نمبر ۱۰۱) سیتلا بخش وتنکر بخش قوم تجھا کر بسین تعلقدار رمیں گڈہ

اسکا تذکرہ خاندانی نمبر ۹۰ پہ مفصل درج ہے اولاد رای معم بال ہی موتعلقہ ڈھگوس بوقت تقسیم علیحدہ قائم ہوا یہ ریاست اوسی تعلقہ کی ایک شاخ ہے تعلقہ میں دیسہ موضع جبھی معہ ... ضلع ریتاب گدہ میں واقع ہیں اور اس خاندان میں اگر مورث اعلی بلا وصیت فوت ہوجاوے تو بموجب آئین معمولی کے انخاص ذیحق وارث ریاست ہوتا

(نمبر ۱۰۲) بابوکشن پرشاد سنگھ قوم تجھا کر منوار تعلقدار چاندی پور پربھر

قریباً پانچسو سال کے موتا ہوی سکھ راج ویو مورث اعلی ضلع عظم گڈھ سے آکر راج جہرو میں آنے اور ریاست اختیار حاصل کیا جب زمانہ بربوزکا منقلب ہوا آسوقت سا دو موضع پرانیا قبضہ کرکے مالک ریاست ہو گئے اور دو فتح یار گیہ موواضعات پر بھی اپنا قبضہ کرتے رہی چند پشتون کے بعد اس خاندان میں ملٹن سنگ ولشکری سنگ موحرض دوسرا برس کا ہوتا ہوکہ ان دونوں میں ریاست تقسیم ہوئی ملٹن سنگ کے خاندان سے یہ تعلقدار و تعلقہ نمبر ۱۰۱ آتا ہے اور لشکری سنگ کے خاندان سے تعلقدار ان نمبر ۱۰۳ و ۱۰۲ کے تعلقدار ان ہیں ۔ اس تعلقہ میں متی موضع اور ماسعہ پچی جبھی سنواہ ضلع فیض آباد میں واقع ہیں اس خاندان میں اولاد واکبر وارث ریاست ہوتا ہے ۔

(نمبر ۱۰۳) بابو ہردت سنگھ قوم منوار تعلقدار بربھر چاندی پور ہوا

یہ تعلقہ ایک شاخ تعلقہ نمبر ۱۰۱ کا ہو حال خاندانی وڈانماز ریاست اعلی ریاست درج نمبر بربھر ہو خاندان سکھ راج ویو مورث اعلی میں یہ ریاست ملٹن سنگ موربث سے متعلقہ و قائم ہوئی جیسے اس خاندان میں قبضہ چلا آتا ہی تعلقہ میں موضع سا متی پچی جبھی موربہ ضلع فیض آباد میں واقع ہیں اولاد واکبر اس خاندان میں وارث ریاست ہوتا ہے ۔

(نمبر ۱۰۴) شمشیر بہادر ولد بابو شیو بریگاش سنگھ قوم مینوار تعلقدار برج بہر راج سلطان پور

یہ تعلقہ ایک شاخ تعلقہ نمبری ۱۰۲ کا ہے مفصل تذکرہ خاندانی و آغاز ریاست اسی نمبر پر درج ہو خاندان سکھراج دیو مورث اعلیٰ مین اللشکری سنگھ مورث سے یہ ریاست قائم ہوئی ہے اس خاندان میں قبضہ جلاآ تا ہو تعلقہ مین اوسی موضع اور درسوپی جمعی موسیٰ سیبچہ ضلع فیض آباد مین واقع ہیں ۔ اولاد اکبر اس خاندان وارث ریاست ہوتا رہا ہے ۔

(نمبر ۱۰۵) ٹھکر این دلیل کنور بیوہ جندبگار شا و قوم مین تعلقدار لہریست پور

قحسالی سو سال میہر سلطنت دہلی ہست ایک وسیع رتبہ کہی ہزار رتبہ ایک اراضی خیر فرزوعدہ کا موجرا خنگل بہری افتاد وہ تھا موریان تعلقدار کہ مرحمت ہوا تھا انھون نے خنگل کو کشور کر آباد کی کرائی اور بنام مزدو بروا تعلقہ قائم کیا عہد نابالکی تہبولیت بنام بروا ہوئی تھی اب بنام بروا ہست اپور تعلقہ مشہور ہو آخرالامر سند تعلقداری گورنمنٹ انگلشیہ سے بنام جندکا بخش مرحمت ہوی تھی بعد وفات اوکی یہ ریاست تابض ہین اور تعلقہ مین لہست موضع سے ٹی جمعی ضلع ہر ودوی مین واقع ہین بسم گدی نشینی اس خاندان مین ہو ۔

(نمبر ۱۰۶) شیو درشٹ نراین سنگھ خلف بابو بیپ نراین سنگھ قوم سوار تعلقدار برج بہر

یہ تعلقہ شاخ تعلقہ نمبر ۱۰۴ کا ہے مفصل تذکرہ خاندانی و آغاز ریاست اسی نمبر پر درج ہی خاندان دیو مورث اعلیٰ مین اللشکری سنگھ سے یہ ریاست قائم ہو حیہے اس خاندان مین قبضہ جلاآ تا ہو اوران تعلقدار زآبنی ریاست مقبوضہ سے تعداد وی ریاست ہوتی جمع مالگذاری کی جاأدا و اسنے پانچ بیوہ نگو منتقل کردی ہی اپنے تصفیہ مین جرف دو موضع اور درصہ ٹی جمعی اٹاملیسہ کی ریکھی مین موضع ضلع فیض آباد مین واقع ہین ۔ اس خاندان مین اولاد اکبر وارث ریاست ہوتا ہی ۔

(نمبر ۱۰۷) گنیش کنور بیوہ ارجن سنگھ قوم کنپوریہ تعلقدار رئیسی

ان کا تذکرہ خاندانی و آغاز ریاست نمبر ۱۷ پر درج ہی یہ ریاست طلبہدار ساہ دوسری ترکی سالہا مین سے علاحدہ قائم ہوئی ہیبے نسلاً بعد نسل قبضہ جلاآ با تعلقہ مین عناموضع جمعی سیملایسہ ضلع سلطان پور مین واقع ہین بہم گدی نشینی اس خاندان مین ہو ۔

(نمبر ۱۰۸) احمد حسین وواحد حسین قوم شیخ تعلقداران گدیہ وگوبلا البتولی

سنہ ۹۹۷ ہجری مین تقاضی بحلا، الدین انصاری مدنی نے اپ اقوام بجہرون سے نپور تغیع اس ریاست کو حاصل کیا با تجا جیبے قبضہ موریان جلاآ با شستہ بعد فصلی مین نراید تعلقداران حال مورثہ نامہائی ہیز خالض اس ریاست کے موریہ بعد وفات اوکی یہ تعلقداران تافیض ریاست مین اور قوم شیخ قدروائی اولاد و تافیض قدروہ سے

معروف ہیں شیخ احمد حسین صاحب ملا امرت سرکار رئیس العبدہ تحصیلداری تنسار ہیں ۔ تعلقہ مین الوقتہ ہی
جمعی دیعہ دارو ۔ اضلاع لکھنؤ وبارہ بنکی میں واقع ہیں اس رئیست مین اگر مورث اعلیٰ بلا وصیت فوت ہوجاوے
تو بموجب آئین معمول کے اشخاص ذیل تحقیق وارث رئیست ہوونگے ۔

(نمبر ۱۰۹) ٹھاکر کلبھدیو بخش خلعت سردار ججبا سنگہ قوم ٹھاکر جھبوار تعلقدار پرسینی واکبر ہری پال کچہ
رہ پرسینی گوٹھاکر چمک چپا راران پور ۔ انکے مورث سبقے سے جبز و ملکیت دار تعلقہ پرسینی کے تھے سردار جھبا سنگہ والد
تعلقدار حال نے بصلہ خیر خواہی ایام مدد رشتا عطیہ تعلقہ اکو ہری گوپال کھیرہ ملکیت منضبط منہا پال سنگہ کو مع خطاب
سردار سبہا در گورنمنٹ انگلشیہ سے عطیہ حاصل کر کے شامل تعلقہ کیا تعلقہ پرسینی کا سند و ربست استرار ی ہو اور
یہ رئیست انہی پانچ تعلقہ داران خیر خواہ کے ہے بعد وفات سردار جھبا سنگہ آپ قابض تعلقہ ہیں ۔ اور تعلقہ مین
کا موقع ایک پٹی جبی مسمی خانپرسیہ اضلاع لکھنؤ ودرای بریلی وانام مین مع ملکیت عطیہ واقع ہیں اس
خاندان میں اولاد اکبر مالک رئیست ہوتا ہے ۔

(نمبر ۱۱۰) ٹھاکر لالتا بخش قوم گور تعلقدار کچھورہ و بجھردا
گیارہ سو برس ہوے ہوے درگہ ناتھ سنگہ مورث اعلیٰ بذریعہ چاکری علامانہ راجہ جج چیندوای قنوج نار کلیبر سے اس جو مین
آئے بعد ازاں اسکے لیکگا سنگہ اپنے باپ کی جگہ عامل مقرر ہوے ۔ انہون نے یہ ملکیت اقوام متہدہ کی جو راجہ قنوج نیچ خرچ
ہوگئی تھی حکمر راجہ بعد قتل وخراج انوام متہدہ راجہ قنوج سے قبال کی جبے آنازاس رئیست کا ہی بھر مورثان تعلقدار
بذریعہ بیع اور میں ترقی و کر صورت تعلقہ قائم کی سند تعلقہ بنام ٹھاکر دال سنگہ ہوئی تھی بعد آنکے اب یہ رئیست قابض
رئیست میں حصہ موقع سے پٹی جبی مسمی معلا الوسیہ اضلاع ہر روئی و ستیاپور مین واقع ہیں اولاد اکبر خاندان مینا
وارث رئیست ہوتا ہے ۔

(نمبر ۱۱۱) سید وصی حیدر قوم سید تعلقدار بھجو گتا پور
سقلہ ہجری مین محمد صغراؤ ودث ہمراہ سلطان شمس الدین اپنی ولایت سے ہند مین آئے اور وہ بیات پر گنہ ملگرام
سجلد وہی نخجیانی سری راجہ مالک سری انگر جواب ملگرام مشہور بہ دربار شاہ ہ سے آنکو عطا ہوئے بھر اولاد محمد صغرا نے
جنگل کشوار بھہ گتا پور آباد کر ایا مین نام سے تعلقہ مشہور بہ گورنمنٹ انگلشیہ سے سند تعلقداری بنام سید محمد ابراہیم انکے
شیے بھائی کو مرحمت ہوئی تھی حسب وصیت آنکے بعد یہ تعلقدار قابض رئیست ہیں ۔ تعلقہ مین تعلقہ موقع ایک پٹی جبی
فصلہ ہر روئی مین واقع ہین رسم آبادی نشینی اس خاندان مین ہے ۔

(نمبر ۱۱۲) ۱ ۔ چودھری محمد اشرف ۲ ۔ محمد زین العابدین ۳ ۔ محمد نائل ۴ ۔ محمد ابرار
انوام سید تعلقداران آصف پور وآصف پور گبھاری و بارگا گنج دو دہو بندیپور خطاب چودھری معین حیات ۔

یہ تعلقہ اران ممنجا نذ ان تعلقہ از نمبر ١١١ کے ہیں آصف پور جٹ کے نام سے تعلقہ مشہور ہی ہی سید آصف مورث نے آباد کیا تھا بعدہ موبیان موذ کیا را سی مقام پر پیٹ مولا فصلی ہین خاذی الدین حیدر شاہ ذوال ملک اورہ نیکہ بنا بنام رفعت علیخان عرف نصیر الدین حیدر شاہ اپنے بھتیجے کے نام مرزا بوکرا یا اور سیط سال تک ہ تحصیل سرکار شاہی کھیا سیگلا یو افصلی ہین ہوری کا کاظم ہین نہان مورث کہ بجہ نذیر سلطنت اورہ ه تجهی نیکگا ه نصیر اله نصیر شاہ ایا سے بذا بجوانی مرحمت ہوا آ سرقت سے تمغه مورثان سراہ جاگہ آرامی هو سید تعلقدار سی گورنمنٹ انگلشیہ سے ... ـ جوہ یا بھا صاحبان سکا نام کچہ باٹی ملی تھی لیکن یا ہم اسطور سے قابض یہ حقو دوسری محمد انشرفت کو تعلقہ آصف پور روال ملا ۔ منبع جمی بیہا موضه محمد زین العابد ین کو تعلقہ تگہاری رسے سنے صیع جمی بالعمده جاحت سید محمد فاضل کو تعلقہ در کار گئے تھے ۔ دفعہ دو جی جمی میں یہا میہ ـ سید محمد مبارکه تعلقہ دعوند پور موضه موضه سے نبی جمی معمله لویٹ ـ یہ تعلقدار ان ایام نهاذ بی نهر خوار سرکار رہتے کہ اسکے جصله ہین گورنمنٹ انگلشیہ ست علاوه عطیه عطیه مرحمت ہوا اب اس تعلقہ ہین سع ملکیت عطیه موسا موانع صرجی جمی اله مده یویلپت فیلع ہرروای ہین واقع ہین ا اس خاندان ہین اولا د اکبر و ارث رسیت ہوتا ہی

(نمبر ١١٣) مرزا محمد علی بیگ توم مغل تعلقدار اورنگ آباد

نمبر در عرصه دو تین سال مرزا مہا دریبیگ ساکن ملک حرب مورث از جانب شاه اورنگ زیب بابشاه دہلی دا سطے تنبیه ومدارک تعلقدار ان ٹبو نخجه وغیره و جو ملک اس ریاست کے تھے اس جوار ہین آنے اور رسیاٹی پس مالکانه قبضه کر لیا اور گدهی بال پور کو منبهه بم کر اسکے مہتا م بابشاه اورنگ آباد آباد کیا جس نامهت یہ تعلقہ مشہور ہی عند نشیتو سنگه بعد ازانکی اولاد ہین محمد بخش و قطبی محمد موسے آنہین علاقه تقسیم ہوا نمبر اکی اولاد یہ تعلقدار قابض رسیت ہین اور نمبر سوای اولاد سے تعلقہ ار قطب نگر نمبری ١٢١ کے ہین اس تعلقہ ہین یوعیسا سوعیع ایک نئی جمی موه میللا مهصه فیلع سیتاپور ہین واقع ہین رہم گدی نشینی اس خاندان ہین ہین موه

(نمبر ١١٤) کاظم حسین نہان خان نزاد وه تعلقدار بجهو پور امو ور دریا پور یه حصه شراکتی

شنه ٩ ہجری عهد محمد بابرشاه ہین شیخ ہین مورث اعلی بجلیدوری حسن خدمات اعطاء جاگیر برگنه بانزی و لسبو ان و فتہیور وصد ریور اس ملک ہین آئے اور بجهو امو خاص ہین بیکومت اختیار کی ٩١٠ ہجری ہین بعہد جهانگیتر شنا بابشاه انکے مورثان کو خطاب بخانی مرحمت ہوا اسکے نه بجوی ہین بہا نهان مورث شاه وقت سے بجنار لاب ممتاز الملاک ممتاز بجوه سے عند نشیتو نکے بعد امام علیخان مورث نے سلادت کو تری ہی آخر الامرث تعلقدار ی نبها بابشاه ہین نهان گورنمنٹ انگلشیہ سے مرحمت ہوئی نیابد وفات اسکے یہ تعلقدار ی قابض رسیت ہین اور یه رئیس ممنجا نذان راجه امیر حسین نهان صاحب تعلقدار متذکره نمبر اکی ہین عہد سلطنت اورہ ه ہین تجل حسین نهان والا ر حسین نهان مورثان و نذیر یه تعلقدار بجی تعلقہ داری عهده نظامت وجلقه داری پر سرفراز رہ ۔ اس تعلقه ہین

یہ موضع سے نئی جمعی یعنی اسلام پالی یہ ضلاع باردہ نیکی و ستیا پور میں واقع ہیں اس خاندان میں رسم گدی نشینی ہوتی ہے۔

(نمبر ۱۵) ٹھاکر ہری ہر بخش قوم بنوار تعلقدار سرودہ

کیفیت خاندانی و آغاز ریاست اس قوم کی نمبر ۱۳ پر درج ہے یہ ریاست کرن دیو موریث اعلیٰ سے جس وقت تقسیم حاصل کیا تھا قائم ہوئی آنکی اولاد میں سادھی سنگھ سے موضع سرودہ جسکے نام سے تعلقہ مشہور ہے۔ سلالہ نصلی میں آباد کیا آنکی چند پشتوں کے بعد رشید تعلقداری نام گنگا بخش گورنمنٹ انگلشیہ پر مرحمت ہوئی۔ بعد وفات آنکے یہ تعلقدار قابض ریاست ہیں۔ تعلقہ میں سہ موضع یعنی نئی جمعی، اطلاع باردہ نیکی و ستیا پور میں واقع ہیں۔ رسم گدی نشینی اس خاندان میں ہوتی ہے۔

(نمبر ۱۶) ٹھاکر فضل علی خان قوم گوری تعلقدار اکبر پور

پہلے سے مالک اس ریاست کے نجت بلی و مہابلی اقوام ٹھاکر گوری منہو ہیں۔ تھے جب بوجہ سرکشی فردوستا پیشگاہ شاہ وقت سے خارج از ملکیت ہوئے اور رویانت رائے سیٹھہ سکنہ نیسوان کو صوبہ اودہ سے یہ ریاست ملکی اس وقت نکلسا ہجری میں نجد نواب شجاع الدولہ بہادر بمقام فیض آباد ہر دو تشخص مشرف با سلام ہوئے اور اپنی ملکیت پر قبضہ یا با جبسہ موزن چلا آیا ہوا مگر بحالت اسلام اوسی نام سابقہ سے مشہور ہے۔ اکبر پور اکبر علی خلف مہابلی نو مسلم کا آباد کیا ہوا ہے یہ تعلقدار اسی خاندان سے ہیں۔ تعلقہ میں ریاست مخرج یعنی نئی جمعی یہ سیٹھا یہ ضلاع سیتا پور میں واقع ہیں۔ رسم گدی نشینی اس خاندان میں ہوتی ہے۔

(نمبر ۱۷) ٹھاکر جواہر سنگھ قوم ٹھاکر بیس تعلقدار اسبی چونبیہ و برہمولی

آغاز قوم بیس بیان کا تذکرہ نمبر ۳ پر درج ہے رشتہ ۱۲۱۲ نصلی میں یہ ریاست ہنگام تقسیم با ہمی علاقہ سجدہ لیا جو ملکیت نواز شاہ موریث کی تھی جبعا نیدیو سنگھ آکے والد کو ہوئی تھی پھر انکھون نے بانٹ کے مع دربن علاقہ کو بہت ترقی ہر دی بعد وفات اونکی یہ تعلقدار قابض ریاست اور رشید تعلقداری بھی گورنمنٹ انگلشیہ سے انہین کے نام مرحمت ہوئی و بصلہ خیر خواہی امام نمدر ۱۸۲۷ء تعلقہ بہ ہوئی گورنمنٹ سے عطیہ حاصل ہوا۔ تعلقہ میں سہ موضع اور یعنی نئی جمعی و سبلیا نوبیہ بالان مع ملکیت عطیہ یعنی سیتا پور میں واقع ہیں اولاد اکبر اس خاندان میں مالک ریاست ہوتا ہے۔

(نمبر ۱۸) ٹھاکر درگا بخش قوم بنوار تعلقدار نیلگا نون وجلالپور

یہ تعلقہ ایک شاخ شانہ تعلقہ نمبر ۱۳ کا ہی دیو کرن دیو موریث اعلیٰ نے وقت تقسیم تعلقہ نمبر ۱۸ سے جدا ریاست حصہ میں حاصل کیے تھے تیزر سومدیس کا عرصہ گذرا ہوا سنبھا ٹھاکر سنگھ موریث نے بزور بازد مرا گئے است نیلگا نون و غیرہ یہ ملکیت اقوام ٹھاکر و کایت ہندی کی تھی جنبہ بزا کر تعلقہ بنام نیلگا نون تمام کیا سنہ ۱۲۵۳ء نصلی میں بنایہ و دیہات پرگنہ بارہ بنکی میں

آباد کی افزونی ریاست کی آخر الامر بجوانیدین مالک ریاست ہوی و خدا رسیدہ ۱۸۶۷ میں خیرخواہ سرکار رہا اور تعلقہ
جلالپور مع سند تعلقداری گورنمنٹ انگلشیہ سے عطیہ حاصل کیا بعد آنکے یہ مرتبہ ان کو ملا اور تعلقہ میں ۔۔۔ موضع
اور دیہی جمعی موضعہ شامل مع ملکیت عطیہ ضلع سیتاپور میں واقع ہیں رسم گدی نشینی اس
خاندان میں ہے ۔

(نمبر ۱۱۹) ٹھاکر دیاراج شنگر قوم ٹھاکر میں تعلقدار کا نمبر ۔۔۔ موضع واد وی پور
انکا خاندان کا خاندانی نمبر ۔۔۔ پر رہ چکا ہے اور یہ تعلقدار منجملہ خاندان و نفر قدیم تعلقہ لبنی نمبر ۱۱ کے ہیں ۔۔۔
رانا پیرجہان مورث ۔۔۔ دیہ کھیرہ سے آکر بمقام بہر بمقام آباد ہوے اور یہاں موضع علاقہ بہر ۔۔۔ زمیداری کنجرہ ۔۔۔
بزور بازو قبضہ حاصل کیا ۔۔۔ سو قت سے قبضہ موروثیان چلا آتا ہے آخر الامر یہی شنگر ۱۸۶۷ ایام خدا رسیدہ ۔۔۔ کی خیرخواہی
میں ۔۔۔ موضعہ مشمولہ تعلقہ گورنمنٹ انگلشیہ سے عطیہ حاصل کیے بعد ذات آنکہ یہ تعلقدار ۔۔۔ ریاست ہیں
تعلقہ میں مع ملکیت عطیہ یہ ۔۔۔ موضع لبنی جمعی ۔۔۔ ضلع سیتاپور و کھیری میں واقع ہیں رسم
گدی نشینی اس خاندان میں ہے ۔

(نمبر ۱۲۰) رائے ابرام طلی قوم کایتھ تعلقدار رام پور خطاب رائے موروثی
شنگہ بجری میں رائے پرتھی راو مورث اعلیٰ ۔۔۔ سلطنت جلال الدین میران شاہ بادشاہ دہلی عہدہ ۔۔۔
پر مامور از موکہ راہ صوبہ دار محمد آباد میں آئے کہ بمقام صدر نشین حاکمان تھا صوبہ دارا اور وہ نے حسب اصلاح انکے
قلعہ و تمہ اقوام بھر کا کر کے اپنی سفارش سے یہ ملکیت رائے پرتھی راو کے سلطنت دہلی سے دلوادی جیسے ۔۔۔ موروثان
چلا آتا ہوا ۔۔۔ تیرہ ہوے میں پشت میں یہ تعلقدار ریاست ہیں اور انکو اختیارات ۔۔۔ ریاست ۔۔۔
اپنے علاقہ میں حاصل ہیں تعلقہ میں اس موضع لبنی جمعی ۔۔۔ ضلع ۔۔۔ بارہ بنکی میں واقع ہیں رسم
گدی نشینی اس خاندان میں ہے ۔

(نمبر ۱۲۱) مرزا احمد علی بیگ قوم سید تعلقدار قطب نگر و کریم نگر
یہ تعلقدار منجملہ خاندان اور رساخ تعلقہ اور نگ آباد و نرنگ آباد و مستذکرہ نمبر ۱۱۳ کے ہیں اس ریاست کو قطعی ۔۔۔ ۔۔۔
اور نگ آباد سے حاصل کیا تھا آخر کار یہ تعلقہ کے سبب ۔۔۔ ہوا ۔۔۔ کی زرعہ زمیں ابراہیم بیگ کو ۔۔۔ کیا بعد وفات
انکی یہ ۔۔۔ بذریعہ تنبیت وراثت ریاست ہوی تعلقہ میں موضع جمعی موضع ۔۔۔ ضلع سیتاپور و ۔۔۔
میں واقع ہیں رسم گدی نشینی اس خاندان میں ہے علاقہ سید تعلقہ بوجہ قرضہ کے نیلام ہوگیا ۔

(نمبر ۱۲۲) مولوی فضل حسین قوم سید تعلقدار جلالپور و راو پور و کیکئی پر دہ پور گر مو پور باون
بستری و محمد پور برتروہ و کسرورہ گنج — سات سو پرس ہوی مورث اعلیٰ جنگی زیارت سند علیہ میں

ہوگی میاں آبرے آنکہ پر اراضی بیقہر رہمانی سلطنت اور ہہ سو معطلہ ہوئی تھی آکی اولاد ہمین سے سید جلال ہہر
آباد کیا وکہ جہن نام معی تعلقہ مشہور ہی میتا الیمن ہہں۔۔۔ جو حہری محمد تقیم نے وجہ لاولدی اپنی سید غلام شریف آبا
حیات شہ کہ مالک ریاست کیا آخری ہیں اس تعلقہ سکے منشی فضل رسول صاحب اﷲ کے مالک سہری چیکہ نام سند تعلقہ
گورنٹ سے مرحمت ہوئی اور آنمہن نے ہجلہ خین خواہی ایام خدمت گذشہ کو ملکیت تعلقہ محمد پر ورہہیہ گورنٹ
انگلشیہ سے عطیہ حاصل کی بعد وفات آنکے یہ رئیں قابض تعلقہ ہین۔ تعلقہ ہین سے موضع سے بھی جبی
ملکیت عطیہ پریدہ ئی واہ نام ویا میتا پور رہ کھیری و لکھنٔو ہین طایح ہین۔ اہ خلا نہایہ
اولاد و اکبر و وارث ریاست ہہ ہوا مرہ۔

(نمبر ۱۲۳) قاضی اکرام احمد قوم شیخ تعلقہ دار ستر کھہ

یہ تعلقہ بہت جدید ہی اور اس ریاست مین جنہ ودبہات آبائی واجدادی تھہ شنہ اﷲ نصلی منہ قاضی میتہ نواز طلقی ہہا
نے ستر کھہ خاص پر تصبہہ پایا اور پھر ملکیت کو یوﮞ فیو مترقی دی بعد ووفات آنکی آریہ قابض ریاست ہین
دہ اﷲ موضع اور اک بھی جبی مدیہ لیا وصیہ فلاع بارہ پنکی ہین واقع ہین اولاد و اکبر اس خاندان ہین مالک
ریاست ہہ ہا ہے۔

(نمبر ۱۲۴) ٹھاکر گھو بیر سنگہ قوم کلہن تعلقہ دار و دہنا وان و بیجنٹ یادری
تذکرہ خاندانی و آغاز ریاست آنکا نمبر ۳۹ پر درج ہو دولہ رامی موریث اعلی کے خاندان سے پرا گذتا موریش نے
یہ ریاست نائم کی جہیہ پہلے الاقصال تبضبہ موریثان آنکا چلا آتا پاہی اور تعلقہ نمبرہ ۱۲۵ اشاخ اس تعلقہ کا ہے۔ اس
تعلقہ ہین مدیب موضع سے بھی جبی ہیہ و ذرایع ہین آتہ ہین گہم گکم نہشنی اہل خاندان ہین ہجہ

(نمبر ۱۲۵) ٹھاکر میر تنجے بخش قوم کلہن تعلقہ دار سیاہ پور رہ کو ٹکا مروتقہ
یہ تعلقہ اک اشاخ تعلقہ دہنا وان نمبری ۱۲۴ کا ہی او تذکرہ خاندانی و آغاز ریاست نمبر ۳۹ پر درج ہو انور پنگہ
غلقہ پرا گذتا تعلقہ دار دہنا وان موریث نے اس ریاست کو بوقت حظرانی گذارہ ہین پایا تھا جہیہ تبضبہ موریثان اکا
چلا آتا ہی کہ تعلقہ ہین سے موضع ہی بھی جبی ہیہ۔ افلاع گونڈہ و ذرایع ہین واقع ہین ارہہم گکہ نہشنی
اس خاندان ہین ہجہ۔

(نمبر ۱۲۶) دیوان ہہر نجل سنگہ قوم بکبوتی تعلقہ دار اور یا تریہ
تذکرہ خاندانی انکا نمبر ۵ پر درج ہی تعلقہ دار اولاد و جگہ سنگہ موریث اعلی ہین اور یہ تعلقہ اک اشاخ چی ریست آبا
نمبری ۵۹ رہ کا ہوا مرہ تعلقہ مین بصرف موضع بھی غلقہہ ضلع ریا گہہ مین جات گہہ ہہ رہم گکہ نہشنی اہل خاندان ہین ہجہ۔

(نمبر ۱۲۷) ا ٹھاکر نست سنگہ و ۲ بشیرشر نجش سنگہ ملا ۔ جگہو بن سنگہ ملا ۔ ارتقہ سنگہ اقوام بکبوتی

تعلقداران دریاپور۔ اِن کا تذکرہ خاندانی نمبر وار بہ ریج بھی اور یہ تعلقہ ایک شاخ بستی سیون آباد نمبر ۷۹ و ۔۔ کا ہی تعلقہ ہیں
موضع مسعود چہپی بکلا میں تیا گکدہ ضلع بریا گکدہ میں واقع ہیں اور اس ریاست میں اگر مورث اعلیٰ بلا وصیت فوت ہو جاوے
تو بموجب آئین معمولی کے اشخاص نزدیکی وارث ریاست ہوتے ہیں ۔

(نمبر ۱۲۸) حکیم کرم علی قوم سید تعلقدار گوگھیا

یہ تعلقہ پیدا کردہ آپ کے مورث کا ہے اور آپ بہت بیدار مغز و رئیس ہیں آپ اپنے تعلقہ میں حکومت آزری مہ ستری
اور اسشٹنٹ کلکٹری سے ممتاز رہے بعد تقسیم کتاب ۔ انہوں نے انتقال کیا اس تعلقہ میں بستی موضع چہپی
ایماں ۔۔ کی ضلع بارہ بنکی میں واقع ہیں اس خاندان میں رسم گدی نشینی ہے ۔

(نمبر ۱۲۹) بابو جدون ناتھ سنگھ قوم منوار تعلقدار بہگوان پہوہ نہ واہو سے پور

یہ تعلقہ ایک شاخ تعلقہ انوگنجہ متذکرہ نمبر ۳۰ کا ہے مفصل تذکرہ خاندانی اوسی نمبر یہ ریج ہی چار سو سال سے
بھگلان دیو مورث اپسر دوم دیو روردہ رای کہ بروقت تقسیم بر ہستا حال موئی تھی جیسے قبضہ موزان برابر
چلا آتا ہی آخرالامر سند تعلقہ گورنمنٹ انگلشیہ سے بنام بابو پرتھی بال سنگھ موئی تھی بعد وفات ان کو آپ قابض
ریاست ہوے اس تعلقہ میں موضع موضع چہپی ۔۔ اضلاع لکھنؤ و بارہ بنکی میں واقع ہیں اس میں رسم
گدی نشینی اس خاندان میں ہے ۔

(نمبر ۱۳۰) ۱۔ محبوب الرحمٰن ۲۔ عنایت الرحمٰن ۳۔ عبدالرحمٰن ۴۔ فضل الرحمٰن اقوام شیخ
تعلقداران بریڑی و گھسیاری ۔ ۸۵۔ ہجری میں بعہد محمد ابراہیم شاہ بادشاہ شرقی خواجہ محمد انتہار طاروئی
مورث اعلیٰ ہمراہ ناٹار خان صوبہ دار واسطے تنبیہ و اخراج اقوام بھر اس ملک میں آئے اور بعد اخراج اقوام کہہ
سب سفارش صوبہ دار بجلید و ہا بحسن خیر خواہی بطیعت موضع فینکگاہ شاہ ۔۔ دہلی سے بطور رعد و معاثر حاصل کیے
پھر شہ ۸۵۔ اہجری میں بعہد نواب ابوالمنصور خان محمد اعظیم مورث نے بذریعہ بیع ریاست میں ریاست کو ترقی دی بکریمہ بنا فرو
بریڑی تعلقہ قائم کیا آخرالامر بعد جند پشتون کے محبوب الرحمٰن بنے بوجہ صغیر سنی اپنی کے سند تعلقداری گورنمنٹ
انگلشیہ سے بنام نظام فرید اپنے چچا کے دلوا دی لیکن نظام فرید صاحب نے با وصف ان ۔۔ کہ یہ تقسیم میں خلا جدا نہیں تھا
منصفہ علاقہ محبوب الرحمٰن کو نصف نیا اپنے لڑکوں نمبر ۲ و ۳ و ۴ کو تقسیم کرکے نام قابضان مندرج سند کرا دیا
کل ملکیت اس تعلقہ میں ۔۔ موضع اور موضع بنی چہپی لا ریاست ۔۔ اطلاع فینض آباد و بارہ بنکی میں واقع ہیں
اس خاندان میں اگر مورث اعلیٰ بلا وصیت فوت ہو جاوے تو بموجب آئین معمولی اشخاص نزدیکی وارث
ریاست ہو ننگے ۔

(نمبر ۱۳۱) محمد نسیم خان قوم جہان تعلقدار سلطانپو

یہ کانون سلسلہ قدیم زمیدداری اقوام مسلمان و کایستھ کا تھا ... فصلی میں فقیر محمد خان ... تعلقدار نے

بذریعہ بیع حاصل کرکے بعد افزونی ریاست تعلقہ قائم کیا اور عہد غازی الدین حیدر شاہ میں یہ عہدہ حکمداری

... بعد وفات انکی یہ تعلقدار راحمد خان مالک ریاست ہوے اور میر و پسران نے بھی ریاست ...

اس ریاست کے مالک ہوے اور راحمد خان کو تعلقہ کمیندی متذکرہ نمبر ۱۸۱ ملا - اس تعلقہ میں ... موضع

حسبی ... فصل مذکور میں واقع ہیں اس خاندان میں اولاد اکبر مالک ریاست ہوتا ہو -

(نمبر ۱۳۲) سیر محمد حسین خان قوم سید تعلقدار راجہ ہیرا پور

یہ تعلقدار قدیم باشندے ضلع بدایون کے ہیں عہد سلطنت اور میں عہدہ کلکٹری ... فوج اور ... کے ممتاز ...

اور اپنی قوت بازو سے بذریعہ بیع و رہن یہ ریاست حاصل کرکے یہ تعلقدار نامزد ہوے - اب تعلقہ میں صرف ایک ...

... ضلع سیتاپور میں واقع ہو اور باقی کل علاقہ نیلام ہوگیا - اولاد اکبر ... خاندان میں وارث ریاست

ہوتا ہے -

(نمبر ۱۳۳) فدا حسین خان قوم سید تعلقدار اپبرلا و چی مڑیادون دیہی مصرپور کوٹہ

آپ قدیم باشندے ضلع بدایون کے ہیں اور تعلقدار نمبر ۱۳۲ کے بجائے ہیں عہد سلطنت اور میں کپتان

فوج تھے اور حکمداری کرتے رہے یہ ریاست ایک عہد بذریعہ تعلقہ نمبر ۱۳ کی ... بذریعہ انتقال خانگی ... قبضہ میں

آئی اور جداگانہ تعلقہ قرار پایا اس تعلقہ میں موضع ... اور دو چی حسبی ... ضلع کھیری ولکھ میں

واقع ہیں اولاد اکبر اس خاندان میں مالک ریاست ہوتا ہے - یہ علاقہ ڈگری عدالت سول کورٹ سے نیلام ہوگیا -

(نمبر ۱۳۴) بابو سکھراج سنگھ قوم ٹھاکر کلمین تعلقدار راٹ

انکا تذکرہ خاندانی و آغاز ریاست نمبر ۱۳ پر درج ہے یہ تعلقدار خاندان دولت راے کے مورث سے ہیں

تعلقہ میں سوا موضع ... دو چی حسبی ... ضلع گونڈہ میں واقع ہیں رسم گدی نشینی ان خاندان میں ہے -

(نمبر ۱۳۵) ٹھیکمین اکلاس ... قوم کلمین تعلقدار ... و ملار

انکا تذکرہ خاندانی نمبر ۱۳ پر درج ہو اور یہ ریاست خاندان دولت راے سے قائم ہی ... اس تعلقہ کا

... انگلشیہ سے بنام نیبال سنگھ ... تھا بعد آنکے یہ ریعیہ زمیدہ انکی قائض ہیں یہ تعلقہ میں ... موضع

... چی حسبی ... ان ملاع گونڈہ و مبارکہ نکی میں واقع ہیں رسم گدی نشینی اس خاندان میں ہے -

(نمبر ۱۳۶) سیّدہ رکسیہ بی بیال و سیتابال ام قوم کھتری تعلقداران مغزل الدین پور و کنگورا

... موہوہ کوریہ ... جنگرہ اور ... کھیرہ ورزنگو یا - عہدہ جارسو بریس کا ہوتا ہو مغزل الدین پور کو مالک

مغزل الدین نے جنگل کٹھا کر نیا مزدوہ اپنے آباد کیا تھا جسکے نام سے تعلقہ مشہور ہو اور پیٹیگاہ ثناء دہلی سے ...

معافی حاصل ہوا اور انکی اولاد میں یہ بشیرتوں اُن کے بعد خانجہاں خانصاحب ریاست ہوئے ایا افضل علی میں لالچی بیشتر موروثہ تعلقہ دار ان کہ معروف ریاضی تصاحب منی خانجہدی سے علاقہ پر قبضہ حاصل ہوا مگر چھ اولاد میں ہذریعہ بیع موروثہ ریاست کو ترقی دیکہ تعلقہ قائم کیا ایسے ہی انفسی میں بعد وفات لالچی مرلی موہر و میشہ بیٹا رام تاقبض ریاست ہوے اب مرلی منوہر کی جگہ سلیم بیٹا بردیال و میٹار ام خود تاقبض تعلقہ میں نمونہ بیٹا قدرشیشہ اہوبیں سرکار کی خیرخواہی کی تھی جلیدہ ہوے اُسکے عہد و بیات بطور عطیہ گورنمنٹ سے شامل کرکے شامل تعلقہ کیا اور اب علاقہ ایسین تقسیم ہوگیا میشہ بردیال حصہ دار ۹ رکے ہیں میشہ بیٹا رام ۔ رکے مالک ایا تعلقہ میں مع ملکیت عطیہ معیسہ مذروعہ ایلای بھی تھی مع حاک ۔ اضلاع عتیا پور و کھیری میں واقع ہیں اس خاندان میں اور اکبر مالک ریاست ہوتا ہو۔

(نمبر ۱۳) دریا و کنور زروجہ پتنا تھہ بخش سنگہ و ٹھاکر اجودھیا بخش سنگہ قوم میں تعلقہ دار زمیندار چیپارہ۔ تذکرہ خاندانی انگلکا نمبر ۱ پر درج ہو یہ علاقہ ایک شاخ تعلقہ نمبر ۱ کا ہو سمبت ۱۸۵۵ میں بجنگ بلی مورث نے رام بخش سے علیحدہ ہوکر یہ موضع جہاں پیشتر جنگل چرا گاہ و موشیان کا تھا ہ آباد کیا اور چیپار نام رکھا اُسوقت سے آنخاں زریاست کای ہی اور بعرصہ دہ میرہ پیش سے یہ موضع بطور معافی سرکار جمعی چلا آتا تھا گورنمنٹ انگلشیہ سے بندوبست تعلقداری بنام ٹھاکر اجودھیا بخش سنگہ و پتنا تھہ بخش سنگہ کے ہوا تھا اب تنا تھہ بخش سنگہ کی جگہ انکی زوجہ و ٹھاکر اجودھیا بخش سنگہ خود مالک ریاست ہیں تعلقہ میں ۱۸۵ موضع جمعی مبلغ ۱۸۵ ۔ اضلاع رای برہلی میں واقع ہیں رسم گدی نشینی اس خاندان میں ہو۔

(نمبر ۱۴) نواب بلینخان قوم شیخ قدرای تعلقدار موضع میلا رای گنج یہ تعلقدار راجہ فرزند علیخان صاحب کے چچا میں نشی ۱۲۱۱ ہجری میں شیخ غلام امیر مورث اسلے نواب شجاع الدولہ بہادر والی لکھنوت سے بشی میلا رای گنج و موضع بھنسریا و درجن پور و غیرہ و حاصل کیا تھا زان بعد شیخ حیدر علی انکے چچانے ریاست کو بذریعہ خریداری اور ترقی دی جیسے جلے الاتصال تہ بندہ موضعان چلا آیا ریاست تعلقہ گورنمنٹ انگلشیہ سے انھیں بکے نام مرحمت ہوئی۔ تعلقہ میں ہو موضع لعہ بنی جمعی سمہ ۔ اضلاع بارہ بنکی میں واقع ہیں رسم گدی نشینی اس خاندان میں ہو۔

(نمبر ۱۵) ٹھاکر امین اوسی نا تھہ کنور زمیوہ ٹھاکر سردار شنگہ قوم میں تعلقہ دار جمیہ پور مو کولا انکا تذکرہ خاندانی نمبر ۱ پر درج ہو یہ تعلقہ ایک شاخ تعلقہ نمبر ۱ کا ہی کمندرای کی مورث کی الادین ہندوشنگہ انکے بجھائی برتھی راج سے علیحدہ ہوکر اس مقام یہ جو بھگوت مشہور تھا آسے اور جنگل کمئو کرہ بہیات آباد کیا اسی نام میشہ پور کو لا قائم کیا اُسوقت سے قبضہ موروثان چلا آیا اب آخر الامر مورث تعلقہ گورنمنٹ انگلشیہ سے

بنام سردار سنگھ مرحمت ہوئی تھی بعد وفات آنکے یہ رئیسہ قابض ہیں ۔ تعلقہ میں بعضے موضع جبھی
اعمال رئیسہ ضلع رائے بریلی میں واقع ہیں ۔ رسم گدی نشینی اس خاندان میں ہے ۔

(نمبر ۱۴۰) بمعہ دہ سنگھ و درشن سنگھ قوم تعلقدار گورا و حسین آباد

اِنکا تذکرہ خاندانی نمبر ۱ میں درج ہے خاندان کرن رائے میں مہند نشیتوں کے بعد مہربان سنگھ مورث
تعلقہ بہار نمبری ۱۹ سے علیحدہ ہوکر اس مقام پر آئے اور جنگل کو کاٹ کر اقوام گورکو آباد کیا اور گورا نام سے تعلقہ
مشہور کیا جیسے قبضہ مہربان پر بابر جلا آتا ہی ہوگا رفنٹ اینگریزی ثبیہ سے سند تعلقہ بنام ستیلا بخش مرحمت
ہوئی تھی بعد دہ و سنگھ ۔ یہ ہر دو صاحبان قابض تعلقہ ہیں ۔ تعلقہ میں نفعہ موضع جبھی سے بار سے رہتے ہیں لاٹ
اور نام ورائے بریلی میں واقع ہیں اس خاندان میں اولا دِ اکبر مالک ریاست ہوتا ہے ۔

(نمبر ۱۴۱) سید رضا حسین قوم سید تعلقدار نزولی

سنہ ۔۔۔ ہجری میں محمد صالح مورث احلی بعہد سلطان ابراہیم شاہ سپہ سالار ہوکر ادہ میں آئے اور بعد
معرکہ اقوام بھر ثبیکاہ سلطان وقت سے بعوضے موضع زمینداری بھروں کی عطیہ حاصل کی اور دردیائی میں
سکونت کرکے جامع مسجد طیارکی پھر عہد سلطان جلال الدین محمد اکبر شاہ دہلی میں سید ابو محمد مورث ثاقب
جودھرایت و خطاب نصرت سلطانی سے موسوم ہوا وآخر الامر گورنمنٹ اینگلیشیہ سے سند تعلقداری بنام
چودھری حسین بخش صاحب والا تعلقدار عطا ہوئی رہی تھی جایسے اونکے یہ رئیس قابض ہیں تعلقہ میں نفعہ
ٹپٹی جبھی میں ۔۔۔ ضلع نجلی میں واقع ہیں ۔ رسم گدی نشینی اس خاندان میں ہے ۔

(نمبر ۱۴۲) فتح سنگھ عرف فتح بہادر خلف چودھری گلاب سنگھ قوم بہار تعلقدار سروہی

عہد ہمایون شاہ میں جب راجہ انونت سنگھ تعلقدار سابق سادات اقوام کے ہاتھ سے قتل ہوا اُس وقت
یہ ریاست ثبیکاہ شاہ دہلی سے اقوام دھموبین کو بطور جاگیر ملکی حبوقت ہمایون شاہ ایران میں
تھے سید نی مل قوم تھا کہ تقریب بیاہ شادی اپنی لڑکی سے اس جگہ میں آیا ہوا تھا زسید باران گورو نواح مدار
دھموبین سے نہایت نارض تھے سید نی مل نے بابا اور اون لوگوں سے دھموبین کو قتل کرکے آپ
قابض ریاست ہوگیا اُنکی ساتوین پشت میں ۱ ۔ سا ہو ۔ ۔ اسمیں ۔ ۔ راناک ۔۔ پھر لید ن
یہ چار بھائی ہوے اِن میں تین سو سال ہوے سے ریاست تقسیم ہوئی ۔ ساہو کو کرڈون ۔
اسمیں کو ۔۔ ریاست ہانک کو سنگر آپور وغیرہ پھر لید ن ۔۔ کو اکھار ۔ یہ تعلقدار اولا و اسمیں
میں اور تعلقہ میں دہ لاٹ موضع جبھی سے ۔۔۔ ضلع اور نام میں واقع ہیں اس خاندان میں
اولا دِ اکبر مالک ریاست ہوتا ہے ۔

(نمبر ۱۴۳) ...

(نمبر ۱۴۴) ...

(نمبر ۱۴۵) بابو اعظم علی خان قوم بھایے سلطان خان زادہ تعلقدار دیوگانوار و محند دوم پور ...

(نمبر ۱۴۶) رام نرائن قوم کایستھ تعلقدار سیابک پور ۔ خطاب چودھری حسین حیاب ...

(نمبر ۱۴۷) بابو پرتھی پال سنگھ قوم بلوار تعلقدار نگھرا ۔

مورث تعلقدار نے خرید کرکے شامل تعلقہ کیا اس تعلقہ میں تعلقدارین متعدد موضع اور معتبر بنی علیٰ شریف کی ضلع فیض آباد میں واقع ہیں — اولادِ اکبر اس خاندان میں مالک ریاست ہوتا ہے ۔

(نمبر ۱۴۸) محمد احمد خان قوم شیخان تعلقدار کسمنڈی خورد

یہ تعلقدار شیخ خاندان و شاخ تعلقدار نمبر ۱۳۱ کے ہیں یہ موضع کسمنڈی ۱۲۴۹ ہجری سے لغایہ ۱۲۵۹ ہجری بدفعات بذریعہ بیع اُنکے والد فقیر محل خان کے قبضے میں آیا تھا بعد اُنہوں نے اور ترقی علاقے کی کی اور عہدِ غازی الدین حیدر شاہ اودھ میں بعہدہ چکلہ داری ممتاز رہے بعد وفات اُنکے یہ تعلقدار حسب تقسیم باہمی مالک اس ریاست کے ہوئے و محمد نسیم خان برادر اُنکے تعلقہ سہالیُو نمبر ۱۳۱ کے مالک ہوئے اس تعلقہ میں للمعہ موضع جمعی عطاء علیٰ شریف ضلع لکھنؤ میں واقع ہیں اس خاندان میں اولادِ اکبر مالک ریاست ہوتا ہے ۔

(نمبر ۱۴۹) مہیش بخش سنگھ قوم سین تعلقدار و بیا دوان ۔ خطاب بابو ۔

رائے بوم بال مورث اعلیٰ اس گروہ نے جبکہ تذکرہ نمبر ۔۔۔ مفصل درج ہے جہ سے ریاست حاصل کی تھی اور وقائع مختلف میں ریاست تقسیم ہوکر متعدد دریا میں فائم ہوگئیں اوسی ریاست سے یہ تعلقہ ایک شاخ ہے ۔ اس تعلقے کی سند گورنمنٹ سے بنام شیو درت سنگھ مورث کے مرحمت ہوئی تھی بعد وفات اُنکے آپ اُن میں اور آپ بہت بڑے مستعد و لائق شخص میں آپنے علم انگریزی اور تہذیب و قانونی سے اپنی جوہر لیاقت سقدر وسعت دی کراب علاوہ اس ریاست کے عہدہ اسسٹنٹ کنشری مالک و دیگر حکمران میں ہیں موضع جمعی معمہ لاطلعہ ضلع بناب گڑھ میں واقع میں رسم گدی نشینی اس خاندان میں ہر

(نمبر ۱۵۰) سرجیت سنگھ قوم شمار حسین تعلقدار شیخ پور جوراسی

اُنکا تذکرہ خاندانی و آغاز ریاست نمبر ۔۔۔ پر درج ہے یہ تعلقہ ایک شاخ تعلقہ ڈگوس نمبر ۔ ۔ کا ہوا آخر الامر مالک اس ریاست کے شمار دھو بکل سنگھ ہوئے جنکے نام گورنمنٹ انگلشیہ سے سند تعلقداری حمیت ہوئی اور ایام غذر رشتہ عیسوی میں خیرخواہ سرکار رہے اوسکے صلہ میں ملکیہ عطیہ حاصل کرکے ترقی ریاست کی کی بعد دھو بکل سنگھ کے یہ تعلقدار قابض ریاست ہوئے ۔ تعلقہ میں معہ ملکیت عطیہ ریاست موضع جمعی صمم ابماہ ضلع بناب گڑھ میں واقع میں رسم گدی نشینی اس خاندان میں ہے

(نمبر ۱۵۱) شمار شیو مہاس تو م لسین تعلقدار سمرانوان ضلع باراہ بنکی ۔

اس تعلقہ میں چودہ موضع آبائی و جدادی تھے اور اُنکے مورث نے دیگر دیہات بذریعہ بیع حاصل کرکے شامل تعلقہ کیے اور ریاست کو ترقی دی گورنمنٹ انگلشیہ سے بندوبست تعلقداری بنام شمار سہاس بے برادرکلان کے ہوا تھا جب اُنہوں نے اولاد وفات پائی یہ تعلقدار قابض ریاست ہوئے

مگر بوجہ بد انتظامی کل تعلقہ فروخت ہوکر یہ قبضہ راجہ فرزند علی خان و نجیبت سنگھ صوبہ دار خیرخواہ سرکار اور رشید شیر پرشاد کے ہے ۔

(نمبر ۱۵۲) مسماة صاحب النساء بیوہ چودھری محمد حسین قوم شیخ تعلقہ اکھڑ گیا عرصہ نوسو سال کا ہے تا کہ مدنان اعلیٰ انکے سہراہ حضرت سہر سالار شہ غزنین سے اس ملک میں آئے اور اقوام سہرذ کا قلعہ فتح کرکے موضع کھڑ کا اوکی ریاست پر اپنا قبضہ کیا یہ موضع کھڑ گا او وقت پر ویرا تھا و سوبرس بعد اسی خاندان میں سے کرم علی مورث نے از سرِ نو آباد کرکے نام قدیم سے مشہور رکھا پھر وقتا فوقتا دیگر مدنان نے سرکی ریاست کرکے ایک تعلقہ بنام کھڑ کا قائم کیا گوہنت انگلشیہ سے سند تعلقہ داری بنام کرم علی چچا محمد حسین کے ہوئی تھی پسِ اولی میں بجلت بغاوت نام او خالص ہوکر بنام محمد حسین بند و سبت علاقے کا ہے بعد وفات محمد حسین یہ رتبہ زوجہ اوکی قائمن علیٰ تعلقہ میں عنہ موضع معہ پُّی جمعی اے ﷼ ضلع بارہ بنکی میں واقع میں اولاد اکبر اس خاندان میں مالک ریاست ہوتا ہے ۔

(نمبر ۱۵۳) میر بنیاد حسین قوم سید تعلقہ دار بھان مٔو ۔
یہ ریاست آبائی و اجدادی عرصہ سات سوسال سے قائم ہے اور آپکے مورث نسلاً بعد نسل قائمن چلے آئے سند تعلقہ بنام سید اولاد حسین انکے والد کے ہوئی تھی بعد وفات اوکے یہ تعلقہ دار کا ریاست میں تعلقے میں شہیہ موضع جمعی للعمل لماطلعہ ضلع نوابگنج بارہ بنکی میں واقع میں اولاد اکبر اس خاندان میں وارث ریاست ہوتا ہے ۔

میر امجاد حسین قوم سید تعلقہ دار سمیل پور
اس تعلقے میں تعہ موضع اور ایک بنی جمعی ـ کی ضلع بارہ بنکی میں واقع میں سم گدی نشینی اس خاندان میں ہے ۔

(نمبر ۱۵۴) ٹھاکر دیپ سنگھ سوم سینبی تعلقہ دار مانج پور و سکران
یہ ریاست قدیم ہے اٹھارہ پشت گذرے میں راجہ سانتن مورث اعلیٰ دہلی سے براے انسان گنگاجی اس نواح میں آئے اور ایک ویرہ ویران متصل قصبہ رسانڈی واقعہ پردولی ضلع ضلع بنام سانتن کھیڑ آباد کرکے سکونت اختیار کی اور دیہات قرب و جوار پر قابض ہو گئے اوکی جتنی پشتا میں راجہ ہوراج کو آباد کے مقیم ہوے راوکی میں پشت میں راجہ دریاو سنگھ آخری ئیس ملک ریاست ہوے بعد وفات انکے زوجہ اوکی وارث ریاست ہوئیں اور سند تعلقداری گوہنت انگلشیہ سی حاصل کی

اور بناء اس نے ان تعلقداروں کو بندوبست بذریعہ تنہیت مالک ریاست کیا ۔ تعلقہ مین سے موضع جمعی مع
اضلاع ہردوئی و سیتاپور مین واقع ہین رسم گردی کی نشینی اس خاندان مین ہے ۔

(نمبر ۱۵۵) بابو اِیشوج سنگھ قوم راجکمار تعلقدار بیوپور ڈہلاوڈ ٹھاٹ حصہ قبضہ ۔ نمبر گکت اللہ سنگھ
نمبرہ ۹ ۔ و سرمایہ بیوپور شراکتی ۔ تذکرہ خاندانی آپ کا نمبر ۔ پر درج ہے ۔ و کیفیت آغاز ریاست
نمبرہ ۳ ۔ پر تحریر ہے ۔ یہ تعلقہ ایک شاخ نمبر ۹۵ کا ہے ۔ اس تعلقہ مین للعشہ موضع مع
جمعی مع ۔ اضلاع سلطانپور و فیض آباد مین واقع ہین اولاد اکبر اس خاندان مین وارث ریاست
ہوتا ہے ۔

(نمبر ۱۵۶) محمد زمان خان و محمد سعید خان و محمد سلطان خان قوم تہیان تعلقداران اماوان
نذرالدین و مصطفے خان سوران اعلی ہمراہ سلطان محمود غزنوی اس ملک مین آئے اور عہدہ دیوان گردی دیہات
پیرگنہ سلاوان حصال کرکے نذرالدین پور و مصطفے آباد اپنے نام سے آباد کیے پھر پشتہ ہجر بین بعد سلطان ابراہیم
محمد اماں خان مورث نے اماوان خاص کی اراضی جو بطور جنگل جبلہ و تھی فتادہ تھی بجلہ و دی حسن ریاست شاہی حصال کرکے
بمناسبت نام اپنی آباد کرکے اماوان نام رکھا و نیز دیگر دیہات بھی آباد کیے اور تعلقہ بنام اماوان قایم کیا
چناںچہ پشتو سنکے بعد سن تعلقداری بنام عبدالحکیم خان و سعادت خان گورنمنت انگلشیہ سے مرحمت ہوئی تھی
بعد اسکے یہ تعلقداران قابض ہوئے تعلقہ مین عطیہ موضع جمعی مع ۔ ضلع راے بریلی مین
واقع ہین اس خاندان مین اولاد اکبر مالک ریاست ہوتا ہے ۔

(نمبر ۱۵۷) ذوالفقار خان و کرم علی خان و اسد علی خان و شہامت خان قوم تہیان تعلقدار اپیو
چھہ سو کچھتر سال ہوے ہینگر خان مورث اعلی ہمراہ شاہ شہاب الدین غوری بنظر قلعہ قطع و فتح اقوام پھر ان
ملک مین آئے اور بعد فتحیابی پیشگاہ شاہ سے چند دیہات مع خطاب مع دیوان عطیہ حصال کیے پھر اف کی اولاد
نے جنگل وغیرہ کو کشواکر اور دیہات آباد کیے بعد عہد اکبر شاہ و تعلقہ قایم ہوگیا جیسے قبضہ موجودان براے جلایا
آخرالامر سند تعلقداری گورنمنت انگلشیہ سے بنام ہر چہار صاحبان مرحمت ہوئی ۔ تعلقہ مین عطیہ موضع
جمعی مع ۔ ضلع راے بریلی مین واقع ہین اس خاندان مین اولاد اکبر مالک ریاست ہوتا ہے ۔

(نمبر ۱۵۸) بھگوان بخش قوم تہاکر بیس تعلقدار اور ہرہ و کسمورا
انکا تذکرہ خاندانی نمبرہ ۔ پر درج ہو ۔ یہ تعلقہ ایک شاخ تعلقہ نمبر ۳۰۳ کا ہو ۔ کاہو ۔ رگھنات سنگھ مورث اعلی نے
اس ریاست کو تعلقہ کوری سدولی سے علیحدہ قایم کیا جیسے براے قبضہ چلا آتا ہو آخرالامر سند تعلقداری
گورنمنت انگلشیہ سے بنام ٹھکر این گلاب کنور عطیہ ہوئی تھی بعد اونکے آپ قابض ہین ۔ تعلقہ مین عطیہ موضع

جمع ... اضلاع رائے بریلی و گونڈہ میں واقع ہیں رسم گدی نشینی اس خاندان میں ہے۔

(نمبر ۱۵۹) مشہین کنور بیوہ بلبھدر سنگھ قوم جنوار تعلقدار پہروڑی وسند... وہمائی سوبرس ... اور گرسین و بترندا ساہ مورث موضع مکون اضلاع بہرائچ سے ... از زمانہ سلطنت تیمو ... میں بنصب حصہ داری پرگنہ کھیرون مقرر ہوے اور رسواضعات مرزاپور وغیرہ کو مالکانہ حاصل کیا اور لقب چودھرا یت پایا آخرالامر دصہ سال ہوے رگھناتھ سنگھ کو بجلہ دوسرے کارگزاری یہ ملکیت بصر وی و دیگر دیہات جیسکے نام سے تعلقہ مشہور ہے معہ منصب قانون گوئی حکومت اور دست سے عطا ہوئی اور گورنمنٹ انگلشیہ سے بندوبست تعلقداری رگھناتھ سنگھ کے نام ہوا بعد وفات اونکی بلبھدر سنگھ اونکے اکٹر کے قابض ریاست ہوئی اوکی وفات کے بعد یہ ریمیسہ زوجہ اُنکی قابض ریاست ہیں۔ تعلقہ میں عصہ موضع جمعی معہ ... اضلاع رائے بریلی میں واقع ہیں اس خاندان میں اولاد اکبر مالک ریاست ہوتا ہے۔

(نمبر ۱۶۰) رائے امین بہادر قوم کرمی تعلقدار پیلا سکھیتو و نوابپور و محمد آباد وخطاب رائے امین حنبا ... اسے قولام والہ تعلقدار کو بجلہ دوسرے خیر خواہی ایام غدر ۱۸۵۷ میں ... علاقہ منفصط واجہ بونی سنگھ تعلقدار متولی گورنمنٹ انگلشیہ سے عطہ حاصل ہوا اتھاب بعد وفات اوکی آپ قابض ریاست ہوئے اوکی تعلقہ میں عصہ موضع جمعی مالک کی اضلاع کھیری میں واقع ہیں۔ اس خاندان میں اولاد اکبر وارث ریاست ہوتا ہے۔

(نمبر ۱۶۱) بابو سیتلا بخش سنگھ قوم راجکمار تعلقدار نانامئو و رام گڑھ و دہند و پور و میرپور و سریا و دناسئو۔ تذکرہ خاندانی آپ کا نمبر ۔ پر درج ہے الیشری سنگھ مورث اعلی اس خاندان کے سلسلہ میں ہر کران دیو مورث تعلقہ ارنے یہ ریاست پیدا کی جیسے قبضہ مورثان چلا آتا ہے للعبہ موضع ... نئی جمعی ... اضلاع سلطانپور و فیض آباد میں واقع ہیں رسم گدی نشینی اس خاندان میں ہے۔

(نمبر ۱۶۲) جہانگیر بخش خان قوم بگبوتی خانزادہ تعلقدار گنگیو و بہمرپور و صدر آباد شاہپور۔ یہ تعلقہ مندرجہ نمبر ۔ کا ہے اولاد ملوک چند عرف ۔۔ تار خان میں چند پشتہ نکے بعد وزیر خان مورث نے تعلقہ حسن پور سے یہ ریاست علیحدہ قائم کی جیسے قبصہ مورثان اس خاندان میں چلا آتا ہے تعلقہ میں عصہ موضع جمعی و دعطیہ ... اضلاع سلطانپور و فیض آباد میں واقع ہیں۔ اولاد اکبر اس خاندان میں مالک ریاست ہوتا ہے۔

(نمبر ۱۶۳) کامتا پرشاد و بشنا تھ سنگھ قوم راجکمار تعلقدار بہد زیان و فاصل پور و دیور سی بہراوپور۔ آپ کا تذکرہ خاندانی نمبر ۔ پر درج ہے الیشری سنگھ مورث اعلی اس خاندان کے ستے اونکے سلسلہ میں

پرچی پت سورٹ تعلقدار نے یہ ریاست پیدا کی اوس وقت سے قبضہ سورٹ خان چلا آتا ہی تاہی بعض موضع

بعد فتح جمعی ہی علاقہ سلطانپور ریاست میں واقع ہیں اولاد اکبر اس خاندان میں وارث ریاست ہوتا آیا

(نمبر ۱۶۴) سہسری پال سنگھ قوم کنپوریہ تعلقدار بردولیا ۔

انکا تذکرہ خاندانی و آغاز ریاست نمبر ۱۲۰ پر درج ہے راج ساہو کی اولاد میں برجموہن سنگھ سورث
تعلقدار نمبر ۱۲۰ سے بابو شیو پرشاد سنگھ سورث تعلقدار قابض حال سے یہ ریاست حاصل کی
تھی اور کی تیسری پشت میں یہ رئیس قابض ریاست ہیں تعلقہ میں یہ موضع جمعی بھدوئی
ضلع سلطانپور میں واقع ہیں رسم گدی نشینی اس خاندان میں ہے ۔

(نمبر ۱۶۵) مسماۃ الہٰی خانم قوم بجگوتی خانزادہ تعلقدار منیار پور و پالی حصہ
یہ علاقہ تذکرہ نمبر ۹ کا ہے اولاد ملوک چند عرف تاتار خان میں چند پشتوں کے بعد حیات خان
مورث سے یہ ریاست قائم ہوئی آخری رئیس اس تعلقہ کے بساون خان ہوئے بعد وفات اُنکے
بی بی صغرا دختر انکی جو کہ زوجہ اول سے تھیں وارث ریاست ہوئیں بعد انتقال بی بی صغرا
اکبر علی خان پسر بساون خان جو زوجہ ثانی سے تھے بذریعہ اس نشینی مالک تعلقہ ہوئے جب انکا
بھی انتقال کیا تو یہ رئیسہ زوجہ اوکی مالک ہوئیں ۔ تعلقہ میں دہ موضع جمعی بنی بھدوئی
ضلع سلطانپور و فیض آباد میں واقع ہیں ۔ رسم گدی نشینی اس خاندان میں ہے ۔

(نمبر ۱۶۶) ۱۔ مسماۃ امتیاز فاطمہ ۔ ۲۔ بھاگ بھری قوم شیخ تعلقداران گوپیا پور
و برہمولا ۔ بعہد تیمور شاہ بادشاہ دہلی شیخ رحیم اللہ صدیقی اصفہانی مورث سلطنت
دہلی میں آکر سپہ سالار و رسالدار فوج ہوئے اوکی اولاد میں نعمت اللہ ہمایوں بادشاہ
کے وقت میں قانون گوئی پر گشتہ گوپیا مؤ کے ہوئے اونہوں نے سر لسکے صدیقی آباد کی
عالمگیر شاہ کے عہد میں شیخ محمد سعید اولاد نعمت اللہ کو بہت دیہات عطا ہوئے جبسے
بنیاد ریاست قائم ہے اور نسلاً بعد نسل قبضہ چلا آتا ہے اور گو یا مؤ خاص کی آبادی
انہے سو سال کی ہے راجہ گوپی ناتھہ سے بنام گوپی مؤآباد کیا بنا کثرت استعمال سے
گویا مؤ مشہور ہے ۔ تعلقہ میں معہ موضع آبے بنی جمعی چبہ سامعہ علاقہ سیتاپور
و ہردوئی میں واقع ہیں اس خاندان میں اولاد اکبر وارث ریاست ہوتا ہے ۔

(نمبر ۱۶۷) بابو سہنوان بخش سنگھ قوم سومبنسی تعلقدار دومی پور ۔

یہ ریاست چھ سو برس سے قائم ہے مورث اعلیٰ اس خاندان کے راجہ بہر سین اس ملک میں

سوے جگہ کا تذکرہ مفصل نمبر ۱۱۔ پر درج ہے آپ اسی خاندان سے ہیں آپ کی ملکیت میں
حصہ موضع جمعی مراطام معظم ۳۰ بیگھہ ضلع پرتاب گڈھ میں واقع ہیں رسم گدی نشینی اس خاندان میں ہے۔

(نمبر ۱۶۸) بابو ہردت سنگھ قوم سوم ہنی تعلقدار پرگنہ گنج ۔

یہ ریاست چھ سو برس سے قائم ہے مورث اعلیٰ اس خاندان کے رائے ہرکرپتی اس
ملک میں ہوسے جگہ کا تذکرہ نمبر ۱۱۔ پر درج ہے آپ ہوسی خاندان سے ہیں آپ کی ملکیت
میں ہے موضع جمعی مراسلہ ضلع پرتاب گڈھ میں واقع ہیں رسم گدی نشینی اس خاندان میں ہے

(نمبر ۱۶۹) اودے راج سنگھ قوم کھٹبنس تعلقدار معینی پایر ۔

مفصل تذکرہ خاندانی وآفاق ریاست کا نمبر ۳۰۳ پر درج ہے پہلے راج گونڈہ بھی اسکے شامل تھا
اگر وہ جاتا رہا اصرف یہ ریاست سورشان تعلقدار کے قبضے میں رہی اور سورشان تعلقدار
اسپر قابض چلے آئے سند تعلقہ کی بنام رانی سرفراز کنور کے گورنمنٹ انگلشیہ سے
مرحمت ہوئی تھی بعد ازدکے آپ قابض ہیں اور موضع یا پرخاص جبکے نام سے تعلقہ
مشہور ہوبحق پربت یہ قبضہ اولاد بردست داران کے سے ہے باللہ موضع ایک بستی جمعی
ادے سامہ ضلع گونڈہ میں واقع ہیں رسم گدی نشینی اس خاندان میں ہے۔

(نمبر ۱۷۰) اہبل رام قوم کچھواہہ تعلقدار پروا ۔

پرتاب مل سنگھ مورث گورکھ پورسے اس ملک میں آکر بمقام موضع گوہانی پرگنہ ڈگسر
مقیم ہوسے عرصہ ایک سوسات سال کا ہوتا ہے یہ ریاست انکے مورثان کو راج گونڈہ
سے بحق برادری حاصل ہوئی تھی جبسے قبضہ اس خاندان میں چلا آتا ہے آخری ایس
اس ملک کے بجسے پرتھی پال سنگھ ہوسے بعد ازدکے ٹھکرائن برج راج کنور دختر
اوکی مالک ریاست ہوئیں بعد وفات ٹھکرائن مذکورہ یہ تعلقدار رشو سراوازدکے
قابض ریاست میں تعلقدین اللعہ موضع اللعہ بستی جمعی لہ سامہ ضلع گونڈہ میں واقع
ہیں رسم گدی نشینی اس خاندان میں ہے۔

(نمبر ۱۷۱) مرزا فیاض بیک تعلقدار برہ گاتون ۔

آپکے مورث اعلیٰ مرزا عباس بیگ صاحب ایک کثر اسسٹنٹ کشنر ملک اودھ تھے جنہوں نے ایام غدر میں شدید
میں بصلہ خیر خواہی گورنمنٹ سے جنہما علاقہ تمنصبط راجہ مستولی یہ تعلقہ حاصل کیا تھا مراحصا مدوج بریتان مانگ
تھے بعد عطا ہوئی علاقہ وحصول انکشن قصد تعلیم ابنہ برادرزادگان کے دلالت کو بھی تشریف لیگئے اور وہاں

تعلیم کرائی بعد والیتی لاینت مذکورہ نے جب انتقال کیا تو آپ کی ہمہ ست نامہ مرزا صاحب وارث تعلقہ قرار پائے اور صاحبزادی مرزا صاحب بھی شریک منافع ہوئیں سات موضع جمعی سلاپیٹھ ضلع سیتاپور میں واقع ہیں ۔ اس خاندان میں اولاد اکبر وارث ہوتا ہے ۔

(نمبر ۱۷۴) بیچی بہادر سنگھ تعلقہ دار شاہ گڑھ قوم سنبل گوتی ۔
یہ تعلقہ ایک شاخ تعلقہ گل گڑھ المعتبی نمبر د کا ہے راجہ بکرم ساہی موروث اعلی راجہ مادھو سنگھ اور سلطان ساہی موروث شاہ اعلے انکے حقیقی بھائی تھے جب سلطان ساہی اوس ریاست سے علیحدہ ہوئے تو تعلقہ شاہ گڑھ اونکو دیا گیا آخر الا بابو بلونت سنگھ کے نام سے سند اس تعلقے کی گورنمنٹ انگلشیہ سے مرحمت ہوئی تھی بعد وفات اوسکے یہ تعلقہ ارقابض ہوئے لعلے موضع دو بڑی جمعی ۔
ضلع سلطانپور میں واقع ہیں رسم گدی کی نشینی اس خاندان میں ہے ۔

(نمبر ۱۷۴) میر احمد جان قوم بچھان تعلقہ دار لکھوپور ۔
یہ ملکیت راجہ شیو داس سنگھ تعلقہ دار جندہ پور کو تھے بوجہ برآمدگی توسہ ضبط سرکار ہوکر گورنمنٹ سے بصلہ خیر خواہی ایام غدر رشتہ ۱۸۵۷ عیسوی میں جعفر علی خان کمیدان کو عطا ہوئی تھی بعد اوسکے آپ قابض ہوئے دو موضع جمعی اعلاسہ کے ضلع رائے بریلی میں واقع ہیں ۔ اور اس خاندان میں اولاد اکبر وارث ریاست ہوتا ہے ۔

(نمبر ۱۷۴) سمیت سنگھ خلف رنجیت سنگھ قوم سنگھ تعلقہ دار کا نتھا ۔
بمرور عرصہ چار سو ارسہ سال گوپال سنگھ موروث اعلے بعد تیمور شاہ اس ملک میں آئے اوکی اولاد میں سے جب کہ ان سنگھ اقوام لودھ کی لڑائی میں مارے گئے دو زوجہ انکی حاملہ باقی رہیں اونسے اسکرم و گرجیو سنگھ اور آستام میں لڑ کو پیدا کیا انہوں نے بعہد شاہ بابر اقوام لودھ سے جنگ کرکے پھر ملکیت کا نتھا کو حاصل کیا اوسی خاندان سے یہ تعلقہ دار قابض ریاست میں ایام غدر رشتہ ۱۸۵۷ میں دیگر برادران قوم نے جو شریک ملکیت تھے گورنمنٹ انگلشیہ سے سرکشی کی اونکے حصہ کی ملکیت ضبط ہوکر رنجیت سنگھ والد تعلقہ دار کو جو خیر خواہ سرکار رہے تھے گورنمنٹ انگلشیہ سے مرحمت ہوئی اور سند تعلقہ داری علی بعد رنجیت سنگھ یہ تعلقہ دار مالک ریاست ہوکر یہ تعلقہ میں لہ موضع سے پچی جمعی بعہدہ سالعہ یہ ضلع اعظم گڑھ میں واقع ہیں ۔ اس خاندان میں اولاد اکبر مالک ریاست ہوتا ہے ۔

(نمبر ۱۷۵) سلطان سنگھ قوم چنیل تعلقدار گنگلہہا مزرعہ پیپر کھیرہ

یہ تعلقدار تقدیم قوم ٹھاکر منیل کا تھا آپ کے والد بجی اسی حصہ دار تھے وہ ایام غدر رشیہ زمین خیر خواہ سرکار رہے اور دیگر رشتہ کیان نے سرکشی کی گورنمنٹ انگلشیہ سے اوذکی حقیقت ضبط ہو کر کل ملکیت ٹھاکر امراؤ سنگھ آپ کے والد کو سرکار سے ملا بلکہ ایام غدر خیر خواہی خدمت سے ہوئی اوذکے بعد آپ جانشین تعلقہ ہیں اس تعلقہ میں پچے موضع جسمی پرچہ بندی میں فصلع اوذنام میں واقع ہیں اس خاندان میں اولاد واکبر مالک یاست ہوتی ہے

(نمبر ۱۷٦) شیخ نوازش علی قوم شیخ تعلقدار بھناپور و پرتاب گنج

پانچسو برس ہوئے محد وم قاضی قندوہ موذثان تعلقدار ولایت روم سے آکر بکر یا دشاہ دہلی اود دہ میں قاضی مقرر ہوئے اور اوذکو باوذن مواضعات سرکار شاہ دہلی سے حاصل ہوئے جو قندوہ دار حلقع بارہ ونیکی مشہور ہے اوذکی آشنوین پشت میں شیخ امیر اللہ کی شادی دختر علی محمد قانوگوئے پرگنہ مسام ہوئے ہو کر علی محمد سے یہ ریاست امیر اللہ حاصل ہوئی جیسے پر ریاست قائم ہے آپ اولاد امیر اللہ سے ہیں سے دفعہ اللہ سے نبی جمی میرعلی محمد اطلاع بہرائچ ربارہ نجلی میں واقع ہیں رسم گدی نشینی اس خاندان میں ہے

(نمبر ۱۷۷) پانڈے شنکر جیت سنگھ قوم برہمن تعلقدار اسدائو

یہ تعلقہ پیشتر اقوام ٹھاکر کیسین کا تھا مگر یہ سال ہوئے بان سنگھ آپ کے دادا نے بذریعہ بیع ریاست کو حاصل کیا اور سلطنت اود میں آپ کی دادا بھادر سنگھ اور داود عمدہ چیکہ داری ممتاز رہے جیسے علی الاتصال قبضہ موذمان چلا آتا ہی آخر الامر آپ مالک تعلقہ ہیں اس تعلقہ میں پچے موضع ارعہ نبی جمی میرعلی محمد دہ نجلی میں واقع ہیں اس خاندان میں رواج گدی نشینی ہے ۔

(نمبر ۱۷۸) شیخ عنایت اللہ وانعام اللہ واکرام علی تعلقداران سیدنپور

رشتہ ہجری میں بہ عہد سلطنت جلال الدین غوری شاہ دہلی سید محمد ابراہیم مورث اعلے کو بجلد ودی بجا آوری مدت اخراج اقوام بھر یہ ریاست علما ہوئی نمی اود سوقت سو مورثان موذمان تعلقدار قابض تعلقہ چلے آتے ہیں آخر الامر سند تعلقداری گورنمنٹ انگلشیہ سے بنام شیخ لطافت اللہ و شیخ وجاہت اللہ ہر دو برادران کے خطا ہوئی تھی بعد وفات ہر دو صاحبان شیخ وجاہت اللہ کی جگہ شیخ عنایت اللہ و شیخ لطافت اللہ کی جگہ انعام اللہ واکرام علی پسران ہر دو صاحبان سر ہوئے پشت مورث اعلے ہیں قابض ریاست ہیں ۔ تعلقہ میں سے موضع اود زمین نجلی جمعی امعلہ دفعہ اللہ سے فصلع نوا گنج میں واقع ہیں ۔ اس ریاست میں اگر مورث اعلی بلا وصیت فوت ہو جاوے تو بموجب آئین معمولی واشخاص ورثیت وارثگانہ س ریاست ہوونگے

(نمبر ۱۷۹) میر فخر الحسن قوم سید تعلقدار نوہرہ

اند و مرشاہ و عادل ملک متوطن جونپور، مورث اعلیٰ بہرہ علی، و عرصہ سانٹھ سو سال بہراہ شاہ و ابراہیم شاہ و حسین پران
سلطان ابراہیم شرقی اعلیٰ بمقام راسے بریلی آ اقوام بھر کا قلع وقمع کرکے جنگل کٹوا کر راسے بریلی کو محکم شاہ و قمع
آباد کیا بحلہ و سے اس خیر خواہی کے عرصے و انضباتی تبلی پور وغیرہ اوز کو سر کار شاہ دہلی سے بطور معافی عطا ہو کیا
اور راسے اکبر الدین پسر کلاں کو عہدہ قاضی مرحمت ہوا و بعد ازوال سلطنت دہلی حکومت تک یہ ریاست اس
خاندان سے ضبط ہوگئی چند پشتون کے بعد اسی خاندان میں میر کرامت حسین، میر حیدر حسین نے بذریعہ ملازمت
شاہی بحلہ و حسن خیر خواہی پھر دوبارہ اس ریاست پر قبضہ حاصل کیا جیسے دو ژمان تعلقہ دار برابر قابض
چلے آتے ہیں آخرالامر بند و بست سرسری بنام تعلقہ دار قابض حال گورنمنٹ انگلشیہ سے ہوا اور قسمہ میں
یہ موضع جسی ہم علاقہ متعہ ضلع راسے بریلی میں واقع ہیں اولاد اکبر اس خاندان میں وارث ریاست ہوتا ہے

(نمبر ۱۸۰) سبھان احمد قوم میواتی تعلقہ دار عزیز آباد

شجرہ فصلی میں شیخ محمد بیجو مورث اعلیٰ انکے پہلے کایستھ مسلمان ہوئے اوسی شجرہ الاصلی میں کمال پور
سیران سید سے اور شجرہ الا فصلی میں موضع عزیز آباد خرید کیا پھر یو نافیو ماترقی ریاست ہوتی ہی اب
یہ موضع جسی ہم علاقہ ضلع راسے بریلی میں واقع ہیں اولاد اکبر اس خاندان میں وارث ریاست
ہوتا ہے ۔

(نمبر ۱۸۱) میرظفر مہدی قوم سید تعلقہ دار علی نگر خطاب میر

سلطنت سلطان محمد تغلق شاہ دہلی سے سید محمد ذکریا مورث اس خاندان کو بوجہ سرتابی راجہ جروال
کل ریاست تعلقہ جروال ماٗلکا نہ مرحمت ہوئی اوزکی آٹھویں پشت میں علی نقی نے علی نگر بنگلا مل قسمہ کیا
اوزکی تیسری پشت میں آپ تعلقہ دار صاحب ہیں بعد موضع معتبہ بڑی جمبی الارض معہ ضلع بہرائچ میں
واقع ہیں اولاد اکبر اس ریاست میں وارث ہوتا ہے

(نمبر ۱۸۲) میر کاظم حسین قوم سید تعلقہ دار دیرا قاضی خطاب میر

سید محمد شاہ مورث اعلیٰ اس خاندان کے سکتھے اوزکی اولاد میں چند پشتون کے بعد سید صفدر حسین ہوئے
اوزکی شادی احمد علیخان تعلقہ دار جروال کی دختر سے ہوئی شجرہ الا فصلی میں صفدر حسین کو یہ ریاست
ترکہ سسرالی سے حاصل ہوئی آپ اولاد صفدر حسین سے ہیں بعض موضع بڑی جمبی معہ پشتہ الارض ضلع بہرائچ میں
واقع ہیں اولاد اکبر اس خاندان میں وارث ریاست ہوتا ہے ۔

(نمبر ۱۸۳) سید رمضان علی قوم سید تعلقہ دار اودنام

سانٹھ سو پچاس برس کا زمانہ ہوا اٹھاکر اودونت نگر دانونت نگر قوم حسین متوطن قنوج از جانب والی تنوج اس ملک میں آئے

اور وہ نام خاص اپنے نام سے آباد کرکے دہان مقیم ہوئے ہر چند دیہات دیگر آباد کرکے رفتہ رفتہ کل دیہات پیکشتہ اوناں پر قابض ہوگئے اوکنوبہا والدین کے جو خاندان سید ابوالقراش سکنہ شہر واسطی سے تھا یہ عوض انتقام خون اپنے باپ کے جومعرکہ تنوج میں ہاتھ افونت سنگہ سے قتل ہوا تھا تیغ کیا بجلدہ وہ اس کا نمایاں سرکار شاہ دہلی سے اور نام خاص جسکے نام سے تعلقہ مشہور ہے مع چند دیہات دیگر بہا والدین کو بطور جاگیر مرحمت ہوئے اور سوقت سے آغاز اس ریاست کا ہے پھر مورثان تعلقہ دارنے بذریعہ آبادی بیع وغیرہ ریاست کی ترقی وی آخر الاکثر افصلی ہیں بند وبست تعلقہ کا بنام وہ دوسری دست علی کو ہوا بعد وفات اونکی یہ تعلقہ دار بحکم عدالت قابض ہیں۔ تعلقہ میں اسہ موضع للعیہ ٹی مبی ضلع اونام میں واقع ہیں اور اس خاندان میں اولا داکبر وارث ریاست ہوتا ہے۔

(نمبر ۱۸۴) بابو جبر زنگ بہادر سنگھ قوم سوم بنسی تعلقہ اربیس پور

یہ ریاست مجہتہ تسو برس سے قائم ہے مورث اعلے اس خاندان کے راجہ بیرستی اس ملک میں ہوئے جنکا تذکرہ مفصل نمبر دوا پر درج ہے آپ اوسی خاندان سے ہیں آپ کی ملکیت میں موضع سو اضافات جمہی للہ عنہ کما عطیہ ضلع پرتابگڈھ میں واقع ہیں رسم گدی نشینی اس خاندان میں ہے

(نمبر ۱۸۵) گردہاری سنگھ برادر خورد کنور بجگونت سنگھ قوم کالیتھہ تعلقہ ارگو کلبپو راسیٹی دیہنیورد یہ موضع اسینی اسکران نامی قوم برہمن کا آباد کیا ہوا ہے جسکے نام سے تعلقہ مشہور ہے اسکان کی اولا دین دیگری بھگو اناس نے بدست کنور بہادر سنگہ مورث تعلقہ دار بیع تعلقہ ارجع کیا تھا اوسوقت سے انکے مورث قابض چلا آتے ہیں تعلقہ میں علمہ دوضع رجی ٹی جی بعلرپتے اضلاع المبوبا وہ نجگی میں واقع ہیں اولا داکبر اس خاندان میں ملاک ریاست ہوتا ہے۔

(نمبر ۱۸۶) شیخ منصب علی قوم شیخ تعلقہ ایسیدا

یہ موضع سیدا ہارخادیم سے شمال قصبہ دیوا تھا اور مورثان تعلقہ ارقدیم سے تعلقہ ارد یو امشہور تھی شتہ افصلی میں بوعلی مورث اعلے نے دریہ ناہالی پر بعد اخراج قبضہ کیرت سنگہ وغیرہ تھا کران بیس بحکم کرنیل سلیمن صاحب بہادر اور بارہ اس ریاست ونیز دیگر دیہات مقبوضہ تھاکران پر قبضہ پا یا اوسوقت سے اس خاندان میں یہ ریاست قائم ہے اور قبضہ مورثان برابر بحال تا نام ہے تعلقہ نمبری ۱۹۹ و ۲۳ اسی خاندان سے علطہدہ قائم ہے۔ اس تعلقہ میں اسہ موضع دوتیہی مبی اضلاع بارہ نجگی میں واقع ہیں اس خاندان میں اولا داکبر ملاک ریاست ہوتا ہے۔ اور اب یہ تعلقہ بالکل فروخت ہوگیا۔

(نمبر ۱۸۷) ستا رام قوم کھتری تعلقہ اربہموپور بیسنا ہمی و تیگاؤ انبکر

سکے پرگنہ فعلی میں زمینداری بھجو پور کنہیالال مورثے نے بذریعہ رہن حاصل کی تھی اور علاقہ تیکر اینکر بصد خیرخواہی
ایام عہد گذشتہ دام تعلقہ دار قابض حال کو گورنمنٹ انگلشیہ سے مرحمت ہوا لیکن قطعہ بھجو پور راہب کا ہے جو گیا علاقہ
تیکر اینکر و بسیندی بھی ملکیت قدیم اب باقی بستے مضبوط اور جمعہ جمی جمی معلوم ہوا ۔ ضلع سیتاپور میں واقع ہیں
اولاد اکبر اس خاندان میں مالک ریاست ہوتا ہے ۔

(نمبر ١٨٨) سید محمد حامد قوم سید تعلقہ دار بیورامی

شجرہ جعری زمانہ سلطنت سلطان شہاب الدین غوری میں سید محمد صالح اسم باسے شہر کرمان سے آکر مقام بھو پور
باد شاہ سے علاقی ہوئے اور موضع بھولی بطور رہنائی جمعیت و دو معاش شاہ سے حاصل کیا بعد وفات اونکے سید محمد
اونکے بیٹے نے حسب استعداد ماسے فرد آنکہ موضع بلور زمینداری مع خطاب خانی شاہ وقت سے علیحدہ پائے پھر
بعد محمد ماہ نے بعد رو عرصہ تین سو سال بیورامی خاص خریدیک کرکے اس نام سے تعلقہ قائم کیا جسے قبضہ مورثان چلا آتا
فی المال یہ تعلقہ دار مالک ریاست ہیں اور تعلقہ میں بچہ موضع آٹھ بی بی معہ تمسک ۔ ضلع بارہ بنکی میں واقع ہیں اس
خاندان میں اولاد اکبر مالک ریاست ہوتا ہے

(نمبر ١٨٩) محمد امیر و غلام عباس قوم شیخ انصاری تعلقہ دار شہاب پور

نتر سال ہوئے جبکے اپکی ریاست قائم ہوئے اور فیض الدین شیخ و شہاب پور و موضع فتح سرائی تین دیہات راجہ رزاق بخش
مالک تعلقہ جہانگیر آباد سے بھجے اب راجہ فرزند طنیان قائم مقام ہیں بذریعہ رہن و بیع مورثان تعلقہ دار نے حاصل کرکے
شامل تعلقہ کیے اب اس تعلقہ میں صد موضع اور سکے بچی بی تمسک ۔ ضلع بارہ بنکی میں واقع ہیں اس خاندان میں
اولاد اکبر مالک ریاست ہوتا ہے

(نمبر ١٩٠) غلام قاسم خان قوم سبین خان زادہ تعلقہ دار عثمان پور

عرصہ جار سو سال کا گذرا ہے کونسل سنگھ مورث علے نے عہد ہمایون شاہ میں بعلہ قطع و قمع اودھ میں بجر ریاست پرگنہ
سندور پر دخل پایا اونکے کوئی اولاد نرسوتی تھی ایک سنقیر سے وہ لتجی اولاد ہوئے اونسے باین شرط و عادی کا اگر تمہارے
دولڑکے پیدا ہوں تو ایک کو مسلمان کرنا چنانچہ اونکے دولڑکے پیدا ہوئے لگن سنگھ و جگن سنگھ لگن سنگھ مسلمان ہوئے
اور لاکھو خان نام رکھ گیا ڈیڑھ سو برس بعد اونکی اولاد میں ہمت خان و غضنفر خان و بہادر خان ہر سہ برادران نے
علاقہ تقسیم کیا غضنفر خان کو یہ تعلقہ عثمان پور ملا آخر الامر سنور خان وارث ریاست ہوئے بعد وفات اونکی سیاہ ظلور الانسا
اونکی زوجہ اور اونکے بعد دشمن زمانخان قابض ریاست ہوئے لیکن بحکم اہل ولایت وہ بیدخل ہوئے اور
بہادر خان برادر زادہ منور خان کو تعلقہ ملا بعد وفات بہادر خان غلام قاسم خان جانشین ہوئے وہ بھی
بعد قضیہ بمرگئے محمد ابراہیم خان و بکار لڑکا بعمر دہ سالہ و ر سماہ رسول النسا اونکی زوجہ مالک تعلقہ ہیں لیکن اس

تعلقہ میں چند حصہ بذریعہ انتقال خانگی اب بقبضہ راجہ فرزند طفیان صاحب ہیں ۔ اور تعلقہ میں دیگر موضع سعہ پٹی مبنی بعلاقہ ۔ ضلع بارہ بنکلی میں واقع ہیں رسم گدی کی نشینی اس خاندان میں ہر

(نمبر ۱۹۱) احسان رسول نلف چودھری عنایت رسول قوم شیخ تعلقدار امیرپور

شکتہ حجوری ہیں بہ عہد سلطان محمود غزنوی سید حسن بعضا مورث ایلے انکے ہمراہ و سید سالار مسعود غازی جمعیت فراہم اقوام بہبر کی اس ملک میں آئے اوسوقت امیرپور وغیرہ دیہات اقوام بہبر دن کے او کمکو عطا ہوئے جیسے یہ ریاست قائم ہوئی ۔ بعد اسکے عہد سلطنت دہلی سے اس خاندان میں لقب چودھرایت ہو۔ اسناد تعلقداری کی گورنمنٹ سے بنام عنایت رسول پدر تعلقدار کے ہوئی ۔ بعد اوسکے آپ تعلقہ دار ہیں ۔ تعلقین حلقہ موضع سلے پٹی مبنی بعلقہ ۹ ضلع بارہ بنکلی میں واقع ہیں ۔ اس خاندان میں الاعلی اللاولا کبر بالمالک ریاست ہوتا ہے ۔

(نمبر ۱۹۲) نظیر حسن قوم سید تعلقدار اہما موذ گدی مسی مہیتیا

تعلقہ اہما بمبکے نام سے یہ ریاست ملقب ہے مساجرانہ دار وقفہ و ابجدیلی کے قبضے میں تھا لصحا خیر خواہی ایام نذہ شدہ ۔ مگر درنث انکلامیہ سے بند و نسبت اسکا بطور عطیہ مالکا نہ بنام اونکے ہوا اور جبر رویہ اغنا ناسرکار سے حاصل ہوتھا اوس سے بقیہ ریاست تعلقہ حاصل ہوئی ہے اب بعد وفات دار وقفہ صاحب آپ تعلقہ ہونے گئے موضع سے پٹی مبنی بعلاقہ ۱۲ کے ضلع مبنی گنون بارہ بنکلی میں واقع ہیں ۔ اور اس خاندان میں اولاد اکبر وارث ریاست ہوگا

(نمبر ۱۹۳) بلبھد رسنگھہ قوم سوم مبنی تعلقدار سوجا گھر خطاب بابو

یہ ریاست مبجہ تنو برس سے قائم ہے مورث ایلے اس خاندان کے راجہ بہر بہتی اس ملک میں ہیں ہوئے فنگلا تذکرہ نمبر ۱ پر مندرج ہے آپ اوسی خاندان سے ہیں تعلقہ میں بلخ موضع مبنی بعلاقہ ۹ ضلع پتا بکذہ دو ہیں واقع ۔ رسم گدی کی نشینی اس خاندان میں ہے

(نمبر ۱۹۴) امید سنگھہ قوم ٹھاکر بجگوتی تعلقدار الیسن پور ۔

اسکا تذکرہ خاندانی نمبر ۱ پر مندرج ہے خاندان چکرہ سنگھہ مورث سے بہ تعلقدار قابض اس ملکیت میں تعلقہ ہیں موضع مبنی بعلاقہ ۹ ضلع پرتاب گڈہ میں واقع ہیں ۔ اولاد اکبر اس خاندان میں وارث ہوتا ہے

(نمبر ۱۹۵) ٹھاکر ارجن سنگھہ و مہیش بخش راجہ قوم ٹھاکر بیس تعلقدار پائن بہا ۔

اسکا تذکرہ خاندانی نمبر ۱۸ پر مندرج ہے کرن رای کے خاندان میں بخت بہادر سنگھہ مورث نے یہ ریاست وقت تقسیم باہمی حاصل کی تھی جیسے قبضہ مورثان برابر چلا آتا ہے ۔ تعلقہ میں حصہ موضع ایک مبنی بعلاقہ ۹ ضلع اونام میں واقع ہیں ۔ اور یہ تعلقدار رئیس قدیم ریاست میں اگر مورث ایلے بلا وصیت فوت ہوجائے تو موجب آئین مولی اشخاص ذیحق وارث ریاست ہونگے

(نمبر ۱۹۶) مادھو سنگھ قوم کنبوریہ تعلقدار نورالدین پور خطاب بابو

اسکا تذکرہ خاندانی نمبر ۱۹۷ پر درج ہے ۔ پانچ سو برس ہوئے بہادر سنگھ مورث اعلیٰ جو راون سنگھ پیسر خورد راجہ کلیان سنگھ کو اپنار اس منشین کرکے مالک ریاست کیا اور انہوں نے ملکیت کو ترقی دی اور نورالدین پور میں سکونت اختیار کی اور کی مچھ پشت کے بعد ۔ بابو دین سنگھ نے بوجہ لاولدی خود دو جاگیریں بخش اپنے بھتیجے کو راس منشین اپنا کیا بعد وفات اسکے ٹھکر دین توم کنبوریہ نے وجہ قابض ریاست ہوئے مُن اسکے بعد یہ تعلقدار اثناء قابض ریاست ہیں ۔ تعلقہ میں درست موضع جیسی معہ ۔۔۔ ضلع رائے بریلی میں واقع ہیں ۔ رسم گدی نشینی اس خاندان میں ہے ۔

(نمبر ۱۹۷) بھیا اوتار سنگھ قوم سورج بنس تعلقدار رانی مؤ

اسکا تذکرہ خاندانی وآغاز ریاست نمبر ۵۹ پر درج ہے ۔ یہ تعلقہ اوسی نمبر ۳۵ کا ایک شاخ ہے ۔ عرصہ دو سو برس کا گذرا اگلال سا مورث سے یہ ریاست علیحدہ وقائم ہوئی جیسے برابر قبضہ اس خاندان میں چلا آتا ہے ۔ سند تعلقداری گورنمنٹ انگلیشیہ سے آپکو مرحمت ہوئی ۔ تعلقہ میں درست موضع صدیپٹی بھی معہ ۔۔۔ ضلع بارہ بنکی میں واقع ہیں اس خاندان میں رسم گدی نشینی ہے ۔

(نمبر ۱۹۸) بھیا ہر رتن سنگھ قوم ٹھاکر بیسین تعلقدار مجھگوان اوریا ڈہیمہ خطاب بھیا

مفصل تذکرہ خاندانی وآغاز ریاست اسکا نمبر ۵۹ پر درج ہے اور آپ کچھ زمیندار سابق بھی تھے بصلہ خیر خواہی ایام غدر شناختہ حق زمینداری اس ملکیت کا آپکو گورنمنٹ انگلشیہ سے مرحمت ہوا ہے اور آپ تعلقدار قرار دیا گیا ۔ موضع صدیپٹی بھی معہ ۔۔۔ ضلع گونڈہ میں واقع ہیں ۔ اس خاندان میں مورث اعلیٰ اگر بلا وصیت فوت ہوجاویں تو بموجب قائدہ خاندان کے اشخاص ذیحق وارث ہونگے ۔

(نمبر ۱۹۹) شیخ ریاست ملی قوم شیخ تعلقدار شیخ پور واقع ضلع بارہ بنکی

یہ تعلقہ شاخ نمبر ۲۶ کا ہے ۔ سمفصل تذکرہ حالات اوسی نمبر پر درج ہے اور اب یہ تعلقہ فروخت ہو گیا بلکہ گذارہ کے سیتقدر اراضی باقی ہے کچھ ریاست باقی نہیں ہے ۔

(نمبر ۲۰۰) مساۃ قطب النسا قوم شیخ تعلقدار گوریا کلان

آپکے مورث شاہ رفیع الدین مدینہ سے ہند میں آباد ہوئے تھے اگر دہلی میں آباد ہوئے تھے باد شاہ بریشاہ میں قوم شیخ انصاری اولاد میں دو ہیں اسکے ۔۔۔ نمی شادی خاندان مالک یوست میں جو کلان افسر فوج سید مسعود حشمتیہ میں ہوئی اوکی اولاد میں سے ۔۔۔ شیخ نظام الدین اور شیخ طاہر تھے شیخ نظام پور نے نظام پور اور شیخ طاہر نے طاہر پور آباد کیا جب شیخ طاہر قاونگو در گنہ ہو تو موضع گوریا کا حق ملکیت حاصل کیا اور شمال اپنی ملکیت کی او قائم کی بنا قائم کی ۔۔۔ اد وقت سے یہ ریاست قائم ہے مساۃ موصوفہ بالا بجا ہے جہانگیر نجبش اپنے شوہر بہ شوہر ہونے کے ۔۔۔ بفض تعلقہ میں اس ریاست میں سو موضع بھی

... ضلع لکھنؤ میں واقع ہیں اور اولاد اکبر اس خاندان میں مالک ریاست ہوتی ہے ۔

(نمبر ۳۰۱) نثار علی خان قوم بھٹی تعلقہ دار نیور و پرگنہ سبوڈھی

نشستہ فصلی میں امام زبر خان و عطے خان ساکنان قدیم بھشم بہ عہد سلطان علاء الدین غوری ہمراہ تاتار خان مصوبہ دار کے تعلقہ بسوڈھی میں مست مہرا دھی اقوام بھر کی آبے بعد فتح کے پرگنہ سبوڈھی و موئی زبر خان کو عطا ہوا اور اسکی اولاد و اسی مناجان اور کالینخان سے مناجان پرگنہ موئی میں اور کالینخان سبوڈھی میں قائم ہوئے یہ حصے ریاست قائم سے سند تعلقہ گورنمنٹ سے بنام شیر خان مرحمت ہوئی تھی بعد اونکے آپ اونکے نشستی قابض یہ بعض ریاست ہوئے ایک موضع سے پنیات جمبی ضلع بابر و بجلی میں واقع ہیں وارث آپ ریاست کا ابقاء تا رسم گدی نشینی قائم ہوتا ہے ۔ اور تعلقہ دار نمبر ۳۰۲ اسی خاندان سے ہیں ۔

(نمبر ۳۰۲) ٹھکدار این دریا و کنور قوم ٹھاکر رابجکمار تعلقہ دار گارب پور

تذکرہ خاندانی آپکا نمبر بزرگ ہے خاندان ایشری سنگ پورش اعلیٰ این گارب دیوسے یہ ریاست قائم ہوئی اور قابض حال اولاد گارب دیوسے سے سنے مست موضع معہ بستی جمبی اعلیٰ ضلع سلطان پور میں واقع ہیں اولاد اکبر اس خاندان میں وارث ریاست ہوتا ہے ۔

(نمبر ۳۰۳) دیاشنکر قوم بابھیبی برہمن تعلقہ دار کروہالو ہرامؤ

آپکے مورث سالمنت اودھ میں ہمیشہ معزز مقرب غلام خانان اودھ میں تصور رہو کرہ عہدہ ہائے نظامت و ضلعہ داری سے فراز رہے اور یہ ریاست زرخرید آپکے مورثان کی ہے دو سہ شریک اپکے نے جب لاولد وفات پائی تو واونکا حصہ بملکیت بھی آپکو منتقل ہوئی اس سند تعلقہ بھی گورنمنٹ سے آپکو عطا ہوئی اس تعلقہ میں نئے موضع اور بستی جمبی سمراؤ نام میں واقع ہیں ۔ اور اس ریاست میں اگر مورث بلا وصیت فوت ہو جاوے تو وراثت بموجب دستور خاندانی اشخاص ذیحق کو پہونچتی ہے ۔

(نمبر ۳۰۴) جاگیر بخش قوم کنپور یہ تعلقہ دار بھون ساہپور

انکا تذکرہ خاندانی نمبر ۱۱ پر درج ہے خاندان رئیس مورث اعلے ہین بھون ساہ مورث نے ساہپور کو اپنے نام پر آباد کیا اور تعلقہ کی بنا قائم کی نشستہ فصلی میں مورثان اس ریاست کو موضع بھگوان سلطنت اودھ سے بموجب خون بہا بابو دری کے سنگہ اونکی ایک اولاد کے عطا ہوا از بانہ حال این سند تعلقہ داری بنام بابو استیلا بخش گورنمنٹ انگلشیہ سے مرحمت ہوئی بعد اونکے یہ تعلقہ دار قابض ریاست ہوئے تعلقہ میں بعہ موضع جمبی صحب اعلیٰ ضلع سلطان پور میں واقع ہیں رسم گدی نشینی اس خاندان میں ہے ۔

(نمبر ۲۰۵) ٹھاکر فتح محمد قوم شیخ قیراطی تعلقدار پشر ہانصاب ٹھاکر

بہت عرصہ ہوا امیانجی مورث انکے ملک مصر سے آئے اور بحیثیت ملازمی سابق صوبہ دار اودہ کے بعہدہ تحصیلداری پرگنہ بھراپچ مین تعینات ہوئے اور بہ ظہور حسن خدمات شیخ سامی خادم امیانجی کو جہتر بھموج قوم برہمن زمیندار سوضع پٹھریہ کی ملکیت بطور پایکا نہ بیشگا ہصوبہ دار اودہ سمے مرحمت ہوئی بھر سالار بخش نے جو بعدہ اولادی مین ہوسے رئیست کو ترقی دی جیسے آپکے موشان نسلاً بعد نسل قابض چلے آتے ہین تعلقہ مین مہوس موضع ایک پٹی جبھی سکمہ عشہ ضلع بھراپچ مین واقع ہین رسم گدی کی نفیئی اس خاندان مین ہے۔

(نمبر ۲۰۶) ٹھاکر نرمان سنگہ قوم گور تعلقدار انچھا پور عمری و سمرا

یہ موضع میسکے نام سے تعلقہ مشہور ہے اہل زمینداری سادات جبرمل کا تھا اشتلاا فصلی مین بنر کیریت سنگہ والا تعلقدار حال کو مظفر مہدی وخیرہ سادات جبرمل سے بذریعہ نیع مع دیگر دیہات حاصل ہوا اتھا او سوقت سے قبضہ چلا آتا ہے اور یہ ریاست جدید ہے تعلقہ مین سے موضع بھی جبھی صمہ سا بیتہ ۹ ارمہ پہ افلاع گونڈہ و بھراپچ مین واقع ہین رسم گدی کی نشینی اس خاندان مین ہے۔

(نمبر ۲۰۷) فتح بہادر خان قوم بھر تھوان خان زادہ تعلقدار بہوندا

یہ بنیس خاندان راجہ کرن سے ہین کہ جنگلا سلسلہ راجہ بکر ماجیت سے ملتا ہے تقریباً سات سو برس گذرے کہ راجہ کرن فرید علاقہ بلو حصہ درا مادی کو دریا تھا اودہین یہ یہ ریاست ہ اور راجہ کرن کی اولاد گدہ یہ ٹھاکر کہلاتے ہین چند پشتوں کے بعد اودتار سنگہ دہلی کو گئے اور دہان مذہب اسلام قبول کیا اور نام خان اظم خان رکھا گیا بھی یہ خان کہلاتے ہین اوسی خاندان سے یہ تعلقدار قابض ریاست مین ہرسے وضع بہوی بنا کموجہ ہیہ ضلع راے بریلی مین واقع ہین رسم گدی کی نشینی اس خاندان مین ہے۔

(نمبر ۲۰۸) ۱۔ ٹھاگہ ناتھ کنور ۲۔ کھرگ کنور اقوام چپگوتی تعلقداران دسرہ اتھہ پور

اکنا نذکرہ خاندانی نمبر ۲۰۲ پر درج ہی یہ تعلقہ ایک شاخ تعلقہ نمبرہ کاہ تعلقہ مین ہے۔۔ موضع جبھی سمہ ضلع پتابگڈھ مین واقع ہین رسم گدی کی نشینی اس خاندان مین ہے۔

(نمبر ۲۰۹) کالکا بخش و زوجہ گنگا بخش قوم ٹھاکر بسوار تعلقدار رام کوٹی و عاجمی پور

یہ عہد شہنشاہ عالمگیر کلیان مل مورث اعلے نے پرگنہ رام کوٹ میسکے نام سے تعلقہ مشہور ہے بطور مورث سا جری حاصل کیا چند عرصہ کے بعد اس خاندان سے یہ ریاست جاتی رہی اور سو بھارا ی قوم گور بطور مساجری قابض ریاست ہوئے اور بعون آزوی سنگہ پریہ کلیان مل کو تشبنی کیا بعد وفات سو بھارا ی فوجی سنگہ مالک ریاست ہوا اور قبولیت

اس علاقہ کی گورنمنٹ اودھ کو لے کر مبسوط ریاست قائم ہوئی ۔ بعد ازاں نواب سعادت علی خان سہر دیو بخش پدر تقی القدر بحال نے
قبضہ پایا ۔ اودھ خوں نے بوجہ لا ولدی خود کالکا بخش کو پرورش کیا تھا کو لکا بخش اصلی لڑکے اپنے پیدا سہر دیو بخش نے
انتقال کیا ۔ اودھ وقت سند تعلقہ داری بوجہ باغی گنگا بخش کالکا بخش کے نام گورنمنٹ انگلشیہ سے مرحمت ہوئی ۔ لیکن بند وبست
گنگا بخش بھی شرکت تعلقہ کیے گئے ۔ اب گنگا بخش نے وفات شدائی اودھ کو دو حصے پر بانٹی زمین قابض ہیں اور کالکا بخش جس کی بقایا ہے شامل ہے
اپنے حصے پر قابض ہیں ۔ یہ تعلقہ میں موضع صدر ٹپی ممبی ۔۔۔ ضلع سیتاپور میں واقع ہیں اس خاندان میں اگر مورث اعلیٰ بلا وصیت
فوت ہو جاوے سے وراثت بوجب دستور خاندانی وارث نزدیک کو پہونچتی ہے ۔

(نمبر ۲۱۰) ٹھاکر جگمو ہن سنگھ قوم ٹھاکر تعلقدار دیو گنا گرد دیو پور

اس تذکرہ خاندانی و آغاز ریاست نمبر ہر پر بھی سہر دیو کے خاندان میں اہلاء ساہ وارث اعلیٰ تعلقہ گو را کو سینی تذکرہ نمبر ۲۰ کی
بلائینے حصے کے علیٰحدہ ہو کر موضع کیرت پور میں جو کہ سرکار شاہی ہائے معاف تھا اگر آباد ہوا اب دو مردان سنگھ بہ تعلقدار حال ملکیت قائم
بنام گرد دیو پور بتعلقہ قائم کیا ۔ اودھ وقت سے برابر قبضہ موروثان چلا آتا ہے ۔ تعلقہ میں سے موضع ممبی سمیت ہائے رائے بریلی ہیں
واقع ہیں اس خاندان میں اولاد اکبر وارث ریاست ہوتا ہے ۔

(نمبر ۲۱۱) مسماۃ جگراج کنور قوم کائستھہ زوجہ گوری شنکر تعلقدار سہر داس پور

ہر داس مورث اعلیٰ اس خاندان کے تھے مگر بعرصہ خبثہ سو سال اودھ خوں نے نکل کر ہوا کہ ہر داس پور جس کے نام سو تعلقہ مشہور ہے
آباد کیا رفتہ رفتہ اودھ مہینے دیوہ کی ترقی سے تعلقہ قائم ہو گیا ۔ پشتین پشت میں جما تھہ کے نام سند تعلقہ گورنمنٹ سے بی
بعد وفات اودھ کے گوری شنکر لڑکا ودھ قابض ہوا اب یہ ریاست ترکہ کئو شوہری پر قابض ہیں موضع ممبی مہ ۔۔۔ ضلع
رائے بریلی میں واقع ہیں اور اولاد اکبر اس خاندان میں وارث ریاست ہوتا ہے ۔

(نمبر ۲۱۲) مہیپال سنگھ قوم ٹھاکر گوتم تعلقدار بارہ

مودہ پشت کا زمانہ گزار کرا رائے سکندر سنگھ وارث اعلیٰ بہ عہد محمد ابراہیم سلطان شرقی بنظر قلع وقمع اقوام سہر اس
ملک میں آئے اور بعد از شکست اس بلکیت اقوام سہر پر قبضہ اپنا حاصل کیا ۔ اودھ خوں نے ایک جدید موضع
کی بنا ڈالی اور اپنے نام پر او سکا نام سکندر پور رکھا اور وہان سکونت اختیار کی اودھ کی تیسری
پشت میں رائے خیال سنگھ مورث بارہ خاص میں مکان بنا کر سکونت پذیر ہو سے
اودھ وقت سے یہ ریاست بارہ کے نام سے مشہور رہے اور قبضہ موروثان چلا آتا ہے ۔
تعلقہ میں سے موضع ممبی معہ تاخیث ضلع رائے بریلی میں واقع ہیں ۔ اس خاندان میں
اگر مورث اعلیٰ بلا وصیت فوت ہو جاوے سے تو بوجب دستور خاندانی اشخاص نزدیک کو
پہونچتی ہے ۔

(نمبر ۲۱۳) درگاہی خان قوم بہالی سلطان خانزادہ و تعلقہ دار ...

تذکرہ خاندانی و آغاز ریاست نمبر ۳۰ ۔ پرورج ہر یہ تعلقہ اسی تعلقہ کی ایک شاخ ہے آخری رئیس اس تعلقہ نبی بخش خان سوت جنگے نام پسند تعلقہ عطا سوئی ابد و فات آنکہ یہ مقدار قابض ریاست ہیں ۔ تعلقہ میں جمع موضع جمعی صمیمہ ... اضلاع سلطان پور و راے بریلی میں واقع میں اس ریاست میں اولاد اکبر مالک ہوتا ہے ۔

(نمبر ۲۱۴) گیا دین سنگھ و سہجت سنگھ قوم ٹھاکر راجکمار تعلقہ دار شہرہ ...

تذکرہ خاندانی قوم راجکار کا نمبر ۵ ۔ پرورج ہر جمیہ سو سال سوہے اندر سا و مورث احلی نے جنگل کشوارہ اس کا نون آباد کیا پھر تقسیم باہمی میں گنگلا و اس مورث کو یہ ریاست ملی آخرالامر سند تعلقہ دار ہی گورنمنٹ سے بنام ٹھکر امین مدت سوئی ابد انکی یہ درئیس تابض تعلقہ میں ہے بعض موضعات سات بنی جمعی ... ضلع فیض آباد میں واقع میں اولاد اکبر اس خاندان میں وارث ریاست ہوتا ہے ۔

(نمبر ۲۱۵) بابو سردون سنگھ قوم پلکمر یا تعلقہ دار انتو وا سردپور ۔

تذکرہ خاندانی و آغاز ریاست نمبر ۵ ۔ و ۳۰ ۔ پرورج ہر یہ تعلقہ نمبر ۳۰ کا ایک شاخ ہے اس تعلقہ میں پانچ موضع جمعی سلطی ... اضلاع پتاب و سلطان پور میں واقع میں رسم گدی نشینی اس خاندان میں ہے ۔

(نمبر ۲۱۶) فرزند علی خان قوم سید تعلقہ دار لکھنوارہ ۔

یہ تعلقہ دار ساکن کوچہ جہان آباد و ملازم فوج سرکار شاہی تھی اور معرکہ بیلی گاڑ ہ میں خیر خواہ گورنمنٹ انگلشیہ رہی بجلد و سے اس خیر خواہی ایام فندق شش ایام یہ ملکیت ینمہار علاقہ منضبط رہا نا ابنی مادہ و بخش سنگھ گورنمنٹ سے عطیہ حاصل سہوی لیکن انکرون نے اب یہ ریاست بنام سید علی اپنے لڑکے کے منتقل کردی ہر تعلقہ میں جار موضع جمعی للمعاملہ ... ضلع راے بریلی میں واقع میں اولاد اکبر اس خاندان وارث ریاست ہوتا ہے ۔

(نمبر ۲۱۷) بخشی ہر پرشاد قوم کایستہ سکسینہ تعلقہ دار بیلوی ۔

آغاز اس ریاست کا سلہ ۱۲ ہجری میں بخشی چنتر سین سے بذریعہ بیع ہوکر رفتہ رفتہ ترقی سہوتی رہی اور موثان انکے سرکار شاہی میں بخشی فوج و مقربان شاہی سے تھے بعد وفات آنکے یہ تعلقہ دار بذریعہ بینت اپنے چنتر سین کے ریاست پر قابض سوے اور آگے گورنمنٹ انگلشیہ نے سند تعلقہ عطا فرمائی ۔ تعلقہ میں آٹھ موضع تین ٹپی جمعی سلہ ... ضلع بارہ بنکی میں واقع میں ۔ اس خاندان میں اولاد اکبر مالک ریاست ہوتا ہے ۔

(نمبر ۲۱۸) نیہور رتن سنگھ قوم کھمو تعلقہ دار بہو نہ ۔

ان تعلقہ دار کا خاندان جو قب راوت سے مشہور ہو گروہ ٹھاکران میں ہے اور انکی ریاست قدیم ترین ریاستوں میں سے ہے ۔ بہار شاہی انکے مورث احلی تھے آنکی اولاد میں بہیرون دا اس میں سوے اسی خاندان سے ...

یہ تعلقدار میں پہلے یہ تعلقہ بہت بڑا تھا مگر تقسیم ہہونے ہونے اس تعلقہ میں اب آٹھ موضع جمعی صاحبہ
ضلع بریلی میں واقع ہیں اس خاندان میں رسم گدی نشینی ہے ۔

(نمبر ۲۱۹) وان بہادر سنگھ قوم رکوار تعلقدار محمد پور ۔

یہ ریاست ایک شاخ رام نگر دھمیری کی تذکرہ نمبر ۳۳۷۔ کی ہے چار سو برس ہوے را ماس مورث
سے علیحدہ ہوکر یہ ریاست قائم کی ۔ پیر مردان سنگھ مورث نے محمد شاہ فقیر کے نام پر اس موضع محمد پور کو آباد
جس کے نام سے تعلقہ مشہور ہے ۔ اس وقت تک علی الاتصال قبضہ موثران چلا آتا ہے ۔ اس تعلقہ میں تین موضع اور
تیس جمعی ضلع سہارن پور ۔ ضلع بجنور میں واقع ہیں اس خاندان میں اولاد اکبر مالک ریاست ہوتا ہے ۔

(نمبر ۲۲۰) دلجیت سنگھ قوم بھگوتی تعلقدار رتھگاواں ۔

کاتذکرہ خاندانی نمبر ۲۰۰۔ پر درج ہے یہ تعلقہ اسی نمبر کا ایک شاخ ہے تعلقہ میں سات موضع جمعی
محل ۔ ضلع پرتاب گڑھ میں واقع ہیں اس خاندان میں اولاد اکبر وارث ریاست ہوتا ہے ۔

(نمبر ۲۲۱) فضل حسین متخلص بابا بی بی قوم رہیان مسلمان تعلقدار کٹوارہ و رام پور گوکل ۔

کاتذکرہ خاندانی نمبر ۲۲۲۔ پر مفصل درج ہے یہ تعلقہ ایک شاخ اسی نمبر ۲۲۲ کا ہے شکستہ فصلی میں
مدار بخش خان مورث نے اس تعلقہ پر قبضہ پایا اور یہ تعلقہ موضع کٹوارہ کی نام سے مشہور ہے ۔ اس وقت تک
برابر قبضہ چلا آتا ہے ۔ سند تعلقہ داری گورنمنٹ انگلشیہ سے بنام بابا بی بی کے ہوئی لاکن انھوں نے فصل حسین
اپنے نو اسہ کو تبنی کیا ہے جنکی تصویر یہ شمال ہے ۔ تعلقہ میں لائچہ موضع جمعی معہ محال ۔ ضلع کھیری میں واقع
ہیں رسم گدی نشینی اس خاندان میں ہے ۔

(نمبر ۲۲۲) محمد شیر خان قوم ابھیان مسلمان تعلقدار رائے پور پیریا ۔

کاتذکرہ خاندانی نمبر ۲۲۱۔ پر مفصل درج ہے یہ تعلقہ اسی نمبر ۲۲۱ کا ایک شاخ ہے اور یہ
موضع رائے پور چکلہ کی نام سے تعلقہ مشہور ہے شکستہ فصلی میں بہ قبضہ جلال الدین مورث آیا تھا
اس وقت سے برابر قبضہ اس خاندان میں چلا آتا ہے ۔ اس تعلقہ میں جمیہ موضع جمعی معہ محال
ضلع کھیری میں واقع ہیں اور اولاد اکبر اس خاندان میں وارث ریاست ہوتا ہے ۔

(نمبر ۲۲۳) مہیپال سنگھ قوم کنپوریہ تعلقدار اسرا ۔

کاتذکرہ خاندانی نمبر ۱۴۱۔ پر درج ہے خاندان راجہ بانک میں اولاد دسمی مورث صورت اعلیہ
یہ تعلقدار میں ۔ تعلقہ میں جمیہ موضع جمعی سمیت معہ محال ۔ ضلع پرتاب گڑھ میں واقع ہیں اس
خاندان میں اولاد اکبر مالک ریاست ہوتا ہے ۔

(نمبر ۲۲۴) میر اشرف حسین قوم سید تعلقدار کشریا۔

عرصہ دو سال سے بندایہ خریدار ہی مورثان اُنکے قابض اس ریاست کے ہوے ۔۔ جبکہ قبضہ اس خاندان نہیں ۔۔ یہ پہلا بیہ آتا ہو آخر الامر میر کرامت حسین مالک ریاست کے ہوے ۔۔ جنکے نام گورنمنٹ انگلشیہ سے سند تعلقہ داری مرحمت ہوئی بعد وفات اونکے یہ تعلقدار قابض ریاست ہیں۔ تعلقہ میں ساتھ ۔۔ موضع اور ساتھ ۔۔ جمعی ۔۔ ضلع فیض آباد میں واقع میں اس خاندان میں اولاد اکبر وارث ریاست ہوتا ہے۔

(نمبر ۲۲۵) وصی الزمان قوم شیخ تعلقدار میان گنج۔

یہ گنج آباد کیا ہوا بیان الماس خواجہ سرا کا تھا ابعدہ وفات اُنکے سرکار شاہ اودہ میں ضبط ہوا اور وہ میں نذرول تمسار یا ۔۔ سنہ ۱۲۶۵ فصلی میں بعد انتزاع سلطنت اودہ ۔۔ بجنگل قوم کا ۔۔ ہوا ابعدہ ضبط سرکار بہادر گورنمنٹ انگلشیہ ۔۔ مولوی حبیب الرحمن کو بعدہ خیر خواہی ایام غدر ۱۸۵۷ء میں ۔۔ ہوا ۔۔ بہادر نے ترقی ریاست کی ۔۔ بعد وفات مولوی صاحب ۔۔ یہ تعلقدار قابض تعلقہ ہیں۔ تعلقہ میں ساتھ موضع آخنہ ۔۔ جمعی ۔۔ ضلع او نام میں واقع میں اس خاندان میں اولاد اکبر وارث ریاست ہوتا ہے۔

(نمبر ۲۲۶) شیو امبر سنگھ قوم کپوریہ تعلقدار رامیپور۔

انکا تذکرہ خاندانی نمبر ۲۱ پر درج ہے یہ خاندان ان راجہ ڈانک میں اولاد و سمس مورث سے یہ تعلقدار میں ۔۔ تعلقہ میں لکہ موضع جمبی سمہ ۔۔ ضلع پرتاب گڑھ میں واقع ہیں اس خاندان میں اولاد اکبر وارث ریاست ہوتا ہو۔

(نمبر ۲۲۷) سردار میرا سنگھ قوم سکھ تعلقدار رجدان۔

سردار جوہر سنگھ صاحب قوم کھتری رئیس پنجاب کو بجلد و سے خیر خواہی ایام غدر ۱۸۵۷ء گورنمنٹ انگلشیہ سے یہ ریاست بنجلد ملکیت منفعت تعلقہ چردہ ہوا کہ مرحمت ہوئی تھی بعد اُنکے یہ رئیس قابض ریاست ہیں تعلقہ میں اکیس موضع ایک کچی جمبی ۔۔ ۱۲ سرہ ۳ مائی ۔۔ ضلع بہرائچ میں واقع میں اس خاندان اولاد اکبر مالک ریاست ہوتا ہو۔

(نمبر ۲۲۸) سردار بگھیل سنگھ قوم سکھ تعلقدار رجھنگا۔

یہ ریاست پہلے اقوام نجبارہ کی تھی بعد کو اقوام جنوبار کے قبضہ میں آکر خیال تعلقہ بجھنگا ہوی پھر بجرم ۔۔ آمدگی توبہ ۔۔ گورنمنٹ انگلشیہ میں ضبط ہوکر سردار بشور سنگھ مورث کو بجلد و سے خیر خواہی ایام غدر ۱۸۵۷ء مرحمت ہوئی بعد اُنکے یہ رئیس قابض تعلقہ ہیں۔ اس خاندان میں اولاد اکبر وارث ریاست ہوتا ہو۔ تعلقہ میں پانچ موضع دو کچی جمبی صدر ۔۔ ضلع بہرائچ میں واقع میں۔

(نمبر ۳۲۹) سید سردار علی قوم سید تعلقدار سی سی سلمون و ابتیاپور۔

آپ کے والد سید محمد خان ایک کمیدان فوج تھے بعد ازاں خیر خواہی ایام مندرجہ شششلہ ءگورنمنٹ انگلشیہ سے یہ ملکیت انکو عطیہ ہوئی حتی کہ بعد وفات انکے آپ تابیض علاقہ ہوے اور آپنے ایک جدہ واس تعلقہ کا جو بنام سی سی سلمون موسوم ہے ... یا س سردار ہیرا سنگھ کے بذریعہ بیع منتقل کر دیا پانچ سوضلع و دیہی جمعی الطلقت ضلع بہرائچ میں واقع ہین اولاد اکبر اس خاندان مین وارث ریاست ہوتا ہے۔

(نمبر ۳۳۰) ۱۔ محمد علی خان ۲۔ حسین علی خان ۱۔ اقوام سید تعلقداران او دیح کا نون۔

موصوفان تعلقدار پہلے سے کمیتقندر ریاست کے زمیندار تھے جبکہ عرصہ سے بشمول ریاست قدیم یہ تعلقہ جدید قائم ہوا گورنمنٹ انگلشیہ سے سند تعلقداری بنام سید علی بید تعلقدار کو مرحمت ہوئی حتی کہ بعد وفات انکے یہ تعلقہدار تابیض ملکیت مین تعلقہ مین پانچ موضع جمعی صحہ بارہ ہے ... ضلع او نام مین واقع ہینا۔ اس خاندان مینا اولاد اکبر وارث ریاست ہوتا ہے۔

(نمبر ۳۳۱) شمس النسا قوم شیخ تعلقدار حسپر املو کپور و سراے شیخ۔

یہ تعلقہ عرصہ تک مجبونت راسے و دولت راسے چچہ و صریان کے قبضہ مین رہا ہمیشہ افصلی مین آپکے شوہر شیخ مظفر علی نے موضع حسپر ا کو جبکے نام سے تعلقہ مشہور ہے خریدہ کیا تھا اب بعد وفات انکے آپ تابیض تعلقہ ہین اس تعلقہ مین چہ موضع دیہی جمعی صحہ لاکھ ہیہ ... کی اضلاع لکھنؤ دوبارہ نبکی مین واقع ہین اس خاندان مین اولاد اکبر مالک ریاست ہوتا ہے۔

(نمبر ۳۳۲) محمد حسین قوم شیخ صدیقی تعلقدار خانی پورہ گنورہ و گو پری خورد۔

یہ تعلقہ موروثی شیخ احمد بخش کا ہے جبکے مورث بوقت ہمایون خاہ لکھنؤ مین آۓ اور شیخ کامیاب ملازم محمد شاہی تھے شیخ ابوالقاسم لکھنؤی کی ہمشیرہ ہے سوئی ابوالقاسم خان سے بوقت اصلاح یہ جائداد جہیر مین ملی شیخ کا بنا ... اولاد مین سے آپ مین گیا رہ موضع ایک دیہا جمعی صحہ معہ لعتہ ... ضلع لکھنؤ دوبارہ نبکی مین آپ کی ملکیت کے واقع مین او را اولاد اکبر اس خاندانین مالک ریاست ہوتا ہے۔

(نمبر ۳۳۳) مرزا جعفر علی خان قوم شیخ تعلقدار بجیثہ دہوس پیرہ۔

مرزا بعض علی خان تعلقدار بجیثہ خاندان حکیم مہدی علیخان و نواب اللہ دیہ ستے مین اور حکیم سید علی خان دیوانیان د لوانیہ اللہ ... وزیر بادشاہ اودھ سے تھے خواجہ تخفیف کشمیری امیر کہ جنہوں نے نوکری کی تھی آمدن الدولہ پانجہین نواب اودھ ... دو اولاد دیہوڑ کر مرہ حکیم مہدی ہادی علی اول نے قضاکی بلا اولاد او دوسرے کے یہاں احمد علی نواب منور الدولہ ...

یہ وا و امرزہ جعفر علی خان موجودہ تعلقدار کے تھے جعفر علی خان اپنی ایک ملکیت بھین و مواضع واقع ضلع بجنور میں حاصل کی اسی میں سے ایک موضع کا نام جعیثہ چکرم جو ہیئہ نام تعلقہ کا مشہور ہی کل اس تعلقہ میں بمعہ موضع مجمعی سلطانہ پورہ کی ضلع لکھنؤ میں واقع میں۔ اور اس ریاست میں اگر مورث اعلیٰ بلا وصیت فوت ہو جاوے تو وارثت بموجب دستور خاندان اشخاص ذی حق کو پہونچتی ہے۔

(نمبر ۲۳۴) شیخ طالب علی خلف چودھری مصاحب علی و کریم بخش تعلقدار دین پناہ ۔

ایک ہندہ و تحصیل دہین موضع سبیلا میں جو اس زمانہ میں اہل منبوا کے قبضہ میں تھا آیا اور عطیہ زمینداری کا اختیار کر کے مواضعات کھنڈ سرہ وغیرہ پر قبضہ پایا اور پھر اپنے نام پر ایک بار میں و دین پناہ کو آباد کیا تھا جس کے نام سے یہ تعلقہ موسوم ہے مالکان موجودہ اہل خاندان چودھریان کرشی سو میں اب یہ تعلقہ بذریعہ رہن منتقل ہوتا جاتا ہے اس تعلقہ میں پانچ موضع ایک بھی مجمعی ... کی منبع بارہ بنکی میں واقع میں اور اولاد مالک ریاست اس خاندان میں ہوتا ہے ۔

(نمبر ۲۳۵) مہپال سنگھ خلف دنیا سنگھ قوم بھین تعلقدار ملونہ ۔

اذکار تذکرہ خاندانی و آنماز ریاست نمبر سہ پر دیا چکرم کرن رس کی تیسری پشت میں بہمان سادہ مورث اعلیٰ نے طلوعہ خاص آباد کیا تھا جیسے یہ ریاست قائم ہے اور قبضہ اس خاندان کا چلا آتا ہے گورنمنٹ انگلشیہ سے سند تعلقہ بنام دیا سنگھ پدر تعلقدار موجودہ مرحمت ہوئی تھی بعد ازنگکے رئیس موجودہ قابض ریاست میں ۔ تعلقہ میں پانچ موضع ایک بھی مجمعی سمت پر طلا علومیہ ضلع او نام میں واقع میں اس خاندانیین اگر مورث اعلیٰ بلا وصیت فوت ہو جاوے تو بموجب دستور خاندانی اشخاص ذی حق کو وراثت پہونچتی ہے ۔

(نمبر ۲۳۶) رو کمن کنور زودہ تحصیل سنگھ تربیدی قوم برہمن تعلقدار تربیدی کا گنج و شکار آباد و تربیدی کا ... و سعید پور بہیلہ ۔

شوہر آنکے محمد حکومت خان ان لاو و حین معززین انصر ون میں سے تصور ہوتے تھے انہوں نے اپنی ذات خاص سے یہ ریاست تربیدی کا گنج حاصل کی اور بعلہ خیر خواہی ایام مفصہ شنثام ملکیت جسکو شکار آباد و تربیدی کا پدر و سعید پور عطیہ گذشتے حاصل ہوئی اور مسبہ وصیت نامہ اپنے شوہر کے یہ رئیسہ قابض تعلقہ میں اس ریاست میں سات موضع اور ایک بھی مجمعی ... کی ضلاع بارہ بنکی و اونام وسکے بریلی میں واقع میں اس خاندان میں اولاد اکبر وارث ریاست ہوتا ہے ۔

(نمبر ۲۳۷) محمد نصیر الدین قوم شیخ تعلقدار میر پور ۔

یہ تعلقدار اہ و تعلقہ خاندان اور تعلقہ نمبر ۲۳۰ سے میں اس تعلقہ میں جو موضع اور ریاست بھی مجمعی مصہ ... کی ضلع بارہ بنکی میں واقع میں ۔ اور اس خاندان میں اگر مورث اعلیٰ بلا وصیت فوت ہو جاوے تو بموجب وراثت دستور

خاندانی کے اشخاص ذی حق کو پہونچتی ہے ۔

(نمبر ۲۳۸)   پرتھی پال سنگھ قوم اسیٹھیا تعلقدار رام نگر ۔

یہ تعلقدار اور تعلقہ خاندان اور تعلقہ نمبر ۱ و سے ہیں ۔ راجہ رام سنگھ مورث اعلیٰ کی جوتھی پشت میں دیورا بنے پوکھرا انصاری سی سے علمدہ ہوکر یہ ملکیت حاصل کی ۔ اسی خاندان سے یہ تعلقدار قابض ریاست میں ۔ سندتعلقہ گورنمنٹ سے بنام بابو ہندی بخشدہ ہوا تعلقدار حال کی ہوئی تھی ۔ یہ وراثنا رئیس قابض علاقہ ہوئے ۔ تعلقہ میں آٹھ موضع اور ایک پٹی جبی معہ ۔۔۔۔۔ سرحد بارہ بنکی میں واقع ہیں ۔ اولاد اکبر اس خاندان وارث ریاست ہوتا ہے ۔

(نمبر ۲۳۹)   بابو لعل بہادر قوم اسیٹھیا تعلقدار اکبیا پور ۔

یہ تعلقہ ایک شاخ تعلقہ پوکھرا انصاری متذکرہ نمبر ۲۱ کا ہے سند تعلقداری بنام سیکم ساہ گورنمنٹ انگلشیہ سے مرمت ہوئی یہ تعلقدار وراثنا قابض ریاست ہیں ۔ تعلقہ میں تین موضع معہ ۔۔۔۔۔ ضلع بارہ بنکی میں واقع ہیں ۔ اولاد اکبر اس خاندان میں وارث ریاست ہوتا ہے ۔

(نمبر ۲۴۰)   وزیر علیخان قوم ہمبئی تعلقدار بیرولی پرگنہ لیسوہ وصی ۔

یہ تعلقہ ایک شاخ تعلقہ نمبر ۲۰۱ کا ہے مفصل تذکرہ اسی نمبر پر دیکھ لیا جاوے اولاد زبر خان میں سے مہنا جان یے پرگنہ سوائی کا قبضہ نمبر ۱۲ سے حاصل کیا اور جب قبصہ برابر اس خاندان میں چلا آتا ہے ۔ تعلقہ میں پانچ موضع سینٹس پٹی ہمبئی معہ ۔۔۔۔۔ ضلع بارہ بنکی میں واقع ہیں ۔ رسم گدی نشینی اس خاندان میں ہے ۔

(نمبر ۲۴۱)   بابو کشن دت قوم ہمبیس تعلقدار پالی ۔

قریب پانچ سو برس کے گذرے جب کہ یہ ریاست لحاظ وسعت ودیگر امور بہ حیثیت موجود وجلی آتی ہے اور سلطنت ہندوستانی میں ہمیشہ مورثان اس ریاست کے بہ لقب تعلقدار موسوم رہے ہیں گورنمنٹ انگلشیہ سے بند و لبست تعلقہ کا بنا تعلقدار قابض حال ہوا ۔ تعلقہ میں ایک موضع ہمبئی معہ ۔۔۔۔۔ ضلع بارہ بنکی میں واقع ہیں ۔ اولاد اکبر اس خاندان میں وارث ریاست ہوتا ہے ۔

(نمبر ۲۴۲)   دیوان کشن کنور قوم کھتری سکھ تعلقدار یعقوب گنج ۔

یہ ملکیت زمانہ عہد ثانی ہی میں یعقوب علیخان خواجہ سراشاہ اردو کی تھی گورنمنٹ انگلشیہ میں منزل قرار پائی اور دیوان حاکم ہے اے صاحب مورث کو بطور عطیہ مرمت ہوئی دیوان حاکم رائے صاحب بہادر نجیب سنگ والی لاہور کے دیوان اعظم تھے تعلقدار حال الحج جانشین میں تعلقہ میں ایک موضع ہمبئی معہ ۔۔۔۔۔ ضلع بارہ بنکی میں واقع اس خاندان میں اولاد اکبر وارث ریاست ہوتا ہے ۔

(نمبر ۲۳۳) مولوی منظر علی تعلقدار سیوا قوم شیخ ۔

یہ ملکیت راجہ مونی سنگھ تعلقدار رتھولی کی بوجہ سرکشی ایام غدر ۱۸۵۷ء منضبط ہوکر بحق مدت شگذاری سرکار
سے رئیس حال کو ناکامیانہ طور پر عطا ہوئی ہے و دو موضع جمعی اسمعیہ ضلع سیتاپور زمین واقع میں ۔
اولاد اکبر وارث ریاست ہوتا ہے ۔

(نمبر ۲۳۴) کالکا بخش قوم ٹھاکر گوڑ تعلقدار جبار سعادت نگر ۔

بصلہ خیرخواہی ایام غدر ۱۸۵۷ء رگھوناتھ سنگھ آپکے مورث کو یہ تعلقہ گورنمنٹ انگلشیہ سے مرحمت ہوا تھا تب
آپ قابض ہیں بابرہ موضع پائے جمعی اسمعیہ ضلع سیتاپور زمین واقع میں ۔ اولاد اکبر وارث ریاست ہوتا ہے ۔

(نمبر ۲۳۵) ٹھاکر رگھوراج سنگھ قوم بیس تعلقدار راجہ پور ۔

اسکا تذکرہ خاندان نمبر ۸۰ ۔ یہ درج ہے کہ رئیس رانانھی با دلو بخش سنگھ باغی تعلقدار فشنکر پور کے صاحبزادہ ہیں ۔
بوجہ ضبطی اصل تعلقہ اسکا سانے نظر مرحمہ خسرو انہ آنگی پرورش و گذارہ کو یہ علاقہ منتقل علاقہ منضبط راجہ جھلاری
اسلت بناوت مرحمت فرما ہے جسمیں اسمعیہ موضع عیسی مطبوعہ ضلع سیتاپور زمین واقع میں جس اس خاندان میں
اولاد اکبر وارث ریاست ہوتا ہے ۔

(نمبر ۲۳۶) ٹھاکر سرجیت سنگھ قوم ٹھاکر کپنہ بابیس تعلقدار پوایاں و سہرورہ

یہ تعلقدار و تعلقہ خاندان و تعلقہ نمبر ۸۰ ۔ سے ہیں اسکے خاندان سامجہند مورث کی اولاد سے یہ تعلقدار قابض
اس ریاست کے ہیں اور عہد نواب منصور علینخان حاکم اودہ میں یہ ریاست منصور گذر ونا م سے موسوم تھی ۔
تعلقہ میں دس موضع جمعی صہبا اسمعیہ اضلاع پہرولی و لکھنؤ زمین واقع میں اس خاندان میں اولاد اکبر وارث
ریاست ہوتا پہ ۔

(نمبر ۲۳۷) صفدر حسین خان تعلقدار سہجانپور قوم پٹھان ۔

یہ رئیس ملک اودہ ضلع راے بریلی میں صدر الصدور میں اور یہ ملکیت بصلہ خیرخواہی ایام غدر گورنمنٹ انگلشیہ
بحکم ڈاکٹ نمبری ۵۱ مورخہ ۱۵ جنوری ۱۸۵۸ء میں آپکو عطا ہوئی ہے و دو موضع جمعی الاسمعیہ ضلع پہرولی
میں واقع میں اور اس ریاست میں اگر مورث اعلی بلاولدیت فوت ہوجاوے تو وارث بموجب دستور خاندان انی
نسبی حق کو پہونچتی ہے ۔

(نمبر ۲۳۸) لالہ اننت رام قوم کایستھ تعلقدار رسولپور ۔

یہ ملکیت راجہ عباس علی تعلقدار نامزدہ بلوام بغاوت ایام غدر ۱۸۵۷ء بوجہ ضبطی بوجہ ضبطی ہوکر بصلہ خیرخواہی
گورنمنٹ انگلشیہ سے آپکو مرحمت ہوا ہے اور بہر تعلقدارنے ترقی املاک کی اب ریاست میں دس موضع اور زمین جمعی الاسمعیہ

ضلع فیض آباد میں واقع ہیں اس خاندان میں اولادِ اکبر وارثِ ریاست ہوتا ہے۔

(نمبر ۹۳۸) شیو راج کنور قوم راجپوت تعلقدار سلطان پور دوسرا وامر متفرق دیوریہ۔

تذکرہ خاندانی آپ کا نمبر پر درج ہے یہ تعلقہ دوسرا ہے بابو راج سنگھ کو بعطیہ خیر خواہی ایام عہدہ شعبہ نذر نسبت الکشمیر مرحمت ہوا تھا عہدہ آپ کی یہ رئیس جانشین ہیں بنیں موضع تین ٹپی جمعی للعصمت سامنہ ضلع سلطان پور میں واقع ہیں اس خاندان میں اولاد واکبر وارثِ ریاست ہوتا ہے۔

(نمبر ۷۵) ہزرامین رام قوم برہمن پانڈے تعلقدار اکبر پورہ نذر سرا۔

یہ تعلقدار خاندان راجہ کرشندت رام تعلقدار سنگھان عینہ متذکرہ نمبر ۳۴ سے ہیں منفصہ چندکہ خاندانی و انکار ریاست اسی نمبر پر درج ہے سلطانِ فصلی میں یہ ملکیت اکبر پورہ جسکے نام سے تعلقہ مشہور ہوا بہار رام انکے راجگان سنگھ تعلقدار گونڈہ قوم لپمین سے خرید کی حتی اس وقت سے برابر قبضہ چلا آتا ہے آٹھہ موضع چاچی جمعی للعصمت لا موضع ضلع گونڈہ میں واقع ہیں اولادِ اکبر اس خاندان میں وارثِ ریاست ہوتا ہے۔

(نمبر ۳۱۸) ہمایوں آنند کنور قوم استھما تعلقدار اودہ۔

یہ کا تذکرہ خاندانی نمبر ۱۸۔ پر درج ہے یہ تعلقہ ایک شاخ تعلقہ نمبر ۳۴ کہدران کا ہے چار سو برس کا زمانہ ہوا بوان سنگھ مورث نے بوقتِ طلع مندگی دیہات متعلقہ اودہ ایک انیو حصہ میں پاک رادساہ خاص میں سکونت اختیار کی آخر الامر بابو شیو امر سنگھ قابض ریاست ہوے بعد وفات انکے یہ رئیسہ زوجہ انکی قابض ریاست میں تعلقہ حیمہ موضع جمعی سلطان للعصمت ضلع راے بریلی میں واقع ہیں رہم گست نشینی اس خاندان میں ہے۔

(نمبر ۳۵۲) مہراج بخش قوم ٹھاکر بیس تعلقدار پلکھا۔

اکا تذکرہ خاندانی نمبرہ پر درج ہے ترمبن شاہ پسر جہارم راجہ ڈومن دیو مورث اعلی کجمور کانون سے علاحدہ ہوکر جنگت پور میں آباد ہوے آکی آٹھویں پشت میں موہن سنگھ تعلقدار نے جنگل کٹوا کر اس موضع کو آباد کیا اور پلکھا نام رکھا جسکے نام سے یہ تعلقہ مشہور ہوا سندہ تعلقداری بھی گورنمنٹ انگلشیہ سے انہیں تعلقدار کو مرحمت ہوئی اگر یہ تعلقہ للبعد بھیجا جارہ ہر تعلقہ میں چار موضع جمعی للعصمت ضلع راے بریلی میں واقع ہیں اس ریاست میں اگر میں خاندانی بلا وصیت خورت موجبا ودر وراثت بموجب دستور خاندانی الخاص کی جب کو پہنچتی ہے۔

(نمبر ۳۵۴) سیتا رام کورمی تعلقدار سہ گانون و بھیم گانون۔

بعہد اکبر بادشاہ ولی نبا ایک رام و پال جی رام مورث اعلی ملازی جسینت ولی بگجرم گانون این آنگی اولاد منہا کامین سنگھ نے سلطنہ فصلی میں ایک موضع بنا ایک پور مورث اصلی نمبرا کے نام پر اور دوسرا موضع پیلیا موضع۔

نمبر ۲۵۳ کے نام پیشتر نسلی میں آباد کیا اور حکیم گاؤں کو آباد کرایا ... ترقی دی کہ سوا موضعات خانپور و پورب گاؤں کے تعلق بہم پہنچے بذریعہ تین گاؤں ملکر اسکا نام سہ گراؤں مشہور ہوا جو اب اسے تعلقہ مشہور ... سند تعلقداری گورنمنٹ انگلشیہ بنام ٹھاکر سنگھ پدر تعلقدار حال ہوئی جو کہ معرکہ بریلی گار دمین خیرخواہ سرکار رہے بعد ازانکے یہ تعلقدار فاضل مین اور یہ تعلقہ بجہیاچارہ ہو سب حصہ داروں کی مقدار حصہ معین ہے۔ تعلقہ مین تین موضع جہبی المعہ ... ضلع رائے بریلی مین واقع مین اس خاندان مین اولاد اکبر وارث ریاست ہوتا ہے۔

(نمبر ۲۵۴) بلبیر سنگھ قوم ٹھاکر بیس تعلقدار کجہری

انکا تذکرہ خاندانی نمبر ۸۔ پر درج ہے اور یہ تعلقہ شاخ تعلقہ نمبر ۷۵ کا ہو یہ ریاست بکر باجیت مورث کو لال سا و خلف بر جو رسا و مورث تعلقدار سر چہا تذکرہ نمبر ۵۷ سے بوقت علمگیری تقسیم میں حاصل ... قبضہ اس خاندان مین برابر چلا آتا ہے۔ تعلقہ مین چار موضع جہبی ... ضلع رائے بریلی مین واقع ... اس خاندان مین اولاد اکبر وارث ریاست ہوتا ہے۔

(نمبر ۲۵۵) ٹھاکر سُخبخش قوم بیس ٹھاکر تعلقدار کسروا

انکا تذکرہ خاندانی نمبر ۸۔ پر درج ہے ہر حصہ ایکسو سال کا گذرتا ہو تلند سنگھ دپہ تاب سنگھ مورثان اعلیٰ نے بجویت مورث تعلقدار گورداست یہ ریاست حصہ مین حاصل کی ہوتی ہے تب قبضہ اس خاندان مین چلا آتا ہے۔ تعلقہ مین چار ... جہبی ان جامعہ ... ضلع رائے بریلی مین واقع ہین۔ اس خاندان مین اولاد اکبر وارث ریاست ہوتا ہے۔

(نمبر ۲۵۶) بابو جگناتھ ورن سنگھ قوم اینتسیا تعلقدار دلی۔

انکا تذکرہ خاندانی نمبر ۱۲۔ پر درج ہے اور یہ تعلقہ شاخ تعلقہ نمبر ۲۲۔ کا ہو نشتر سال کا عرصہ سوا ... جبکہ نئے مورث نے اس ریاست کو راجہ آنمر و سنگھ برا و مورث کلان خود و مورث تعلقدار کھہراوان سے بلوہ گزار حاصل کرکے عامدہ و تعلقہ قائم کیا جیسے اس خاندان مین قبضہ چلا آتا ہے تین موضع جہبی سمت ... ضلع رائے بریلی مین واقع مین اس خاندان مین اولاد اکبر وارث ریاست ہوتا ہے۔

(نمبر ۲۵۷) گنگا بختش مسر قوم برہمن تعلقدار بنیا بارکشرہ

سنہ ... یو نسلی مین راجہ مہران سنگھ نے شیمو راجہ بی والد راجہ ہیرالال مصر ناظم نفاست دلمر و بریلی نے اس ... کہ خریدہ کر یانتہا جیسے نمبہ چلا آتا ہے ایک۔ موضع جہبی الاربعہ ... ضلع رائے بریلی مین واقع ہوے ... اور اس ... سند مین اگر مورث اعلیٰ بلا ریاست فوت ہو جاوے تو وراثت بوجب دستور خاندانی اشخاص ذوی حق ... کر یہو نعمتی ہے۔

(نمبر ۲۵۸) محمد محسن و محمد شفیع اقوام سید تعلقدار علی پور چکانی ۔

یہ علاقہ منجملہ علاقہ منضبطہ رانا بینی ما وصو نجبش سنگہ بائی کے بسلہ خیر خواہی ایام غدر شہیع سید عبد الحکیم صاحب والد تعلقدار ان حال کو گورنمنٹ انگلشیہ سے مرحمت ہوا تھا اور سید صاحب اکسٹر اسسٹنٹ ملک تھے دہ تھے بعد حصول پنشن و نصف لیگی وفات پائی اب بعد اونکے یہ صاحبان قابض و وارث ہیں اور محمد شفیع صاحب نائب عہدہ رشتہ داری منطبہ بانکی میں ملازم سرکار ہیں تعلقے میں ۔ صہ ۔ موضع دوٹی جمعی سمہ لما لعہ ضلع بریلی رسے ضلع میں واقع ہیں اس خاندان میں اگر مورث اعلی بلا وصیت فوت ہو جاوے تو وراثت بوجب دستور خاندانی اشخاص ذیحق کو پہونچتی ہو ۔

(نمبر ۲۵۹) بینی پرشاد قوم چھتری تعلقدار دھگانواں تحت گانون ہر دوئی ۔

یہ ملکیت بسلہ خیر خواہی ایام غدر شہیع گجراج سنگہ انکے والد کو گورنمنٹ انگلشیہ سے منجملہ ملکیت منضبطہ رانا بینی ما وصو نجبش سنگہ بانی کے عطا ہوئی تھی بعد وفات اونکے آپ قابض ہیں ایک موضع جمعی لما للعہ رسے ضلع رای بریلی میں واقع ہے اور اس ریاست میں اگر مورث اعلی بلا وصیت فوت ہو جاوے تو وراثت بوجب دستور خاندانی کے اشخاص نحق کو پہونچتی ہو ۔

(نمبر ۲۶۰) نبیو بش سنکر سنگہ وارجن سنگہ قوم جوار تعلقدار سرتاب پور و سادی پور کوٹوا انصف حصہ ۔

انکا تذکرہ خاندانی وا آغازر یاست نمبر ، پر درج ہو اولاد بریا سنگہ و لکھو کھی سنگہ انکے مورث انکے تھے اور کی چیلاشپٹوں کے بعد موبین ساہی کو یہ ریاست وقت تقسیم بابھی خاندان سے حاصل ہوئی تھی جبکہ قبضہ موضان اس خاندان میں برابر چلا آتا ہی ۔ تعلقے میں دو موضع حطہ پٹی جمعی معمعہ لا وطع رسے ضلع سلطانپور و لسے بریلی میں واقع ہیں اس ریاست میں اگر مورث اعلی بلا وصیت فوت ہو جاوے تو وراثت بوجب دستور خاندانی اشخاص نحق کو پہونچتی ہو ۔

(نمبر ۲۶۱) شنیو گوبند تیواری قوم برہمن تعلقدار ہبہ جھوانی ۔

عرصہ تیس سال کا ہوا غریب سنگہ و دھری جیو سابق مالک ریاست اور بہیرا لال مورث اعلی تعلقدار قابض حال سے قرابت داری ہوئی او سی ذریعہ سے مورثان انکے یہاں شامل کھیرو سے اس مقام پر آکر آباد ہوے پھر بہادین والاد بہیرا لال کی نار شہ میں ایسر دین خلف غریب سنگہ نے یہ ملکیت بر بہادین کو عطا کی جب سے آغازر یاست کا ہوا اور موران تعلقدار قابض چلے آتے ہیں تعلقے میں ۔ صہ ۔ موضع دوٹی جمعی معمعہ جایسے رسے ضلع اونام میں واقع ہیں اولاد اکبر اس خاندان میں وارث ریاست ہوتا ہی ۔

(نمبر ۲۶۲) زوجہ نعمت اللہ خان قوم اہبان مسلمان تعلقدار مرزا پور و جلال پور ۔

مسلمان کو لی و سولی مورثان علی جوار دکھن پہ اس ملک میں کے اور نبروز بازان ران سابقہ سے اولائیان کے ریاست سید کی انکے خاندان میں زر سنگہ دید اور راوجی بہان ساہ و لچانی بہ دے زر سنگہ دیو لگدی نشین راج متولی ہوے جنکے خاندان سے راجہ لوئی سنگہ باغی تھے جنکا تعلقہ منضبط ہو گیا اور راوجی بہان ساہ نے موضع کنٹوار میں

قیام کرکے نو سو نواسی دیہات گرد و نواح پرگنہ وار و قبضہ پا کر تعلقہ بنام کھجوروارہ قائم کیا اوکی تیسری پشت میں جہان شاہ
ہوے اُن کے دولہ کے نبیرہ وگلاسی نے صحبت میں ۱۰۷۵ھ بعد تجدید رنگ مذہب اسلام قبول کرکے سند زمیداری نو سو اُسی
مواضعات کی شاہ سے حاصل کی چنانچہ بنیرہ کی اولاد سے جملہ اہلیان سلمان ہیں اور گلاسی اولاد مگر گیا رشتہ فصلی
عہد جہانگیر شاہ شیر میں یہ ریاست اس قوم کی تبضے سے جاتی رہی تھی پھر ۱۱۸۸ھ افسری میں حکام شاہی سے چند مواضعا
اس خاندان کو بطور دوبعانی حاصل ہوئی بعد کو موہن شان نے ترقی ریاست کی جب سے آغاز ریاست موہ کر برابر تہذیبہ چلا آتا ہے
پھر تقسیم باہمی میں چند تعلقہ اس ریاست کے خاندان میں ہو گئے چنانچہ نمبر ۱۲ و ۲۲ ۳۲۔ کے تعلقدار اسی خاندان سے
علیحدہ قائم ہوئے تھے اس تعلقے میں آخرالامر سند تعلقداری گورنمنٹ انگلشیہ سے بنام نعمت اللہ خان وحمت ہولی
تھی بعد وفات اُن کی یہ ریاست و جواں کی قابضہ ریاست ہیں اور تعلقہ میں بعد موضع جمعی سمہ لاکھ ضلع کھیری میں
واقع ہیں رسم گدی نشینی اس خاندان میں ہے۔

(نمبر ۔) نواب محمد باقر علیخان قوم مغل تعلقدار کندوان کہ خطاب نواب مورثی۔
خواجہ نفیع کشمیری امیر ملازم نواب آصف الدولہ باد حاکم اودہ کے تھے اُن کی دوسری پشت میں نواب والا ہاد جو عہد تک وزیر سلطنت اودھ رہے بنا اس ریاست کی نواب صاحب ممدوح کی ذات سے بذریعہ رہن و بیع کے ہولی
پھر نواب مجد علیخان صاحب خلف نواب صاحب موصوف نے ترقی ریاست فرمائی بعد و نیکے آپ قابض میں بعض
موضع پلے ٹی جمعی ریاست ۱۲ ۔ کسر ضلع سیتاپور میں واقع ہیں رسم گدی نشینی اس خاندان میں ہے۔

(نمبر ۔) میجر ہی بی آر صاحب قوم یورپین تعلقدار لود دھواری۔
آپ ملک اود دھر میں قبل یام بغاوت بعہدہ ڈٹی کلکٹری ضلع بریلی میں حکمران تھے بصلہ خیر خواہی ایام غدر شریع
میں یہ تعلقہ گورنمنٹ انگلشیہ سے آپ کو وحمت ہوا وجہ تسمیہ لود دھواری کہ یہ قوم لود دھواس تعلقہ میں پشتہ آباد ہیں
بعض موضع جمعی معہ ضلع بریلی میں واقع ہیں انکا علاقہ کل فروخت ہوگیا۔

(نمبر ۔) ایل ڈی ہرسی صاحب قوم یورپین تعلقدار کمیا بزرگ و ندپور و رانی جاگیرہ سیتل پور۔
یہ تعلقہ کپتان ولیم رسیم صاحب کو منجلہ ملکیت منضبط راجہ لونی سنگھ تعلقدار متولی باغی گورنمنٹ انگلشیہ سے وحمت
ہوا تھا عبارت ۲۳۔ موضع و بٹی جمعی معہ ضلع کھیری میں واقع ہیں۔ اس خاندان میں اولاد اکبر وارث ریاست ہوتا ہے۔

(نمبر ۔) شہزادہ شہید یونسنگہ قوم سکہ خطاب شہزادہ تعلقدار بندڑی پور و بنتی و گوکل پور وغیرہ۔
شاہ مغدرل کے خاندان کی فہرست در بارہ میران شہزادہ کا نام درج چوہندڑی گنیش حسکے نام سے یہ تعلقہ مشہور ہے
آباد کردہ گنیش قوم بربمن تیواری کا ہے جو شامل تعلقہ بنی یا دھو بخش باغی تعلقدار شنکر پور کے تھا یہ قبضہ ضبطی تعلقہ
بنی یا دھو بخش پشیگاہ و گورنمنٹ سے آپ کو وحمت ہوا آپ مہارا جہ نجیت سنگھ صاحب بہادر حاکم پنجاب کے پوتے ہیں

بعض موضع سے پٹی جمعی سادہ وغیرہ ،ضلع رائے بریلی میں واقع ہیں اولاد اکبر ۔ خاندان میں وارث ریاست ہوتا ہے ۔

(نمبر) الگزنڈر میکلس آر صاحب قوم یورپین تعلقہ دار ایرا ۔

تعلقہ ایرا و ڈگرا و تیر الوجھی مشترکہ مسٹر رور صاحب کو بجلہ وہی حسن خدمات ایام غدر منجملہ علاقہ منضبطہ اغیان شدہ ١٨۔۔۔ کے گورنمنٹ انگلشیہ سے مرحمت ہوا تھا ۔ اب تعلقہ ایرا پر آپ قابض ہیں بسوب موضع جمعی موضع وغیرہ ، ضلع کھیری میں واقع ہیں اولاد اکبر اس خاندان میں وارث ریاست ہوتا ہے ۔

ضمیمہ   پولیس آنامی آر صاحب تعلقہ دار نگرا ۔

یہ تعلقہ ایک شاخ تعلقہ مستندکرہ بالا کا ہے بسوب موضع جمعی معرلات ، ضلع کھیری میں واقع ہیں ۔

ضمیمہ   یوپوز رافضی آر صاحب تعلقہ دار ہیر الوجھی ۔

یہ تعلقہ ایک شاخ تعلقہ مستندکرہ صدر ایرا کا ہے ایک موضع جمعی ہا ص موضع ، ضلع کھیری میں واقع ہے ۔

(نمبر) راجہ جگناتھہ بخش سنگھہ قوم گور خطاب راجہ مسرور قی تعلقہ دار وزیر نگر ۔

آپ کا تعلقہ فروخت ہو گیا لیکن آپ ضلع شاہجہانپور میں مالک غربی و شمالی میں بھی علاقہ دار ہیں ۔

(نمبر) راجہ شیو پانتھہ سنگھہ قوم بہمن کشمیری خطاب راجہ حین حیات تعلقہ دار بیتہر ۔

یہ ملکیت چند کا بخش تعلقہ دار بیتہر کی تھی جو بوجہ سرکشی ایام غدر دائم المحبس ہوا اور اسکے تعلقے میں سے کچھ علاقہ راجہ گور دکنر مستندکرہ نمبر ١۵ کو اور ایک ذریعہ اس موضع بیتہر کا بلدیو سنگھہ رسالدار کو اور بیتہر خاص آپ کو گورنمنٹ انگلشیہ سے مرحمت ہوا ۔ اس تعلقے میں ردو موضع جمعی البتہ ماوست ، ضلع اودھ میں واقع ہیں اس خاندان میں اولاد اکبر وارث ریاست ہوتا ہے ۔

(نمبر) ایچ جبرت سنگھہ ، بہچمن کنور اقوام سکھہ خطاب سردار تعلقہ داران ۔ چھاباری وسکردرہ شاہ معزول کے خاندان کی فہرست میں یہ سردار ہیں ۔ آپ خاندان ہمارا جہر نجیب سنگھہ بہادر رئیس لاہور ہیں گورنمنٹ سے سردار فتح سنگھہ اور سردار رایاست سنگھہ کو یہ ملکیت عطیہ ہوئی تھی اب آپ صاحبان در اثنا قابض ہیں بسبب موضع جمعی رایاست ، اضلاع گونڈہ و بہرایچ میں واقع ہیں ۔ اس خاندان میں اولاد اکبر وارث ریاست ہوتا ہے ۔

(نمبر) بینی ماہو بخش سنگھہ قوم ٹھاکر ہیں تعلقہ دار اکبر پور ضلع اودا و ۔

آپ کا تعلقہ بالکل بچ و رہن ہو گیا اور آپ بیدخل ہیں البتہ یہ گاہ اراضی گذارے کے واسطے آپ کے قبضہ میں ہے ۔

(نمبر) مہیبال سنگھہ قوم ٹھاکر چندیل تعلقہ دار جامو ضلع اودام ۔

اس تعلقدار کے سبب تفرق حکم عدالت دیوانی لیلنڈ مارگیج بنک کے واقع انگریزوں کے ہاتھہ فروخت ہو گئے جا جامو خاص کی اراضی ہیں صرف موضع گاہ سیرہ قبضہ تعلقدار باقی ہے ۔

Lachhman Kunwar Taluqdar of Chhariari

Beni Madho Bakhsh Taluqdar of Akbarpur

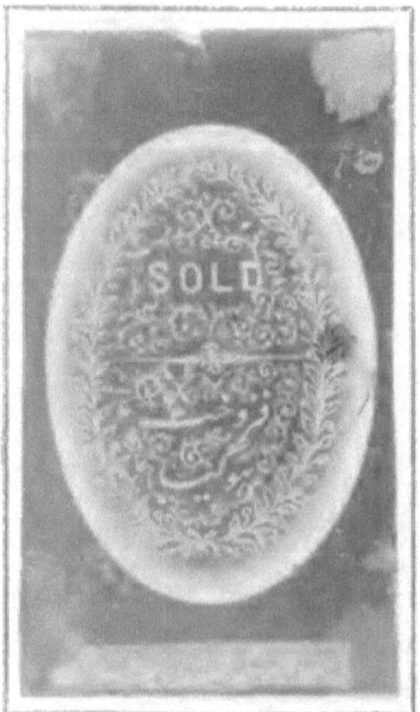

Mahpal Singh Taluqdar of Jajmau

Alexander Douglas Taulluqdar of Airn

Pauline Annie Orr Taulluqdar of Nagra

Louisa Fanny Orr Taulluqdar of Jirabughi

Sardar Jaggat Singh Taulluqdar of Chhachari

L. B. Hazary Taalluqdar of Kiman Buzurg

Shahzada Shahdeo Singh Taalluqdar of Bhandri
Ganesh

Raja Jagar Nath Singh Taalluqdar of Wazirnagar

Lala Shoo Nath Singh Taalluqdar of Bihtar

261— Shoo Gobind Tiwari Taalluqdar of Bi'ta Bhawani

262—Widow of Narmat-ul-lah Khan Taalluqdar of Mirzapur

Nauwab Muhammad Baqar Ali Khan Taalluqdar of Kunwan Khera

Major A. P. Grii Taalluqdar of Lonawali

Singh Taalluqdar of Alipur Chabal

750.—Beni Prashad Taalluqdar of Mahgaon

26 ...—Sheo Shamsir Singh Taalluqdar of Pratabpur

26 .—Arjun Singh Taalluqdar of Pratabpur